PENGUIN  CLAS

SWEET THURSDAY

JOHN STEINBECK (1902–1968) was born in Salinas, California, in 1902, and grew up in a fertile agricultural valley about twenty-five miles from the Pacific coast—and both valley and coast would serve as settings for some of his best fiction. In 1919 he went to Stanford University, where he intermittently enrolled in literature and writing courses until he left in 1925 without a degree. During the next five years he supported himself as a laborer and journalist in New York City and then as a caretaker for a Lake Tahoe estate, all the time working on his first novel, *Cup of Gold* (1929). After marriage and a move to Pacific Grove, he published two California fictions, *The Pastures of Heaven* (1932) and *To a God Unknown* (1933), and worked on short stories later collected in *The Long Valley* (1938). Popular success and financial security came only with *Tortilla Flat* (1935), stories about Monterey's *paisanos*. A ceaseless experimenter throughout his career, Steinbeck changed courses regularly. The powerful novels of the late 1930s focused on the California laboring class: *In Dubious Battle* (1936), *Of Mice and Men* (1937), and the book considered by many his finest, *The Grapes of Wrath* (1939). Early in the 1940s, Steinbeck became a filmmaker with *The Forgotten Village* (1941) and a serious student of marine biology with *Sea of Cortez* (1941). He devoted his services to the war, writing *Bombs Away* (1942) and the controversial play-novelette *The Moon Is Down* (1942). *Cannery Row* (1945), *The Wayward Bus* (1947), *The Pearl* (1947), *A Russian Journal* (1948), another experimental drama, *Burning Bright* (1950), and *The Log from the Sea of Cortez* (1951) preceded publication of the monumental *East of Eden* (1952), an ambitious saga of the Salinas Valley and his own family's history. The last decades of his life were spent in New York City and Sag Harbor with his third wife, with whom he traveled widely. Later books include *Sweet Thursday* (1954), *The Short Reign of Pippin IV: A Fabrication* (1957), *Once There Was a War* (1958), *The Winter of Our Discontent* (1961), *Travels with Charley in Search of America* (1962), *America and Americans* (1966), and the posthumously published *Journal of a Novel: The East of Eden Letters* (1969), *Viva Zapata!* (1975), *The Acts* of *King Arthur and His Noble Knights* (1976), and *Working Days: The Journals of* The Grapes of Wrath (1989). He died in 1968, having won a Nobel Prize in 1962.

ROBERT DEMOTT, recipient of the 2006 Trustees Award from the National Steinbeck Center, is the Edwin and Ruth Kennedy Distinguished Professor at Ohio University, the author of *Steinbeck's Typewriter*, an award-winning book of critical essays, and the editor of *Working Days*, a *New York Times* Notable Book. He lives in Athens, Ohio.

JOHN STEINBECK

Sweet Thursday

Introduction by
ROBERT DEMOTT

PENGUIN BOOKS

PENGUIN BOOKS

Published by the Penguin Group

Penguin Group (USA) Inc., 375 Hudson Street, New York, New York 10014, U.S.A.
Penguin Group (Canada), 90 Eglinton Avenue East, Suite 700, Toronto, Ontario, Canada M4P 2Y3
(a division of Pearson Penguin Canada Inc.)
Penguin Books Ltd, 80 Strand, London WC2R 0RL, England
Penguin Ireland, 25 St Stephen's Green, Dublin 2, Ireland (a division of Penguin Books Ltd)
Penguin Group (Australia), 250 Camberwell Road, Camberwell, Victoria 3124, Australia
(a division of Pearson Australia Group Pty Ltd)
Penguin Books India Pvt Ltd, 11 Community Centre, Panchsheel Park, New Delhi - 110 017, India
Penguin Group (NZ), 67 Apollo Drive, Rosedale, North Shore 0632, New Zealand
(a division of Pearson New Zealand Ltd)
Penguin Books (South Africa) (Pty) Ltd, 24 Sturdee Avenue, Rosebank, Johannesburg 2196, South Africa

Penguin Books Ltd, Registered Offices:
80 Strand, London WC2R 0RL, England

First published in the United States of America by The Viking Press 1954
Published in Penguin Books 1979
This edition with an introduction by Robert DeMott published 2008

LIBRARY OF CONGRESS CATALOGING IN PUBLICATION DATA
Steinbeck, John, 1902–1968.
Sweet Thursday / John Steinbeck ; introduction by Robert DeMott.
p. cm.—(Penguin classics)
Sequel to: Cannery Row.
Includes bibliographical references (p.).
ISBN 978-0-14-303947-1
1. Monterey (Calif.)—Fiction. I. Title.
PS3537.T3234S9 2008
813'.52—dc22   2008016040

Printed in the United States of America
Set in Sabon

For
ELIZABETH
with love

Contents

Introduction

*"I found it irresistible. It's quite a performance. I bet
some of it is even true, and if it wasn't, it is now."*
—John Steinbeck's dust jacket blurb on Gypsy Rose
Lee's memoir, *Gypsy* (1957)

John Steinbeck was born in the agricultural community of
Salinas, California, on February 27, 1902, to middle-class
parents: John Ernst Steinbeck, a businessman who would later
become Monterey County treasurer, and Olive Hamilton Steinbeck, a former schoolteacher. Steinbeck grew up in Northern
California and was influenced from his earliest days by the region's diverse geographical landscape and its common people,
which, along with his interest in democratic principles and social justice, remained foundations of his art for the rest of his
life. Steinbeck attended Salinas High School, where he was an
undistinguished but bookish student, then enrolled sporadically
at Stanford University from 1919 to 1925. An English-
journalism major, he took a short-story-writing class from Professor Edith Mirrielees and was published in Stanford's
undergraduate literary magazine, but because he was restless
and craved adventure, he never finished his degree. He held a variety of temporary jobs during the next four years (laborer and
cub reporter in New York City, fisheries manager, and resort
handyman and caretaker at a private estate near Lake Tahoe),
eventually publishing his first novel, *Cup of Gold*, in 1929. The
book, a historical novel about the seventeenth-century pirate
Henry Morgan, scarcely sold, but Steinbeck's choice of vocation
was sealed. He never again held a traditional nine-to-five job.
Beginning in 1930, with the support and encouragement of his
parents and especially of his first wife, Carol Henning Steinbeck,

whom he had married that year, writing became Steinbeck's daily occupation, and it continued so through lean and flush times for the remainder of his life. When Steinbeck, who had left California in the early 1940s, died in New York City on December 20, 1968, he had managed to support himself and his families (he was married three times and had two sons and one stepdaughter) exclusively on his writing-based income, primarily from the thirty books of fiction, drama, film scripts, and nonfictional prose he published between 1929 and 1966, many of them translated into numerous foreign languages worldwide. In 1962 Steinbeck was awarded the Nobel Prize in Literature, "for his realistic and imaginative writings, combining as they do sympathetic humour and keen social perception," according to the Swedish Academy, which administers the award. Steinbeck was only the seventh American writer to have been chosen since the prestigious prize's inception in 1901, yet his election provoked vehement and highly publicized reactions among his critics, who wondered aloud whether he deserved the award. In his acceptance speech, delivered on December 10, 1962, in Stockholm, the humble and self-deprecating Steinbeck confessed, ". . . there may be doubt that I deserve the . . . award . . . over other[s] whom I respect and reverence—but there is no question of my pleasure and pride in having it for myself."

John Steinbeck is best known for his hard-hitting, socially conscious novels of the 1930s, especially the three novels that form his "labor trilogy": *In Dubious Battle* (1936), *Of Mice and Men* (1937), and *The Grapes of Wrath* (1939), all of which depict the tragic economic and social conditions for migrant agricultural workers during the Depression era in his native state. One of the most searing indictments of California as a promised land ever written, *The Grapes of Wrath* (often considered among the greatest of twentieth-century novels) was such a controversial best seller that the reclusive and private Steinbeck experienced a personal backlash from its unprecedented and unanticipated success: "I have always wondered why no author has survived a bestseller," he told John Rice in a June 1939 interview. "Now I know. The publicity and fan-fare are just as bad as they would be for a boxer. One gets self-conscious and that's the end of one's writing." Steinbeck did not give up writing altogether, as he once threatened to do, but after 1940 much of his important work centered on new topics: ecological issues, scientific discourse, and the interrelatedness of nature and culture in two brilliant books, *Sea of Cortez: A Leisurely Journal of Travel and Research* (1941), cowritten with Ed Ricketts, and *Cannery Row* (1945); the implications of individual choice, heroism, and moral action in *The Pearl* (1947), *East of Eden* (1952), *Viva Zapata!* (1952), and *The Winter of Our Discontent* (1961); and nonfiction narratives in *Travels with Charley in Search of America* (1962) and *America and Americans* (1966), both of which engage in a kind of lover's quarrel with America. Steinbeck, a prophetic postmodernist given to literary experimentation, explored the paradoxes of the creative process itself in *Sweet Thursday* (1954), and in the posthumous *Journal of a Novel: The* East of Eden *Letters* (1969) and *Working Days: The Journals of* The Grapes of Wrath (1989).

For all his dark pessimism and tragic vision, Steinbeck loved writing comedic fiction. *Tortilla Flat* (1935), *Cannery Row*, and *The Short Reign of Pippin IV* (1957) come immediately to mind. *Sweet Thursday*, which started life as an unfinished novel–cum–musical comedy called "Bear Flag," is Steinbeck's happiest, most lighthearted fiction and formed the basis for Richard Rodgers and Oscar Hammerstein's short-lived 1956 Broadway musical, *Pipe Dream*. A novelistic sequel to *Cannery Row*, *Sweet Thursday* is among Steinbeck's least-known works (despite having provided much plot action and characterization for David Ward's 1982 romantic film *Cannery Row*, which starred Nick Nolte and Debra Winger).

From the late 1930s onward Steinbeck was generally assured of popular and commercial success no matter what he published. *Sweet Thursday* was no exception—it sold remarkably well. One day alone—on June 15, 1954—Viking Press sold two thousand copies, which prompted Pascal Covici, Steinbeck's editor, to predict it would top one hundred thousand for the year, and later to exult: "the book keeps on selling!" Covici's claims were optimistic. According to Meghan Mahan, *Sweet Thursday* was on the best-seller list for five weeks, and was the seventh-best-selling fiction work of 1954, ultimately accounting for over sixty thousand copies. Among professional reviewers and cultural tastemakers, however, Steinbeck's novel garnered a less friendly (and often hostile) reception. But a few level-headed critics, such as Hugh Holman writing in the *New Republic* on June 7, 1954, struck a balanced appraisal that put the novel in perspective:

> I think we have been wrong about Steinbeck. We have let his social indignation, his verisimilitude of language, his interest in marine biology lead us to judge him as a naturalist. . . . Steinbeck is . . . a social critic . . . occasionally angry but more often delighted with the joys that life on its lowest levels presents. I think *Sweet Thursday* implicitly asks its readers to take its author on such terms. If these terms are less than we thought we had reason to hope for from *The Grapes of Wrath*, they are still worthy of respect.

As Holman advises, this quirky but raffish, ebullient, and pleasurable short novel deserves to be taken on its own terms. Who knows but that it will "set free" another reader or writer, as it did prolific crime novelist Elmore Leonard when he read it in 1954?

In *John Steinbeck*, biographer Jay Parini claims that Steinbeck "was not always writing realistic fiction. . . . His imagination was puckish, and he worked by charm, incantation, invocation, and philosophical musing." *Sweet Thursday*'s multiple layers of meaning, its self-confessed "reality below reality," its rambunctious tone, and its blurring of historical reality and actual persons with invented scenarios and made-up actions took precedence over traditional novelistic methods. The fictional Mack (based on a real-life person), upon reading some unflattering reviews of *Cannery Row*, claims to "have laid out a lot of time on critics" and wonders whether they all read the same book: "Some of them don't listen while they read, I guess," he states, because they are more interested in assigning handy catchwords to a work—"overambitious," "romantic," "naturalistic doggavation"—than in "understanding."

In the truncated, forty-seven-line version that became *Sweet Thursday*'s published prologue, Mack's suggestions about chapter headings, character descriptions, and loose-limbed hooptedoodle are laid out as matters of personal preference, not as punitive markers, but they are incorporated in the novel to undercut aesthetic distance and to facilitate the audience's willing participation in the story. Steinbeck is in on the con game and is part of its web of artful intrigue: marginalized characters in an earlier roman à clef, *Cannery Row*, discuss a novel in which they appeared; its real-life author follows their advice in a fictional sequel in which they once again appear as dramatis personae commenting on their earlier experiences as though they were real. Steinbeck's April 1, 1959, letter to film director Elia Kazan summarizes his postwar aesthetic belief: "Externality is a mirror that reflects back to our mind the world our mind has created of the raw materials. But a mirror is a piece of silvered glass. There is a back to it. If you scratch off the silvering, you can see through the mirror to the other worlds on the other side. I know that many people do not want to break through. I do, passionately, hungrily."

Steinbeck's post–World War II fictions differ from his earlier realism. Think of the *Monty Python* mantra: "Now for something completely different." His radical shift toward a more self-referential style occurred after 1947. Following his third trip to Russia, his interest in a communal vision of human organization (the bedrock of his earlier fiction) waned. His new Cold War–inspired thinking that totalitarian groupthink is the enemy of democracy is exemplified in his June 8, 1949, letter to novelist John O'Hara, in which he relinquishes his earlier mode: "I believe one thing powerfully—that the only creative thing our species has is the individual, lonely mind. . . . The group ungoverned by individual thinking is a horrible destructive principle. The great change in the last 2,000 years was the Christian idea that the individual soul was very precious. Unless we can preserve and foster the principle of the preciousness of the individual mind, the world of men will either disintegrate into a screaming chaos or will go into a gray slavery."

Following this pronounced shift in political orientation, Steinbeck composed four experiments between 1950 and 1954: the play-novelette *Burning Bright*, the film script *Viva Zapata!*, the epic *East of Eden*, and the comic *Sweet Thursday*. These "deeply personal" texts, as he called them, constitute a different order of writing from their more famous proletarian predecessors. By calling attention to their own literariness through such elements as literary allusions and references, language play, and artful framing devices, these works demonstrate Steinbeck's turn toward an incipient postmodernism, a condition of textual openness and metafictional high jinks where the act of writing becomes its own valid end. "If a writer likes to write," he claimed in "Critics, Critics, Burning Bright" in 1950, "he will find satisfaction in endless experiment with his medium. He will improvise techniques, arrangements of scenes, rhythms of words, and rhythms of thought. He will constantly investigate and try combinations new to him, sometimes utilizing an old method for a new idea and vice versa. Some of his experiments will inevitably be unsuccessful but he must try them anyway if his interest be alive. This experimentation is not criminal . . . but it is necessary if the writer be not moribund."

In its original form, *Sweet Thursday* was consciously proposed as a tonal, thematic counterbalance to the "weight" of *East of Eden*, Steinbeck told Elizabeth Otis, his literary agent and the dedicatee of *Sweet Thursday*, on September 14, 1953: "it is kind of light and gay and astringent." A boisterous sequel to Steinbeck's more famous *Cannery Row*, which appeared nine years earlier (treating Monterey's prewar era), *Sweet Thursday* shares the same Monterey Peninsula location in Northern California and many of the same characters as *Cannery Row*, but it takes up the post–World War II life of Doc (based on Steinbeck's soul mate, Edward F. Ricketts, who had died in an auto-train crash on Ocean View Avenue in May 1948). The novel emphasizes Doc's difficulties in reestablishing his Western Biological Laboratory business, his struggles with writing a scholarly treatise on octopi, and his rocky off-again, on-again relationship with an angry, tough-talking, golden-hearted hooker-turned-waitress named Suzy. It also features the burlesque-like antics of the Row's Palace Flophouse denizens (Mack, Hazel, and others) and Fauna, the madam of the Bear Flag, who—playing Cupid for Doc and Suzy—wants to ensure a romantic fairy-tale ending for the incompatible but otherwise smitten couple.

As this brief summary suggests, when approached from a rigidly analytical position, *Sweet Thursday* can be considered sentimental (like most other hookers at Fauna's Bear Flag brothel, Suzy's indelible goodness erases her stigma as a prostitute, even a half-assed one at that), reductive (Doc imagines he cannot be happy without a woman to complete his identity), and improbable (the plot hinges on coincidences and convenient superficialities). Such flaws—trumpeted by many critics and scholars as indisputable proof of Steinbeck's declining powers—have made the book an easy target for snipers, as it was for the unnamed *Time* reviewer who, in its June 14, 1954, issue, held nothing back: "*Sweet Thursday* is a turkey with visible Saroyanesque stuffings. But where [William] Saroyan might have clothed the book's characters and incidents with comic reality, Steinbeck merely comic-strips them of all reality and even of very much interest."

But to arrive at the deeper significance of this oddball fiction, questions of character motivation and realism need to be contextualized. *Sweet Thursday* is important for what it reveals of Steinbeck's continuing aesthetic and philosophical changes and for his attitude toward the necessity of fictive experimentation in the unsettling wake of a postwar depletion (symbolized by the decline of sardines in Monterey Bay), and a pervasive exhaustion that influenced all levels of Cannery Row's existence.

Steinbeck understood the corrosive nature of discontent and disaffection. There was a span in his career, beginning in mid-1948, when he was cut adrift from accustomed moorings by the death of Ed Ricketts and by his divorce shortly afterward from Gwyn Conger, his second wife, whom he married in 1943 and with whom he had two children, Thom and John IV. On and off for over a year, Steinbeck was mired in enervation, isolation, misogyny, and self-pity, and his self-identity as a writer seemed splintered, fragmented, even fraudulent, as Jackson Benson has graphically documented in *The True Adventures of John Steinbeck*. After *The Pearl* and *The Wayward Bus*, both published in 1947, this customarily resilient writer found it increasingly difficult to settle on his next project (the many versions of *Zapata*, for instance, the false starts on *East of Eden*, and the several unwritten plays he planned during this period). Steinbeck's personal disarray and emotional discontentedness, coupled with his awakening reaction to America's Cold War intellectual climate, which called into question the validity of socialist economies, set him on a road toward an end he could not yet envision but whose allurements he apparently could not refuse. In the feverish and sometimes blind searches of that period from 1948 through the early 1950s, he underwent deep readjustments toward many things, not the least of them his own art.

In his relationship with his third wife, Elaine Anderson Scott, whom he met in May 1949 and married in December 1950, Steinbeck discovered healing powers in love and mutual domestic attachment that in turn had a direct, exponential bearing on his work energy and anticipation and, by his own admission, may have saved him from despair and worse. His May 30, 1951, entry in *Journal of a Novel* puts it all on the line: "And what changes there have been. I did not expect to survive them and I don't think I would have. Every life force was shriveling. Work was non-existent. The wounds were gangrenous and mostly I just didn't give a dam [*sic*]. Now two years later I have a new life and a direction. I am doing work I like."

Steinbeck validated his recovery by repeating it. In *Sweet Thursday*, Steinbeck's own emotional and creative processes became the novel's subject. In writing about Doc trying to write his scholarly essay, and in portraying indomitable Suzy as a catalyst for self-awareness and conjugal fulfillment, Steinbeck turned out to be narrating nothing less than the symbolic story of his own emotional rescue and artistic refashioning. Steinbeck probably realized that blurring himself and Ricketts would be problematical: "Wouldn't it be interesting if Ed was us and that now there wasn't any such thing or that he created out of his own mind something that went away with him," Steinbeck wrote Ritch and Tal Lovejoy right after Ricketts's death in May 1948. "I've wondered a lot about that. How much was Ed and how much was me and which was which[?]" In the process of writing *Sweet Thursday*, Steinbeck did not "purposefully . . . destroy or deprecate Doc," as Peter Lisca maintained in *The Wide World of John Steinbeck*. Instead, Steinbeck replaced Doc with himself; in recasting his portrait of the artist, he did so in an entirely familiar scale, which is perhaps why he confessed to Elizabeth Otis on September 14, 1953, that the new work is "a little self indulgent."

Steinbeck took enormous pleasure in producing this blissful novel. He exorcised his painful marriage with second wife Gwyn in *Burning Bright* and *East of Eden*, whose characters reflect aspects of his own tortured relationship. In *Sweet Thursday* he allowed himself the luxury to indulge in the happiness of his present moment and his transformative new life with Elaine. Rationalization or not, as a person who labored with words day in and day out, year after year, he often spoke of his need for his task to be "fun." "There is a school of thought among writers which says that if you enjoy writing something it is automatically no good and should be thrown out," he told Elizabeth Otis. "I can't agree with this." If *Cannery Row* represented the way things were, he explained in November 1953 to Harold Bicknell and Grant Mclean (the real-life models of Gabe and Mack), then his new project became the way things "might have happened to Ed and didn't." The two propositions ("one can be as true as the other") are necessary for a holistic view of the novelist's mind and for an understanding of what the spirit of Ed Ricketts meant to Steinbeck, who didn't "seem able to get over his death," as he told former Stanford classmate Carlton A. Sheffield on November 2, 1953.

Significantly rooted in personal experience, memory, longing, and emotion, *Sweet Thursday* foregrounds the struggle of individual consciousness in (and through) language. In doing so, Steinbeck keeps a good part of Ed Ricketts and his legacy alive. In chapter 6, "The Creative Cross," Doc's tribulations in researching and writing his proposed scholarly essay, "Symptoms in Some Cephalopods Approximating Apoplexy," mirror aspects of Steinbeck's preparatory stages in his own creative regime; Doc's prewriting jitters and inability to concentrate are colored as well by Steinbeck's wrenching artistic and personal upheavals of the late 1940s and his awareness of the need for emotional fulfillment:

For hours on end he sat at his desk with a yellow pad before him and his needle-sharp pencils lined up. Sometimes his wastebasket was full of crushed, scribbled pages, and at others not even a doodle went down. Then he would move to the aquarium and stare into it. And his voices howled and cried and moaned. "Write!" said his top voice, and "Search!" said his middle voice, and his lowest voice sighed, "Lonesome! Lonesome!" He did not go down without a struggle. He resurrected old love affairs, he swam deep in music, he read the *Sorrows of Werther*; but the voices would not leave him. The beckoning yellow pages became his enemies.

Writing, like so many other endeavors in life, including romance and courtship, Steinbeck shows, is less a condition of mastery than it is hard work, full of self-doubt, false steps, insecurities, angers, frustrations, and disruptions. Steinbeck suggests that success lies as much in the marshaling of conjunctive forces and ambient fortune as it does in the completion of the scholarly project. Paradoxically, there is a telling difference in ends, because the form Steinbeck adopts for *Sweet Thursday* takes on a life of its own, borrows heavily from other literary works, and veers away from the kind of objective, autonomous document a practicing scientist would be expected to produce. Steinbeck must have realized, as he reread and reimagined the Doc of *Cannery Row* and "About Ed Ricketts" (1951), that only by embracing comedy and tragedy, realism and fabulation, the inarticulate "transcendental sadness" of *Cannery Row* and the "frabjous" expression of joy of *Sweet Thursday*, could Steinbeck lay to rest the ghost of Ed Ricketts, which, by this time, had become the symbol of Steinbeck himself.

Steinbeck playfully names chapter 10 "There's a Hole in Reality through which We Can Look if We Wish," demonstrating that in the seesaw form of *Sweet Thursday*, Steinbeck was able to bring both the narrative plot and the process of reflexive commentary into a single work. The performance appears to be made up on the spot, and its spontaneity undercuts the novel's pretensions and dismantles the rules of its own invention: "There are people who will say that this whole account is a lie, but a thing isn't necessarily a lie even if it didn't necessarily happen," the narrator claims at the end of chapter 8. In various characters' use of malapropisms and in Mack's humorous use of Latin phrases and exalted language, *Sweet Thursday* questions the representational ability of language (and class) while it validates the process by which such mysteries emerge without ever being fully concluded. Steinbeck demystifies the role of the artist by emphasizing the prewriting process, the elusiveness of language, and the necessity for human bonding, rather than the finished result (Doc has yet to write his essay as the book ends, but he has been awarded a research grant by Old Jingleballicks). That characters as diverse as Doc; Joe Elegant, the Bear Flag's cook, who is writing a Freudian novel called "The Pi Root of Oedipus"; and Fauna, who not only writes horoscopes but authors Suzy's conduct and manners ("I should write a book. . . . 'If She Could, I Could,' " she boasts in chapter 22), all wrestle with compositional acts and problems of inscription highlights Steinbeck's perception that the tangled wilderness of language (whether of speech, writing, sexuality, body gesture, or masquerade dress) is one of the few frontiers left to us in a discontented, uncentered, apocalyptic age. Writing, like Gypsy Rose Lee's stripping, Steinbeck reminds us, is a performance; both are fueled by desire, and they can be nouns as well as verbs.

To aid and abet his novel's satire and literary referentiality, Steinbeck stripped bare a small library of useful works. In the populist echoes and literary parodies, mimicries, puns, wordplays, resonances, and allusions to the Bible, Shakespeare's *Twelfth Night*, *The Little Flowers of Saint Francis*, the Welsh *Mabinogion*, Coleridge's "Kubla Khan," Robert Louis Stevenson's *Child's Garden of Verses*, and especially Lewis Carroll's *Alice's Adventures in Wonderland*, as well as his "Jabberwocky" and "The Walrus and the Carpenter" from *Through the Looking Glass*, and Walt Disney's iconic *Snow White and the Seven Dwarfs*, *Sweet Thursday* is enriched by Steinbeck's eclectic browsing in these favorite titles. (Consult the notes to this edition for further information.) Perhaps more than anything else, however, Steinbeck's avowed reading of Al Capp's enormously popular, extremely inventive *Li'l Abner* comic strip, which he and his family followed assiduously in newspapers at home and abroad, propelled *Sweet Thursday* toward its cultural shape. "Yes, comic strips," he told Sidney Fields in a 1955 interview

reprinted in *Conversations with John Steinbeck*. "I read them
avidly. Especially Li'l Abner. Al Capp is a great social satirist.
Comic strips might be the real literature of our time. We'll never
know what literature is until we're gone. But more people read
comic strips than books or anything else."

In 1953, the same time he was working on "Bear Flag," the
precursor of *Sweet Thursday*, Steinbeck introduced Capp's book-
length collection, *The World of Li'l Abner*. Steinbeck did not
habitually provide blurbs or introductions to the work of other
writers, but when he did, it was for a strong reason. He told
Elizabeth Otis on June 17, 1952, that he would "love to do" the
introduction, which he was certain he could write "in a very
short time because I have thought of [Capp] a lot." As with many
of Steinbeck's lesser-known or fugitive items, this brief piece reveals much about his creative bearings, influences, and purposes.
Beneath his jaunty, ironic, tongue-in-cheek tone there are numerous revelations that bear directly on *Sweet Thursday*'s zany style
and technique. Indeed, *Sweet Thursday* may be considered Steinbeck's attempt at writing a literary comic book, his conscious attempt "to get into Capp's act."

Steinbeck boasts that Al Capp "may very possibly be the best
writer in the world today" and "the best satirist since Laurence
Sterne." Like Dante, who redefined the established traditions of
literature in his time by writing in Italian rather than in Latin,
Capp too is a pioneer, perhaps even a visionary. The literature
of the future, Steinbeck asserts, might eventually depart from
the "stuffy" adherence to "the written and printed word in poetry, drama, and the novel" and eventually include popular
forms of cultural discourse such as the comic book, Capp's
métier. Steinbeck asks:

> How in the hell do we know what literature is? Well, one of the
> diagnostics of literature should be, it seems to me, that it is read,
> that it amuses, moves, instructs, changes and criticizes people.
> And who in the world does that more than Capp? . . . Who
> knows what literature is? The literature of the Cro Magnon is
> painted on the walls of the caves of Altamira. Who knows but
> that the literature of the future will be projected on clouds? Our

present argument that literature is the written and printed word
has no very eternal basis in fact. Such literature has not been with
us very long, and there is nothing to indicate that it will continue.
If people don't read it, it just isn't going to be literature.

In Capp's ability to "invent" an entire world in Dogpatch, to give
it memorable characters, recognizable form, and unique spoken
language, he created that quality of aesthetic participation Steinbeck aimed for in all his fictions. The unbridled license to make
up in any way that fits the artist's or the medium's immediate,
compulsive demands—not those of a critical blueprint—is what
Capp and Steinbeck share.

Indeed, Steinbeck's description of the key elements of the *Li'l
Abner* strip can also be applied to *Sweet Thursday*: the latter's
plot has a "fine crazy consistency" of (il)logic; it satirizes the "entrenched nonsense" of blind human striving, respectable middle-
class life, and normal male/female courting rituals; it constructs
an entire fictive world in the Palace Flophouse and its larger do-
main, Cannery Row itself (where, like in Capp's Dogpatch, realistic outside rules of physics and morality don't necessarily apply);
and it also contains suitably exaggerated situations (Capp's Sadie
Hawkins Day parallels Steinbeck's accounts of the annual return
of monarch butterflies to Pacific Grove and the Great Roque
War), as well as characters whose names are distinctive, colorful,
and unique (Steinbeck's Whitey No. 1, Whitey No. 2, and Joseph
and Mary Rivas; Capp's Hairless Joe and Moonbeam McSwine,
for example). Finally, in Hazel's ludicrous run for the United
States presidency, we catch Steinbeck's nod to Zoot Suit Yokum's
improbable presidential nomination in 1944. Moreover, in its optimistic, life-affirming treatment of the roller-coaster love affair
between Doc and Suzy, Steinbeck playfully reflects not only his
own relationship with Elaine but also the courtship and marriage
of the recalcitrant Li'l Abner and the bountiful Daisy Mae. There
are numerous examples of passages, such as the one in chapter 16
in which Mack believes he can heal the psychosomatic diseases of
rich women, that not only pay homage to Capp (there are echoes
in Mack's proposal of Marryin' Sam's "perspectus" for expensive
weddings), but also underscore Steinbeck's own self-mimicking

method, his application of Capp's satiric "tweak with equal pressure on all classes, all groups," and his appreciation for the "resounding prose" of Capp's folk dialogue.

Perhaps more than anything else, however, one scene in particular serves as a special indication of Capp's influence. *Sweet Thursday* is the only novel by Steinbeck whose chapters are titled. The often parodic or incongruent titles are analogous to Capp's boldfaced commentary and frame headings in his comic strip; the chapters themselves are short and easily comprehended, like cartoon strip panels, which is one of the features Mack called for in his prologue. In chapter 28, "Where Alfred the Sacred River Ran," Steinbeck lampoons Samuel Taylor Coleridge's poem "Kubla Khan" in his title, then describes a wild party and Doc's reaction to it in a way that can best be understood if we imagine ourselves to be reading a comic strip or cartoon (perhaps under the influence of some stimulant or other), blissfully participating in its "preposterous" spatiality. The following scene, a masquerade on the theme of *Snow White and the Seven Dwarfs*, suggests the flavor and dimensions of Steinbeck's boundary-breaking recitation:

A fog of unreality like a dream feeling was not in him but all around him. He went inside the Palace and saw the dwarfs and monsters and the preposterous Hazel all lighted by the flickering lanterns. None of it seemed the fabric of sweet reality. . . .

Anyone untrained in tom-wallagers might well have been startled. . . . Eddie waltzed to the rumba music, his arms embracing an invisible partner. Wide Ida lay on the floor Indian wrestling with Whitey No.2, at each try displaying acres of pink panties, while a wild conga line of dwarfs and animals milled about. . . .

Mack and Doc were swept into the conga line. To Doc the room began to revolve slowly and then to rise and fall like the deck of a stately ship in a groundswell. The music roared and tinkled. Hazel beat out rhythm on the stove with his sword until Johnny, aiming carefully, got a bull's eye on Hazel. Hazel leaped in the air and came down on the oven door, scattering crushed ice all over the floor. One of the guests had got wedged in the grandfather clock. From the outside the Palace Flophouse seemed to swell and subside like rising bread.

This festive carnivalesque passage, which occurs in what Mack calls a "veritable fairyland," is one of Steinbeck's most pleasurable fictive moments. It revels in a sense of fancifulness, in luxurious staging and fluid movement that join sacred and profane experience in memorable ways. Steinbeck's reversals of gender expectations and his conscious abdication of the "fabric of sweet reality" account for the exaggerated swelling house, the improvisatory instances of cross-dressing ("all over the Row the story was being rewritten to fit the wardrobe"), and the homosociality and sexual impersonation ("one of the queerest scenes Steinbeck ever imagined," scholar Leland Person claims); and they reflect the unpredictable loops and digressions of the novel's structure, its topsy-turvy abandonment of overtly linear or "literary" progression in favor of a quantum randomness, and its one-dimensional (but not necessarily simplistic) characterizations. This hilarious scene is an example of Steinbeck's belief that "technique should grow out of theme," as he told Pascal Covici in early 1956, and his advice to humorist Fred Allen: "Don't make the telling follow a form."

Furthermore, Steinbeck's postwar change of aesthetic sensibility made all the difference between his treatment of Doc, whose "transcendent sadness" and essential loneliness closed *Cannery Row*, and this portrayal, which ends with the partially incapacitated but romantically redeemed Doc riding off with the no less reformed and eager Suzy (she is driving) into the sunset of a day that is "of purple and gold, the proud colors of the Salinas High School." Steinbeck continues, "A squadron of baby angels maneuvered at twelve hundred feet, holding a pink cloud on which the word J-O-Y flashed on and off. A seagull with a broken wing took off and flew straight up into the air, squawking, 'Joy! Joy!'" That over-the-top moment gives *Sweet Thursday* the same fanciful, buoyant quality Steinbeck found in *The World of Li'l Abner*: "such effective good nature that we seem to have thought of it ourselves." Inevitably, Doc and Suzy's fairy-tale relationship is not so much a smarmy act of denouement as it is a proof of Steinbeck's belief in the necessity for human beings to willingly open themselves to the demands of mutual love, and his abiding sense of the "joy" of creative drives to address human desire. *Sweet Thursday* conjoins writing and sexuality, which creates an exquisite "satisfaction" that comes when "words and sentences" and "good and shared love" combine, as he announced in a short essay called "Rationale." "Believe me, I have nothing against fairy tales," he told Otis and his drama agent Annie Laurie Williams on April 7, 1962. "God knows I've written enough of them. My point is that no fairy tale is acceptable unless it is based on some truth about something. You can make it as light and airy and full of whimsy as you wish but down underneath there has to be a true thing." Love, considered emotionally, physically, and as a form of creativity, Steinbeck suggests, is the "true thing" that has the potential to heal the split between man and woman, self and world, language and life, text and audience. The pejorative *Time* magazine review was only partly—and unintentionally—correct in its assessment of *Sweet Thursday*. Steinbeck did "comic-strip" his characters of reality, but that was his desire; far from being proof of his decline into an undifferentiated Saroyanesque landscape, his appropriation of Al Capp's free-form inventiveness, vivid technique, exaggerated scenarios, and "dreadful folk poetry" helped further in the novel what Steinbeck saw in *Li'l Abner*: a "hilarious picture of our ridiculous selves."

Thus "Sweet Thursday" functions as a double signifier—at once private and public utterance, reference and object, process and product. The name refers to a "magic kind of day" when all manner of unanticipated, random events occur on Cannery Row (to which Steinbeck devotes three contiguous, titled chapters—19, 20, 21—at the midpoint of his novel, and one—39—at the very end). Then, refracted, "Sweet Thursday" (a time, a place in the mind, a historical context) becomes, like Hawthorne's symbolic "Scarlet Letter" or Melville's multimeaning "Moby-Dick," the title of the book Steinbeck brings into being. The title operates in turn as a looking glass, a hole in reality, that reflects, distorts, enlarges, and/or magnifies the implicit ethereality and quantum activities of the "magic day" by borrowing a sense of its own disruptive form from the uninhibited carnival quality of life on the Row and from a number of literary texts that play into the mix. That inherent duality and fluid interchangeability of word and world and fiction and fact symbolizes Steinbeck's imaginative concerns and method. When in chapter 20 Fauna tells Joe Elegant, "When a man says words he believes them, even if he thinks he is lying," she is suggesting that language (not only experience) is a reality, and a seductive one at that.

Far from being a pooped-out failure because he abandoned critical realism after *The Grapes of Wrath*, Steinbeck was a prophetic postmodernist, a journeyer in a literary fun house, and a traveler in the land behind the mirror of art. In *Sweet Thursday* the mirror had become nearly silverless, so that we see his hand at work behind the curtain of realism, calling attention to the house of words he is building. For that reason, traditional disciplinary literary criticism won't work effectively with a textual construct like *Sweet Thursday* or, for that matter, with much of what Steinbeck wrote in the last phase of his career. Authoring these texts, he authored himself anew and vice versa.

Perhaps *Sweet Thursday* is not an overstuffed turkey but more like the gull that presides over the novel's conclusion— earthbound on occasion but still capable of some startling flights of fancy, humor, and goodwill. Pascal Covici was correct—the novel sold with abandon—and while its commercial success justified Covici's faith in Steinbeck as an enduring popular writer, just as its success fueled some critics' scorn, there is, as with all Steinbeck's work, a historical and personal context that provides background for understanding this delightful satiric novel. *Sweet Thursday*, the last book Steinbeck ever wrote about California, became at once an elegy to the departed Ricketts and a demonstration of creativity, as well as an homage to Steinbeck's newly found emotional existence with Elaine and a farewell to the beloved landscape of his native state.

ROBERT DEMOTT

Suggestions for Further Reading

PRIMARY WORKS BY JOHN STEINBECK

Note: Steinbeck's long-lost handwritten manuscript of *Sweet Thursday* and a portion of early drafts of its predecessor, "Bear Flag," which he gave to Broadway producer Ernest H. Martin, were discovered among Martin's possessions in 2004 and subsequently auctioned by Pacific Book Auction Galleries in 2007. See http://www.pbagalleries.com. The typescript, carbon copy, and unrevised galley proofs of *Sweet Thursday* are housed at the Harry Ransom Humanities Research Center, University of Texas, Austin, in Works, 1926–1966, Box 8, Folders 2–5. See http://www.hrc.utexas.edu/research/fa/steinbeck.html#works.

Steinbeck, John. "About Ed Ricketts." *The Log from the Sea of Cortez*. New York: Viking Press, 1951, vii–lxvii.
———. *Cannery Row*. New York: Viking Press, 1945.
———. "Critics, Critics, Burning Bright" (1950). *Steinbeck and His Critics: A Record of Twenty-five Years*. E. W. Tedlock and C. V. Wicker, eds. Albuquerque: University of New Mexico Press, 1957, 43–47.
———. "Introduction." *The World of Li'l Abner* by Al Capp. Foreword by Charles Chaplin. New York: Farrar, Straus, and Young with Ballantine Books, 1953, i–vi.
———. "Introduction Mack's Contribution." Unpublished autograph manuscript, typescript, and galley proofs of original extended Prologue to *Sweet Thursday*. Harry Ransom Humanities Research Center, University of Texas, Austin, TX.
———. "Rationale." In Tedlock and Wicker's *Steinbeck and His Critics*, 308–9.

Steinbeck, John, and Edward F. Ricketts. *Sea of Cortez: A Leisurely Journal of Travel and Research*. New York: Viking Press, 1941.

CORRESPONDENCE, INTERVIEWS, ADAPTATIONS

Fensch, Thomas. *Steinbeck and Covici: The Story of a Friendship*. Middlebury, VT: Paul S. Eriksson, 1979.

Rodgers, Richard, and Oscar Hammerstein II. *Pipe Dream*. New York: Viking Press, 1956.

Steinbeck, John. *Conversations with John Steinbeck*. Thomas Fensch, ed. Jackson: University Press of Mississippi, 1988.

———. *Letters to Elizabeth: A Selection of Letters from John Steinbeck to Elizabeth Otis*. Florian J. Shasky and Susan F. Riggs, eds. Foreword by Carlton Sheffield. San Francisco: Book Club of California, 1978.

———. *Steinbeck: A Life in Letters*. Elaine Steinbeck and Robert Wallsten, eds. New York: Viking Press, 1975.

Ward, David S. *Cannery Row*. Hollywood: MGM, 1982. 120 mins.

BIOGRAPHIES, MEMOIRS, BACKGROUND, AND APPRECIATIONS

Note: An exhaustive chronology of Steinbeck's life is available in Robert DeMott and Brian Railsback, eds., *Travels with Charley and Later Novels, 1947–1962* (New York: Library of America, 2007), 955–73. Chief Internet sites devoted to John Steinbeck are http://www.steinbeck.sjsu.edu/home/index.jsp at the Martha Heasley Cox Center for Steinbeck Studies at San Jose State University, and http://www.steinbeck.org at the National Steinbeck Center, Salinas, California. The Cannery Row Foundation, Monterey, California, maintains a useful Web site relevant to the setting, history, and background of Steinbeck's Monterey novels, http://www.canneryrow.org. Search http://www.topix.net/who/john-steinbeck for regularly updated news on John Steinbeck.

Astro, Richard. *John Steinbeck and Edward F. Ricketts: The Shaping of a Novelist*. Minneapolis: University of Minnesota Press, 1974.

Benson, Jackson J. *The True Adventures of John Steinbeck, Writer*. New York: Viking Press, 1984.

Davis, Kathryn M. "Edward F. Ricketts: Man of Science and Conscience." *Steinbeck Studies* 15 (Winter 2004): 15–22.

DeMott, Robert. *Steinbeck's Reading: A Catalogue of Books Owned and Borrowed*. New York: Garland Publishing, 1984.

Hemp, Michael Kenneth. *Cannery Row: The History of Old Ocean View Avenue*. Monterey, CA: History Company, 1986.

Leonard, Elmore. "Elmore Leonard on John Steinbeck." In *20 Years of Publishing America's Best*. Preface by Cheryl Hurley. New York: Library of America, 2002, 9–11.

Parini, Jay. *John Steinbeck: A Biography*. New York: Henry Holt, 1995.

Ricketts, Edward F. *Breaking Through: Essays, Journals, and Travelogues of Edward F. Ricketts*. Katherine A. Rodger, ed. Foreword by Susan F. Beegel. Berkeley: University of California Press, 2006.

————. *Renaissance Man of Cannery Row: The Life and Letters of Edward F. Ricketts*. Katharine A. Rodger, ed. Tuscaloosa: University of Alabama Press, 2002.

Sheffield, Carlton. *John Steinbeck, the Good Companion*. Terry White, ed. Introduction by R. A. Blum. Berkeley, CA: Creative Arts, 2002.

Shillinglaw, Susan. *A Journey into Steinbeck's California*. Photographs by Nancy Burnett. Berkeley, CA: Roaring Forties Press, 2006.

Tamm, Eric Enno. *Beyond the Outer Shores: The Untold Odyssey of Ed Ricketts, the Pioneering Ecologist Who Inspired John Steinbeck and Joseph Campbell*. New York: Four Walls Eight Windows, 2004.

CAREER OVERVIEWS, REVIEWS, AND REFERENCE WORKS

Ditsky, John. *John Steinbeck and the Critics*. Rochester, NY: Camden House, 2000.

Li, Luchen, ed. *John Steinbeck: A Documentary Volume*. Volume 309 of *Dictionary of Literary Biography*. Detroit: Thomson Gale, 2005.

McPheron, William. *John Steinbeck: From Salinas to Stockholm*. Stanford, CA: Stanford University Libraries, 2000.

Railsback, Brian, and Michael J. Meyer, eds. *A John Steinbeck Encyclopedia*. Westport, CT: Greenwood Press, 2006.

Riggs, Susan F. *A Catalogue of the John Steinbeck Collection at Stanford University*. Stanford, CA: Stanford University Libraries, 1980.

Schultz, Jeffrey, and Luchen Li, eds. *Critical Companion to John Steinbeck: A Literary Reference to His Life and Work*. New York: Facts on File, 2005.

CRITICAL COMMENTARY ON *SWEET THURSDAY*

Note: An extensive bibliography of secondary sources on Steinbeck, prepared by Greta Manville for San Jose State University's Martha Heasley Cox Center for Steinbeck Studies, is accessible at http://www.steinbeckbibliography.org/index/html.

Astro, Richard. "Steinbeck's Bittersweet Thursday." *Steinbeck Quarterly* 4 (Spring 1971): 36–48. Reprinted in *The Short Novels of John Steinbeck: Critical Essays with a Checklist to Steinbeck Criticism*. Jackson J. Benson, ed. Durham, NC: Duke University Press, 1990, 204–15.

DeMott, Robert. "The Place We Have Arrived: On Writing/Reading toward Cannery Row." In *Beyond Boundaries: Rereading John Steinbeck*. Susan Shillinglaw and Kevin Hearle, eds. Tuscaloosa: University of Alabama Press, 2002, 295–313.

————. "Steinbeck's Typewriter: An Excursion in Suggestiveness." In *Steinbeck's Typewriter: Essays on His Art*. Troy, NY: Whitston Publishing, 1996, 287–317.

Ditsky, John. "'Stupid Sons of Fishes': Shared Values in John Steinbeck and the Musical Stage." *Steinbeck Studies* 15 (Winter 2004): 107–16.

Gladstein, Mimi. "Straining for Profundity: Steinbeck's *Burning Bright* and *Sweet Thursday*." In *The Short Novels of John Steinbeck: Critical Essays with a Checklist to Steinbeck Criticism*. Jackson J. Benson, ed. Durham, NC: Duke University Press, 1990, 234–48.

Levant, Howard. "Hooptedoodle." In his *Novels of John Steinbeck: A Critical Study*. Columbia: University of Missouri Press, 1974, 259–72.

Lisca, Peter. *The Wide World of John Steinbeck*. New Brunswick, NJ: Rutgers University Press, 1958, 276–84.

Mahan, Meghan. *Sweet Thursday*. *20th-Century American Bestsellers*. http://www3.isrl.uiuc.edu/~unsworth/courses/bestsellers.

McElrath, Joseph, Jesse S. Crisler, and Susan Shillinglaw, eds. *John Steinbeck: The Contemporary Reviews*. New York: Cambridge University Press, 1996, 406–25.

Metzger, Charles R. "Steinbeck's Version of the Pastoral." *Modern Fiction Studies* 6 (Summer 1960): 115–24. Reprinted in *The Short Novels of John Steinbeck: Critical Essays with a Checklist to Steinbeck Criticism*. Jackson J. Benson, ed. Durham, NC: Duke University Press, 1990, 185–95.

Millichap, Joseph. *Steinbeck and Film*. New York: Frederick Ungar, 1983, 172–75.

Morsberger, Robert. "Steinbeck's Happy Hookers." *Steinbeck Quarterly* 9 (Summer–Fall 1976): 101–15.

Newfield, Anthony. "Pipe Dream Memories." *Steinbeck Studies* 15 (Winter 2004): 117–28.

Owens, Louis. "Critics and Common Denominators: Steinbeck's *Sweet Thursday*." In *The Short Novels of John Steinbeck: Critical Essays with a Checklist to Steinbeck*

Criticism. Jackson J. Benson, ed. Durham, NC: Duke University Press, 1990, 195–203.

———. "*Sweet Thursday*: Farewell to Steinbeck Country." In his *John Steinbeck's Re-Vision of America*. Athens: University of Georgia Press, 1985, 190–96.

Person, Leland S. "Steinbeck's Queer Ecology: Sweet Comradeship in the Monterey Novels." *Steinbeck Studies* 15 (Spring 2004): 7–20.

Railsback, Brian. "Evolution of a Hero." In his *Parallel Expeditions: Charles Darwin and the Art of John Steinbeck*. Moscow: University of Idaho Press, 1995, 121–27.

Simmonds, Roy S. "*Sweet Thursday*." In *A Study Guide to Steinbeck (Part II)*. Tetsumaro Hayashi, ed. Metuchen, NJ: Scarecrow Press, 1979, 139–64.

Timmerman, John. "The Cannery Row Novels." In his *John Steinbeck's Fiction: The Aesthetics of the Road Taken*. Norman: University of Oklahoma Press, 1986, 168–82.

Sweet Thursday

Prologue

One night Mack lay back on his bed in the Palace Flophouse and he said, "I ain't never been satisfied with that book Cannery Row. *I would of went about it different."*

And after a while he rolled over and raised his head on his hand and he said, "I guess I'm just a critic. But if I ever come across the guy that wrote that book I could tell him a few things."

"Like what?" said Whitey No. 1.

"Well," said Mack, "like this here. Suppose there's chapter one, chapter two, chapter three. That's all right, as far as it goes, but I'd like to have a couple of words at the top so it tells me what the chapter's going to be about. Sometimes maybe I want to go back, and chapter five don't mean nothing to me. If there was just a couple of words I'd know that was the chapter I wanted to go back to."

"Go on," said Whitey No. 1.

"Well, I like a lot of talk in a book, and I don't like to have nobody tell me what the guy that's talking looks like. I want to figure out what he looks like from the way he talks. And another thing—I kind of like to figure out what the guy's thinking by what he says. I like some description too," he went on. "I like to know what color a thing is, how it smells and maybe how it looks, and maybe how a guy feels about it—but not too much of that."

"You sure are a critic," said Whitey No. 2. "Mack, I never give you credit before. Is that all?"

"No," said Mack. "Sometimes I want a book to break loose with a bunch of hooptedoodle. The guy's writing it, give him a

PROLOGUE

*chance to do a little hooptedoodle. Spin up some pretty words
maybe, or sing a little song with language. That's nice. But I
wish it was set aside so I don't have to read it. I don't want
hooptedoodle to get mixed up in the story. So if the guy that's
writing it wants hooptedoodle, he ought to put it right at first.
Then I can skip it if I want to, or maybe go back to it after I
know how the story come out."*

Eddie said, "Mack, if the guy that wrote Cannery Row
comes in, you going to tell him all that?"

*Whitey No. 2 said, "Hell, Mack can tell anybody anything.
Why, Mack could tell a ghost how to haunt a house."*

*"You're damn right I could," said Mack, "and there
wouldn't be no table-rapping or chains. There hasn't been no
improvement in house-haunting in years. You're damn right I
could, Whitey!" And he lay back and stared up at the canopy
over his bed.*

"I can see it now," said Mack.

"Ghosts?" Eddie asked.

"Hell, no," said Mack, "chapters. . . ."

What Happened In Between

When the war came to Monterey and to Cannery Row everybody fought it more or less, in one way or another. When hostilities ceased everyone had his wounds.

The canneries themselves fought the war by getting the limit taken off fish and catching them all. It was done for patriotic reasons, but that didn't bring the fish back. As with the oysters in *Alice*, "They'd eaten every one." It was the same noble impulse that stripped the forests of the West and right now is pumping water out of California's earth faster than it can rain back in. When the desert comes, people will be sad; just as Cannery Row was sad when all the pilchards were caught and canned and eaten. The pearl-gray canneries of corrugated iron were silent and a pacing watchman was their only life. The street that once roared with trucks was quiet and empty.

Yes, the war got into everybody. Doc was drafted. He put a friend known as Old Jingleballicks in charge of Western Biological Laboratories and served out his time as a tech sergeant in a V.D. section.

Doc was philosophical about it. He whiled away his free hours with an unlimited supply of government alcohol, made many friends, and resisted promotion. When the war was over, Doc was kept on by a grateful government to straighten out certain inventory problems, a job he was fitted for since he had contributed largely to the muck-up. Doc was honorably discharged two years after our victory.

He went back to Western Biological and forced open the water-logged door. Old Jingleballicks hadn't been there for years. Dust and mildew covered everything. There were dirty pots and pans in the sink. Instruments were rusted. The live-animal cages were empty.

Doc sat down in his old chair and a weight descended on him. He cursed Old Jingleballicks, savoring his quiet poisonous words, and then automatically he got up and walked across the silent street to Lee Chong's grocery for beer. A well-dressed man of Mexican appearance stood behind the counter, and only then did Doc remember that Lee Chong was gone.

"Beer," said Doc. "Two quarts."

"Coming up," said the Patrón.

"Is Mack around?"

"Sure. I guess so."

"Tell him I want to see him."

"Tell him who wants to see him?"

"Tell him Doc is back."

"Okay, Doc," said the Patrón. "This kind of beer all right?"

"Any kind of beer's all right," said Doc.

Doc and Mack sat late together in the laboratory. The beer lost its edge and a quart of Old Tennis Shoes took its place while Mack filled in the lost years.

Change was everywhere. People were gone, or changed, and that was almost like being gone. Names were mentioned sadly, even the names of the living. Gay was dead, killed by a piece of anti-aircraft fallback in London. He couldn't keep his nose out of the sky during a bombing. His wife easily remarried on his insurance, but at the Palace Flophouse they kept Gay's bed just as it was, before he went—a little shrine to Gay. No one was permitted to sit on Gay's bed.

And Mack told Doc how Whitey No. 1 took a job in a war plant in Oakland and broke his leg the second day and spent three months in luxury. In his white hospital bed he learned to play rhythm harmonica, an accomplishment he enjoyed all the rest of his life.

Then there was the new Whitey, Whitey No. 2, and Mack was proud of him, for Whitey No. 2 had joined First Marines and gone out as a replacement. Someone, not Whitey No. 2, said he had won a Bronze Star, but if he had he'd lost it, so there was no proof. But he never forgave the Marine Corps for taking his prize away from him—a quart jar of ears pickled in brandy. He'd wanted to put that jar on the shelf over his bed, a memento of his service to his country.

Eddie had stayed on his job with Wide Ida at the Café La Ida. The medical examiner, when he looked at his check sheet and saw what was wrong with Eddie, came to the conclusion that Eddie had been technically dead for twelve years. But Eddie got around just the same, and what with the draft taking everybody away he very nearly became a permanent bartender for Wide Ida. Out of sentiment he emptied the wining jug into a series of little kegs, and when each keg was full he bunged it and buried it. Right now the Palace is the best-endowed flophouse in Monterey County.

Down about the middle of the first quart of Old Tennis Shoes, Mack told how Dora Flood had died in her sleep, leaving the Bear Flag bereft. Her girls were brokenhearted. They put on a lady-drunk that lasted three days, stuck a "Not Open for Business" sign on the door, but through the walls you could hear them doing honor to Dora in three-part harmony—"Rock of Ages," "Asleep in the Deep," and "St. James Infirmary." Those girls really mourned—they mourned like coyotes.

The Bear Flag was taken over by Dora's next of kin, an older sister who came down from San Francisco, where for some years she had been running a Midnight Mission on Howard Street, running it at a profit. She had been a silent partner all along and had dictated its unique practices and policies. For instance, Dora had wanted to name her place the Lone Star, because once in her youth she had spent a wonderful weekend in Fort Worth. But her sister insisted that it be called the Bear Flag, in honor of California. She said if you were hustling a state you should do honor to that state. She didn't find her new profession very different from her old, and she thought of both as a public service. She read horoscopes and continued, after hours at least, to transform the Bear Flag into a kind of finishing school for girls. She was named Flora, but one time in the Mission a gentleman bum finished his soup and said, "Flora, you seem more a fauna-type to me."

"Say, I like that," she said. "Mind if I keep it?" And she did. She was Fauna ever afterward.

Now all this was sad enough, but there was a greater sadness that Mack kept putting off. He didn't want to get to it. And so he told Doc about Henri the painter.

Mack kind of blamed himself for Henri. Henri had built a boat, a perfect little boat with a nice stateroom. But he'd built it up in the woods, because he was afraid of the ocean. His boat sat on concrete blocks and Henri was happy there. One time, when there wasn't much else to do, Mack and the boys played a trick on him. They were bored. They went down to the sea rocks and chiseled off a sack of barnacles and took them up and glued them on the bottom of Henri's boat with quick-drying cement. Henri was pretty upset, particularly since he couldn't tell anybody about it. Doc could have reassured him, but Doc was in the Army. Henri scraped the bottom and painted it, but no sooner was the paint dry than the boys did it again, and stuck a little seaweed on too. They were terribly ashamed when they saw what happened. Henri sold his boat and left town within twenty-four hours. He could not shake the persistent and horrifying notion that the boat was going to sea while he was asleep.

And Mack told how Hazel had been in the Army too, although you couldn't get anybody to believe it. Hazel was in the Army long enough to qualify for the G.I. bill, and he enrolled at the University of California for training in astrophysics by making a check mark on an application. Three months later, when some of the confusion had died down, the college authorities discovered him. The Department of Psychology wanted to keep him, but it was against the law.

Hazel often wondered what it was that he had gone to study. He intended to ask Doc, but by the time Doc got back it had slipped his mind.

Doc poured out the last of the first bottle of Old Tennis Shoes, and he said, "You've talked about everything else. What happened to you, Mack?"

Mack said, "I just kind of stayed around and kept things in order."

Well, Mack had kept things in order, and he had discussed war with everybody he'd met. He called his war the Big War. That was the first one. After the war the atom-bomb tests interested

him, in a Fourth-of-July kind of way. The huge reward the government offered for the discovery of new uranium deposits set
off a chain reaction in Mack, and he bought a second-hand
Geiger counter.

At the Monterey bus station the Geiger counter started
buzzing and Mack went along with it—first to San Francisco,
then to Marysville, Sacramento, Portland. Mack was so scien-
tifically interested that he didn't notice the girl on the same bus.
That is, he didn't notice her much. Well, one thing led to another, which was not unique in Mack's experience. The girl was
taking the long way to Jacksonville, Florida. Mack would have
left her in Tacoma if his Geiger counter hadn't throbbed him
eastward. He got clear to Salina, Kansas, with the girl. On a hot
muggy day the girl lunged at a fly on the bus and broke her
watch, and only then did Mack discover that he had been following a radium dial. Romance alone was not enough for Mack
at his age. He arrived back in Monterey on a flatcar, under a
tarpaulin that covered a medium-sized tank destined for Fort
Ord. Mack was very glad to get home. He had won a few dollars from a guard on the flatcar. He scrubbed out the Palace
Flophouse and planted a row of morning glories along the
front, and he and Eddie got it ready for the returning heroes.
They had quite a time when the heroes straggled back.

Over Doc and Mack a golden melancholy settled like autumn
leaves, melancholy concocted equally of Old Tennis Shoes and
old times, of friends lost and friends changed. And both of
them knew they were avoiding one subject, telling minor stories
to avoid a major one. But at last they were dry, and their subject
confronted them.

Doc opened with considerable bravery. "What do you think
of the new owner over at the grocery?"

"Oh, he's all right," said Mack. "Kind of interesting. The
only trouble is he can't never take Lee Chong's place. There was
never a friend like Lee Chong," Mack said brokenly.

"Yes, he was wise and good," said Doc.

"And tricky," said Mack.

"And smart," said Doc.

"He took care of a lot of people," said Mack.

"And he took a few," said Doc.

They volleyed Lee Chong back and forth, and their memories built virtues that would have surprised him, and cleverness and beauty too. While one told a fine tale of that mercantile China-man the other waited impatiently to top the story. Out of their memories there emerged a being scarcely human, a dragon of goodness and an angel of guile. In such a way are the gods cre-ated.

But the bottle was empty now, and its emptiness irritated Mack, and his irritation oozed toward Lee Chong's memory.

"The son-of-a-bitch was sneaky," said Mack. "He should of told us he was going to sell out and go away. It wasn't friendly, doing all that alone without his friends to help."

"Maybe that's what he was afraid of," said Doc. "Lee wrote to me about it. I couldn't advise him—I was too far away—so he was safe."

"You can't never find out what a Chink's got on his mind," said Mack. "Doc, who would of thought he was what you might say—plotting?"

Oh, it had been a shocking thing. Lee Chong had operated his emporium for so long that no one could possibly have fore-seen that he would sell out. He was so mixed up in the feeding and clothing of Cannery Row that he was considered perma-nent. Who could have suspected the secret turnings of his para-doxical Oriental mind, which seems to have paralleled the paradoxical Occidental mind?

It is customary to think of a sea captain sitting in his cabin, planning a future grocery store not subject to wind or bottom-fouling. Lee Chong dreamed while he worked his abacus and passed out pints of Old Tennis Shoes and delicately sliced ba-con with his big knife. He dreamed all right—he dreamed of the sea. He did not share his plans or ask advice. He would have got lots of advice.

One day Lee Chong sold out and bought a schooner. He wanted to go trading in the South Seas. He dreamed of palms and Polynesians. In the hold of his schooner he loaded the entire stock of his store—all the canned goods, the rubber boots, the caps and needles and small tools, the fireworks and calendars, even the glass-fronted showcases where he kept gold-plated collar buttons and cigarette lighters. He took it all with him. And the last anyone saw of him, he was waving his blue naval cap from the flying bridge of his dream ship as he passed the whistle buoy at Point Pinos into the sunset. And if he didn't go down on the way over, that's where he is now—probably lying in a hammock under an awning on the rear deck, while beautiful Polynesian girls in very scanty clothes pick over his stock of canned tomatoes and striped mechanics' caps.

"Why do you suppose he done it?" Mack asked.

"Who knows?" said Doc. "Who knows what lies deep in any man's mind? Who knows what any man wants?"

"He won't be happy there," said Mack. "He'll be lonely out among them foreigners. You know, Doc, I figured it out. It was them goddam movies done it. You remember, he used to close up every Thursday night. That's because there was a change of bill at the movie house. He never missed a movie. That's what done it, the movies. I and you, Doc, we know what liars the movies are. He won't be happy out there. He'll just be miserable to come back."

Doc gazed at his run-down laboratory. "I wish I were out there with him," he said.

"Who don't?" said Mack. "Why, them South Sea Island girls will kill him. He ain't as young as he used to be."

"I know," said Doc. "You and I should be out there, Mack, to help protect him from himself. I'm wondering, Mack, should I step across the street and get another pint or should I go to bed?"

"Why don't you flip a coin?"

"You flip the coin," said Doc. "I don't really want to go to bed. If you flip it I'll know how it's going to come out."

Mack flipped, and he was right. Mack said, "I'd just as lief step over for you, Doc. You just set here comfortable—I'll be right back." And he was.

The Troubled Life of
Joseph and Mary

Mack came back with a pint of Old Tennis Shoes and he poured some in Doc's glass and some in his own.

Doc said, "What kind of a fellow is the new owner over there—Mexican, isn't he?"

"Nice fellow," said Mack. "Classy dresser. Name of Joseph and Mary Rivas. Smart as a whip, but kind of unfortunate, Doc—unfortunate and funny. You know how it is, when a pimp falls in love it don't make any difference how much he suffers— it's funny. And Joseph and Mary's kind of like that."

"Tell me about him," said Doc.

"I been studying him," said Mack. "He told me some stuff and I put two and two together. He's smart. You know, Doc, there's a kind of smartness that cuts its own throat. Haven't you knew people that was so busy being smart they never had time to do nothing else? Well, Joseph and Mary is kind of like that."

"Tell me," said Doc.

"I guess you couldn't find no two people oppositer than what you and him is," Mack began. "You're nice, Doc, nice and egg-heady, but a guy would have to be nuts to think you was smart. Everybody takes care of you because you're wide open. Anybody is like to throw a sneak-punch at Joseph and Mary just because he's in there dancing and feinting all the time. And he's nice too, in a way."

"Where'd he come from?" Doc asked.

"Well, I'll tell you," said Mack.

Mack was right. Doc and Joseph and Mary were about as opposite as you can get, but delicately opposite. Their differences balanced like figures of a mobile in a light breeze. Doc was a man whose whole direction and impulse was legal and legitimate. Left to his own devices, he would have obeyed every law, down to pausing at boulevard stop signs. The fact that Doc was constantly jockeyed into illicit practices was the fault of his friends, not of himself—the fault of Wide Ida, whom the liquor laws cramped like a tight girdle, and of the Bear Flag, whose business, while accepted and recognized, was certainly mentioned disparagingly in every conceivable statute book.

Mack and the boys had lived so long in the shadow of the vagrancy laws that they considered them a shield and an umbrella. Their association with larceny, fraud, loitering, illegal congregation, and conspiracy on all levels was not only accepted, but to a certain extent had become a matter of pride to the inhabitants of Cannery Row. But they were lamblike children of probity and virtue compared to Joseph and Mary. Everything he did naturally turned out to be against the law. This had been true from his earliest childhood. In Los Angeles, where he had been born, he led a gang of pachucos while he was still a child. The charge that he lagged with loaded pennies, if not provable, at least seems reasonable. He rejected the theory of private ownership of removable property almost from birth. At the age of eight he was a pool hustler of such success that Navy officers had been known to put him off limits. When the gang wars started in the Mexican district of Los Angeles, Joseph and Mary rose above pachucos. He set up an ambulatory store, well stocked with switch knives, snap guns, brass knuckles, and, for the very poor, socks loaded with sand, cheap and very effective. At twelve he matriculated at reform school, and two years later emerged with honors. He had learned nearly every criminal technique in existence. This fourteen-year-old handsome boy with sad and innocent eyes could operate the tumblers of a safe with either fingers or stethoscope. He could make second stories as though he had suction cups on his feet. But no sooner had he mastered these arts than he abandoned them, reasoning that the odds were too great. He was always a smart boy. Joseph and Mary was looking for a profession wherein the victim was the partner of the predator. The badger game, the swinging panel, and the Spanish treasure were nearer to his ideal. But even they fell short. He had never made a police blotter and he wanted to keep it that way. Somewhere he felt there was a profession illegal enough to satisfy him morally and yet safe enough not to outrage his instinctive knowledge of the law of averages. You might have said he was well launched on his career when, suddenly, puberty smote him, and for a number of years his activities took a different direction.

In the fields of larceny and fraud Joseph and Mary vegetated for a number of years. He was a man when the fog cleared from before his eyes and he could see again. Then just when he was set to go, the Army got him and kept him as long as it could in good conscience. It is said that his final dishonorable discharge is a masterpiece of understatement.

J and M never could get set. He started again on his career and took a wrong turning, for he fell under the influence of a young and understanding priest, who drew him into the warm bosom of Mother Church, into which Joseph and Mary had been born anyway. Now Joseph and Mary Rivas approved of confession and forgiveness, and he felt, as perhaps François Villon had, that under the protection of the cloth he might find some outlet for his talent. Father Murphy taught him the theory of honest labor, and when Joseph and Mary had got over the shock of the principle he decided to give it a try. He was still malleable, and he succeeded, where Villon had failed, in keeping his hands off church property. With the help of Father Murphy, who had influence in the city government, Joseph and Mary found himself the possessor of a city job, a position of dignity, with a monthly check to be cashed without fear of fingerprinting.

The Plaza in Los Angeles is a pretty square, ornamented with small gardens, palms in great pots, and many, many flowers. It is a landmark, a tourist center, a city pride, for it preserves a Mexican-ness unknown in Mexico. Joseph and Mary, then, was in charge of watering and cultivating the plants in the Plaza—a job that was not only easy and pleasant but kept him in direct touch with those tourists who might be interested in small packets of art studies. Although Joseph and Mary realized he could never get rich in this job, he took a certain pleasure in being partly legal. It gave him the satisfaction most people find in sin.

At about this time the Los Angeles Police Department had a puzzle on its hands. Marijuana was being distributed in fairly large quantities and at a greatly reduced price. The narcotics squad conducted raid after raid without finding the source. Every vacant lot was searched from San Pedro to Eagle Rock. And then the countryside was laid out on graphing paper and the search for the pointed leaves of the marijuana went on in ever-widening circles: north past Santa Barbara; east to the Colorado River; south as far as the border. The border was sealed, and it is well known that muggles does not grow in the Pacific Ocean. Six months of intensive search, with the cooperation of all local officials and the state police, got absolutely nowhere. The supply continued unabated, and the narcotics squad was convinced that the pushers did not know the source.

Heaven knows how long the situation might have continued if it had not been for Mildred Bugle, thirteen, head of her class in Beginning Botany, Los Angeles High School. One Saturday afternoon she crossed the Plaza, picked some interesting leaves growing around a potted palm, and positively identified them as Cannabis Americana.

Joseph and Mary Rivas might have been in trouble but for the fact that the Los Angeles Police Department was in worse trouble. They could not bring him to book. How would it look if the newspapers got hold of the story that the Plaza was the source of supply? that the product had been planted and nurtured by a city employee, freshened with city water, and fed with city manure?

Joseph and Mary was given a floater so strongly worded that it singed his eyelashes. The police even bought him a bus ticket as far as San Luis Obispo.

Doc chuckled. "You know, Mack," he said, "you're almost building a case for honesty."

"I always put in a good word for it," said Mack.

"How did he get in the wetback business?" Doc asked.

"Well, he was casing the field for a career," said Mack, "and wetbacks looked like a gold-brick cinch. Joseph and Mary figured the angles and the percentage. You look at it and you see it couldn't flop." He put up his fingers to count facts, then took a quick drink to tide him over the period when his hands would be tied up.

Mack touched the little finger of his left hand with his right forefinger. "Number one," he said. "J and M talks Mexican because his old man and his old lady was Mexican before they come to L.A." He touched his third finger. "Number two, the wetbacks come in by theirself. Nobody makes them come. There's a steady supply. Number three, they can't talk English and they don't know a cop from a bucket. They *need* somebody like Joseph and Mary to take care of them and get them jobs and take their pay. If one of them gets mean, all J and M got to do is call the federal men, and they deport him without no trouble to J and M. That's what he was always looking for—a racket with the percentage stacked for the house. He figures he's got three or four crews working in fruit and vegetables and he can kind of lay back and rest, the way he always wanted. That's why he bought out Lee Chong. He figured to make the grocery a kind of labor center, where he could rest up his men and sell them stuff at the same time. And what he's doing ain't very much against the law."

Doc said, "I can tell, from your tone, it didn't work. What happened?"

"Music," said Mack.

Now it is true that Joseph and Mary did know all the angles, averages, and percentages. His systems couldn't lose, but they did. The odds are against making your point with the dice, and that law holds until magic intervenes and someone makes a run.

There were literally millions of wetbacks in the country—quiet, hard-working, ignorant men, content to bend their backs over the demanding earth. It was a setup; it couldn't lose. How did it happen, then, that in Joseph and Mary's crew there should be one tenor and one guitar player? Under his horrified eyes an orchestra took shape—two guitars, a guitarón, rhythm and maraca men, a tenor, and two baritones. He would have had the whole lot deported if his nephew, Cacahuete, had not joined them with his hot trumpet.

Joseph and Mary's wetbacks abandoned the carrot and cauliflower fields for the dance floors of the little towns in California.

They called themselves the Espaldas Mojadas. They played "Ven a Mi, Mi Chica Dolorosa" and "Mujer de San Luis" and "El Nubito Blanco que Llora."

The Espaldas Mojadas dressed in tight *charro* costumes, wore huge Mexican hats, and played for dances in the Spreckel Fireman's Hall, the Soledad I. O. O. F., the Elks of King City, the Greenfield Garage, the San Ardo Municipal Auditorium. Joseph and Mary stopped fighting them and started booking them. Business was so good he screened new wetbacks for talent. It was Joseph and Mary's first entrance into show business, and its native dishonesty reassured him that his course was well chosen.

"So, you see," said Mack, "it was music done it. You can't trust nothing no more. You take Fauna now—the Bear Flag ain't like any hookshop on land or sea. She makes them girls take table-manner lessons and posture lessons, and she reads the stars. You never seen nothing like it. Everything's changed, Doc, everything."

Doc looked around his moldy laboratory, and he shivered. "Maybe I'm changed too," he said.

"Hell, Doc, you can't change. Why, what could we depend on! Doc, if you change a lot of people are going to cash in their chips. Why, we was all just waiting around for you to get back so we could go on being normal."

"I don't feel the same, Mack. I'm restless."

"Now you get yourself a girl," said Mack. "You play some of the churchy music to her on your phonograph. And then I'll come in and hustle you for a couple of bucks. Make a try, Doc. You owe it to your friends."

"I'll try," said Doc, "but I have no confidence in it. I'm afraid I've changed."

3
Hooptedoodle (1)

Looking back, you can usually find the moment of the birth of a new era, whereas, when it happened, it was one day hooked on to the tail of another.

There were prodigies and portents that winter and spring, but you never notice such things until afterward. On Mount Toro the snow came down as far as Pine Canyon on one side and Jamesburg on the other. A six-legged calf was born in Carmel Valley. A cloud drifting in formed the letters O-N in the sky over Monterey. Mushrooms grew out of the concrete floor of the basement of the Methodist Church. Old Mr. Roletti, at the age of ninety-three, developed senile satyriasis and had to be forcibly restrained from chasing high-school girls. The spring was cold, and the rains came late. Velella in their purple billions sailed into Monterey Bay and were cast up on the beaches, where they died. Killer whales attacked the sea lions near Seal Rocks and murdered a great number of them. Dr. Wick took a kidney stone out of Mrs. Gaston as big as your hand and shaped like a dog's head, a beagle. The Lions' Club announced a fifty-dollar prize for the best essay on "Football—Builder of Character." And last, but far from least, the Sherman rose developed a carnation bud. Perhaps all this meant nothing; you never notice such things until afterward.

Monterey had changed, and so had Cannery Row and its denizens. As Mack said, "The tum-tum changes, giving place to new. And God tum-tums himself in many ways."

Doc was changing in spite of himself, in spite of the prayers of his friends, in spite of his own knowledge. And why not? Men do change, and change comes like a little wind that ruffles the curtains at dawn, and it comes like the stealthy perfume of wildflowers hidden in the grass. Change may be announced by a small ache, so that you think you're catching cold. Or you may feel a faint disgust for something you loved yesterday. It may even take the form of a hunger that peanuts will not satisfy. Isn't overeating said to be one of the strongest symptoms of discontent? And isn't discontent the lever of change?

Before the war Doc had lived a benign and pleasant life, which aroused envy in some gnat-bitten men. Doc made a living, as good a living as he needed or wanted, by collecting and preserving various marine animals and selling them to schools, colleges, and museums. He was able to turn affable and uncritical eyes on a world full of excitement. He combined the beauty of the sea with man's loveliest achievement—music. Through his superb phonograph he could hear the angelic voice of the Sistine Choir and could wander half lost in the exquisite masses of William Byrd. He believed there were two human achievements that towered above all others: the *Faust* of Goethe and the *Art of the Fugue* of J. S. Bach. Doc was never bored. He was beloved and preyed on by his friends, and this contented him. For he remembered the words of Diamond Jim Brady who, when told that his friends were making suckers of him, remarked, "It's fun to be a sucker—if you can afford it." Doc could afford it. He had not the vanity which makes men try to be smart.

Doc's natural admiration and desire for women had always been satisfied by women themselves. He had few responsibilities except to be a kindly, generous, and amused man. And these he did not find difficult. All in all, he had always been a fulfilled and contented man. A specimen so rare aroused yearning in other men, for how few men like their work, their lives—how very few men like themselves. Doc liked himself, not in an adulatory sense, but just as he would have liked anyone else. Being at ease with himself put him at ease with the world.

In the Army there had been times when he longed for his music, for his little animals, and for the peace and interest of his laboratory. Coming home, forcing open the water-swollen door, was a pleasure and a pain to him. He sighed as he looked at his bookshelves. It took him ten minutes to decide which record to play first. And then the past was gone and he was faced with the future. Old Jingleballicks had kept the little business going in a manner even more inefficient than Doc had, and then had left it to founder. The stocks of preserved animals were depleted. The business contacts had lapsed. The bank that held his mortgage was no longer checked by patriotism. There was some question whether Doc could ever build back his marginal business. In the old days he would have forgotten such considerations in multiple pleasures and interests. Now discontent nibbled at him— not painfully, but constantly.

Where does discontent start? You are warm enough, but you shiver. You are fed, yet hunger gnaws you. You have been loved, but your yearning wanders in new fields. And to prod all these there's time, the bastard Time. The end of life is now not so terribly far away—you can see it the way you see the finish line when you come into the stretch—and your mind says, "Have I worked enough? Have I eaten enough? Have I loved enough?" All of these, of course, are the foundation of man's greatest curse, and perhaps his greatest glory. "What has my life meant so far, and what can it mean in the time left to me?" And now we're coming to the wicked, poisoned dart: "What have I contributed in the Great Ledger? What am I worth?" And this isn't vanity or ambition. Men seem to be born with a debt they can never pay no matter how hard they try. It piles up ahead of them. Man owes something to man. If he ignores the debt it poisons him, and if he tries to make payments the debt only increases, and the quality of his gift is the measure of the man.

Doc's greatest talent had been his sense of paying as he went. The finish line had meant nothing to him except that he had wanted to crowd more living into the stretch. Each day ended with its night; each thought with its conclusion; and every morning a new freedom arose over the eastern mountains and lighted the world. There had never been any reason to suppose it would be otherwise. People made pilgrimages to the laboratory to bask in Doc's designed and lovely purposelessness. For what can a man accomplish that has not been done a million times before? What can he say that he will not find in Lao-Tse

or the *Bhagavadgita* or the Prophet Isaiah? It is better to sit in
appreciative contemplation of a world in which beauty is eter-
nally supported on a foundation of ugliness: cut out the support, and beauty will sink from sight. It was a good thing Doc
had, and many people wished they had it too.

But now the worm of discontent was gnawing at him. Maybe
it was the beginning of Doc's middle age that caused it—glands
slackening their flow, skin losing its bloom, taste buds weaken-
ing, eyes not so penetrating, and hearing dulled a little. Or it
might have been the new emptiness of Cannery Row—the silent
machines, the rusting metal. Deep in himself Doc felt a failure.
But he was a reasonably realistic man. He had his eyes examined, his teeth X-rayed. Dr. Horace Dormody went over him
and discovered no secret focus of infection to cause the restlessness. And so Doc threw himself into his work, hoping, the way
a man will, to smother the unease with weariness. He collected,
preserved, injected, until his stock shelves were crowded again.
New generations of cotton rats crawled on the wire netting of
the cages, and four new rattlesnakes abandoned themselves to a
life of captivity and ease.

But the discontent was still there. The pains that came to Doc
were like a stir of uneasiness or the flick of a skipped heartbeat.
Whisky lost its sharp delight and the first long pull of beer from
a frosty glass was not the joy it had been. He stopped listening
in the middle of an extended story. He was not genuinely glad
to see a friend. And sometimes, starting to turn over a big rock
in the Great Tide Pool—a rock under which he knew there
would be a community of frantic animals—he would drop the
rock back in place and stand, hands on hips, looking off to sea,
where the round clouds piled up white with pink and black
edges. And he would be thinking, What am I thinking? What
do I want? Where do I want to go? There would be wonder in
him, and a little impatience, as though he stood outside and
looked in on himself through a glass shell. And he would be
conscious of a tone within himself, or several tones, as though
he heard music distantly.

Or it might be this way. In the late night Doc might be working at his old and battered microscope, delicately arranging

plankton on a slide, moving them with a thread of glass. And there would be three voices singing in him, all singing together. The top voice of his thinking mind would sing, "What lovely little particles, neither plant nor animal but somehow both—the reservoir of all the life in the world, the base supply of food for everyone. If all of these should die, every other living thing might well die as a consequence." The lower voice of his feeling mind would be singing, "What are you looking for, little man? Is it yourself you're trying to identify? Are you looking at little things to avoid big things?" And the third voice, which came from his marrow, would sing, "Lonesome! Lonesome! What good is it? Who benefits? Thought is the evasion of feeling. You're only walling up the leaking loneliness."

Sometimes he would leave his work and walk out to the lighthouse to watch the white flail of light strike at the horizons. Once there, of course, his mind would go back to the plankton, and he would think, It's a protein food of course. If I could find a way to release this food directly to humans, why, nobody in the world would have to go hungry again. And the bottom voice would sing, "Lonesome, lonesome! You're trying to buy your way in."

Doc thought he was alone in his discontent, but he was not. Everyone on the Row observed him and worried about him. Mack and the boys worried about him. And Mack said to Fauna, "Doc acts like a guy that needs a dame."

"He can have the courtesy of the house anytime," said Fauna.

"I don't mean that," said Mack. "He needs a dame around. He needs a dame to fight with. Why, that can keep a guy so goddam busy defending himself he ain't got no time to blame himself."

Fauna regarded marriage with a benevolent eye. Not only was it a desirable social condition, but it sent her some of her best customers.

"Well, let's marry him off," said Fauna.

"Oh no," said Mack. "I wouldn't go that far. My God! Not Doc!"

Doc tried to solve his problem in the ancient way. He took a long, leisurely trip to La Jolla, four hundred miles south. He traveled in the old manner, with lots of beer and a young lady companion whose interest in invertebrate zoology Doc thought might be flexible—and it was.

The whole trip was a success: weather calm and warm, tides low. Under the weed-wreathed boulders of the intertidal zone Doc found, by great good fortune, twenty-eight baby octopi with tentacles four or five inches long. It was a little bonanza for him if he could keep them alive. He handled them tenderly, put them in a wooden collecting bucket, and floated seaweed over them for protection. An excitement was growing in him.

His companion began to be a little disappointed. Doc's enthusiasm for the octopi indicated that he was not as flexible as she. And no girl likes to lose center stage, particularly to an octopus. The four-hundred-mile trip back to Monterey was made in a series of short dashes, for Doc stopped every few miles to dampen the sack that covered the collecting bucket.

"Octopi can't stand heat," he said.

He recited no poetry to her. The subject of her eyes, her feelings, her skin, her thought, did not come up. Instead Doc told her about octopi—a subject that would have fascinated her two days before.

Doc said, "They're wonderful animals, delicate and complicated and shy."

"Ugly brutes," said the girl.

"No, not ugly," said Doc. "But I see why you say it. People have always been repelled and at the same time fascinated by octopi. Their eyes look baleful and cruel. And all kinds of myths have grown up around octopi too. You know the story of the kraken, of course."

"Of course," she said shortly.

"Octopi are timid creatures really," Doc said excitedly. "Most complicated. I'll show you when I get them in the aquarium. Of course there can't be any likeness, but they do have some traits that seem to be almost human. Mostly they hide and avoid trouble, but I've seen one deliberately murder another. They appear to feel terror too, and rage. They change color when they're disturbed and angry, almost like the rage blush of a man."

"Very interesting," said the girl, and she tucked her skirt in around her knees.

Doc went on, "Sometimes they get so mad they collapse and die of something that parallels apoplexy. They're highly emotional animals. I'm thinking of writing a paper about them."

"You might find out what causes human apoplexy," said the girl, and because he wasn't listening for it, Doc didn't hear the satire in her tone.

There's no need for giving the girl a name. She never came back to Western Biological. Her interest in science blinked out like a candle, but a flame was lighted in Doc.

The flame of conception seems to flare and go out, leaving man shaken, and at once happy and afraid. There's plenty of precedent of course. Everyone knows about Newton's apple. Charles Darwin and his *Origin of Species* flashed complete in one second, and he spent the rest of his life backing it up; and the theory of relativity occurred to Einstein in the time it takes to clap your hands. This is the greatest mystery of the human mind—the inductive leap. Everything falls into place, irrelevancies relate, dissonance becomes harmony, and nonsense wears a crown of meaning. But the clarifying leap springs from the rich soil of confusion, and the leaper is not unfamiliar with pain.

The girl said good-by and went away, and Doc did not know she was gone. For that matter he did not know she had been with him.

With infinite care Doc scrubbed out a big aquarium, carpeted it with sea sand, and laid in stones populated with sponges and hydroids and anemones. He planted seaweeds and caught little crabs and eels and tide-pool Johnnys. He carried buckets of sea water from the beach and set up a pump to circulate the water from tank to aquarium and back. He considered every factor within his knowledge—relations of plant and animal life, food, filtering, oxygenation. He built an octopus world within walls of glass, trying to anticipate every octopus need and to eliminate every octopus enemy or danger. He considered light and heat.

Eight of his octopi were dead, but the twenty living ones scuttled to the bottom of their new home and hid themselves, throbbing and blushing with emotion. Doc drew a stool close and peered into the little world he had made, and his mind was filled with cool green thoughts and stately figures. For the moment he was at peace. The pale expressionless eyes of the octopi seemed to be looking into his eyes.

In the days that followed, Doc's disposition was so unpredictable that Mack exhausted every other possibility before he moved in on Western Biological for the two dollars he thought he needed.

Mack's campaign was probably the most elaborate of his career. It began quietly, and only after a thorough preparation did it begin to take shape. Then spinnerets of emotion laced in and the heavy notes of tragic necessity began to be faintly heard. Drama grew, as it should, out of its inherent earth. Mack's voice was controlled and soft—no trembling yet—just a reasonable, clear, but potentially passionate growth. Mack knew he was doing well. He could hear himself, and he knew that if he were on the receiving end he would find it impossible not to weaken. Why, then, did not Doc turn his eyes from the dimly lit aquarium? He had certainly said "hello" when Mack came in. A little shakily Mack cut in the *vox angelica*, the *vox dolorosa*, and finally a *bendiga stupenda* so moving that Mack himself was in tears.

Doc did not turn his head.

Mack stood stunned. It is a frightening thing to lay out everything you have, to finish, and have no response. He didn't know what to do next. He said loudly, "Doc!"

"Hello," said Doc.

"Don't you feel good?"

"Sure, Mack. How much do you want?"

"Two dollars."

Doc reached in his hip pocket for his wallet without lifting his eyes. Mack's great performance had been wasted. He might just as well have simply come in and asked for the money. He knew he could never reach such a height again. A sudden anger came over him, and he considered refusing the money, but his natural good sense saved him. He stood there rolling the dollar bills between his fingers. "What's got into you, Doc?" he said.

Doc turned slowly toward him. "There's going to be one great difficulty," he said. "How am I going to light them? It's always a problem, but in this case it might be insuperable."

"Light what, Doc?"

"We start with two obvious problems," Doc continued. "First, they can't stand heat, and second, they are to a certain extent photophobic. I don't know how I'm going to get enough cold light on them. Would it be possible, do you suppose, to condition them, to light them constantly, so that the photophobia subsides?"

"Oh sure," said Mack uneasily.

"Don't be too sure," said Doc. "The very process of conditioning might, if it did not kill them, change their normal reactions. It's always difficult to evaluate responses that approximate emotions. If I place them in an abnormal situation, can I trust the response to be normal?"

"No," said Mack.

"You cannot dissect for emotion," Doc went on. "If a human body were found by another species and dissected, there would be no possible way of knowing about its emotions or its thoughts. Now, it occurs to me that the rage, or rather the symptom that seems like rage, must be fairly abnormal in itself. I have seen it happen in aquariums. Does it occur on the sea bottom? Is the observed phenomenon not perhaps limited to the aquarium? No, I can't permit myself to believe that, or my whole thesis falls."

"Doc!" Mack cried. "Look, Doc, it's me—Mack!"

"Hello, Mack," said Doc. "How much did you say?"

"You've already given it to me," said Mack, and he felt like a fool the moment he'd said it.

"I need better equipment," said Doc. "Goddam it, I can't see without better equipment."

"Doc, how's about you and me stepping over and getting a half-pint of Old Tennis Shoes?"

"Fine," said Doc.

"I'll buy," said Mack. "I've got a couple of loose bucks."

Doc said sharply, "I'll have to get some money. Where can I get some money, Mack?"

"I told you, I'll buy, Doc."

"I'll need a wide-angle binocularscope and light. I'll have to find out about light—maybe a pinpoint spot from across the room. No, they'd move out of that. Maybe there are new kinds of lights. I'll have to look into it."

"Come on, Doc."

Doc bought a pint of Old Tennis Shoes and later sent Mack out with money to buy another pint. The two of them sat in the laboratory side by side, staring into the aquarium, resting their elbows on the shelf, and they got to the point where they were mixing a little water with the whisky.

"I got an uncle with an eye like them," said Mack. "Rich old bastard too. I wonder why, when you get rich, you get a cold eye."

"Self-protection," said Doc solemnly. "Conditioned by relatives, I guess."

"Like I was saying, Doc. Everybody in the Row is worried about you. You don't have no fun. You wander around like you was lost."

"I guess it's reorientation," said Doc.

"Well, some people think you need a dame to kind of nudge you out of it. I know a guy that every time he gets feeling low he goes back to his wife. Makes him appreciate what he had. He goes away again and feels just fine."

"Shock therapy," said Doc. "I'm all right, Mack. Don't let anybody give me a wife though—don't let them give me a wife! I guess a man needs a direction. That's what I've been needing. You can only go in circles so long."

"I kind of like it that way," said Mack.

"I'm going to call my paper 'Symptoms in Some Cephalopods Approximating Apoplexy.'"

"Great God Almighty!" said Mack.

4

There Would Be No Game

As he got to know him, Joseph and Mary regarded Doc with something akin to love—for love feeds on the unknown and unknowable. Doc's honesty was exotic to Joseph and Mary. He found it strange. It attracted him in spite of the fact that he could not understand it. He felt that there was something he had missed, though he could not figure what it was.

One day, sitting in Western Biological, Joseph and Mary saw a chess board and, finding that it was a game and being good at games, he asked Doc to teach him. J and M easily absorbed the characters and qualities of castles and bishops and knights and royalty and pawns. During the first game Doc was called to the telephone, and when he returned he said, "You've moved a pawn of mine and your queen and knight."

"How'd you know?" the Patrón asked.

"I know the game," said Doc. "Look, Joseph and Mary, chess is possibly the only game in the world in which it is impossible to cheat."

Joseph and Mary inspected this statement with amazement. "Why not?" he demanded.

"If it were possible to cheat there would be no game," said Doc.

J and M carried this away with him. It bothered him at night. He looked at it from all angles. And he went back to ask more about it. He was charmed with the idea, but he couldn't understand it.

Doc explained patiently, "Both players know exactly the same things. The game is played in the mind."

"I don't get it."

"Well, look! You can't cheat in mathematics or poetry or music because they're based on truth. Untruth or cheating is just foreign, it has no place. You can't cheat in arithmetic."

Joseph and Mary shook his head. "I don't get it," he said.

It was a shocking conception, and he was drawn to it because, in a way, its outrageousness seemed to him like a new, strange way of cheating. In the back of his mind an idea stirred. Suppose you took honesty and made a racket of it—it might be the toughest of all to break. It was so new to him that his mind recoiled from it, but still it wouldn't let him alone. His eyes narrowed. "Maybe he's worked out a system," he said to himself.

5
Enter Suzy

It is popular to picture a small-town constable as dumb and clumsy. In the books he plays the stock bumpkin part. And people retain this attitude even when they know it's not true. We have so many beliefs we know are not true.

A constable, if he has served for a few years, knows more about his town than anyone else and on all levels. He is aware of the delicate political balance between mayor and councilmen, Fire Department and insurance companies. He knows why Mrs. Geltham is giving a big party and who is likely to be there. Usually he knows, when Mabel Andrews reports a burglar, whether it is a rat in the dining room, a burglar, or just wishful thinking. A constable knows that Mr. Geltham is sleeping with the schoolteacher and how often. He knows when high-school boys have switched from gin to marijuana. He is aware of every ripple on the town's surface. If there is a crime the constable usually knows who didn't do it and often who did. With a good constable on duty a hundred things don't happen that might. Sometimes there's a short discussion in an alley; sometimes a telephone call; sometimes only his shadow under a street light. When he gets a cat down out of a tree he knows all about the owner of the cat. And many weeping, parent-prodded little boys and girls put small things, stolen from the Five-and-Dime, in the constable's hands, and he, if he is a good constable, gives them a sense of mercy-in-justice without injuring the dignity of the law.

A stranger getting off the Del Monte Express in Monterey wouldn't be aware that his arrival was noted, but if something happened that night he would know it all right.

Monterey's Joe Blaikey was a good constable. He wouldn't ever be chief—didn't much want to be. Everybody in town liked Joe and trusted him. He was the only man in town who could stop a husband-and-wife fight. He came by his techniques in both social life and in violence from being the youngest of fifteen nice but violent children. Just getting along at home had been his teacher. Joe knew everyone in Monterey and he could size up a stranger almost instantly.

When a girl named Suzy got off the Greyhound bus, she looked up and down the street, fixed her lipstick, then lifted her beat-up suitcase and headed for the Golden Poppy Restaurant. Suzy was a pretty girl with a flat nose and a wide mouth. She had a good figure, was twenty-one, five-feet-five, hair probably brown (dyed blond), brown cloth coat, rabbit-skin collar, cotton print dress, brown calf shoes (heel taps a little run over), scuff on the right toe. She limped slightly on her right foot. Before she picked up her suitcase she opened her brown purse of simulated leather. In it were mirror, comb with two teeth missing, Lucky Strikes, matchbook that said "Hotel Rosaline, San Francisco," half pack of Peppermint Life Savers, eighty-five cents in silver, no folding money, lipstick but no powder, tin box of aspirin, no keys.

If there had been a murder that night Joe Blaikey could have written all that down, but now he wasn't even aware that he knew it. Joe acted pretty much by instinct. He got into the Golden Poppy just as the waitress was putting a cup of coffee on the counter in front of Suzy.

Joe slipped onto the stool next to her. "Hi, Ella," he said to the waitress. "Cup of coffee."

"Coming up," said Ella. "How's your wife, Joe?"

"Oh, pretty good. Wish she'd get her strength back, though."

"Takes it out of you," said Ella. "Man can't understand that. Give her a tonic and let her rest. I'll have fresh coffee in a minute if you want to wait."

"Yeah," said Joe.

Ella went to the head of the counter, put coffee in the Silex, and filled the bowl.

Joe said quietly to Suzy, "What's on your mind, sister?"

"Not a thing," said Suzy. She didn't look at him but she could see him in the shine of a malted machine behind the counter.

"Vacation?"

"Sure."

"How long?"

"Don't know."

"Looking for a job?"

"Maybe."

Ella started toward them, saw what was happening, and got busy at the other end of the counter.

Joe asked, "Know anybody here?"

"I got an aunt here."

"What's her name?"

"That your business?"

"Yep."

"All right, I got no aunt."

Joe smiled at her, and Suzy felt better. She liked a guy who was worried about his wife.

He said to her, "On the bum?"

"Not yet," said Suzy. "You gonna give me trouble, mister?"

"Not if I can help it," said Joe. "You got a Social Security card?"

"Lost it," said Suzy.

Joe said, "It's a tough town. All organized. Don't work the street. The authorities won't have it. If you need a buck to blow town, come to me. My name's Joe Blaikey."

"Thanks, Joe. But I ain't hustling, honest."

"Not yet, you ain't," said Joe. "It's a hell of a town to get a job in since the canneries closed. Take it easy." He stood up and stretched. "I'll get the coffee later, Ella," he said and went out.

Ella's work seemed to be all done. She mopped the counter with a damp cloth. "Swell fella," she said. "More coffee? Fresh is ready."

"Seemed like," said Suzy. "Yeah."

Ella brought a fresh cup. "Where you staying?"

"Don't know yet."

"My sister rents rooms—pretty nice. Four dollars a week. I can give her a ring, see if she's got one vacant."

"I think I'll look around town a little," said Suzy. "Say, mind if I leave my suitcase here? It's kind of heavy."

"Sure. I'll put it back of the counter here."

"Well, s'pose you're off shift when I come back?" Ella looked levelly at Suzy. "Sister," she said, "I ain't never off shift."

Suzy looked in the store windows on Alvarado Street and then she went to the wharf and watched the fishing boats at their moorings. A school of tiny fish always lay in the shade of the pier and two little boys fished with hand lines and never caught anything. About four o'clock she strolled along deserted Cannery Row, bought a package of Lucky Strikes at the grocery, glanced casually at Western Biological, and knocked on the door of the Bear Flag.

Fauna received her in the combination bedroom and office.

"I'll tell you the truth," said Fauna, "business ain't been good. It may pick up some in June. I wish I could put you on. Ain't you got a hard-luck story that would kind of sway me?"

"Nope," said Suzy.

"You broke?"

"Yep."

"But you don't make nothing of it." Fauna leaned back in her swivel chair and squinted her eyes. "I used to work a Mission," she said. "I know hard-luck stories from both ends. I guess if you laid all the hard luck I've heard end to end, why, the Bible would look short. And some of them stories was true. Now, I could make a guess about you."

Suzy sat silent—posture, hands, face, noncommittal.

"Lousy home," said Fauna. "Fighting all the time. Probably you wasn't more than fifteen or sixteen when you married the guy, or maybe he wouldn't. Done it just to get away from the fighting."

Suzy made no reply.

Fauna looked away so that she wouldn't see the hands slowly grip each other. "Got in a family way right off," said Fauna.

"That made the guy restless, and he powdered. What did you say?"

"I didn't say nothing," said Suzy.

"Where's the baby?"

"I lost it."

"Do you hate the guy?"

"I got nothing to say," said Suzy.

"Okay with me. I ain't really very interested. There's some dames born for this business. Some are too lazy to work and some hate men. Don't hardly none of them enjoy what they're doing. That would be like a bartender that loves to drink. You don't look like a natural-born hustler to me. You ain't lazy. Why don't you get a job?"

"I worked waitress and I worked Five-and-Dime. Only difference is, you get took to a movie instead of three bucks," said Suzy.

"You trying to make a stake?"

"Maybe."

"Got a boy?"

"Nope."

"Hate boys?"

"Nope."

Fauna sighed. "You got me, sister. I can feel myself being got. You're a tough kid. Doing your own time, like an old con. I like that. It works better with me than a hard-luck story. Tell me, you hot?"

"Huh?"

"Under raps, I mean. Anybody got anything on you?"

"Nope."

"Ever done time?"

"Once. Thirty days. Vagrancy."

"Nothing else on the blotter?"

"Nope."

"Can you give off a smile? You'd freeze the customers." Suzy grinned at Fauna.

"Good God Almighty!" said Fauna. "You look like somebody's sister! I'm afraid you'll cost me. Why do I have to be a pushover? Ever worked a house?"

"Nope."

"Well, it ain't as bad as the street. Doc Wilkins will be in tomorrow."

Suzy asked, "Can I get my suitcase?"

"I guess so." Fauna opened a wallet on her desk. "J. C. Penney's is open till six. Get yourself a dress—fancy but cheap. Get a new toothbrush. And when you come back, for God's sake go to work on your hair. You could be a good-looking kid if you worked it up."

"I been riding a bus," said Suzy.

"That'll do it," said Fauna. "We eat at half-past six. How long since you ate?"

"Yesterday."

"Beef stew tonight, creamed carrots, cherry Jell-O for dessert."

On her way to the door Suzy paused and her hand patted the doorframe. "Cop worked me over today," she said. "Name's Joe Blaikey."

"He's a nice fella. Why, he'd lend you dough," said Fauna.

"That's what he said," Suzy replied. "I love beef stew."

At the Golden Poppy, Ella handed the suitcase over the counter. "You look like a kid with a job," said Ella.

"Looks like. Say, where's J. C. Penney?"

"Turn right and go a block and a half. Yellow front. Be seeing you."

"Sure," said Suzy.

On the sidewalk Joe Blaikey fell into step beside her and took her suitcase from her hand. "That's a good woman," he said. "You just keep your nose clean and you'll be all right."

"How'd you know?" Suzy asked.

"She called me," said Joe. "See you around."

"Okay," said Suzy.

She took her suitcase from him and turned into J. C. Penney's.

"Can I help you?"

"Dress. Not too dear."

"Over here."

"I like that tomatoey one."

"That's a new shade, 'Love Apples.' "

"Tomato color."

"It's rayon. It'll give you good service."

"It better. Size twelve."

"Shoes to match?"

Suzy took a very deep breath. "Yes, by God!" she said.

6

The Creative Cross

For days the flame burned in Doc, his phoenix thought. True, he didn't have a proper microscope, but he had eyes and he had, thank God, an analytic mind that could slough off sensations, emotions, pains. As he stared at the octopi his thesis took form. With a glass needle he stimulated one to fear and rage until it attacked and killed its brother. He removed one passive octopus to a separate jar where he subjected it to mild solutions of menthol, of Epsom salts, sickening it a little and then bringing it back to health again. Then he aroused rage, and when the body colors pulsed and changed he introduced a small amount of cocaine sulphate and saw the emotion disappear into sleep, if you can say an octopus sleeps. Then he aroused it with saline and touched it here and there with the frustrating needle, noted the flush, the growing intensity of color, the uncertain whipping and groping of the arms, until suddenly it collapsed and died. Doc removed the body and dissected the tissue, trying to find burst vesicles.

"It works!" he said aloud. "I haven't proper equipment to see how it happens, but this animal dies with the appearance of apoplexy. There must be leakage even if I can't see it. I can start my paper with observation."

Doc bought a package of yellow pads and two dozen pencils. He laid them out on his desk, the pencils sharpened to needle points and lined up like yellow soldiers. At the top of a page he printed: OBSERVATIONS AND SPECULATIONS. His pencil point broke. He took up another and drew lace around the O and the B, made a block letter of the S and put fish hooks on each end. His ankle itched. He rolled down his sock and scratched, and that made his ear itch. "Someone's talking about me," he said and looked at the yellow pad. He wondered whether he had fed the cotton rats. It is easy to forget when you're thinking.

Watching the rats scrabble for the food he gave them Doc remembered that he had not eaten. When he finished a page or two he would fry some eggs. But wouldn't it be better to eat first so that his flow of thought would not be interrupted later? For some days he had looked forward to this time of peace, of unbroken thought. These were the answer to his restlessness: peace and the life of the mind. It would be better to eat first. He fried two eggs and ate them, staring at the yellow pad under the hanging light. The light was too bright. It reflected painfully on the paper. Doc finished his eggs, got out a sheet of tracing paper, and taped it to the bottom of the shade below the globe. It took time to make it neat. He sat in front of the yellow pad again and drew lace around all the letters of the title, tore off the page, and threw it away. Five pencil points were broken now. He sharpened them and lined them up with their brothers.

A car drove up in front of the Bear Flag. Doc went to the window and looked out. No one he knew, but he saw Mack go into the grocery. He remembered he wanted to ask Mack something.

It's always hard to start to concentrate. The mind darts like a chicken, trying to escape thinking even though thinking is the most rewarding function of man. Doc could take care of this. When you know what you're doing you can handle it. He set his jaw and was starting to turn back to his desk when he saw out of the corners of his eyes the flash of a skirt. He looked out the window again. A girl had come out of the Bear Flag and was walking along Cannery Row toward Monterey. Doc couldn't see her face, but she had a fine walk, thigh and knee and ankle swinging free and proud, no jerk and totter the way so many women walked as they fell from step to step. No, this girl walked with her shoulders back and her chin up and her arms swinging in rhythm. It's a gay walk, Doc thought. You can tell so much by a walk—discouragement or sickness, determination. There are squinched-up mean walks and blustering walks, shy creeping walks, but this was a gay walk, as though the walker were going happily to a meeting with someone she loved. There was pride in the walk too, but not vanity. Doc hoped she would not turn the corner, but she did. There was a flick of skirt and she was gone. But Doc could see in his mind her swinging limbs, the melody of her lithe, swift movement. Probably ugly as a mud fence, he thought, and then he laughed at himself. "That's full circle," he said. "Mind, I congratulate you. You jumped me to sex, translated it to aesthetics, and ended with sour grapes. How dishonest can I be? And all because I don't want to go to work. I'll work my head off to avoid work. Come, mind. This time you don't get away with it—back to the desk."

He picked up a pencil and wrote, "The observed specimens were twenty small octopi taken in the intertidal zone near the town of La Jolla. Specimens were placed in a large aquarium under conditions as nearly approximating their natural habitat as possible. Sea water was continuously filtered and replaced every twenty-four hours. Animals from a typical ecological community were introduced, together with sand, rock, and algae taken from the collecting point. Small crustaceans were supplied. In spite of precautions, five individuals died within one week. The remaining fifteen seemed to become acclimatized and readily captured and consumed the small grapsoid crabs placed in the aquarium. The lights—" His pencil point broke. He took another, and it broke with a jerk, making a little tear in the paper. He read what he had written; dull, desiccated, he thought. Why should I presume that an animal so far removed from the human—perhaps I'm fooling myself. The middle voice sang subtly, "Looking for yourself in the water—searching, little man, among the hydroids for your soul—looking for contentment in vanity. Are you better than Mack that you should use the secret priestly words of science to cover the fact that you have nothing to say?"

And the bottom voice mourned, "Lonesome! Lonesome! Let me up into the light and warmth. Lonesome!"

Doc jumped up and went to the aquarium and stared into the lighted water. From under a rock an octopus looked out and one of its arms flicked rhythmically, as though it led an orchestra, and the beat was gay and free and fluid—like the swinging thigh and knee and ankle.

Doc put his face in the palm of his hand and pressed blackness on his eyes until specks of green and red light swarmed on his vision. And then he got up and went across the street for beer.

Tinder Is as Tinder Does

Joseph and Mary Rivas liked Fauna, even admired her. But he did feel that it was a little indecent for a woman to own the Bear Flag, a paying institution with a steady income. Operate it, yes, but not own it. The proprieties told Joseph and Mary there should be a man in the background to drain off the profits. It was his observation that when women had access to money they got nervous. To his mind, a healthy woman was a broke woman. A dame with money was a kind of a half-assed man. She stopped working at being a woman, and, as everybody knows, the finest thing about a woman is that she is a woman.

Joseph and Mary had given some thought to relieving Fauna of the responsibility of the profits: if he owned the Bear Flag and Fauna ran it, there would be a natural and practical balance. Fauna had so far figured her way out from under his philanthropy, but Joseph and Mary did not give up, particularly when it was no trouble not to.

A good stock manipulator reads the financial page and looks for the stock he has, but he also notices other quotations too, just in case. Joseph and Mary kept that kind of eye on the Bear Flag. He felt that someday Fauna might look away from the dealer for a moment. Now that his own affairs ran smoothly, he was able to cast a benevolently rapacious eye about him. He knew about Suzy before she had even got her clothes washed, and he felt that Fauna was slipping.

"You got a quail there," he told Fauna. "That's Mary trouble if I ever seen it."

"I guess so," said Fauna.

"Why'd you take her on?"

"I let myself make a mistake once in a while," said Fauna. "She ain't a good hustler, but when I get through with her she might make somebody a damn fine wife."

"She's making a patsy of you," said the Patrón.

"People got to be a patsy now and then," said Fauna. "You never feel real good if you never been a sucker. Once I went missionary down in South America."

"Why?" asked the Patrón.

"Can't remember right off."

"What did you do?"

"Taught them to love one another."

"What did they do?"

"Taught me to shrink heads."

"Savages!" said the Patrón.

"No they wasn't. Them headhunters was pretty nice people—honest too. When they sell you a head they give good value. But there's always a wise guy. Like this Athatoolagooloo—a natural-born head-hustler. He'd worked out a way to push monkey heads. Gave them a close shave, didn't have to shrink them much. There's people will buy anything."

"I know," said the Patrón.

"Well, the Bishop come through," said Fauna, "and he give me holy hell for buying up them monkey heads."

"You mean to say *you* bought them?" said the Patrón.

"Sure I bought them. I got a box of them in the woodshed. Everybody said I was a fool, but it paid off."

"How'd it pay off?"

"Well, look," said Fauna. "My bunch was honest and they shrunk honest heads. S'pose a shipment goes out and this joker Athatoolagooloo slips in a couple of his monkey heads—pretty soon nobody don't trust nobody. Why, people would get to looking asspants at a real nice head. I bought them up to keep them off the market. I had my reputation to think of."

"Yeah, but this joker—" the Patrón began.

"I know what you're going to say—and he done it too. He

had me. He charged me more for them monkey heads than I paid for the real article. He knew he had me."

"That's what I thought. Anybody would," said the Patrón.

"Oh, it all worked out," said Fauna. "If you ever buy a Chungla head you'll know you got the best."

"Yeah, but how about the joker?" said the Patrón.

Fauna opened up her desk drawer and took out a beautiful little item, black as polished ebony and no bigger than a lemon. "He made up real nice, didn't he?" said Fauna.

The Patrón looked nervously away. "I got to get back," he said. "I left my nephew in the store."

"Don't he play trumpet?"

"Drives me crazy," said Joseph and Mary. "Got a new trumpet. Can't get away from it. Made him go practice down on the beach. Figured the waves and the sea lions would kind of drown him out. The other night he give a passing signal to a Navy tug, and they're still looking for what passed them. But last night was the worst. He was practicing down on the beach and he aimed his damn trumpet into the sewer pipe. Got resonance, he said. I don't know if it's true, but I heard that every toilet in the whole neighborhood give off with 'Stormy Weather.' Old lady Somers was taking an enema. I don't believe what they said happened. I got to get back. That kid can break glass with a high note."

"Come over and visit again," said Fauna.

"You mind what I said about Suzy."

"I will," said Fauna.

It's a funny thing, but you never like to trade at your own place. The store across the street has always got fresher cigarettes than you have. The girls at the Bear Flag never got cigarettes from the slot machine at the Bear Flag. When they wanted Luckies or a 7 Up they went to the Patrón's. For that matter, nearly everyone in Cannery Row went nearly every place in Cannery Row nearly every day.

Joseph and Mary had hardly got back to the grocery before Suzy came in. You wouldn't recommend Joseph and Mary as a celebrator of God's loveliest creation, but if you wanted a quick assay on a babe you couldn't ask for better than Joseph and Mary's. If he was not involved in an emotional way he was good. Between the time Suzy got change and the time she pushed the Lucky Strike button on his cigarette machine, each had gone over the other and registered the result.

Suzy's note: "Greaseball, smart and mean. Look out if he gives you something. A percentage boy. Smiles with his mouth. Eyes like a snake. May trip himself someday by being too smart."

Patrón's note: "Lousy risk for a house. A character. Won't play the rules. Might reverse the field. Too friendly. If she likes a guy she might toss in her roll."

The Patrón would have kicked her out of the Bear Flag. He knew that the only person you can trust is an absolutely selfish person. He always runs true to form. You know everything he'll do. But you take somebody with an underlying kindness, and he might fool you. The only satisfactory sucker is the one who is entirely selfish. You never have any trouble with that kind. Fauna was laying herself wide open.

Joseph and Mary tabulated Suzy the way he might have bought a used car. Pretty good figure, good ankles and legs, too light in the butt and too heavy in the chest. That's a bad sign: a good hustler is flat-chested. Face kind of pretty if she felt like it. Face reflected how she felt. Good-looking if she felt good. A good hustler has a mask, looks the same to everybody, pretty, but you don't remember what she looked like the next morning. Suzy you wouldn't forget. A real bad risk. Suzy liked people or she didn't like them. That in itself was bad.

Cacahuete, the Patrón's nephew, was dusting shelves, and he flashed a gold smile at Suzy.

Suzy lighted up. She didn't smile—she grinned. Her lips were full and mouth wide, and when she grinned her eyes crinkled and something warm and scary came out of her. That's a bad risk. On top of this was toughness, but not dependable dull toughness. Suzy might take a poke at Jack Dempsey. She wasn't smart. All in all, Joseph and Mary would've dumped Suzy in a minute. She'd be the kind of dumb dame who'd fall for some guy without finding out his bank balance. She was the kind, he thought, who'd give one guy a helluva lot of trouble but who'd be lousy playing the field. She had something of the same quality Doc had. The Patrón decided to warn Fauna again. This kid could be pure murder in a hookshop. Such was the Patrón's reasoned opinion, and the Patrón was a professional. If you'd take a doctor's advice about a disease, you'd surely take the Patrón's about a hustler. Both could be wrong, of course.

The appraisals and judgments were almost instantaneous, so that by the time Suzy had opened her cigarettes, put one in her mouth, and lighted it, the judgment was complete.

"How are you?" Joseph and Mary asked.

"Okay," said Suzy. "Fauna wants some yellow pads and a couple of pencils—soft pencils."

The Patrón laid them out. "She does a lot of writing," he said. "She's used six pads in about a month."

"She's doing astrology."

"You believe that stuff?"

"No, but it don't do no harm."

"I knew a guy made a good living with it," said the Patrón.

"Oh, she don't charge nothing," said Suzy.

"I know," said the Patrón. "I can't figure why not. Fauna ain't dumb."

"She sure ain't," said Suzy.

Doc came in with two empty beer bottles. "Get a couple of cold ones back on the ice, will you?" he asked.

Suzy glanced at him, took him in, and looked away. His beard shocked her a little. She didn't stare at him the way you don't stare at a cripple.

The Patrón said, "Why don't you put in an icebox? Then you can take a case at a time."

"It's easier to let you keep the ice," said Doc.

"You know Suzy here? She's new at the Bear Flag."

"How do you do?" said Doc.

"How do you do?" said Suzy. She would have said "Hi" to anyone else.

When Doc had gone the Patrón said, "That's a funny guy."

"It takes all kinds," said Suzy.

"He knows stuff I ain't even heard of." The Patrón was defending Doc the way everyone did.

"Kind of hoity-toity?" asked Suzy.

"Hell no! That's the way he always talks. He don't know no other way."

"Well, I guess it takes all kinds," said Suzy.

"He gets bugs and stuff out of the ocean and sells them."

"Who to?"

"Why, there's people'll buy anything," said the Patrón.

"I guess so. Why don't other people do it?"

"Too much work, and you got to know what to get."

"Say, why does he wear that beard? I used to know a wrestler wore one."

"I don't know why," said the Patrón. "Why'd the wrestler?"

"Thought it made him look tough."

"Well, maybe Doc the same—but no, he don't want to be tough." The Patrón went on, "In the Army they made a guy with a beard shave it off. Said a guy with a beard wanted to be different, and the best way to not get along in the barracks is to be different."

"Maybe that's it," said Suzy. "I don't mind a different guy if he ain't too different."

"Dames can take it," said the Patrón. "They don't like it but they can take it. What the hell am I doing all this talking for? I got work to do!"

Suzy asked, "You Mexican?"

"American. My old man was Mexican."

"Can you talk that spick talk?"

"Sure."

"Polly-voo?"

"That ain't the same kind," said the Patrón.

"Be seeing you," said Suzy, and she went out and let the screen door slam.

She ain't a bad kid, the Patrón thought, but I'd sure kick her the hell out of the Bear Flag.

————

Doc looked out the window of Western Biological. He watched Suzy walk past the vacant lot and up to the front porch of the Bear Flag. Just as she was about to climb the steps she turned and looked around. She thought someone was looking at her. She didn't see Doc.

8

The Great Roque War

Pacific Grove and Monterey sit side by side on a hill bordering
the bay. The two towns touch shoulders but they are not alike.
Whereas Monterey was founded a long time ago by foreigners,
Indians and Spaniards and such, and the town grew up higgledy-
piggledy without plan or purpose, Pacific Grove sprang full
blown from the iron heart of a psycho-ideo-legal religion. It
was formed as a retreat in the 1880s and came fully equipped
with laws, ideals, and customs. On the town's statute books a
deed is void if liquor is ever brought on the property. As a result, the sale of iron-and-wine tonic is fantastic. Pacific Grove
has a law that requires you to pull your shades down after sun-
down, and forbids you to pull them down before. Scorching on
bicycles is forbidden, as is sea bathing and boating on Sundays.
There is one crime which is not defined but which is definitely
against the law. Hijinks are forbidden. It must be admitted
that most of these laws are not enforced to the hilt. The fence
that once surrounded the Pacific Grove retreat is no longer in
existence.

Once, during its history, Pacific Grove was in trouble, deep
trouble. You see, when the town was founded many old people
moved to the retreat, people you'd think didn't have anything
to retreat from. These old people became grumpy after a while
and got to interfering in everything and causing trouble, until a
philanthropist named Deems presented the town with two
roque courts.

Roque is a complicated kind of croquet, with narrow wickets
and short-handled mallets. You play off the sidelines, like bil-
liards. Very complicated, it is. They say it develops character.

In a local sport there must be competition and a prize. In Pacific Grove a cup was given every year for the winning team on the roque courts. You wouldn't think a thing like that would work up much heat, particularly since most of the contestants were over seventy. But it did.

One of the teams was called the Blues and the other the Greens. The old men wore little skullcaps and striped blazers in their team colors.

Well, it wasn't more than two years before all hell broke loose. The Blues would practice in the court right alongside the Greens but they wouldn't speak to them. And then it got into the families of the teams. You were a Blue family or a Green family. Finally the feeling spread outside the family. You were a partisan of the Blues or a partisan of the Greens. It got so that the Greens tried to discourage intermarriage with the Blues, and vice versa. Pretty soon it reached into politics, so that a Green wouldn't think of voting for a Blue. It split the church right down the middle. The Blues and the Greens wouldn't sit on the same side. They made plans to build separate churches.

Of course everything got really hot at tournament time. Things were very touchy. Those old men brought a passion to the game you wouldn't believe. Why, two octogenarians would walk away into the woods and you'd find them locked in mortal combat. They even developed secret languages so that each wouldn't know what the other was talking about.

Well, things got so hot and feeling ran so high that the county had to take notice of it. A Blue got his house burned down and then a Green was found clubbed to death with a roque mallet in the woods. A roque mallet is short-handled and heavy and can be a very deadly weapon. The old men got to carrying mallets tied to their wrists by thongs, like battle-axes. They didn't go anyplace without them. There wasn't any crime each didn't charge the other with, including things they'd outgrown and couldn't have done if they'd wanted to. The Blues wouldn't trade in Green stores. The whole town was a mess.

The original benefactor, Mr. Deems, was a nice old fellow. He used to smoke a little opium, when it was legal, and this kept him healthy and rested so that he didn't get high blood pressure or tuberculosis. He was a benevolent man, but he was also a philosopher. When he saw what he had created by giving the roque courts to the Pacific Grove retreat he was saddened and later horrified. He said he knew how God felt.

The tournament came July 30, and feeling was so bad that people were carrying pistols. Blue kids and Green kids had gang wars. Mr. Deems, after a period of years, finally figured that as long as he felt like God he might as well act like God. There was too much violence in town.

On the night of July 29 Mr. Deems sent out a bulldozer. In the morning, where the roque courts had been, there was only a deep, ragged hole in the ground. If he'd had time he would have continued God's solution. He'd have filled the hole with water.

They ran Mr. Deems out of Pacific Grove. They would have tarred and feathered him if they could have caught him, but he was safe in Monterey, cooking his yen shi over a peanut-oil lamp.

Every July 30, to this day, the whole town of Pacific Grove gets together and burns Mr. Deems in effigy. They make a celebration of it, dress up a life-size figure, and hang it from a pine tree. Later they burn it. People march underneath with torches, and the poor helpless figure of Mr. Deems goes up in smoke every year.

There are people who will say that this whole account is a lie, but a thing isn't necessarily a lie even if it didn't necessarily happen.

9

Whom the Gods Love
They Drive Nuts

To a casual observer Cannery Row might have seemed a series of self-contained and selfish units, each functioning alone with no reference to the others. There was little visible connection between La Ida's, the Bear Flag, the grocery (still known as Lee Chong's Heavenly Flower Grocery), the Palace Flophouse, and Western Biological Laboratories. The fact is that each was bound by gossamer threads of steel to all the others—hurt one, and you aroused vengeance in all. Let sadness come to one, and all wept.

Doc was more than first citizen of Cannery Row. He was healer of the wounded soul and the cut finger. Strongly entrenched in legality though he was, he found himself constantly edged into infringements by the needs of his friends, and anyone could hustle him for a buck without half trying. When trouble came to Doc it was everybody's trouble.

What was Doc's trouble? Even he didn't know. He was deeply, grievingly unhappy. For hours on end he sat at his desk with a yellow pad before him and his needle-sharp pencils lined up. Sometimes his wastebasket was full of crushed, scribbled pages, and at others not even a doodle went down. Then he would move to the aquarium and stare into it. And his voices howled and cried and moaned. "Write!" said his top voice, and "Search!" sang his middle voice, and his lowest voice sighed, "Lonesome! Lonesome!" He did not go down without a struggle. He resurrected old love affairs, he swam deep in music, he read the *Sorrows of Werther*, but the voices would not leave him. The beckoning yellow pages became his enemies. One by one the octopi died in the aquarium. He had worn thin the excuse of his lack of a proper microscope. When the last octopus died he leaped on this as his excuse. When his friends visited him he would explain, "You see, I can't go on without specimens, and I can't get any more until the spring tides. As soon as I have specimens and a new microscope I can whip the paper right off."

His friends sensed his pain and caught it and carried it away with them. They knew the time was coming when they would have to do something.

In the Palace Flophouse a little meeting occurred—occurred, because no one called it, no one planned it, and yet everyone knew what it was about.

Wide Ida brooded hugely. The Bear Flag was represented by Agnes, Mabel, and Becky. All the boys were accounted for. The meeting began casually and obliquely, as all meetings should.

Hazel said, "Wide Ida throwed out a drunk last night and sprained her shoulder."

"I ain't as young as I used to be," Wide Ida said gloomily.

"The drunk dared her," said Hazel. "He didn't even touch the sidewalk going out. If they was an Olympic event for A and C, Wide Ida would win it easy."

"Sprained my shoulder up," said Wide Ida.

They kept skirting their problem.

Mack said, "How's Fauna been?"

"Pretty good. She got problems," said Agnes.

Becky was delicately picking off nail polish. "That Fauna," she said, "she's a wonder. She's giving us tablesetting lessons. I bet if they was thirty-five forks, she'd know what every one of them was for."

"Ain't they to eat with?" Hazel asked.

"Jesus, what a ignorant!" said Becky. "I bet you don't know a dessert fork from a hole in the ground."

Hazel said belligerently, "You know what a Jackson fork is for?"

"No, what?"

"Just leave it lay and see who's a ignorant," said Hazel.

Wide Ida asked, "Any change with Doc?"

"No," said Mack. "I went over to see him last night. I wisht there was something we could do."

They fell to musing. If the times were hard on Doc, they were equally hard on his friends who loved him. Once he had been infallible. There was nothing he could not do because there was nothing he wanted to do very much. And in spite of themselves a little contempt for him was growing in his friends—a kind and loving contempt that might never have happened if he had not once been so great. People who had once spoken his name with awe now felt better than he because he was no better than they.

"I ain't got an idea's how to proceed," said Mack.

Hazel said, "How's about if we ask Fauna to do his horoscope? She's doing me right now."

"You ain't got no future," said Mack.

"I have too," said Hazel. "I bet Fauna could tell us what to do about Doc."

Mack looked interested. "It's better than nothing," he said. "Hoc sunt. Eddie, you dig up one of them kegs you buried during the war. Hazel, you ask Fauna to come over for a drink. Tell her to bring her star stuff."

"Maybe she's got me finished," said Hazel.

It was a matter of some sorrow to Fauna that she didn't entirely believe in astrology, but she had found that nearly everyone wants to believe that the stars take notice of us. Her science gave her a means for telling people what they ought to do, and Fauna had definite ideas about what everybody ought to do.

In spite of her secret skepticism, every once in a while she turned up a reading that astonished her. Hazel's horoscope had her breathless and baffled. She seriously considered burning it and never telling him.

Hazel led her to the Palace Flophouse and Mack poured her a drink from the keg. She tossed it off, still deep in thought.

"You got my stars wrote down?" Hazel demanded anxiously.

Fauna regarded him sorrowfully. "I don't want to tell you," she said.

"Why not? Is it bad?"

"Awful," said Fauna.

"Come on, tell me. I can take it."

Fauna sighed. "I've checked it over and over," she said. "You sure you give me your true birthday?"

"Sure."

"Then I don't see how it can be wrong." She turned wearily and faced the others. "The stars say Hazel's going to be President of the United States."

There was a shocked silence.

"I don't believe it," said Mack.

"I don't want to be President," Hazel said, and he didn't.

"There is no choice," said Fauna. "The stars have spoke. You will go to Washington."

"I don't want to!" Hazel cried. "I don't know nobody there."

"I wonder where we could all go," said Whitey No. 2. "I seen some islands in the Pacific that was pretty nice. But hell, Hazel would have them too. The U.S. got a mandate."

"I won't take it," said Hazel.

Mack said, "We could kill him."

"His stars don't say it," Fauna said. "He's going to live to seventy-eight and die from a spoiled oyster."

"I don't like oysters," said Hazel.

"Maybe you'll learn in Washington."

Mack said, "Maybe you made a mistake."

"That's what I hoped," said Fauna. "I went over and over it. No, sir! Hazel is going to be President."

"Well, we've weathered some pretty bad ones," Eddie offered forlornly.

"Ain't they no way I can tell them I won't do it? Hell, I'll hide out!" said Hazel desperately.

Fauna shook her head dismally. "I'll check again," she said, "but I don't think you got a prayer. You got nine toes, Hazel?"

"I don't know."

"Well, count."

Hazel took off his shoes and moved his lips. "Nine," he said bitterly.

"That's what the horoscope said. We can only pray it's for the best."

"Lord!" said Whitey No. 2. "That's what I call a nine-to-one prayer. Fauna, now you've went and made a president out of a sow's ear, how about getting Doc's paper wrote?"

"Who's a sow's ear?" Hazel demanded.

"William Henry Harrison."

"Oh!" said Hazel. "Oh, yeah!"

Agnes piped up in her hoarse soprano, "Doc just ain't himself. I took him a pint and he didn't hardly pass the time a day. Just set there looking at that yellow paper. Know what was on that paper?"

"Eggs," said Whitey No. 1.

"No. I don't like to tell. It ain't nice."

"Hot damn!" said Mack. "Maybe he's getting well. Go on—what?"

"Well," said Agnes in a shocked voice, "he'd drew a picture of a lady without no clothes on, and right beside that was one of them damn devilfish, only it was smoking a pipe. Don't hardly seem like the old Doc."

Wide Ida shook herself out of a mountainous lethargy. "He used to be the easygoingest guy in the world. Now he's got a wild hair. Anybody else but Doc, I'd figure it was a dame. But hell! Doc can take dames or let them alone."

Mack said, "He could even take dames *and* let them alone."

Fauna put her hands on her hips. "You fellas sure there ain't a girl hiding out where he can't get to her?"

"No," said Hazel. "I wisht he'd snap out of it. Go over and talk to him, and he don't say nothing and he don't listen."

"Let's run a few dames past him and see if he picks up," said Whitey No. 2.

Mack said, "I don't believe in it but I wish Fauna would do a job on Doc. Might give us an idea."

Fauna said, "I never seen nobody that wanted me to do a horoscope that believed in it. I ain't sure I believe in it myself. Sure I'll do Doc. When's his birthday?"

With surprise they realized that no one could remember.

"Seems like it was in autumn," said Eddie.

"Got to have it," Fauna said. "Mack, you think you could find out?"

"I guess so. Say, Fauna, if you ain't got too much integrity, could you maybe rig it a little?"

"How do you mean?"

"Well, kind of tell him to lay off his goddam paper and get back to horsing around."

"What's wrong with his paper if only he gets it wrote?" Hazel demanded.

Mack scratched his stomach. "I guess we got to face it," he said. "Doc wants to write that crazy paper. Driving himself nuts with it. Know what I think? Doc ain't never going to write that paper."

Hazel stood up. "What d'you mean?"

"Well, you know them kind of people they call accident prone? No matter what they do they get hurt. It's like they *want* accidents. Well, I think Doc don't really want to write that paper."

Whitey No. 1 said, "He sure goes about it the hard way."

"Ever hear of a substitute?" said Mack.

"You mean like on the bench at football?" Eddie asked.

"Hell no!" said Mack. "I mean like a guy is using something to cover up something else—and maybe he don't even know it himself."

Hazel demanded, "You running Doc down?"

"Take it easy," said Mack. "I think Doc's scared to write that paper because he knows it's crazy. Quod erat demonstrandum."

"Huh?" asked Fauna.

"Q.E.D.," said Mack.

"Oh!" said Fauna. "Sure."

10

There's a Hole in Reality through which We Can Look if We Wish

Doc had made changes. His desk was drawn in front of the window. He sat writing rapidly on his yellow pad. "Color change," he wrote, "seems to be not only a concentration of fluids to the surface but also a warping of tissue, which, perhaps, refracts the light, giving an impression of color."

A door slammed. Doc looked out at the street. Fauna was teetering down the chicken walk that led from the Palace Flophouse.

Doc looked back at his pad. There were footsteps on the pavement. He looked up. Wide Ida was going toward her bar. Joseph and Mary came out of the Heavenly Flower and crossed the street, climbed the stairs of Western Biological, and knocked.

"Come in," Doc cried, and there was relief in his voice.

"Thought I'd shovel the dirt a little. That band of mine is practicing upstairs. Drives me crazy."

"Well, I'm pretty busy," said Doc.

J and M gazed about the room. "Why do you keep snakes?"

"To sell."

"Who'd buy snakes?" said J and M. "Say, what you looking at?" He craned his neck. "That's the new dame. She's going to give Fauna trouble. Little Mary trouble."

"Who?" Doc asked.

"You wasn't listening, I guess."

"I must get to work," said Doc.

"You know, I still don't get it."

"What?"

"There must be some way to kind of bend the odds in chess."

"There isn't. I've got to go."

"What's the rush?"

"Tide!" said Doc.

Doc walked on the beach beyond the lighthouse. The waves splashed white beside him and sometimes basted his ankles. The sandpipers ran ahead of him as though on little wheels. The golden afternoon moved on toward China, and on the horizon's edge a lumber schooner balanced.

On Doc's left the white sand dunes rounded up, and behind them the dark pine trees seemed to hold a piece of night throughout the day.

Doc thought, Under stimulation there is increased pulsing like a man under physical or emotional strain, something like the release of adrenaline—but no way to prove it. No more specimens until spring tides.

His middle voice argued, "Maybe you don't believe any of it. Why can't you laugh at yourself? You could once. You're trapped in a cage of self-importance."

"Lonesome!" the low voice cried in his guts. "No one to receive from you or give to you. No one warm enough and dear enough."

Doc wanted desperately to go back to his old life—the hopeless wish of a man wanting to be a little boy, forgetting the pain of little boys. Doc dropped to his knees and dug a hole in the damp sand with a scooped hand. He watched the sea water seep in and crumble the sides of the hole. A sand crab scuttled away from his digging fingers.

From behind him a voice said, "What are you digging for?"

"Nothing," said Doc without looking around.

"There are no clams here."

"I know it," said Doc. And his top voice sang, "I just want to be alone. I don't want to talk or explain or argue or even to listen. Now he'll tell me a theory he's got on oceanography. I won't look around."

The voice behind him said, "There's so much metal in the

sea. Why, there's enough magnesium in a cubic mile of sea water to pave the whole country."

I always get them, Doc thought. If there's a bughouser within
miles he's drawn to me.

"I'm a seer," said the voice.

Doc rocked angrily back on his heels. "Okay," he said. "It's
just my business but you tell me about it." He didn't remember
ever having been discourteous to a stranger before.

This one was a big, bearded stranger with the lively, innocent
eyes of a healthy baby. He wore ragged overalls and a blue shirt
washed nearly white, and he was barefooted. The straw hat on
his head had two large holes cut in the brim, proof that it had
once been the property of a horse.

Doc found his interest rising.

"It is my custom to invite a stranger to dinner," said the seer.
"Not original, of course. Harun al-Rashid did the same. Please
follow me."

Doc stood up from his squatting position. The tendons in back
of his knees creaked with pain. The seer towered above him, and
on closer inspection it was true that his blue eyes had the merry
light of a wise baby. But his face was granitic—chiseled out of the
material of prophets and patriarchs. Doc found himself wondering if some of the saints had not looked like this. From the ragged
sleeves of the blue shirt wrists like big grapevines protruded, and
hands sheathed in brown calluses crisscrossed with barnacle cuts.
The seer carried a pair of ancient basketball shoes in his left hand,
and, seeing Doc look at them, he said, "I only wear them in the
sea. My feet aren't proof against urchins and barnacles."

In spite of himself Doc felt surrounded by the man. "Harun,"
said Doc, "was visited by djinni and the spirits of earth, fire, and
water. Do the djinni visit you?" Doc thought, Oh Lord! Am I
going to play along with this nonsense? Why can't I cross my
fingers and spit and walk away? I can still walk away.

The seer looked downward at an angle into Doc's face. "I live
alone," he said simply. "I live in the open. I hear the waves at
night and see the black patterns of the pine boughs against the
sky. With sound and silence and color and solitude, of course I
see visions. Anyone would."

"But you don't believe in them?" Doc asked hopefully.

"I don't find it a matter for belief or disbelief," the seer said. "You've seen the sun flatten and take strange shapes just before it sinks in the ocean. Do you have to tell yourself every time that it's an illusion caused by atmospheric dust and light distorted by the sea, or do you simply enjoy the beauty of it? Don't you see visions?"

"No," said Doc.

"From music, don't forms of wishes and forms of memory take shape?"

"That's different," said Doc.

"I don't see any difference," said the seer. "Come along—dinner's ready."

In the dunes there are deep little creases where the wind-crouching pines have made a stand against the moving sand, and in one of these, only a hundred yards back from the beach, the seer had his home. The little valley was protected from the wind. The pine boughs covered it, and the sand was deeply carpeted with sweet pine needles. Once down in the little cup you could hear the wind sweeping the pine tips overhead, and a perpetual dusk hung under the warped trees. The pines survived only by following the suggestions of the stronger forces—crouching low and growing their limbs in the direction of the wind, nourishing the little trailing plants which slow up the pace of the walking dunes. Under the trees a fire was burning, and on a hearth of flat stones blackened tin cans steamed.

"This is my home," the seer said. "You are welcome here. I have a wonderful dinner." He brought a tin box from the fork of a tree, took out a loaf of French bread and sliced off two thick slices. Then he brought sea urchins from a dripping sack, cracked them on a rock, and spread the gonads on the bread. "The males are sweet and the females sour," he said. "I like to mix the two."

"I've tasted them," said Doc. "The Italians eat them. It's about as strong a protein as you can get. Some people think it's aphrodisiac."

There was an iron simplicity in the seer. He was like a monolith of logic standing against waves of angry nonsense.

"Next we'll have steamed limpets," said the seer. "I have a pin here to eat them with. Do you like sea lettuce? It's an acquired taste. And then I have a stew—a kind of universal bouillabaisse—I won't tell you what's in it. You'll see."

"Do you take all of your food from the sea?"

The seer smiled at him. "No, not all. I wish I could. It would be simpler. I take all the protein I need, and more, but my human stomach still craves starch. I want a little bread and some potatoes. I love acid with the protein. See—I have a bottle of vinegar and some lemons. And last, I indulge myself with herbs: rosemary and thyme and sage and marjoram."

"How about sugars?" Doc asked. "You won't find sugars in a tide pool."

The seer dropped his eyes and watched a black ant try to climb an avalanche of sand, losing ground all the way. When he spoke his voice was shy and ashamed. "I steal candy bars," he said. "I can't seem to help it."

"The flesh is weak," said Doc.

"Oh, I don't mind that," the seer cried. "Appetites are good things. The more appetites a man has, the richer he is, but I was taught not to steal. I don't believe in stealing. It hurts my feelings when I do, and I don't enjoy the candy bars as much as I would if I didn't steal them, but I love Baby Ruths and Mounds."

They picked the limpets from their shells with pins and dipped them in lemon juice. The stew contained mussels and clams and crabs and little fish, seasoned with garlic and rosemary.

"Some people don't like it," said the seer.

After they had finished Doc lay back in the pine needles, and a fine peacefulness settled on him. The air, the softness of the needles, the odors of kelp and pine and yerba buena, the music of surf against wind-plucking pine needles, the fullness of belly, made a little room of contentment around him.

He said, "I'm surprised they don't lock you up—a reasonable man. It's one of the symptoms of our time to find danger in men like you who don't worry and rush about. Particularly dangerous are men who don't think the world's coming to an end."

"It's coming to an end, all right," the seer said. "That started the moment it was born."

"I don't know why they don't put you in jail. It's a crime to be happy without equipment."

"Oh, they do," said the seer, "and they put me under observation every once in a while."

"I forgot," said Doc. "You are crazy, aren't you?"

"I guess so," said the seer, "but not dangerous. And they've never caught me stealing candy bars. I'm very clever at that, and I steal only one at a time."

"Don't ever gather disciples," said Doc. "They'd have you on a cross in no time."

"There's not much danger of that. I don't teach anybody anything."

"I'm not so sure," said Doc. "The doctrine of our time is that man can't get along without a whole hell of a lot of stuff. You may not be preaching it, but you're living treason."

"I'm lazy," said the seer. "Did you ever drink yerba buena tea?"

"No."

"It's strong and aromatic and a mild physic. Can you drink it out of a beer bottle?"

"I don't know why not."

"Look out! The bottle's hot! Here, wrap a twig around it."

After a while the seer asked, "What's aching you, or don't you want to talk about it?"

"I'd just as soon talk about it if I knew what it was," said Doc. "As a matter of fact, it's gone away for the moment."

"Ah, one of those," said the seer. "Do you have wife or children?"

"No."

"Do you want wife or children?"

"I don't think so."

The seer said, "I saw a mermaid last night. You remember, there was a half moon and a thin drifting mist. There was color in the night, not like the black and gray and white of an ordinary night. Down at the end of the beach a shelf of rock reaches out, and the tide was low so that there was a smooth bed of kelp. She swam to the edge and then churned her tail, like a salmon leaping a rapid. And then she lay on the kelp bed and made dancing figures with her white arms and hands. She didn't go away until the rising tide covered the kelp bed."

"Was she a dream? Did you imagine her?"

"I don't know. But if I did I'm proud that I could imagine anything so beautiful. What is it you want?"

"I've tried to think," said Doc. "I want to take everything I've seen and thought and learned and reduce them and relate them and refine them until I have something of meaning, something of use. And I can't seem to do it."

"Maybe you aren't ready. And maybe you need help."

"What kind of help?"

"There are some things a man can't do alone. I wouldn't think of trying anything so big without—" He stopped. The heavy waves beat the hard beach, and the yellow light of the setting sun illuminated a cloud to the eastward, a clot of gold.

"Without what?" Doc asked.

"Without love," said the seer. "I have to go see the sunset now. I've come to the point where I don't think it can go down without me. That makes me seem needed." He stood up and brushed the pine needles from his threadbare overalls.

"I'll come to see you again," said Doc.

"I might be gone," the seer replied. "I've got a restlessness in me. I'll probably be gone."

Doc watched him trudge over the brim of the dune and saw the wind flip up the brim of his straw hat and the yellow sun light up his face and glisten in his beard.

Hazel's Brooding

After Mack left the Palace Flophouse (and, incidentally, did not find Doc at home), Hazel sat brooding. Things came through slowly to Hazel. He had heard Mack advance his theory about how Doc would never get his paper written, but the impact of the statement did not strike home until he was alone. It is true that all over Cannery Row the feeling was growing that Doc was not infallible, but the news had not seeped through to Hazel. He knew that Doc was in trouble, but the friendly feeling of contempt had not penetrated. If Hazel had wanted to know the day and hour of the world's demise, he would have gone to Doc and Doc's answer would have been final. Alone he brooded, not about Doc's weakness, but about the treachery of Doc's friends who could question him, who would *dare* to question him.

Hazel beat his hand on the arm of his rocking chair for a while and then he got up and went to Wide Ida's. Eddie was behind the bar, so Hazel had two shots of whisky and paid for a Coke.

He walked between two canneries to the beach. A seagull with a broken wing engaged his kindly interest. He chased it, trying to help it, until it swam to sea and drowned.

Hazel had experienced an earthquake and he searched for the shaker. He walked along the rocks to Pacific Grove Beach, and even the brown young men standing on their hands for the girls did not hold interest. He went up the hill and toured the basement of Holman's Department Store. The floor manager accompanied him, an honor and a precaution few people received. But Hazel didn't even see the shining display of small tools.

You cannot cut the ground from under a man and expect him to act normally. On his way back to Cannery Row, Hazel passed a funeral home where an impressive group was gathering. Ordinarily Hazel would join any kind of celebration with enthusiasm. But now he watched the mounds of gladiolas being carried out and no sense of participation stirred in him. The festive dead would have to be buried without Hazel.

In New Monterey, Hazel walked, not around, but right through a dog fight. All the preceding manifestations would have troubled his friends, but if they had known what Hazel was thinking they would have been horrified.

Thinking is always painful, but in Hazel it was heroic. A picture of the process would make you seasick. A gray, whirling furor of images, memories, words, patterns. It was like a traffic jam at a big intersection with Hazel in the middle trying to get something to move somewhere.

He strolled back to Cannery Row but he did not go to the Palace Flophouse. By instinct, he crept under the branches of the black cypress tree in the vacant lot where he had lived for so many years in pre-Palace days. Hazel's thoughts were not complicated. It was just remarkable that he had them at all.

Hazel loved Doc. Doc was in trouble. Somebody was responsible. Who? That it might be a situation rather than a person was beyond his grasp. The person who was hurting Doc must be made to stop it even if he had to be killed. Hazel had nothing against murder. That he hadn't killed anybody was only because he hadn't needed to or wanted to. He tried to recall everything he had heard concerning Doc's frustration, and it was all nebulous, all vague, except for one thing: Mack had said Doc couldn't write his paper. That was the only clear statement that had been made. Mack was the one. If Mack knew about it, he must be responsible for it. This was a matter of sorrow to Hazel, because he liked Mack very much. He hoped he wouldn't have to kill him.

It was getting dark under the cypress tree, too dark to read. Hazel always judged light by whether or not you could read by it, in spite of the fact that he never read anything. The front-porch light of the Bear Flag came on. Western Biological was still dark. Up the hill in the Palace Flophouse the kerosene lantern made a dim glow through the windows. Again and again, Hazel tried to turn to sweet thoughtlessness, but it was no use. Mack was responsible. Mack had to do something about it.

Hazel got up and brushed the cypress dirt from his clothes. He walked up past the rusty pipes and the empty boiler, crossed the railroad track, and went up the chicken walk. Behind him, muffled by the canneries, he could hear Cacahuete playing "Stormy Weather" on his trumpet and the sea lions on China Point barking.

In the Palace, Mack and the boys were playing tick-tack-toe with a piece of chalk on the floor. The wining jug was set conveniently near.

"Hi, Hazel," said Mack. "Draw up."

"Mack," Hazel said sadly, "I want you should step outside with me and put up your dukes."

Mack rocked back on his heels. "What!"

"I'm going to beat the holy hell out of you," said Hazel.

"Why?" Mack asked.

This was just the question Hazel was afraid of. He tried to find a quick, tough answer. "You just step out and you'll find out," he said.

"Hazel—" Mack stood up. "Hazel baby, what's eating you? Tell me. See if I can't make it right."

Hazel felt the whole situation leaving his hands. "You can't treat Doc that way," he said fiercely. "Not Doc!"

"What way am I treating him? I ain't done nothing to Doc, except maybe hustle him a little. But we all done that—even you tried."

"You said he can't write his paper, that's what you done."

"Oh, for God's sakes!" said Mack.

"You're yellow then."

"Okay, I'm yellow. Sometime when I ain't feeling yellow I'll paddywhack you. Sit down. Have a jolt from the jug."

They babied Hazel and pampered him until his eyes were damp with appreciation. But when Hazel's mind dug in it would not let loose. "You got to help him," he repeated. "He ain't happy, he just mopes. You got to help him."

Mack said, "It ain't entirely our fault. Trouble is, Doc lets concealment like a worm in the bud feed on his damask cheek."

"He sure as hell does," said Whitey No. 2.

"I ain't going to stand for no excuses," said Hazel.

Mack studied the problem from every angle. "Hazel's right," he said at last. "We've been selfish. We never in our lives had such a good friend as Doc, and we're letting him down. Makes me feel ashamed. It's Hazel showed the way. If I was in trouble I wouldn't want Hazel to do no figuring but I sure would like to have him for a friend."

Hazel ducked his head in embarrassment. In his life so few compliments had come his way that he didn't know how to cope with them.

Mack went on, "I make a solemn move we all stand up and drink a toast to Hazel—a noble, noble soul!"

"Aw, hell, fellas," said Hazel, and he wiped his eyes on his sleeve.

They stood in a circle around him, Mack and Eddie, Whitey No. 1 and Whitey No. 2, and each one tipped the jug over his elbow and drank to Hazel. Good feeling was running so high they did it again, and were about to do it a third time when Hazel said, "Ain't there something we can drink to so I can get a drink?"

"To Lefty Grove!" said Eddie.

That broke the ice. An era of good feeling set in. They dug up another keg of the private stock Eddie had saved during the war. He started the bung and smelled it delicately.

"I remember this one," he said. "They was some guys up from South America and they brought in a bottle of absinthe."

"Perfumes the whole house," said Mack.

It was like old times, they reminded one another. If Gay were only here—let's drink a toast to good old Gay, our departed friend.

The absinthe had soothed the mixture in the keg and added something sweet and old-fashioned. A courtliness crept into the speech of the dwellers of the Palace Flophouse, an old-world courtesy. Everyone vied to be last, not first, at the refilled jug.

"Next dough we get we'll go up to Woolworth's and get some glasses," said Mack.

"Hell," said Whitey No. 2, "they'll just get broke. But I see what you mean."

Somehow they felt they were living in a moment when history pauses and takes stock and changes course. They knew they would look back on this night as a beginning. At such times men feel the nudge toward oratory.

Mack steadied himself against the stove and begged their attention by rapping on the stovepipe. "Gentlemen," he said, "let us here highly resolve to get Doc's ass out of the sling of despond."

Eddie said, "Remember we done something like that once and damn near ruined him."

Mack's golden mood held. "We were younger then," he said. "This time we're going to think her out and she's going to be foolproof."

Hazel was so far won back into comradeship that he had relaxed into happy incoherence. "To Lefty Grove!" he said.

Mack opened the oven door and sat on it. "I've give it a lot of thought," he said. "Lately I done hardly nothing else."

"You never do hardly nothing else," said Whitey No. 2.

Mack ignored him. "I got a theory—"

"Aw, shut up!" said Eddie.

"Who you talking to?" said Whitey No. 2.

"I don't know," said Eddie innocently, "but if the shoe fits—"

"I got a theory, if you ain't too pie-eyed to listen," said Mack. When he had them quiet he went on, "When you hear my theory you might get kind of violent. I want you to sleep on it before you talk. I think Doc needs a wife."

"*What!*"

"Well, hell, he don't have to marry her," said Mack. "You know what I mean . . ." If the absinthe had not given them tolerance he might have had a series of fights right then. "Kindly do not interrupt," he said. "I will now review the dame situation in the U.S. You take a look at divorces and the reasons for them and you can only think one thing: the only guy that shouldn't have nothing to do with picking out a wife is the guy that's going to marry her. That's a fact. It's a fact that if he's left alone a guy practically always marries the wrong kind of dame."

"Play it safe and don't marry nobody," said Whitey No. 2.

"There's some guys can't operate that way," said Mack.

"Are you suggesting we turn Doc, our true friend, in?"

"I asked you not to shoot off your face until you slept on it," said Mack with dignity.

Hazel tugged at his sleeve. "Ain't you joking, Mack?"

"No," said Mack, "I ain't joking."

"If anything bad come to Doc, you know what I'd do to you?" Hazel asked.

"Yes," said Mack. "I think I do—and I think I'd have it coming."

Hazel's bed was a four-poster on which the bedposts were two-by-fours topped by a quilt. He had built it from memory of a moving picture. When the Palace Flophouse was quiet at last, Hazel lay in his bed and looked up at the log-cabin pattern of his canopy. His mind was whirling. He wished there were some simpler way to help Doc than by the major operation Mack had suggested. Once he got up and looked out the door and saw that the green shaded light was on in the laboratory.

"The poor bastard," he whispered.

He didn't sleep well and his dreams were shaped liked mushrooms.

Flower in a Crannied Wall

Joe Elegant was a pale young man with bangs. He smoked foreign cigarettes in a long ebony holder and he cooked for the Bear Flag. The girls said he made the best popovers in the world, and he could give a massage that would shake the kinks out of a Saturday night when the fleet was in. He sneered most of the time, and except at mealtime kept to himself in his little lean-to behind the Bear Flag, from which the rattle of his typewriter could be heard late at night.

One morning soon after she had come Suzy was having her coffee while Joe Elegant cleared the table of crumbs from earlier breakfasts.

"You make good coffee," Suzy said.

"Thank you."

"You don't look like a guy who would work here."

"It's temporary, I assure you."

"I got a wonderful recipe for gumbo. Want me to give it to you?"

"Fauna designs the meals."

"You ain't very friendly."

"Why should I be?"

He was passing behind her. Suzy reached up, hooked her fingers in his shirt collar, twisted and yanked his face down level with her own. "Listen you," she began, and she scowled into his popping eyes. "Oh, the hell with it," said Suzy and released him.

Joe Elegant stepped back and massaged his throat and smoothed his shirt.

"Sorry," said Suzy.

"It's quite all right."

"What makes you so mean?"

"You said it. I don't belong here."

"Where do you belong?"

"I don't think you'd understand."

"You too good for the place?"

"Let's say I'm different."

"No kidding!" said Suzy.

"I'm writing a novel."

"You are? What about? I love novels."

"You wouldn't like this one."

"Why not?"

"You wouldn't understand it."

"Then what good is it?"

"It isn't intended for the mass."

"I'm the mass, huh? I guess you got something there. I bet you could write a pretty nice hunk of stuff."

Joe Elegant swallowed and his face twitched convulsively. "Sometime I'll read you some of it."

"Say, that would be nice. But you said I couldn't understand it."

"I'll explain it as I go along."

"I'd like that. There's one whole hell of a lot I don't understand."

"Do you like brownies?" he asked.

"I love them."

"I'll make you some. Maybe you'll come to my apartment some afternoon. I could give you a cup of tea."

"Say, you're a nice fella! Got any more coffee?"

"I'll make a fresh pot."

Parallels Must Be Related

Doc spent a restless night. His head was full of yellow pads and seers and octopi. Ordinarily he would have worked or read since he couldn't sleep, but now if he turned on a light he would see the yellow pad and the marshaled pencils.

As the dawn crept over the bay he decided to go for a very long walk, perhaps to follow the shoreline all the way around to Carmel. He arose, and since it was still dusky in the laboratory he turned on the lights to make his coffee.

Wide Ida, from the entrance of La Ida, saw his lights come on. She put an unlabeled pint bottle of brown liquor in a paper bag and crossed the street to Western Biological.

"Doc," she said, "would you work this stuff over?"

"What is it?"

"They say it's whisky. I just want to know if it'll kill anybody. I got a pretty good buy. They make it up in Pine Canyon."

"That's against the law," said Doc.

"Killing people is against the law too," said Wide Ida.

Doc was torn between bootlegging and murder. He thought sadly that he was always involved in something like this—not good or bad but bad and less bad. He made a fairly quick analysis. "It's not poison," he said, "but it won't build good healthy stomachs. There's some fusel oil in it. But I guess it's no worse than Old Tennis Shoes."

"Thanks, Doc. What do I owe you?"

"Oh, maybe a quart—but not this stuff."

"I'll send over some Old Taylor."

"You don't have to go off the deep end," said Doc.

"Doc, I hear you got trouble."

"Me? What kind of trouble?"

"I just heard," said Wide Ida.

Doc said angrily, "I've got no trouble. What's all the talk! God Almighty, everybody treats me as though I had a disease. What kind of trouble?"

"If there's anything I can do," she said and went out quickly, leaving the pint behind.

Doc took a sip of it, made a face, and took a swig. His heart was pounding angrily. He could not admit that the pity of his friends only confirmed his frustration. He knew that pity and contempt are brothers. He set his chin. "I *will* get the spring tides at La Jolla," he said to himself. "I *will* get a new microscope." And the very lowest voice whispered, "Somewhere there's warmth."

He sat down at his desk and wrote viciously: "Parallels must be related." He took another drink from the pint and opened yesterday's mail. There was an order for six sets of slides— starfish, embryonic series, for the Oakland Polytechnic High School. He was almost glad to do the old and practiced work. He got his collecting buckets together, threw rubber boots in his old car, and drove out to the Great Tide Pool.

Lousy Wednesday

Some days are born ugly. From the very first light they are no damn good whatever the weather, and everybody knows it. No one knows what causes this, but on such a day people resist getting out of bed and set their heels against the day. When they are finally forced out by hunger or job they find that the day is just as lousy as they knew it would be.

On such a day it is impossible to make a good cup of coffee, shoestrings break, cups leap from the shelf by themselves and shatter on the floor, children ordinarily honest tell lies, and children ordinarily good unscrew the tap handles of the gas range and lose the screws and have to be spanked. This is the day the cat chooses to have kittens and housebroken dogs wet on the parlor rug.

Oh, it's awful on such a day! The postman brings overdue bills. If it's a sunny day it is too damn sunny, and if it is dark who can stand it?

Mack knew it was going to be that kind of a day. He couldn't find his pants. He fell over a box that had crept out in his path. He cursed each brother in the Palace Flophouse, and on his way across the vacant lot he went out of his way to kick a dandelion flower. He was sitting gloomily on a pipe when Eddie came by, and so naturally he walked with Eddie to Wide Ida's to try to do something about it. He hung around waiting for Wide Ida to go so that Eddie could slip him a drink. But Wide Ida was bending over the bar, cursing a letter.

"Taxes," she said. "Every time you get going there's more taxes. You're lucky, Mack. You don't own nothing and you don't make nothing. Until they start taxing skin, you're safe."

"What's the beef?" he asked.

"City and county taxes," said Wide Ida.

"On what?"

"On this place. It ain't much, but I was fixed to put a down payment on a new Pontiac."

It was a statement that ordinarily would have aroused a detached compassion in Mack, together with mild self-congratulation that he was not burdened with taxable assets. But now a nagging worry fell on him, and he went back to the Palace Flophouse to worry in greater comfort. He went over the history of the Palace in his mind.

It had belonged to Lee Chong. Long before the war Mack and the boys had rented it from him for five dollars a month, and, naturally enough, they had never paid any rent. Lee Chong would have been shocked if they had. Then Lee Chong sold out to Joseph and Mary. Did the Palace go with the rest? Mack didn't know, but if it did, the Patrón didn't know it. He was no Lee Chong. He would have demanded the rent. But if the Patrón did own the place, he would get a tax bill. If he got a tax bill, he was sure to be on the necks of Mack and the boys. The Patrón was not a man to pay out money without getting more money back, that was certain.

It seemed very unjust. Their home, their security, even their social standing, were cast in the balance. Mack lay on his bed and considered what could be done. Suppose the Patrón demanded back rent—clear back for years. You couldn't trust a man like that. What a lousy day it was! Mack didn't know what to do, so he called a meeting of the boys, even sent Hazel to bring Eddie back from Wide Ida's bar.

It was a grim and shaken assembly. Mack explained all the angles until even Hazel seemed to understand the danger. The boys studied their fingers, looked at the ceiling, blew on their knuckles. Eddie got up and walked around his chair to change his thinking luck.

At last Whitey No. 2 said, "We could steal his mail so he won't get no tax bill."

"It ain't practical," said Mack. "Even if it wasn't a crime."

Hazel offered, "We could kill him."

"You ain't heard that's against the law too?" Mack asked.

"I mean, make it like an accident," said Hazel. "He could fall off Point Lobos."

"Then somebody else inherits the joint and we don't even know who."

The injustice in the theory of private ownership of real estate was descending on them.

"Maybe we could get Doc to talk to him. He likes Doc." This was Whitey No. 1's offering.

"That would only draw it to his attention," said Mack. "Hell, he might even raise the rent."

"He might even try to collect it," said Eddie.

Hazel was going into a slow but luminous burn. He gazed about the whitewashed walls of the Palace Flophouse, at the Coca-Cola calendar girls, at the great and ancient woodstove, at the grandfather clock, at the framed portrait of Romie Jacks. There were honest, unabashed tears in Hazel's eyes. "The son-of-a-bitch," he said. "After all our work he takes away our home—the only place where I ever been happy. How can a guy be so goddam mean?"

"He ain't done it yet," said Mack. "He don't even know about it maybe."

"I wish Doc owned the place," said Eddie. "We wouldn't have no trouble with Doc."

Mack looked at him quickly. "What put that in your head?" he demanded.

"Hell, Doc don't open his mail for weeks on end. Doc would forget to collect the rent and he'd forget to open a tax bill."

Excitement shone in Mack's eyes. "Eddie," he said, "maybe you put your finger in it."

"In what?"

"I got to think it over," said Mack, "but just maybe our darling Eddie here is a genius."

Eddie blushed with pleasure. "What'd I do, Mack?"

"I can't tell you now."

"Hell, Mack, I want to know what I done."

"It was smart," said Mack. "It was a stroke of just pure

wonderful. Now let's give the Patrón a going-over. How much guts you think he's got?"

"Plenty," said Hazel. "And he's plenty wise."

Mack spoke slowly, thinking aloud. "Let's see. Joseph and Mary, you might say, is a con man in a general kind of way—"

"He's a nice dresser," said Hazel.

"A con man can't make enemies unless, of course, he wants to get out of town. He got to keep everybody happy and friendly."

"Come on, Mack," Whitey No. 1 demanded. "Tell us!"

"Fellas," said Mack, "if I blowed it now and it wasn't no good, why, you'd kind of lose face in me. I want to think this one out and see if I can't kind of surround him. But if we do her, you'll all have to help."

"Do what?"

"Let me alone now, boys," said Mack, and he went back to his bed and put his head on his crossed hands and studied the rafters of the Palace Flophouse.

Hazel came quietly to his bedside. "You won't let nobody take our home away, will you, Mack?"

"I promise!" said Mack fervently. "Where's Eddie?"

"Went back to Wide Ida's."

"Will you do something for me, Hazel?"

"Sure, Mack."

"Take that lard can over there and see can Eddie fill it full of beer without too much fuss. It'll help me to think better."

"You'll get your beer," said Hazel. "You just keep thinking, Mack. Say, Mack, how do you think Eddie always got a stroke of genius even when he don't know it and I don't never have none?"

"Come again?" said Mack.

"How come—oh, the hell with it!" said Hazel.

The Playing Fields of Harrow

Fauna had made a success of three improbable enterprises. More than likely she could have held her own in steel or chemicals, maybe even in General Electric, for Fauna had the proper ingredients for modern business. She was benevolent and at the same time solvent, public-spirited and privately an individualist, open-handed but with a delicate sense of doubly-entry bookkeeping, sentimental but not soft. She could easily have been chairman of the board of a large corporation. And Fauna took a deep personal interest in her girls.

Shortly after she took over the Bear Flag, Fauna set aside and decorated the Ready Room. It was a large and pleasant apartment with three windows overlooking the vacant lot. Fauna put in deep chairs and couches covered with bright, flower-littered glazed chintz. The drapes matched the furniture, and the pictures were designed to soothe without arousing interest—engravings of cows in ponds, deer in streams, dogs in lakes. Wet animals seem to serve some human need.

For recreation Fauna provided a table-tennis set, a card table, and a Parcheesi board. The Ready Room was a place to relax, to read, to gossip, to study, and some of these things were actually done by the girls of the Bear Flag.

One wall was dominated by a large framed board on which were pasted enormous gold stars, and this was Fauna's personal pride. The Ready Room was gay and feminine. It had an exotic, Oriental odor from the incense which burned in the blackened lap of a crouching plaster Buddha.

At about a quarter to three Agnes and Mabel and Becky were relaxing in the Ready Room. It was a time of languor. The vacant lot was washed in clear pale sunshine, which made even the rusty pipes and the old boiler look beautiful. The tall mallow weeds were as sweetly green as a garden. A sleek, gray, lazy Persian cat hunted gophers in the grass and didn't care whether she caught one or not.

Mabel stood at the window. She said, "I heard some people used to live in that old boiler."

Agnes was painting her toenails and waving her feet to dry the enamel. "That's before your time," she said. "Mr. and Mrs. Malloy, they had it fixed up nice—awning out front, Oriental rug. Once you got inside, through the fire-door, it was real nice. She was a homemaker."

"Why'd they leave?" Becky asked.

"They got to arguing. She kept wanting curtains. He wouldn't let her because there wasn't no windows. When they argued it kind of echoed in there and got on their nerves. He said there wasn't room inside to take a swing at her. He's in the county jail now—trusty. Mrs. Malloy's slinging hash in a grease joint over at Salinas, waiting for him to get out. They was real nice people. He's a high Elk."

Mabel moved away from the window. "You heard the Rattlesnake Club is coming from Salinas tonight? Took the whole house over."

"Yeah," said Becky. "They're having a memorial meeting for dead members. Fauna give them a rate."

Agnes lifted her left leg and blew on her toenails. "Like this color?" she asked.

"It's nice," said Becky. "Looks a little like you was rotting. Say, where in hell is Suzy? She'll find out when Fauna says three o'clock she means three o'clock. Gee, Fauna's a funny name."

Mabel said, "Her name used to be Flora. What is a fauna anyway? I never knew nobody named that."

"Oh, it's like a baby deer," said Becky. "I don't think Suzy'll be here long. She's kind of nuts—got a nuts look in her eye. Goes out walking."

Mabel said, "Well, it's two minutes to three. Suzy better get here."

On the stroke of three a door opened and Fauna came in from her bedroom. A silver headband was tied around her orange hair, and it made her look like a certain social leader recently deceased. Fauna had the elegance found only in the drawing rooms of the old rich and in *haute monde* brothels. She was heavy but she moved with light, deft steps. She carried a large basket.

"Where's Suzy?" she asked.

"I don't know," said Mabel.

"Well, look in her room."

Mabel went out.

Fauna moved to the Parcheesi board. "Somebody's been shooting craps with the Parcheesi dice," she said.

"How'd you know?" Becky asked.

"There's two bucks in the corner bucket. I don't want gambling in the Ready Room. If a young lady wants to run a few passes with a customer, that's different, but I don't want to find no more pencil marks on the lump sugar either. Gambling's a vice. I knew many a good hooker with a future that's throwed it away on games of chance."

"Hell, Fauna, you play poker," said Becky.

"Poker ain't a game of chance," said Fauna. "And you watch your language, Becky. Vulgarity gives a hookshop a bad name." She took a linen tablecloth from her basket and spread it over the Parcheesi board. Then she laid out a napkin, a plate, wineglasses, and a heap of flat silver.

Mabel and Suzy came in.

Fauna said, "I don't like my young ladies to be late." She took a teacher's pointer from her basket. "Now, what young lady wants to be first?"

Agnes said, "I'll do her."

"You done it yesterday," said Mabel. "Goddam it, it's my turn!"

Fauna said sternly, "Young ladies, suppose some nice dumb young fellow was to hear you. Now, Mabel—" She indicated the items on the tablecloth with a pointer, and Mabel began, like a child reciting poetry, "Oyster fork . . . salad fork . . . fish fork . . . roast fork . . . savory fork . . . dessert fork . . . plate . . . dessert knife . . . savory knife . . . roast knife . . . fish knife—"

"Good!" said Fauna. "Now here." And Mabel went on, "Water . . . white wine . . . claret . . . burgundy . . . port . . . brandy."

"Perfect," said Fauna. "Which side does the salad go on?"

"Left side, so you can get your sleeve in the gravy."

Fauna was deeply gratified. "By God, that's good! I wouldn't be surprised if Mabel wasn't one of them stars before too long." She indicated the gold stars on the wall.

"What are they?" Suzy asked.

Fauna said proudly, "Every one of them stars represents a young lady from the Bear Flag that married, and married well. That first star's got four kids and her husband's manager of an A and P. Third from the end is president of the Salinas Forward and Upward Club and held the tree on Arbor Day. Next star is high up in the Watch and Ward, sings alto in the Episcopal church in San Jose. My young ladies go places. Now, Suzy—"

"Huh?"

"What's that?"

"That funny kind of fork?"

"What's it for?"

"I don't know."

"Cooperate, Suzy. What do you eat with it?"

Suzy mused, "You couldn't get much mashed potatoes on it. Pickles maybe?"

"It's a clam fork," said Fauna. "Now say it. *Clam fork.*"

Suzy said vehemently, "I wouldn't eat a clam if you was to give me a scoop shovel."

"What a mug!" said Agnes.

Suzy turned on her. "I ain't no mug!"

Mabel cried, "Double negative! Double negative!"

"What you talking about?" said Suzy.

Mabel said, "When you say you ain't no mug, that means you're a mug."

Suzy started for her. "Who's a mug?"

Fauna bellowed, "If certain young ladies don't come to order they're going to get a paste in the puss! Now—posture. Where's the books?"

Agnes said, "I think Joe Elegant's reading them."

"Damn it," said Fauna, "I picked them books special so's nobody'd take them. What's he reading them for? *Breeder's Journal, California Civil Code,* and a novel by Sterling North—what the hell is there to read? Well, we'll just have to use the basket, I guess. Agnes, put the basket on your head."

Fauna inspected her. "Now look here, young ladies," she said. "Just because you got your ankles together and your hips flang forward—that don't necessarily mean posture. Agnes, tuck in your butt! Posture's a state of mind. Real posture is when a young lady's flat on her ass and still looks like she got books on her head."

There came a knock on the door and Joe Elegant handed Fauna a note. She read it and sighed with pleasure. "That Mack," she said. "What a gent! I guess he'd drain the embalming fluid off his dead grandma, but he'd do it nice."

"Is his grandma dead?" Agnes asked.

"Who knows?" said Fauna. "Listen to this, young ladies. 'Mack and the boys request the pleasure of your company at their joint tomorrow aft. to drink a slug of good stuff and talk about something important. Bring the girls. R.S.V.P.'" Fauna paused. "He could of yelled outside the window, but not Mack—he requests the pleasure of our company." She sighed. "What a gent! If he wasn't such a bum I'd aim one of you young ladies at him."

Agnes asked, "What's the matter with Mack's grandma?"

"I don't even know he's got a grandma," said Fauna. "Now when we go over there tomorrow, you young ladies keep your traps shut and just listen." She mused, "Something important—well, it might be like Mack needs twenty bucks, so just keep your heads shut and let me do the thinking."

Suddenly Fauna beat her forehead with the heel of her hand. "I nearly forgot! Joe Elegant baked a great big goddam cake. Suzy, you take four cold cans of beer and that cake and go over and give them to Doc to cheer him up."

"Okay," said Suzy. "But it'll probably molt in his stomach."

"His stomach ain't none of your business," said Fauna.

And when Suzy had gone Fauna said, "I wisht I could stick up a star for that kid. She don't hardly pull her own weight here."

The Little Flowers of Saint Mack

Doc laid ten big starfish out on a shelf, and he set up a line of eight glass dishes half filled with sea water. Although he was inclined to carelessness in his living arrangements his laboratory technique was immaculate. The making of the embryo series gave him pleasure. He had done it hundreds of time before, and he felt a safety in the known thing—no speculation here. He did certain things and certain other things followed. There is comfort in routine.

His old life came back to him—a plateau of contentment with small peaks of excitement but none of the jagged pain of original thinking, none of the loneliness of invention. His phonograph played softly, played the safe and certain fugues of Bach, clear as equations. As he worked, a benign feeling came over him. He liked himself again as he once had; liked himself as a person, the way he might like anyone else. The self-hatred which poisons so many people and which had been irritating him was gone for the time. The top voice of his mind sang peacefulness and order, and the raucous middle voice was gentle; it mumbled and snarled but it could not be heard. The lowest voice of all was silent, dreaming of a warm safe sea.

The rattlesnakes in their wire cage suddenly lifted their heads, felt the air with their forked tongues, and then all four set up a dry buzzing rattle. Doc looked up from his work as Mack came in.

Mack glanced at the cage. "Them new snakes ain't got used to me yet," he said.

"Takes a little time," said Doc. "You haven't been here much."

"Didn't feel no welcome here," said Mack.

"I'm sorry, Mack. I guess I've been off my feed. I'll try to do better."

"You going to let up on them devilfish?"

"I don't know."

"They was making you sick."

Doc laughed, "It wasn't the octopi. I guess it was trying to think. I'd got out of the habit."

"I never got the habit," said Mack.

"That's not true," said Doc. "I never knew anyone who devoted more loving thought to minusculae."

"I never even heard of them," said Mack. "Say, Doc, what do you think of the Patrón—your honest, spit-in-the-lake opinion?"

"I don't think I understand him. We're kind of different."

"You ain't kidding," said Mack. "He ain't honest."

Doc said, "I'd call that expert testimony."

"What do you mean?"

"I mean you bring some experience to bear."

"Oh, I know what you mean," said Mack earnestly, "but you search your heart, Doc, and see if I ain't dishonest in a kind of honest way. I don't really fool nobody—not even myself. And there's another thing—I know when I'm doing it. Joseph and Mary can't tell the difference."

"I think that might be true," said Doc.

"What I'm wondering is—well, I don't think the Patrón wants any trouble around here, do you?"

"Nobody wants any trouble."

"He's got a stake here," Mack went on. "If the whole Row took a scunner to him, why, he just couldn't take that chance, don't you think?"

"If I knew what you were talking about, it might help," said Doc.

"I'm just trying to figure something," said Mack.

"Well, if you mean that the Patrón is in kind of a sensitive position—"

"That's what I do mean," said Mack. "He can't afford to have no enemies."

"Nobody wants enemies," said Doc.

"I know. But he could get his ass in a sling. He got a business and he's got property."

"I see what you mean," said Doc. "You're going to pressure him and you want to know what he'll do. What are you going to try to take away from him, Mack?"

"I'm just thinking," said Mack.

"I never knew you to think idly. When you think, somebody gets hurt."

"I never hurt nobody, Doc."

"Well, not bad. I will say your bite is not deadly."

Mack was uneasy. He had not intended the conversation to turn to him. He changed the subject.

"Say, Doc, did you hear? The whole country club took a loyalty oath on the eighteenth green. Whitey No. 2 was caddying. Them members all took off their hats and swore they would not destroy the U.S. government."

"I'm glad," said Doc. "I was worried. Did the caddies take the oath too?"

"Some of them did, but not Whitey. He's kind of an idealist, you might say. He says if he gets an idea to burn down the Capitol he don't want no perjury rap to stand in his way. They won't let him caddy no more."

"Does he want to burn down the Capitol?" Doc asked.

"Well, no. He says he don't want to now, but he don't know what he'll want to do next month. He gives us quite a talk about it. Says he was a Marine, went through a lot of fighting for the country, figures he's got a kind of personal interest. He don't want nobody to tell him what to do."

Doc laughed. "So he can't carry golf clubs anymore because of his ideals?"

"They say he's a security risk," said Mack. "Whitey claims he ain't got a good enough memory to be a security risk. Besides, they don't talk about nothing out there on the golf course except money and dames."

Doc said, "Heroes always get punished at first."

"Speaking of dames, Doc—"

"Let's," said Doc.

"Whatever happened to that swell-looking babe in the fur coat used to come over?"

"She's not been very well."

"That's too bad," said Mack. "What's she got?"

"Oh, something obscure. Can't seem to track it down."

"I guess with that kind of dough—"

"What do you mean?"

"I seen it happen so many times," said Mack. "You take a dame and she's married to a guy that's making twenty-five bucks a week. You can't kill her with a meat ax. She's got kids and does the washing—may get a little tired but that's the worse that can happen to her. But let the guy get raised to seventy-five bucks a week and she begins to get colds and take vitamins."

"That's a new theory of medicine," said Doc.

"It ain't new. Hell, just use your eyes. Guy gets up to a hundred a week and this same dame reads *Time* magazine and she's got the newest disease before she even finished the page. I've knew dames that can give doctors cards, spades, and big casino about medicine. They got stuff called allergy now. Used to call it hay fever—made you sneeze. Guy that figured out allergy should of got a patent. A allergy is, you get sick when there's something you don't want to do. I've knew dames that was allergic to dishwater. Married guy starts making dough—he's got a patient on his hands."

"You sound cynical," said Doc.

"No, I ain't. You just look around and show me one well dame with her old man in the chips."

Doc chuckled. "You think that's what happened to my friend?"

"Oh, hell no," said Mack. "That's big stuff. When you get dough like that it's different. She got to have something that don't nobody know what it is. She can't have nothing common that you can take salts for. She goes around puzzling doctors. They stand around her and they shake their heads and they scratch and they never seen nothing like her case before."

"I haven't heard you go on like this for a long time," said Doc.

"You ain't been in the mood to listen. You think them doctors is honest?"

"I haven't any reason to doubt it. Why?"

"I bet I could fix rich dames up," said Mack. "At least for a while."

"How would you go about it?"

"Well, sir, first I'd hire me a deaf-and-dumb assistant. His job is just to set and listen and look worried. Then I'd get me a bottle of Epsom salts and I'd put in a pretty little screw-cap thing and I'd call it Moondust. I'd charge about thirty dollars a teaspoonful, and you got to come to my office to get it. Then I'd invent me a machine you strap the dame in. It's all chrome and it lights colored lights every minute or so. It costs the dame twelve dollars a half-hour and it puts her through the motions she'd do over a scrub board. I'd cure them! And I'd make a fortune too. Of course they'd get sick right away again, so I'd have something else, liked mixed sleeping pills and wake-up pills that keeps you right where you was when you started."

Doc said, "Thank God you haven't got a license to practice!"

"Why?"

"As a matter of fact, I don't know why," said Doc. "How about preventive medicine?"

"You mean how to keep them from getting sick?"

"Yes."

"That's easy," said Mack. "Stay broke!"

Doc sat silent for a while. He glanced at the starfish and saw the reproductive fluid beginning to ooze from between their rays. "Say, Mack," he asked, "did you come over to try to get something out of me?"

"I don't think so," said Mack. "If I did I've forgot what it was. I'm sure glad you got over it, Doc."

"Got over what?"

"Oh, them goddam sooplapods."

"Look, Mack!" Sudden anger welled up in Doc. "Don't get

any funny ideas. I am going to write that paper. I am going to La Jolla for the spring tides."

"All right, Doc, all right. Have it your own way."

But back in the Palace Flophouse Mack reported to the boys, "Seemed like he was better, but he ain't over the hump yet. We got to help him not to write that goddam paper."

Suzy Binds the Cheese

Suzy was light on her feet. She was up the stairs and knocking on the door of Western Biological before the snakes rattled. Doc called, "Come in," without looking up from his microscope.

Suzy stood in the doorway. She held a gigantic flop cake on one hand and carried a paper bag of canned beer in the other. "How do you do?" she said formally.

Doc looked up. "Oh, hello. For God's sake, what's that?"

"A cake. Joe Elegant made it."

"Why?" Doc asked.

"I think Fauna told him to."

"Well, I hope you like cake," said Doc.

Suzy laughed. "I don't think this is a eating cake. This is a looking cake. Fauna sent you some beer."

"That's more like it," said Doc. "What's Fauna want?"

"Nothing."

"That's funny."

"Where shall I put the cake?" said Suzy.

Now Doc looked at Suzy and Suzy looked at Doc and they both had the same thought and they burst into laughter. Tears streamed from Suzy's eyes. "Oh Lord!" said Suzy. "Oh Lord!" She laughed with her mouth wide and her eyes pinched shut. Doc slapped his leg and threw back his head and roared. And the laughter was so pleasant they tried to keep it going after its momentum was spent.

"Oh Lord," said Suzy, "I got to wipe my eyes." She put the cake down on top of the rattlesnake cage, and hysterical rattling filled the room. Suzy jumped back. "What's that?"

"Rattlesnakes."

"What you got them for?"

"I take their venom and sell it."

"I'd hate to live with a bunch of dirty snakes."

"They're not dirty. They even change their skins. That's more than people do."

"I hate them," said Suzy, and she shuddered.

"You wouldn't, once you knew them."

"Well I ain't likely to get to know them," said Suzy. "They're dirty."

Doc leaned back in his chair and crossed his legs. He said, "You know, this interests me. Snakes are cleaner than most animals. Wonder why you call them dirty?"

Suzy looked at him levelly. "You want to know why?"

"Sure I do."

"Because you run Fauna down."

"Wait a minute," said Doc. "What's that got—I did not!"

"You said Fauna's trying to get something out of you. She just done it to be nice."

Doc nodded his head slowly. "I see. So you got even by calling snakes dirty."

"You got it, mister. Nobody don't run Fauna down when I'm around."

"It was just a joke," said Doc.

"Didn't sound like no joke to me."

"Why, Fauna's one of my best friends," said Doc. "Let's have a can of beer and make peace."

"Okay," said Suzy. "You make the first move."

Doc said, "Tell Joe Elegant it's an incredible cake."

"Got marshmallow frosting," said Suzy.

"And tell Fauna the beer saved my life."

Suzy's face relaxed. "Okay," she said. "I guess that's okay. Where's the opener?"

"Right in the sink back there."

Suzy brought the two punched cans to Doc's work table. "Say, what you doing?"

"Making slides. When I started I put starfish sperm and ova in each of these glasses. Then every half-hour I kill one glass of the developing embryos, and when I have the whole series, I mount them on slides like this, and one slide shows the whole development."

Suzy bent over the dishes. "I don't see nothing."

"They're too small. I can show you in the glass."

Suzy backed up. "What do you do it for?"

"So students can see how starfish get to be."

"Why do they want to know?"

"Well, I guess because that's the way people get to be."

"Then why don't they study people?"

Doc laughed. "It's a little difficult to kill unborn babies every half-hour. Here, take a look." He pushed a glass dish under the microscope.

Suzy peered in the eyepieces. "God Almighty!" she said. "Did I look like that once?"

"Something like."

"Sometimes I feel like that now. Say, Doc, you got a funny business—bugs and all like that."

"There are funnier businesses," he said sharply.

She stiffened. "Meaning my business? You don't like my business, huh?"

"It doesn't matter whether I like it or not. There it is. But it does seem to me a kind of sad substitute for love—a kind of lonesome substitute."

Suzy put her hands on her hips. "And what've you got, mister? Bugs, snakes? Look at this dump! It stinks. Floor ain't been clean in years. You ain't got a decent suit of clothes. You probably can't remember your last hot meal. You sit here breeding bugs—for Chrissake! What do you think that's a substitute for?"

In the old days Doc would have been amused, but now his guard was down and he caught her anger like a disease. "I do what I want," he said. "I live the way I want. I'm free—do you get that? I'm free and I do what I want."

"You ain't got nothing," Suzy said. "Bugs and snakes and a dirty house. I bet some dame threw you over. That's what you're substituting for. Got a wife? No! Got a girl? No!"

Doc found himself shouting, "I don't want a wife. I have all the women I want!"

"Woman and women is two different things," said Suzy. "Guy knows all about women he don't know nothing about a woman."

Doc said, "This guy is happy that way."

"Now you're happy!" said Suzy. "You're a pushover! If no dame's got you it's because no dame wants you. Who the hell would want to live with bugs and snakes in a joint like this?"

"Who'd want to go to bed with anybody that's got three bucks?" said Doc cruelly.

Suzy said icily, "A smart guy. A real smart guy. He's got what he wants. Seems to me I heard you're writing a great big god-dam highfalutin paper."

"Who told you that?"

"Everybody knows about it. Everybody's laughing at you be-hind your back—and you know why? Because everybody knows you're kidding yourself. You ain't never going to write that paper because you can't write that paper. You're just sitting here like a kid playing wish games."

She saw her words go home as surely as though she had watched arrows drive into his chest, and misery and shame overwhelmed her. "I wish I didn't say that," she spoke softly. "I wish to God I never said that."

"It might be true," said Doc quietly. "Maybe you put your finger on the truth. Is everybody laughing at me? Is everybody laughing—?"

"My name's Suzy," she said.

"Are they laughing, Suzy?"

"They got no right to," she said. "I was just fighting back— honest to God I was. I didn't mean any of that stuff I said."

"I love true things," said Doc. "Even when they hurt. Isn't it better to know the truth about oneself?" And he asked it of himself. "Yes, I think it is. I think it is. You're quite right, I've got nothing. That's why I built up the whole story about my pa-per until I believed it myself—a little man pretending to be a big man, a fool trying to be wise."

"Fauna will kill me," Suzy moaned. "She'll wring my neck. Say, Doc, you got no right to take mad talk from a two-bit hustler—you got no right."

"What's it matter where the truth comes from," he said, "if it's the truth?"

Suzy said, "Doc, I never felt so lousy in my life. Get mad at me, won't you?"

"Why should I get mad? Maybe you've stopped a bunch of nonsense. Perhaps you've nipped a fool in the bud."

"Get mad at me," she begged. "Here! Take a punch at me."

Doc chuckled. "I wish it could be that easy."

Suzy said sadly, "Then I ain't got any choice," and she shrilled at him, "Why you goddam bum! You lousy stinking fool! Who the hell d'you think you are?"

There was a flutter of footsteps and the door burst open.

It was Becky. "Suzy! You're late. The Rattlesnakes are here. Come on! Get into your tomato dress."

"It's called 'Love Apples,'" said Suzy quietly. "So long, Doc," and she followed Becky out.

Doc watched them go. He said aloud, "That's probably the only completely honest human I have ever met." His eyes wandered to the table and suddenly he bellowed, "*Goddam it!* She made me miss the time. The dirty bitch! I've got to do it all over." And he dumped the contents of the glass dishes into his slop bucket.

A Pause in the Day's Occupation

Not the least important and valuable custom Fauna brought to the Bear Flag was the little time of rest and contemplation in the Ready Room after work and before sleep. Grievances were brought out and inspected, quarrels were settled, and all the little matters of interest and despair were turned over and examined for their actual value. Then praise or blame were assigned and plans for improvement were laid out with lore and tact learned in other fields. Fauna warped and nudged and bunted her young ladies toward good nature and kindliness, which are the parents of restful sleep. It was not unusual for light refreshments to be served, and on occasion the young ladies' voices joined in song—"Home Sweet Home," "Old Black Joe," "Down by the Old Mill Stream," "Harvest Moon." Dogwatch in the Ready Room was a medicine to weary nerves and frayed bodies.

The Bear Flag was shorthanded the night of the memorial meeting for dead members sponsored by the Rattlesnake Club of Salinas. Helen and Wisteria were doing sixty days for a lady fight that is still discussed with admiration in Cannery Row.

When the last Rattlesnake had gone and the big front door was closed, the girls wandered wearily into the Ready Room, sat down, and kicked off their shoes. Becky said, "One of them Rattlesnakes tonight called us an institution and a landmark."

Agnes said acidly, "We get a few more like Suzy and it'll be a institution all right. I got an uncle in a institution. He goes right on fighting the battle of San Juan Hill. Where is Suzy?"

"I'm right here," said Suzy, entering. "I was getting that cracked record out of the jukebox. Am I pooped! Let's put it in the sack."

"Before Fauna gives us good night? You crazy?" Mabel said. "She'd bust a gut."

Becky sighed. "What a night! This is one time the group rate paid off. Them Rattlesnakes ain't turned a trick since midnight but they sure was active."

"They was going fine until they run out of liquor," said Mabel. "That new stuff Wide Ida sent in must be made of jumping beans."

Suzy said, "I figured if that short one told me once more how his little boy cut a worm in two with a shovel—"

"Oh, you got it too, huh? Know what the little bastard said? Only four years old too. He said, 'I cut a wum.' Now if he said he cut a camel I could listen to it three or four times."

"That bald one!" said Mabel. "Did *his* wife have an operation! They turned her inside out. Sounded like they was pelting her. He got crying so hard I never did find out what she had."

"A malignant artichoke," said Becky. "I made him say it slow."

Agnes asked, "Say, who is this guy Sigmund Ki they was singing about?"

"Never heard of him," said Becky. "I once knew a dame said she was the original Frankie though."

"I've personally knew three original Frankies," said Mabel. "Suzy, you got to stop arguing with the customers."

Suzy said, "If that's the live members of the Rattlesnake Club, the dead ones is what I call dead. I can scream twice at a rubber lizard and then the hell with it."

Fauna came out of the bedroom office and stood in the doorway, rubbing lotion into her hands. She had changed to a peach-colored dressing gown. She said seriously, "Young ladies, you can make fun of the Rattlesnakes if you want to, but if you ever get in the administration end you will welcome good solid citizens like them. Why, there was some very important people here from Salinas! I give them a good rate, but you notice there's no busted furniture. Them free-spending sailors last Saturday night cost me eighty-five dollars in repairs. That nice boy give Becky a five-dollar tip—but he busted two windows and run off with the deer-antler halltree."

Suzy said, "God, I'm sleepy."

Fauna said sharply, "Suzy, I got one rule: never let the sun rise on a cross word or an unbalanced book." She scratched her nose with a pencil. "I just wish there was more Rattlesnakes," she said.

"I wish there was more dead members," Suzy said.

"That's a cross word, Suzy!" said Fauna. "The birds are chirping happily, so why can't we? Now let's relax. Who wants a beer?"

Becky said, "If I say I want it I'll have to get it for everybody. My dogs are tired! You know what I was dancing? A quadrille!"

Fauna said dryly, "I seen you. I'll have to give you some lesson, I guess. You done a kootch quadrille. It ain't your feet should be tired. After all the posture lessons I give you, you still dance like a harlot."

"What's a harlot?" Becky asked.

"A whore," said Mabel.

"Oh, harlot, huh?" said Becky.

Agnes said, "Fauna, I want you should tell Suzy when she goes on errands she should come back. She stayed over Doc's about an hour while the Rattlesnakes was really active."

Suzy asked, "Say, Fauna, what's wrong with Doc?"

"Wrong? Ain't nothing wrong with him," said Fauna. "He's one of the nicest fellas ever lived on Cannery Row. You'd think he'd turn bitter the way everybody hustles him. Wide Ida gets him to analyze her booze, Mack and the boys throw the hook into him for every dime that sticks out, a kid cuts his finger on the Row and he goes to Doc to get it wrapped up. Why, when Becky got in a fight with that Woodman of the World and got bit in the shoulder, she might of lost her arm if it wasn't for Doc. Show her the scar, Becky."

Suzy asked, "Don't Doc never come here?"

"No, he don't. But don't let nothing ever give you the idea he's strange. There's girls goes in there with fur coats and stuff and he plays that churchy kind of music. Doc's all right. He gets what he wants. Dora said every girl made a play for him. I put a stop to that."

"Why'd you do that?" Suzy asked.

"I'm saving him—that's why. You look at them gold stars over there—every star, one of my girls has married well."

Suzy said, "Who marries hustlers?"

"Now that's a bad attitude to take," Fauna said coldly. "That's the kind of attitude I try to discourage. You look at that third star from the end over there. I admit she's kind of snooty, but why shouldn't she be? She's a reader in a big church in San Luis Obispo. I tell you, my girls marry, and marry well!"

Suzy said, "What's that got to do with Doc?"

"I got him staked out for Miss Right," said Fauna. "Someday I'll draw a bead on him."

"Hell," said Suzy, "he said he don't want to marry nobody."

"Watch your language, Suzy," said Fauna. And then with interest she asked, "How'd you get along with him?"

"We got in a hassle," said Suzy. "He made me mad and I made him mad. All them goddam bugs—and a paper about nervous breakdowns in devilfish! Someday a guy in a white coat's going to tap him on the shoulder."

Fauna said, "Don't believe it! Why, some of them bugs he gets as much as ten bucks for."

"Not *apiece*?" said Suzy.

Fauna went on, "Why he takes an old beat-up cat he paid a quarter for and he shoots red and blue and yellow paint in it and he gets fifteen bucks for it."

"Why, for Chrissake?" Suzy asked.

"Suzy, if you don't watch your language I'll wash out your mouth. Now you just get up and bring the beer for that. You're an ignorant girl but I'll be goddamned if I'll let you get common."

Suzy went out, and Fauna said, "I wonder if she might be for Doc—she's got an awful big mouth. She'd talk her way out of an apple dumpling."

Suzy came back with a tray of beer bottles.

Becky said, "Fauna, why don't you read Suzy's horoscope?"

"You mean stars and like that?" said Suzy. "What for?"

Becky said, "To see if you're going to marry Doc."

Suzy said angrily, "I like a joke as good as anybody but don't get rough with me."

Becky said, "Who's rough?"

"I don't believe that crap about stars," said Suzy. "And you lay off talking about Doc. He's been to college—he's read so many books he can't count 'em—and not comic books neither. You lay off talking about him and me."

Fauna said, "That will be enough, miss. You see that chart? Just look at them gold stars. And look particular at that gold star that's got a gold star on it. That young lady is married to a professor at Stanford. He's got about a million books, and she used to take all day Sunday figuring out Jiggs and Maggie. You know what she does? If somebody points to all them books and says, 'Does the little lady read all of them?' she just smiles kind of quiet and mysterious. When they ask her a question, you know what she does? You can learn, Suzy, if you just pay attention. She repeats the last three words anybody says, and first thing you know, they think she said it. Why, her own husband thinks she can read and write! You get smart, Suzy. Doc don't want no dame that knows as much as him. What would he have to talk about? Let him tell you for once. Don't tell him."

Becky said, "She won't. She loves to shoot off her face."

"She damn well better learn to shut up or she won't be no gold star," said Fauna. "That's a good idea about the horoscope. When's your birthday, Suzy?"

"February twenty-third."

"What time was you born?"

"God knows, but I think it was leap year."

Agnes said, "I bet she was born at night. I can always tell."

Fauna went into her room and brought back a chart and pinned it to the wall. And she brought out her schoolroom pointer again. "Now this here's you, Pisces—that's fish."

Suzy said, "You mean I'm fish?"

"You're fish," said Fauna.

"I don't believe a goddam word of it. I don't even like fish," Suzy said. "Why, hell, I break out if I look at a fish!"

"Don't look at them then," said Fauna. "But if you ain't lied about your birthday you're fish. Now let's see—fish is to Jupiter, carry two in the Saturn, and three left over in the House of Venus—"

"I don't believe none of it," Suzy said.

Fauna looked up from her figuring. "Tell her some of that stuff I done, Mabel."

Mabel said, "I seen her do wonderful stuff. I had a pup one time. Fauna, she done a horoscope on him. It says on that pup's third birthday, ten o'clock, he's going explode."

Suzy asked, "Did he?"

"Well, no. Something went haywire with the chart, I guess. Ten o'clock on that dog's third birthday he caught fire. I was taking a lemon rinse."

"You could use one now," Fauna said.

"What caught him on fire?" Suzy asked.

"He just caught. Spontaneous something or other. He was a pretty good dog but he wasn't very bright. Never could house-break him. He used to wet on Joe Elegant."

Suzy said, "I bet Joe Elegant set him on fire."

"That's a lie!" said Mabel. "Joe Elegant was in the hospital."

Suddenly Fauna clapped her hands to her brow. "God Almighty!"

"What is it?" said Becky. "What's the matter?"

Fauna said impressively, "Suzy, you know what you're going to marry? You're going to marry a Cancer!"

"Thought you caught it," said Suzy. "I didn't know you had to marry it."

"Don't get funny," said Fauna. "Cancer, that's a crab—and that's also July. Now you just think—who works with crabs and stuff like that?"

Becky said, "Joe Anguro's fish market."

Fauna exploded, "Doc! And if his birthday's in July he's a gone goose. Agnes, when's Doc's birthday?"

"I don't know. Mack's gonna ask him."

"Well, we'll have to find out. Can't let him know why we want to know."

Agnes said, "Mack will find out. Mack's used to hustling Doc."

"Well, I want to know right away. Now you young ladies get some sleep, you hear me? You know what's coming in today?"

Fauna stuck the pencil in her hair. "A great big fat juicy destroyer! And you know what day it is?"

The girls spoke in a chorus. "Lord-God-Almighty," they said, "payday!"

It took Fauna about five minutes to put up her hair and then she was ready to make her final rounds to see that the garbage was out and all the lights turned off. In the dark Ready Room she saw a glowing cigarette.

"Who's there?" she called.

"Me," said Suzy.

"Why ain't you in bed?"

"I was thinking."

"Now I know you'll never make a hustler. What you thinking about, your horoscope?"

"Yeah."

"You like Doc, huh?"

"I put the knife in him. He made me mad."

"Whyn't you let me handle it?" said Fauna. "I think I could maybe get him for you."

"He don't want a wife, and if he did, he don't want nobody like me."

"People don't know what they want," said Fauna. "They got to be pushed. Why would guys in their right mind want to get married? But they do."

"Maybe they fall in love," said Suzy.

"Yeah—and that's the worst that can happen. Know something, Suzy? When a man falls in love it's ninety to one he falls for the dame that's worst for him. That's why I take matters in my own hands."

"How do you mean?" Suzy asked.

"Well, when a guy picks out a dame for himself he's in love with something in himself that hasn't got nothing to do with the dame. She looks like his mother, or she's dark and he's scared of blondes, or maybe he's getting even with somebody, or maybe he ain't quite sure he's a man and has to prove it. Fella that studied stuff like that told me one time—a man don't fall for a dame. He falls for new roses, and he brings his own new roses. The best marriages are the ones pulled off by someone that's smart but not sucked in. I think you'd be good for Doc."

"Why?"

"Because you ain't like him. You want I should try?"

"No," said Suzy. "I wouldn't sandbag no guy. Especially Doc."

"Everybody sandbags everybody," said Fauna.

Suzy said softly, "You know, you was right, Fauna. I was sixteen when it happened. But you know, he talked to me like I was a girl. I can't even remember how it sounds—talked to like a girl."

Fauna put her hand on Suzy's shoulder. "Maybe you'll find out again," she said. "If I pull this off I'll put a red ring around your gold star. You ready to go to sleep now?"

"I guess so," said Suzy. "Let's don't sandbag Doc."

Suzy waited until Fauna had rustled to her bed and then she crept out the front door. The light was still burning in Western Biological. She went across the street, past the street light, and up the stairs, and she tapped with her fingertips. Doc didn't answer. She opened the door and saw him sitting at his table, his eyes red, the glass dishes in front of him. He looked very tired and the skin above his beard was gray.

"You're working late," she said.

"Yes. You made me ruin the first set. I had to do it over. It takes time."

"I'm sorry. Doc, you got to write that paper. I don't know nothing about it, but you got to write it."

"I think you were right the first time," he said. "Maybe I can't."

"Sure you can," said Suzy. "You can do anything you want to."

"Maybe that's it. Maybe I don't want to."

"I want you to."

"What have you got to do with it?"

Suzy blushed and looked at her fingers for an answer. "Everybody wants you to," she said. "You'll let everybody down if you don't do it."

He laughed. "That's not a good reason, Suzy."

She tried another tack. "Everybody hates a coward—"

"If I'm a coward, whose business is it?"

"You got to write it, Doc."

"I won't!"

"I'd help you if I could."

"What in the world could you do?"

Her face flamed. "Maybe give you a kick in the ass. Maybe that's what you need."

"Why can't you leave me alone?" he said. And then, "Goddam it! You've done it again—you made me pass over the time!"

"You done it yourself," said Suzy, "you lousy stiff! You blame everybody else. You done it yourself."

"Get on back to the whorehouse!" he shouted. "Go on! Get out!"

In the doorway she stopped and looked back. "God, how I hate a fool!" she said, and she slammed the door behind her.

In a moment there was a tap on the glass.

"Go on home!" Doc shouted.

Mack opened the door. "It ain't Suzy, it's me."

"You were listening."

"No, I wasn't. Say, Doc, would you say a piece of property on Cannery Row was a good investment?"

"No," said Doc.

"She's quite a dame," said Mack.

"I thought you said you weren't listening."

"Listen, Doc, nobody in this block listening—but everybody heard. You know, they say there's three good reasons for marrying a hustler."

"What are you talking about?" said Doc.

Mack counted on his fingers. "Number one, she ain't likely to wander—she's done all her experimenting. Number two, you ain't likely to surprise her or disappoint her. And number three, if a hustler goes for you she ain't got but one reason."

Doc watched him, hypnotized. "What reason?"

"She likes you. Good night, Doc."

"Sit down—have a drink."

"I can't. I got to get some sleep. I got work to do tomorrow. 'Night Doc."

Doc looked at the door after Mack had closed it. The grain of the unpainted pine seemed to squirm to his weary eyes.

19
Sweet Thursday (1)

Looking backward in time, you can usually find the day it started, the day of Sarajevo, the day of Munich, the moment of Stalingrad or Valley Forge. You fix the day and hour by some incident that happened to yourself. You remember exactly what you were doing when the Japanese bombed Pearl Harbor.

There is no doubt that forces were in motion on that Thursday in Cannery Row. Some of the causes and directions have been in process for generations. There are always some people who claim they felt it coming. Those who remember say it felt like earthquake weather.

It was a Thursday, and it was one of those days in Monterey when the air is washed and polished like a lens, so that you can see the houses in Santa Cruz twenty miles across the bay and you can see the redwood trees on a mountain above Watsonville. The stone point of Frémont's Peak, clear the other side of Salinas, stands up nobly against the east. The sunshine had a goldy look and red geraniums burned the air around them. The delphiniums were like little openings in the sky.

There aren't many days like that anyplace. People treasure them. Little kids are likely to give off tin-whistle screams for no reason, and businessmen find it necessary to take a drive to look at a piece of property. Old people sit looking off into the distance and remember inaccurately that the days of their youth were all like that. Horses roll in the green pastures on such a day and hens make a terrible sunny racket.

Thursday was that magic kind of day. Miss Winch, who took pride in her foul disposition before noon, said good morning to the postman.

Joe Elegant awakened early, intending to work on his novel, on the scene where the young man digs up his grandmother to see if she was as beautiful as he remembered. You will recall his novel, *The Pi Root of Oedipus*. But Joe Elegant saw the golden light on the vacant lot and a dew diamond in the heart of every mallow leaf. He went out in the damp grass in his bare feet and scampered like a kitten until he got to sneezing.

Miss Graves, who sings the lead in the butterfly pageant in Pacific Grove, saw her first leprechaun up in back of the reservoir—but you can't tell everything that happened every place on that Sweet Thursday.

For Mack and the boys it was the morning of Truth, and since Mack was to bear the brunt of it, his friends cooked him a hot breakfast and Eddie mixed real bourbon whisky in the coffee. Hazel polished Mack's shoes and brushed his best blue jeans. Whitey No. 1 brought out his father's hat for Mack to wear—a narrow-brimmed black hat, the crown peaked up to a point. Whitey No. 1's father had been a switchman on the Southern Pacific, and this hat proved it. He stuffed toilet paper in back of the sweatband until it fitted Mack perfectly.

Mack didn't talk. He knew how much depended on him, and he was brave and humble at the same time. The boys put the carefully printed tickets in his hand and saw him off, and then they sat down in the weeds to wait. They knew Mack was quaking inside.

Mack went down the chicken walk and across the railroad track. He passed the old boiler and rapped on the rusty pipes in a wild show of bravado.

In front of the grocery he studied a display of screw drivers with loving intensity before he went in.

Cacahuete was behind the counter, studying a copy of *Down Beat*. He wore a purple windbreaker with gold piping. A lean and handsome boy, he had the wild and sullen light of genius in his eyes.

"Hi!" said Mack.

"Jar!" said Cacahuete.

"Joseph and Mary around?"

"Upstairs."

"I want to see him personal," said Mack.

Cacahuete gave him a long, surly stare, then went to the back of the store and called, *"Tío mío!"*

"What do you want?"

"Mack wants to see you."

"What about?"

"Who knows?"

Joseph and Mary came down the stairs in a pale blue silk bathrobe.

" 'Morning, Mack. These kids have no manners."

Cacahuete shrugged and took his *Down Beat* to the top of the potato bin.

"You're out early," said the Patrón.

Mack began with ceremonial seriousness, "You ain't been here long, Joseph and Mary, but you've made a lot of friends, good friends."

The Patrón inspected this statement and made a note of its slight inaccuracy. Still, he had nothing to lose by going along with it. "I like the people around here," he said. "They treat me good." His eyelids lowered sleepily, which meant he was as alert as a radar screen.

Mack said, "In a little town you get kind of hidebound. But you're a man of the world. You been all over. You know how things is."

The Patrón smiled and acknowledged his wisdom and waited.

"I and the boys want to ask your advice," said Mack. "You ain't likely to get a wild hair."

A vague uneasiness stirred in the Patrón. "What's it about?" he asked tentatively.

Mack drew a deep breath. "A smart businessman like you might think it was silly, but maybe you been here long enough to get it. It's a sentimental thing. It's about Doc. I and the boys owe Doc a debt we ain't never going to be able to repay."

"How much?" asked the Patrón. He upended a broom and tore out a straw with which to pick his teeth. "Take a powder," he said softly to Cacahuete, and his nephew slithered upstairs.

"It ain't money," said Mack, "it's gratitude. For years Doc's took care of us—get sick he cures us, get broke he's there with a buck."

"Everybody says the same," the Patrón observed. He could not put his finger on the attack, and yet he felt there was an attack.

The sound of his own voice had a warming, reassuring effect on Mack. He was the professional practicing his profession. "We might of went right on hustling Doc for years," he said, "if only Doc didn't get his ass in a sling."

"He's in trouble?"

"You know he's in trouble," said Mack. "Poor bastard sits there beating his brains out with them sooplapods."

"You told me."

"Well, us boys want to do something about it. We ain't going to see our darling friend crap out if we can help it. I bet he done a couple of nice things for you too."

The Patrón said, "Do you know you can't rig a chess game?"

"We had that out," said Mack impatiently. "Doc's business ain't been good. He can't crack open them sooplapods without he gets a great big goddam microscope—cost about four hundred bucks."

The Patrón said hastily, "If you're passing the hat I'll throw in ten bucks."

"Thanks!" said Mack passionately. "I knew you was a good guy. But that ain't it. I and the boys want to do it ourself. We don't want your ten bucks—we want your advice."

The Patrón went behind the counter, opened the icebox, took out two cans of beer, speared them open, and slid one up the counter to Mack.

"Thanks," said Mack, and he beered down his dry mouth and throat. "Haaah!" he said. "That's fine. Now here's what we want to know. We got something and we want to raffle it. Then we want to take that raffle money and get that microscope for Doc. We want you should give us a hand with the tickets and stuff like that."

"What you going to raffle?" the Patrón asked.

This was the moment, the horrible moment. Mack's hand shook a little as he poured down the second half of the cool sharp beer. His insides quaked. "The Palace Flophouse—our home," he said.

The Patrón took a pocket comb out of stock and ran it through his black shining hair. "It ain't worth four hundred bucks," he said.

Mack nearly cried with relief. He could have kissed the Patrón's hand. He loved Joseph and Mary. A strong and tender tone issued from his throat. "We know that," he said, "but it's our home. Oh, I know it ain't very valuable, but when you got something that ain't worth much—why, you raffle it, don't you? If you got a good cause you can raffle an old pair of socks."

A new respect showed in the Patrón's eyes. "You got something there," he said, and then, "Who's going to win it?"

Mack felt confident now. He knew his man. He was ready to use his knowledge. He said confidentially, "I don't never try to kid a smart hombre. I could tell you we was going to draw honest but you'd know that was double malarky. No, we got a idear."

The Patrón leaned forward. Some of his wariness was lulled. He was still no pushover but he was softened up. "What's the idear?" he asked.

"Well, we got to have someplace to live, don't we? Now this is between I and the boys and you—okay?"

"Okay," said the Patrón.

"We'll sell Doc a ticket or maybe just put a ticket in his name, and we'll rig the raffle so he wins."

"I don't get it," said the Patrón.

"Look!" said Mack. "Doc gets his microscope, don't he? And we go right on habiting in the Palace Flophouse but it's Doc's. It's a sap to his old age—a kind of insurance. I and the boys figure that's the least we can do for him."

"S'pose he sells it?" said the Patrón.

"Oh, not Doc! He wouldn't put us out in the street."

A smile spread over the Patrón's large handsome face. He could find no fault with it. "I guess I never give you proper credit," he said. "You're smart. Maybe we can do some business—I mean, later. You got the raffle tickets?"

"We made them up last night." Mack laid a little pile of cards on the table.

"How much apiece?"

"Says right on them," Mack said. "Two bucks."

"My first offer still stands," said the Patrón. "I'll take five and you can leave me some to sell."

"Think you could use twenty?"

"I could unload nearly fifty," said the Patrón. "I'll put them out with the Espaldas Mojadas."

Mack's knees were weak as he went up the chicken walk. His glazed eyes stared straight ahead. He walked right past the boys and into the Palace Flophouse and sat down heavily on his bed. The boys trooped in behind him and stood around.

"Got him!" said Mack. "He don't know he owns it. He bought five tickets and he's going to sell fifty to his wetbacks!"

There is a point of relief and triumph in which words have no place. Eddie went outside, and they could hear his shovel strike the ground. Mack and the boys knew Eddie was digging up a keg.

And this was only one of the happenings on that Sweet Thursday.

20

Sweet Thursday (2)

Fauna always drew the shades of her bedroom tight down. Because of the late hours of business, she had to sleep until noon to get her proper rest. On the morning of Sweet Thursday the sun played a trick on her. The windowshade had a hole in it no bigger than the point of a pin. The playful sun picked up the doings of Cannery Row, pushed them through the pinhole, turned them upside down, and projected them in full color on the wall of Fauna's bedroom. Wide Ida waddled across the wall upside down, wearing a print dress sewn with red poppies and on her head a black beret. The Pacific Gas & Electric truck rolled across her wall upside down, its wheels in the air. Mack strode toward the grocery store head down. And a little later, Doc, weary, feet over his head, walked along the wallpaper carrying a quart of beer that would have spilled if it had not been an illusion. At first Fauna tried to go back to sleep, but she was afraid she might miss something. It was the little colored ghost of upside-down Doc that drew her from her couch.

It is a common experience that a problem difficult at night is resolved in the morning after the committee of sleep has worked on it. And this had happened to Fauna. She was glad when she raised the shade and saw how beautiful was the day. The roof of the Hediondo Cannery where seagulls had perched glowed like a pearl.

Fauna brushed her hair severely back and put on a close-fitting hat of black sequins. She wore her dark-gray knitted suit and carried gloves. In the kitchen she put six bottles of beer in a paper bag, and then, as an afterthought, she rooted out one of the shrunken monkey heads as a present. When she climbed the stairs of Western Biological and stood at the top, puffing a little, you might have thought she was soliciting for the Red Cross instead of for the Bear Flag.

Doc was frying sausages, sprinkling a little chocolate over them. It gave them an odd and Oriental flavor, he thought.

"You're up early," he greeted Fauna.

"I figured one quart of beer wouldn't last long."

"It didn't," said Doc. "Have a couple of sausages?"

"Don't mind if I do," said Fauna. For she knew that he who gives to you is in debt to you. "This here's a monkey head that I picked up in my travels."

"Interesting," said Doc.

"You know, there's some folks think they're people's heads," said Fauna.

"Don't see how they could. See the shape of the eyes and ears? Look at the nose."

"Oh, some folks don't look at people very close," said Fauna. "I'll have a bottle of beer with you."

The taste of the chocolate sausages intrigued her. "I never tasted nothing like it," she observed. "Did you ever eat grasshoppers, Doc?"

"Yes," said Doc. "In Mexico. They're kind of peppery."

Fauna was not one to beat around bushes. "You must get sick of everybody wanting something from you," she said.

Doc smiled. "I'd be sicker if they didn't," he said. "What can I do for you? Say, thanks for the cake and the beer last night!"

Fauna asked, "What did you think of the kid?"

"Strange," said Doc. "Somehow I can't see her working at the Bear Flag."

"Neither can I," said Fauna. "She ain't no good at it but it looks like I'm stuck with her. Trouble with Suzy is, she's got a streak of lady in her and I don't know how to root it out."

Doc munched his sausages and sipped his beer thoughtfully. "I never thought of it, but that could be a drawback," he said.

"She's a nice kid," said Fauna. "I like her fine. But she's a liability in a business way."

"Why don't you kick her out?"

"Oh, I can't," said Fauna. "She's had a tough time. I never had no gift for kicking people out. What I'd like is if she'd pick up and go. She got no future as a floozy."

"She threw the book at me," said Doc.

"You see?" said Fauna. "She's a character. That ain't no good in a house."

"She slapped me in the face with a few basic truths," said Doc. "That's a quick eye she's got."

"And a quicker tongue," said Fauna. "Would you do me a favor?"

"Why, of course," said Doc. "Anything I can."

"I can't go to nobody else," Fauna went on, "they wouldn't understand."

"What is it?"

"Doc," said Fauna, "I knocked around and I seen all kinds. I tell you, if you got a streak of lady in you it spoils you for anything else. Now you never come over to the Bear Flag. You play the field. I personally think that costs you more but I ain't one to mess in the way people want to live."

"I don't think I'm following you," said Doc.

"Okay, I'll lay out the deck. When you're making a play for one of them babes, them amateurs, you got to do quite a lot of talking before you make the sack—ain't that right?"

Doc smiled ruefully. "Right," he said.

"Well, do you always mean every word of it?"

Doc pinched his lower lip. "Why—why—I guess right at the moment I do."

"But afterward?"

"Afterward, if I were to think about it—"

"That's what I mean," said Fauna. "So if you happen to tell a little teensy-beensy bit of baloney you don't blow your brains out."

"You'd do well in the analysis business," said Doc. "What do you want me to do?"

"This kid Suzy's lousy with new roses. She ain't a good hustler because of that streak of lady. I don't know if she'd make a good lady or not. I want her off my neck. Doc, would it do you any harm to make a play for her? I mean, like you do with them dames that come in here."

"What good could that possibly do?" he asked.

"Well, maybe I'm wrong, but the way I figure it, you can use new roses if you want to. If you made a pitch for the kid, like she was a lady, why, she might turn lady on you."

"I still can't see what good it would do," said Doc.

"It would get her the hell out of the Bear Flag," said Fauna. "She wouldn't want to congregate with no more floozies."

"How about me?" said Doc.

"You don't marry them others, do you?"

"No, but——"

"Take a whang at her, will you, Doc?" Fauna begged. "Can't do you no harm. Why, hell, she might scram out of here and take up typewriting or telephone operating. Will you do that for me, Doc?"

He said, "It doesn't seem honest."

Fauna changed her tack. "I was talking to her last night and she said she couldn't remember when a guy had treated her like a girl. What harm would that do?"

"Might make her miserable."

"Might make her fly the coop."

"Maybe she likes it the way it is."

"She don't. I tell you she's a blowed-in-the-glass lady. Look, Doc, you take her out to dinner and I'll buy the dinner. You don't have to make no pass. Just be nice to her."

"I'll have to think about it."

"Think you might do it?"

"I might."

"That's a good kid if you treat her right. You'd be doing me a big favor."

"Suppose she won't go?"

"She will. I won't give her no choice."

Doc looked out the window and a warmth crept through him, and suddenly he felt better than he could remember feeling.

"I'll think about it," he said.

"I'll throw in three bottles of champagne whenever you say the word," said Fauna.

After lunch Joe Elegant read Fauna his latest chapter. He explained the myth and the symbol. "You see," he said, "the grandmother stands for guilt."

"Ain't she dead and buried?"

"Yes."

"That's a kind of a messy guilt."

"It's the reality below reality," said Joe Elegant.

"Balls!" said Fauna. "Listen, Joe, whyn't you write a story about something real?"

"Maybe *you* can tell *me* about the *art* of writing?" he said.

"I sure as hell can," said Fauna. "There's this guy, and he makes love to this dame."

"Very original," said Joe.

"When a man says words he believes them, even if he thinks he's lying."

"For goodness' sake! What are you talking about?"

"I bet I get rid of a certain person and put up a new gold star. You want to take that bet?"

"How did Doc like the cake?" Joe Elegant asked.

"He loved it," said Fauna.

And this was the second event of that Sweet Thursday.

21

Sweet Thursday Was One
Hell of a Day

Fission took place in the Palace Flophouse, and from there a chain reaction flared up in all directions. Cannery Row caught fire. Mack and the boys had the energy and the enthusiasm of plutonium. Only very lazy men could have done so much in so short a time. Oh, the meetings, the messages carried, the plans and counterplans! Mack had to make more and more raffle tickets. What started as a kind of gentle blackmail assumed the nature of an outpouring of popular love for Doc. People bought tickets, sold tickets, traded tickets. Emissaries covered the Southern Pacific Depot, the Greyhound Bus Station. Joe Blaikey, the constable, carried tickets in his pocket and canceled parking summonses if the lawbreaker bought a two-dollar chance on the Palace Flophouse.

Whitey No. 1 invaded the foreign and fancy purlieus of Pebble Beach and Carmel and the Highlands. Whitey No. 2's method was characteristically direct. The first man to refuse him got a rock through his windshield, and the news traveled.

To the boys it had become a crusade. And the winning ticket, of course, with Doc's name on it, was in a tomato can, buried in the vacant lot. By tacit agreement no one mentioned the raffle to Doc. To Doc's friends Mack and the boys mentioned the rigging of the lottery, but to strangers—who cared? It was a perfect example of the collective goodness and generosity of a community.

But if communities have a group Good Fairy they also have an Imp who works parallel with and sometimes in collaboration with the Good Fairy. Cannery Row's Imp saw the Good Fairy stirring to life, and he sprang to action. Into the ears of his clients he whispered a few words, and his constituents grinned with evil pleasure and their thoughts went like this: The Patrón is a wise guy. He's a newcomer, nice clothes, makes his money off poor helpless wetbacks because he's smart. Lee Chong must have sold him the Palace Flophouse and he's forgot it or he never knew it. Once Doc wins it the Patrón won't dare make a move.

It is such fun to outsmart a smart guy. The Imp of the Row had a good professional time and for once his job seemed almost virtuous. People bought more tickets from the Patrón than from anyone else. They wanted to watch his face so they could compare it with his face when he found out.

Now ordinarily Mack and the boys would have strung out the ticket sales over weeks, but time was breathing down their necks. If the Patrón got his tax bill from the county their plan would blow up in their faces. They had to take a chance with Friday—Saturday was the deadline. The boys spread the word that there would be medium-heavy refreshments at the Palace Flophouse on Saturday night and that contributions of any nature would be welcome.

Mack called on Doc the afternoon of Sweet Thursday. "If you ain't doing anything Saturday night," he said, "I and the boys are throwing a little wing-ding. R.S.V.P."

"*Moi, je respond oui.*"

"Come again?"

"I'll be there," said Doc.

Then Mack remembered a mission with which he had been entrusted. "I guess I could squirm it out of you, Doc, like I done once before," he said, "but I'll come right out in the open. When's your birthday?"

A shudder went through Doc. "Please don't give me a party," he begged. "The last one you gave nearly ruined me."

"This hasn't got nothing to do with a party—it's a bet," said Mack. "I stand to win a buck. When is it?" Mack prodded him.

Doc picked the first date that came to him. "July fourth," he said.

"Why, that's like the Fourth of July!"

"A little," said Doc, and he felt greatly relieved.

Later that afternoon Fauna and the girls called formally at the Palace Flophouse in answer to the note Mack had sent asking them to drink a jolt of good stuff. Suzy did not attend. She had been quiet all morning, and then she mooned away on the path that leads along the sea to the lighthouse on Point Pinos. She looked in the tide pools, and she picked a bunch of the tiny flowers that grow as close to the ocean as they can. Suzy was restless and unhappy. She felt excitement and nausea at the same time. She wanted to smile and she wanted to cry, and she was scared and happy and hopeless. Doc had asked her to have dinner with him, at Sonny Boy's on the pier, and Fauna had urged her to go.

Suzy's first reaction had been violent. "I won't do it!" she said.

"Sure you'll go," said Fauna. "I may have to persuade you with a indoor-ball bat—but you'll go."

"You can't make me."

"Want to test that? Why, I've wore my brain down to the knuckles, trying to do something nice for you."

"I ain't got nothing to wear," said Suzy.

"Neither has Doc. If he can go like he does, what right's a chippy to get grand?"

"But hell, Fauna, he's—he's got it inside. People like me got to put on a puff because they got nothing else. I'm afraid I'll turn mean because I don't know how to be nice."

"Suzy," said Fauna, "I'm going to give you a piece of advice, and if you won't take it, I may just call Joe Blaikey and get you floated right out of town. Don't throw the first punch! Wait'll you're hit before you put up your dukes. Most of the time they ain't nobody laid a glove on you."

"Suppose I could wear my suit? It's got a big spot," said Suzy.

"Ask Joe Elegant to spot-clean it and press it. Tell him I said so."

And thus it was that Suzy went walking out lighthouse way on Sweet Thursday.

The meeting in the Palace wasn't really necessary, for word of the raffle had got around and Fauna had bought ten tickets and made each girl buy one.

Eddie had borrowed glasses from Wide Ida's—for once, with her permission. She was invited to the meeting too, and she brought two quarts of Pine Canyon whisky.

"It don't cost hardly nothing," she explained.

Formality took hold of the meeting. Agnes and Mabel kept their knees together when they sat down, and Fauna's look of thunder made Becky snap hers shut so quickly she spilled her drink.

"She's going to be a wallager," said Mack. "I can't wait to see Doc's face when he wins."

Wide Ida asked, "How you going to explain it to him he wins when he didn't buy no ticket?"

"Why, we'll say a friend did it and don't want his name mentioned. I saw Doc a little while ago. He said he'd sure be here."

Fauna said, "Did you find out when is his birthday?"

"Sure. July fourth."

Fauna exhaled with the sound of escaping gas. "Holy apples! He's a gone goose. He got a born-on Oregon boot. I never seen nothing work out so nice!"

"What're you talking about?" said Mack.

Fauna's eyes were misty. "Mack," she said huskily, "I don't want to horn in on your party, but why couldn't we make it an engagement party too?"

"Who's engaged?"

"Well, they ain't yet—but they will be."

"Who?"

"Doc and Suzy. It's right in their horoscopes."

"S'pose they won't?"

"They will," said Fauna. "You can just depend on that—they will!"

The little group sat in silence, and then Mack said softly, "Did I say it was going to be a wallager? This here's a *tom*-wallager!

They ain't been nothing so stupendous since the Second World War! You *sure* Doc'll go for it?"

"You let me take care of that—and don't none of you blab it to him. One time I managed a fighter, Kiss of Death Kelly, welterweight. I'll have Doc in the ring."

Eddie asked, "How about Suzy?"

"Suzy's already in the ring," said Fauna.

They parted quietly, but in their breasts a flame of emotion burned. There never was a day like that Sweet Thursday. And it wasn't over yet.

22

The Arming

At four-thirty in the afternoon Fauna ordered Suzy to the office bedroom with full field equipment. Suzy dumped her clothes on Fauna's bed.

"That's a hell of a way to keep wrinkles out," Fauna observed. She picked up the gray woolen skirt and jacket, laid them out, inspected them for spots, smelled them for cleaning fluid. "Nice piece of goods," she said.

"Community chest," said Suzy. "I was in the charity ward."

"Well, somebody wasn't." Her eyes noted the brown shoes. She went to the door and yelled, "Joe! Joe Elegant!"

He looked in. "I'm not supposed to be on duty," he said.

"I'm a thorn in the side of the worker," said Fauna. "You run up the street to Wildock's and get new heel taps on these here. Tell them to fix this scuffed place and give them a nice shine. Wait and bring them back."

Joe complained as he went, but he went.

Fauna said to Suzy, "You got any gloves?"

"No."

"I'll lend you some. Here—these white ones. And here's a handkerchief. I don't want no lipstick marks on it. Now you listen to me, Suzy girl—take care of your shoes, wear clean gloves, carry a white handkerchief, and keep your stocking seams straight. If you do that you can get away with murder. This here's a nice suit—the kind of cloth that the older it gets the better it looks—if your heels ain't run over. Call Becky in!"

When Becky entered Fauna said, "Ain't you got a white piqué dickey and cuffs?"

"I just done them up."

"I want you to lend them to Suzy. Get some thread and sew the cuffs in this here jacket."

"She'll have to wash them."

"She will."

While Becky basted in the cuffs Fauna said, "Turn out your purse, Suzy." She inspected the pile on the bed. "You don't need that aspirin. Here, take my comb—throw that one away. Ain't nothing tackier than a comb missing teeth. Put these here Kleenex in. Here, use my compact and touch up that shine on your nose once in a while. Let's see your nails! Hmmm, pretty good. You washed your hair?"

"Get her a wig," said Becky, and she bit the thread.

"Don't get smart. Come on now—get off your behind and do something with her hair, and not fancy neither." To Suzy she said, "Becky got a light hand with hair. You can't take that coat. Community chest slipped up there." She tapped her teeth with a pencil and then went to her closet and brought out two baum martens that were biting each other's heads off. "Just hand these here bo' martens over your shoulder," Fauna said. "And if you lose them or hurt them I'll cut your tripes out. Now, where are we? No perfume. Douse some of this Florida water on—kind of old-fashioned and young-smelling."

Becky stood behind Suzy's chair, brushing and combing and molding. "She got big ears," Becky said. "Maybe I can kind of hide them a little."

"You got a nice hand with hair," Fauna said.

The final briefing took place at six o'clock, with the bedroom door closed.

"Turn around," said Fauna. "Keep your ankles close together. Now, walk! That's good. You got a real nice walk. Like I said, you're a good-looking kid if you work at it a little."

Suzy looked at herself in the mirror and she smiled, for it seemed to her that she really was pretty, and the idea startled her and pleased her too, and when she looked pleased she was even prettier. Then her mouth turned down and blind panic came over her.

"What's the matter?" Fauna demanded.

"What can I talk about? Fauna, I don't want to go! I don't

belong with a guy like Doc. Jesus, Fauna, tell him I'm sick. I ain't going."

Fauna let her talk herself out and then she said quietly, "Maybe you'd like to cry now and get your eyes red after all my trouble? Go on, cry!"

"I'm sorry," said Suzy. "You been nice. I ain't no good, Fauna. You're just wasting your time. I know what I'll do—minute he says something I don't understand I'll get mad. I'm scared."

" 'Course you're scared," said Fauna. "But if you didn't care nothing about Doc you wouldn't be scared. You didn't invent it. There ain't never been no dame went out first time with a guy she liked that wasn't scared. Maybe Doc's scared too."

"Oh nuts!" said Suzy.

Fauna said, "If I was your age with your face and shape and what I know, there wouldn't be no man in the world could get away! I got the know-how—but that's all I got. Oh well! I'm going to tell you a few thousand things, Suzy, that if you would listen you'd get anything you want. But hell, you won't listen! Nobody listens, and when they learn the hard way it's too late. Maybe it's a good thing—I don't know."

"I'll listen."

"Sure, but you won't learn. You know, Suzy, they ain't no way in the world to get in trouble by keeping your mouth shut. You look back at every mess you ever got in and you'll find your tongue started it."

"That's true," said Suzy. "But I can't seem to stop."

"You got to learn it like you learn anything else—just practice. Next thing is opinions. You and me is always busting out with opinions. Hell, Suzy, we ain't got no opinions! We just say stuff we heard or seen in the movies. We're scared we'll miss something, like running for a bus. That's the second rule: lay off opinions because you ain't really got any."

"You got them numbered, huh?" said Suzy.

"I should write a book," said Fauna. "*If She Could, I Could.* Now take number three. There don't hardly nobody listen, and it's so easy! You don't have to do nothing when you listen. If you do listen it's pretty interesting. If a guy says something that pricks up your interest, why, don't hide it from him. Kind of try to wonder what he's thinking instead of how you're going to answer him back."

"You're sure putting the finger on me," Suzy said softly.

"I only got a little more, but it's the hardest of all, and the easiest."

"What number?"

"I lost track. Don't pretend to be something you ain't, and don't make like you know something you don't, or sooner or later you'll fall on your ass. And there's one more part to this one, whatever number it is: they ain't nobody was ever insulted by a question. S'pose Doc says something and you don't know what it means. Ask him! The nicest thing in the world you can do for anybody is let them help you."

Suzy was silent, looking down at her hands.

Fauna said, "You got nice nails. How do you keep them so nice?"

Suzy said, "That's easy. My grandma taught me. You keep a old lemon rind, and every time you wash your hands you scrounge your fingernails around in it. And then you shake a little face powder on your hand and you polish your nails on the ham of your hand and you push down the quick with a little piece of lemon wood."

"See what I mean?" said Fauna.

"What?"

"I just asked you a question."

Suzy blushed, "I sure fell into that."

"No, you didn't. I wanted to know. It's best if you ask when you want to know."

"Thanks," said Suzy. "You're a hell of a dame. I wonder if I could learn?"

"You can if you just remember a lot of things: first, you got to remember you're Suzy and you ain't nobody else but Suzy. Then you got to remember that Suzy is a good thing—a real valuable thing—and there ain't nothing like it in the world. It don't do no harm just to say that to yourself. Then, when you got that, remember that there's one hell of a lot Suzy don't know. Only way she can find out is if she sees it, reads it, or asks it. Most people don't look at nothing but themselves, and that's a rat race."

"What's the fourth thing?" Suzy asked.

"I'm proud of you!" Fauna said. "You listened. The next thing you'll have to do some thinking about. Nobody don't give a particular damn about Suzy one way or the other. It's hard to get them thinking about you because they're too busy thinking about themselves. There's two, three, copper-bottom ways to get their attention: Talk about them. If you see something nice or good or pretty, tell them. Don't make it a fake though. Don't fight nobody unless there ain't no other way. Don't never start a fight, and if one starts, let it get going good before you jump in. Best way in the whole world to defend yourself is to keep your dukes down! Now, when you got their attention, first thing they want is to do something for you. Let them. Don't get proud and say you don't need it or want it. That's a slap in the puss. Thing people like most in the world is to give you something and have you like it and need it. That ain't sloppy. That works. You give it a try."

"You think Doc would fall for that stuff?"

"Just give it a try."

Suzy said, "Fauna, didn't you never get married?"

"No."

"Why not?"

Fauna smiled. "Time I learned what I just told you, it was too late."

"I love you," said Suzy.

"Now you see! You got me softened up like butter. I want you should keep them furs."

"But—"

"Watch it!"

"Yeah, I see. I sure do thank you. And would you maybe write down all that stuff so I can get it by heart?"

"Sure I will. Now look, Suzy—tonight, just before you say something, say it first to yourself, and kind of dust it off."

"You mean cussing?"

"I mean cussing and I mean—well, sometimes if you look at it you don't say it. One whole hell of a lot that passes for talk is just running off at the mouth. I guess you're about ready now."

"Is there anything I can do for you, Fauna?"

"Yes. I want you should repeat after me, 'I'm Suzy and nobody else.'"

"'I'm Suzy and nobody else.'"

"'I'm a good thing.'"

"'I'm a good thing.'"

"'There ain't nothing like me in the whole world.'"

"'There ain't nothing'—goddam it, Fauna, now my eyes'll be red!"

"They look pretty that way," said Fauna.

At seven o'clock Doc, dressed in an open-collared shirt, leather jacket, and army pants, rang the bell at the Bear Flag. He looked at Suzy and he said, "I've got to make a telephone call, do you mind?" And he ran back to the laboratory.

Ten minutes later he returned. He had on clean slacks, a tweed jacket, and a tie he hadn't used in years.

Fauna saw him standing under the porch light.

"Honey," she said to Suzy, "you win the first round on points."

23

One Night of Love

Sonny Boy is truly the only Greek born in America named Sonny Boy. He operates a restaurant and bar on the wharf in Monterey. Sonny Boy is plump and getting plumper. Although he was born near Sutro Park in San Francisco and went to public schools, Sonny Boy has singlehandedly kept alive the mystery of the Near East. His perfectly round face hints Orient Express and beautiful spies. His bushy voice is congenitally confidential. Sonny Boy can say "good evening" and make it sound like an international plot. His restaurant makes friends for him and supports him. Perhaps Sonny Boy, in one sense, wears a long black cape and dines with Balkan countesses where two seas kiss the Golden Horn—but he also runs a good restaurant. He probably knows more secrets than any man in the community, for his martinis are a combination truth serum and lie detector. *Veritas* is not only *in vino* but regularly batters its way out.

Doc stopped his old car in front of Sonny Boy's, got out, walked around, opened the door, and helped Suzy out.

She was a little shocked but she remained silent. The sentence, "You think I'm a cripple, for Chrissake!" rose to her throat, but she followed Fauna's advice—whispered it and pushed it back. The fact of his hand on her elbow did a magic thing to her, pushed back her shoulders and raised her chin. The gritty light of resistance went out of her eyes.

Doc opened the door of the bar and stood aside to let Suzy enter. The regulars on the stools turned to look. The eyes crept from pretty face to pretty legs, took in the martens on the way. For one second panic halted her, but she saw no look of recognition in the eyes of the regulars.

Sonny Boy turned sideways to get around the end of the bar. " 'Evening, folks," he said. "Your table is ready. Would you like to have a cocktail here, or shall I send one over?"

"Oh, let's sit at the table," said Doc.

Sonny Boy bowed Suzy through the door to the restaurant, and she strolled ahead with her nice walk. Sonny Boy, rolling along beside Doc, said in a conspiratorial whisper, "Your secretary called. It's all fixed. You got a secretary, Doc?"

Doc overcame his surprise. "Part time," he said.

"Who's the lady? She new around here?"

"She's new around here," said Doc. He caught up with Suzy.

"This way," said Sonny Boy. He led them to a round table in front of the stone fireplace. A pine fire crackled and sent out its fragrance. The table had a centerpiece of wild iris. The bread-sticks stood like soldiers in their glasses. The napkins were folded to make little crowns. It was the best table in the house, private, but downstage and well lighted.

Suzy's eyes darted around the room. No other table had flow-ers. Something wonderful happened in Suzy. She didn't walk around the table and sit down. She waited, and when Doc held her chair she seated herself, looked smiling up at him, and said, "Thank you."

Sonny Boy hovered over the table. "Good you telephoned," he said. "I had trouble getting pompano, but I got it. How's about a cocktail? The wine's cooling."

Doc said, "One time I had some kind of—"

"I remember!" said Sonny Boy. "The Webster F. Street Lay-Away Plan—a martini made with chartreuse instead of ver-mouth. Very good."

"Very effective, as I remember it," said Doc. "Two doubles."

"Coming right up," said Sonny Boy. "I told Tony to be here to play piano like you said, but he's sick."

Doc looked at Suzy to see whether she knew Fauna had made the arrangements. She didn't.

It is probable that if Doc hadn't ordered the Webster F. Street Lay-Away Plans he would have got them anyway. They arrived with a speed that indicated they were already mixed.

The shock of a necktie was leaving Doc. He looked across

the table and smiled at Suzy and he wondered, What is beauty in a girl that it can come and go? This Suzy did not faintly resemble the tough hustler who had screamed at him the night before. He raised the cocktail glass. "You're pretty," he said. "I'm glad you came with me. Here's to both of us."

Suzy swallowed a gulp, held back her tears, and waited for the spasm to pass.

"I should have warned you," said Doc, "there's a rumor that this drink is made of rattlesnake venom and raw opium."

Suzy got her breath. "It's good," she said. "But I was watching its right hand and walked into a left hook!"

Her mind cried, I shouldn't of said that! I forgot already. Then she saw Doc's amusement and it was all right.

Suzy noticed a waiter drifting delicately within earshot. She had discovered something for herself. When in doubt, move slowly. Her head turned toward the waiter and he drifted away. She was delighted with her discovery—everything-in-slow-motion. She then lifted her glass slowly, looked at it carefully, then sipped and held it a moment before she put it down. S-l-o-w-ness—it gave meaning to everything. It made everything royal. She remembered how all the unsure and worried people she knew jumped and picked and jittered. Just doing everything slowly, forcing herself, she felt a new kind of security. Don't forget, she told herself. Don't ever forget this. Slow! Slow!

Doc gave her a cigarette and held a match, and she leaned forward so slowly that the flame was touching her fingers before she had lighted it. A lovely warmth stole through her body. She felt bold, not defensively bold, but safe.

She asked, "Do they know—what I am?"

The Lay-Away Plan works equally on all. Doc said, "They know you're with me. That's all they need to know. Shall we have one more?"

It came before he got his finger raised for attention. If this was conspiracy, Sonny Boy wanted to be in on it. If felicity, he liked that too.

"I like a fire," Suzy said. "Once we had a fireplace where I lived."

Doc said, "You're pretty. Yes, by George! You're pretty!"

Suzy swallowed the first words that rose and swallowed the second ones and ended up by dropping her eyes and saying "Thank you" softly.

Sonny Boy personally escorted the waiter, who carried the ice bucket with the chilled Chablis. Then he stood back and surveyed the table. "How is everything, Doc?"

"Just fine," said Doc.

"You ready to eat?"

"Any time," said Doc.

And Suzy's discovery continued to hold good: Take it slow and keep your eyes open and your mouth shut.

The cold, cracked crab, the pompano, were new to her, and they required an eating technique she didn't know. She did everything a little behind Doc, and he wasn't conscious that she watched every move he made.

When champagne and fruit and cheese arrived, Suzy knew she had to be alone. A thought so overwhelming had come to her that her knees shook and the blood pounded in her temples. Slow! she warned herself. Take it easy. She looked at the leaping flames and then pivoted her head to Doc. "Will you excuse . . . ?"

"Of course!" He jumped up and drew back her chair. Suzy moved regally toward the Ladies' Room. She could not feel her feet against the floor.

Doc watched her passage. Strange, strange, he thought. What is it? "Maidenly" is the word. A kind of lonely and terrible modesty. What has made the change? Then he thought, It's an act. Fauna coached her. But he knew that wasn't true. Acting couldn't get into the eyes like that. Coaching couldn't draw the blood to her cheeks. He spun the champagne bottle in its bucket, and he found himself wishing she would hurry back. His eyes found a window that reflected the door to the Ladies' Room.

Behind that door Suzy dampened a paper towel and put it against her forehead. She stared at herself in the mirror and she didn't know the face. She thought of the dinner. "I hate fish," she said out loud. "It makes me break out. But I ain't broke out." Finally she was ready to inspect the thought that had sent her out: the symbol, the mystery, the signpost with an inexorable pointing finger. It was so plain no one could miss it. Fate was not only pointing the way but booting from behind. She thought of the dishes being taken away: the heaped legs and claws of crab and—They had eaten their horoscopes! Cancer and Pisces—fish and crab.

"Great God Almighty!" she said, and she was limp in the hands of Fate.

Sonny Boy came to the table. "Everything all right?"

"Fine," said Doc.

"Just like you ordered."

"Huh?"

"Your secretary told me."

"Fine," said Doc, "just the way I wanted it."

When Suzy came back she was dedicated. You can only fight Fate so far, and when you give in to it you're very strong; because all of your force flows in one direction.

Doc held her chair and then he popped the champagne cork and smelled it.

Suzy said, "Can I have it?"

"Of course."

Suzy turned the cork in her fingers and looked at it. It was very beautiful. She put it in her purse and took an iris from the vase.

"Do you like champagne?"

"I love it," she said and wondered what it would taste like. And she did love it.

Doc said, "You know, out in the sand dunes there are little valleys covered with pines. Sometime, when you can, let's take meat and things out there and cook our supper. It's very nice."

"The fire reminded you," said Suzy.

"That's clever of you—so it did."

She said, "Doc, will you sometime teach me about the stuff you got in your place?"

"Sure I will." A surge of affection filled him. But he was a little afraid too of her terrible modesty. He looked away from her eyes to the wild iris in her hand. "There's an old Welsh story," he said. "It's about a poor knight who made a wife completely out of flowers—"

The wine was strong in Suzy now. She said the sentence twice to herself before she said it aloud to Doc. "I hope she didn't wilt."

The low voice of Doc's guts burst through at last. "I'm lonely," he said. He said it as a simple matter of fact and he said it in wonder. Then he apologized. "I guess I'm a little drunk." He felt very shy. He filled the glasses. "What the hell! Let's have some brandy too."

Suzy turned half away from him so that her face was outlined in leaping pine flames. "You know that place you said—out in the sand dunes?"

"Yes."

"Could we look at it?"

"Whenever you want."

"On our way home?"

"You'll ruin your shoes."

"I know," said Suzy.

"You could take them off."

"I will," said Suzy.

24

Waiting Friday

Not everyone believes that Friday is unlucky, but nearly everybody agrees it is a waiting day. In business, the week is really over. In school, Friday is the half-open gate to freedom. Friday is neither a holiday nor a workday, but a time of wondering what Saturday will bring. Trade and amusement fall off. Women look through their closets to see what they have to wear. Supper is leftovers from the week.

Joe Elegant ordered sand dabs for supper at the Bear Flag. The Espaldas Mojadas returned from their latest triumph and were ushered with great courtesy to the rooms over the grocery. The Patrón distributed bottles of tequila. Also, he kept a saucer of Seconal at hand. Sometimes a passion of homesickness got into his wetbacks. Sleep, he thought, was better than fighting.

Doc slept late, and when he went to the grocery for his morning beer he found Joseph and Mary alert and gay, and the sound of singing drifted down the stairs.

"Have a good time?" the Patrón asked.

"What do you mean?" Doc demanded.

"Didn't you have a nice party last night?"

"Oh sure," said Doc. He said it with finality.

"Doc, I'd like you to teach me more of that chess."

"You still think you can cheat at it, do you?"

"No, I just like to figure it out. I got a case of Bohemia beer from Mexico, all cold."

"Wonderful!" said Doc. "That's the best beer in the Western Hemisphere."

"It's a present," said the Patrón.

"Why?"

"I don't know. Maybe I just feel good."

"Thanks," said Doc. He began to feel uneasy.

There were eyes on him. Going back to Western Biological, he felt eyes on him. It's the brandy, he thought. I shouldn't drink brandy. Makes me nervous.

He scrambled two eggs and shook curry powder over them. He consulted the tide chart in Thursday's *Monterey Herald*. There was a fair tide at 2:18 P.M., enough for chitons and brittlestars if the wind wasn't blowing inshore by then. The Bohemia beer settled his nerves without solving his restlessness. And for once the curried eggs didn't taste very good.

Fauna knocked and entered. She flicked her hand at the rattlesnakes. "How do you feel, Doc?"

"All right."

"Get drunk?"

"A little."

"How was the dinner?"

"Wonderful. You know what to order."

"I ought to. Say, you want to box or should we lay it on the line? See what I mean about her?"

"Yes. How does she feel?"

"She ain't up yet."

"I'm going collecting."

"Want me to tell her that?"

"Why should you? Wait—I've got her purse. Want to take it to her?"

"Hell, she ain't crippled. Maybe she'll want to get it herself."

"I won't be here."

"You'll be back."

"Say," he said, "what the hell is this?"

She knew he might turn angry now. "I got a lot to do. You ain't mad at me?"

"Why should I be?"

"Well, if you need anything, let me know."

"Fauna," he began. "Oh, let it go."

"What do you want?"

"I was going to ask you something—but I don't want to know."

Suzy was hunched over a cup of coffee when Fauna got back.

" 'Morning," said Fauna. And then, "I said good morning."

"Oh yeah," said Suzy. " 'Morning."

"Look at me!"

"Why not?" Suzy raised her eyes.

"You can look down now," said Fauna.

"You don't know nothing," said Suzy.

"Okay, I don't know nothing. When did I ever get nosy with you? Joe," she called, "bring me a cup of coffee!" She slid a tin box of aspirins across the oilcloth tablecover.

"Thanks." Suzy took three and washed them down with coffee.

"He's going out collecting bugs," said Fauna quietly.

"You went over there?"

"I met him in the street. Have a nice time?"

Suzy looked up at her with eyes so wide that she seemed to be turned inside out. "He didn't make no pass," she said breathlessly. "Went out on the sand dunes and he didn't make no pass."

Fauna smiled. "But he talked nice?"

"Didn't talk much, but he talked nice."

"That's good."

"Maybe I'm nuts, Fauna, but I told him."

"Oh, you ain't nuts."

"I told him everything. He didn't even ask."

Fauna asked quietly, "What did he talk about?"

"He said there's a fella in old times made a wife out of flowers."

"What for, for God's sake?"

"Well, I don't know. But it was all right when he said it."

"What else did he say?"

Suzy spoke slowly. "Out in the sand dunes I done most of the talking. But he give me a boost every now and then when I run down."

Fauna said, "He can do that better than anybody."

Suzy's eyes were shining with excitement. "I almost forgot," she said. "I never took no stock in stars and stuff like that, but you know what we had for dinner?"

"Champagne?"

"Fish and crab!" said Suzy. "And I didn't break out."

"Well?"

"Remember what you said, how I'm fish and he's crab?"

Fauna turned her head away. "I got something up my nose," she said. "I wonder if I'm catching cold."

"Do you think that's a sign, Fauna? Do you?"

"Everything's signs," said Fauna. "Everything."

There was a glory in Suzy's eyes. "Right after we ate we was talking, and he said, 'I'm lonely.'"

"Now that ain't like him," Fauna said. "That's a dirty trick!"

"No, ma'am," Suzy contradicted her. "He didn't say it like that. I heard that one before too. He said it like it was pushed out of him. It surprised him, like he didn't know he was going to say it. What do you think, Fauna? Tell me, what do you think?"

"I think there's going to be like a new gold star."

"Well, s'pose—and there ain't no harm in supposing—s'pose I moved over there. It would be—well, it would be right across the street from here. Everybody knows I worked here. Wouldn't that kind of bother him?"

"He knows you work here, don't he? Suzy girl, you got to promise me something. Don't you never try to run away from nothing, because you can't. If you're all right nobody ain't going to tear you down. Guy that runs away, why, he's a fugitive. And a fugitive never gets away."

"How about Doc?" said Suzy.

"Look, if you ain't good enough for him, he ain't good for you."

"I don't want to lay no bear trap for him, Fauna."

Fauna was smiling to herself. She said, "I guess a man is the only kind of varmint sets his own trap, baits it, and then steps in it. You just set still, Suzy girl. Don't do nothing. Nobody can't say you trapped him if you don't do nothing."

"Well, he didn't really say—"

"They never do," said Fauna.

Suzy said weakly, "I can't hardly breathe."

"You know, you ain't cussed once this morning," Fauna said.

"Ain't I?"

"Some of my gold stars was damn good hookers," said Fauna.

"But when I put up your gold star, Suzy, the whoring business ain't lost nothing. Like the Patrón says, you're too small in the butt and too big in the bust."

"I don't want nobody to get the idea I'm hustling Doc."

"You're damn right you ain't. I'll see to that." She looked speculatively at Suzy. "You know, I'd like you to get out of town tonight and kind of freshen up."

"Where'll I go?"

"You could go on an errand for me to San Francisco if you wanted to. I got a little package up there in a safe-deposit box. I'll give you some dough. And I want you should buy some clothes and a hat. Get a nice suit. It'll last you for years. Look! Walk up and down Montgomery Street and see what the nice-looking dames is wearing—you know, the kind of material. They're pretty smart women up there. Before you buy, look around a little—make it nice. Come on back tomorrow."

Suzy said, "You getting me out of the way?"

"Yeah," said Fauna. "You got the idea."

"Why?"

"Suzy girl, that ain't none of your business. There's a two o'clock bus and a four o'clock bus."

"I'll take the four o'clock."

"Why?"

"Well, you said Doc's going out collecting bugs. Maybe while he's gone I could kind of swamp out his joint. It ain't had a scrubbing for years."

"That might make him mad."

"I'll start him a nice stew cooking slow," said Suzy. "I make a real nice stew." She came around the table.

"Get your hands off me!" said Fauna. "Go on now! And don't you ever say that thing again that made a sucker out of me. My best fur!"

"You mean, 'I love you'?"

"That's it. Don't you say it."

"Okay," said Suzy.

Old Jingleballicks

Doc got back from his collecting about four-thirty. He had over a hundred chitons bound with string to little glass plates to keep them from curling, and submerged in sea water in his collecting buckets were hundreds of brittlestars.

Now, killing is one of the delicate operations of a marine zoologist. You want the animal to resemble its living self, but this is impossible. In death the color changes, just as it does with us. Also, if any violent means of killing is used there is constriction, and in the case of brittlestars the death struggle causes the animal to shed its arms.

In the front room of Western Biological, Doc poured out part of the sea water from his wooden bucket. Then he moved the brittlestars to a large, flat-bottomed glass dish and poured some sea water on top of them. The little animals with the snakelike arms whipped about for a moment and then settled down. When they were quite still and resting Doc added a little fresh water to the dish. The arms stirred nervously. He waited a while and then added a little more fresh water. To a sea animal, fresh water is a poison, and if it is slowly introduced it is as subtle as morphine. It relaxes and soothes until the little creature goes to sleep and dies without violence.

Doc sat down to wait for the poison to act. He sensed that there was something wrong. What could it be? Had he forgotten something? He felt all right, the small hangover of the morning was gone. Of course! It was the case of Bohemia beer over at the Patrón's. His subconscious must have been reminding him of the beer. He looked out the window toward the grocery. And there was something wrong with that too. And finally he saw. His windows were clean. He turned and looked around the laboratory. The records were piled neatly on the shelves, not falling all over themselves. The floor was shining, and that smell—that was soap.

He moved to the kitchen. His dishes were clean, the pans scoured and shining. A delicious odor came from a pot on the gas stove. He lifted the lid. Brown meat juice bubbled up through carrots and onions, and a stick of white celery swam like a fish.

Doc went back to his table and sat down. His cot was made up and smooth and the turned-down sheet was clean. Suddenly a sense of desolation came over him—a great sadness that was like warmth. The toes of his lined-up shoes peeked out at him from under the bed.

The poor kid, he thought. Oh, the poor damn kid! I wonder if she's trying to repay—I hope I haven't done anything bad. My God, I hope she didn't misunderstand anything! What did I say? I know I didn't do anything, but what did I say? I wouldn't hurt Suzy for the world. He glanced around again. She sure does a job of cleaning, he thought. The stew smells wonderful too. He poured a little more fresh water into the glass dish. The arms of the brittlestars were arranging themselves in small spirals. They hardly moved when the fresh poison was introduced.

The clean laboratory made Doc nervous and apprehensive. And there was something missing from himself, something lost. The lowest voice of all was still. In his black depths he was somehow comforted. He went to the record shelf: not Bach . . . no, not Buxtehude . . . not Palestrina either. His hand strayed to an album not used in a long time. He had opened it before he knew what he was doing. And then he smiled and put the first record on the turntable: Mozart's *Don Giovanni*. It started its overture, and Doc, still smiling, went to the kitchen and stirred the stew. "Don Giovanni," he said. "Is that what I think of myself? No! I do not. But why do I feel so good, and so bad?" He looked at his desk. The yellow pads were piled neatly and the pencils were sharpened. "I believe I'll try." And at that point there were fumbling steps on his porch and Old Jingleballicks burst in.

It is madness to write about Old Jingleballicks, but since he came in at this point it is necessary. People coming out of a session with Old Jay felt slightly dizzy, and the wise ones, after a time, just didn't believe it. His name cannot be mentioned, for it occurs on too many bronze plaques that begin, "Donated by——."

Old Jay was born so rich that he didn't know he was rich at all. He thought everybody was that way. He was a scientist, but whether brilliant or a screwball nobody ever knew, and since he had contributed to so many learned foundations and financed so many projects and served on so many boards of trustees, nobody dared openly to wonder. He gave millions away but he was likely to sponge on a friend. His scholastic honors were many, and there were people who thought privately and venomously that they were awarded in hope of a donation, that he was, in fact, like a football player whose grades have little relation to his scholarship.

He was a stubby man with a natural tonsure of yellow hair. His eyes were bright as a bird's eyes, and he was interested in everything. He was so close to reality that he had completely lost touch with realism. Sometimes he amused Doc, and at other times his endless and myopic enthusiasms could drive a man to despair. Old Jingleballicks shouted at everyone under the impression that this made for clarity.

"Did you get my wire?" he cried.

"No."

"Came for your birthday. Always remember it. Same day they burned Giordano Bruno."

"It's not my birthday," said Doc.

"Well, what day is this?"

"Friday."

"Oh! Well, I'll wait over."

"It's in December. I only have one cot."

"All right. I'll sleep on the floor." He wandered to the kitchen, took the lid off the pot, and began eating the stew—blowing on it violently to cool it.

"That's not done," said Doc, and he was irritated to find that he was shouting back.

"Done enough!" cried Old Jay and went on eating.

Doc said, "Hitzler came through. He said you were seen on a

lawn in Berkeley, on your knees, pulling a worm out of the ground with your teeth."

Old Jay swallowed a half-cooked carrot. "Not so!" he shouted. "Say, this stew's not done."

"That's what I told you."

"Oh! Well, you see I've watched robins getting worms. Little beggars dig in their heels, so to speak. I got to wondering how much actual pull was involved. Had a scale with a clamp in my teeth. Average night crawler resists to the extent of one pound six ounces. I tried forty-eight individuals. Think of it! A three-ounce bird pulls twenty-two ounces, over seven times his own weight. No wonder they eat so much. Just eating keeps them hungry. Like robins?"

"Not particularly," said Doc. "Are you going to eat all my dinner?"

"I guess so," said Old Jingleballicks. "But it's not done. You got anything to drink?"

"I'll get some beer," said Doc.

"Fine! Get a lot."

"Don't you want to contribute a little?"

"I'm short," said Old Jay.

Doc said, "You are not. You're a freeloader."

"Oh!" said Jingleballicks.

"I said, don't you want to contribute!"

"I'm a little short," said Old Jay.

Doc said angrily, "You are not. You're a freeloader. You never pay. You ran the lab while I was in the Army and damn near bankrupted me. I don't say you stole most of the museum glass, I just say it's missing. Did you take those specimen jars?"

"Well, yes," said Old Jingleballicks. And then he said thoughtfully, "I wish you were a charity or an institution."

"What!"

"Then I could endow you," said Old Jingleballicks.

"Well, I'm not an institution. So what do you do? You go to a lot of trouble to keep from paying a couple of dollars for beer." And suddenly despair and humor crashed head-on in Doc and he burst into weary laughter. "Oh Lord," he said, "you're just not possible! You're a ridiculous idea."

"Your stew is burning," said Old Jingleballicks.

Doc leaped to the stove and pulled the pot from the burner. "You ate all the juice," he said bitterly. "Of course it burned!"

"It was very good," said Old Jay.

In the grocery Doc said, "Give me a dozen cans of beer."

"Don't you want the Bohemia?"

"Hell no!" Doc said. "I have a guest who—" And then an evil thought came to him. "A very interesting man," Doc said. "Why don't you come over and have a drink with us? Old—I mean, my friend can explain chess to you better than I can."

"Why not?" said the Patrón. "Maybe I better bring a little liquor."

"Why not?" said Doc.

Crossing the street, the Patrón asked, "You going to the party tomorrow?"

"Sure."

"I like you, Doc, but I don't get you. You ain't real," said the Patrón.

"How do you mean?"

"Well, everything you do is—well, you're like that chess. I don't get you at all."

Doc said, "Do you suppose nobody's real to anybody else? You're going to meet a man who can't possibly exist."

"Don't talk like that," said the Patrón nervously.

Old Jay shouted as they went up the stairs, "I bring you tidings of great joy. The human species is going to disappear!"

"This is Joseph and Mary Rivas," said Doc. "Joseph and Mary, this is Old Jingleballicks."

"Why can't you rig a chess game?" the Patrón asked.

"Oh, you can, you can! Or at least you can rearrange your opponent. Comes to the same thing. Now, where was I? Oh yes—we are about to join the great reptiles in extinction."

"Good!" said Doc.

"You mean there ain't gonna be no more people?" said the Patrón.

"Right, young man. We have played the final joke on ourselves. Open the beer! Man, in saving himself, has destroyed himself."

"Who's destroyed?" the Patrón demanded.

"There must be chuckling on Olympus," said Old Jingleballicks. "We go not to Armageddon but to the gas chamber, and we generate our own gas—"

Doc said, "I intended to work on my paper."

"Good! I'll help," said Old Jingleballicks.

"Oh God! *No!*" said Doc.

"Man has solved his problems," Old Jay went on. "Predators he has removed from the earth; heat and cold he has turned aside; communicable disease he has practically eliminated. The old live on, the young do not die. The best wars can't even balance the birth rate. There was a time when a small army could cut a population in half in a year. Starvation, typhus, plague, tuberculosis, were trusty weapons. A scratch with a spear point meant infection and death. Do you know what the incidence of death from battle wounds is today? One percent. A hundred years ago it was eighty percent. The population grows and the productivity of the earth decreases. In a foreseeable future we shall be smothered by our own numbers. Only birth control could save us, and that is one thing mankind is never going to practice."

"Broth-er!" said the Patrón. "What makes you so damn happy about it?"

"It is a cosmic joke. Preoccupation with survival has set the stage for extinction."

"I didn't get one goddam word of that," said Joseph and Mary.

Doc's hands were full. In his left he held a small glass of whisky and in his right a can of beer. He sipped from the one and gulped from the other. "Every instinct tells me to stay out of this," he said, "and every impulse makes me want to get into it."

"Good!" said Old Jay. "Is that whisky?"

"Old Tennis Shoes," said Joseph and Mary. "Want some?"

"Perhaps a little later."

"Okay."

"It's a little later now," said Old Jingleballicks.

"I guess you can hustle with anything," said the Patrón. "I got a feeling I'm being took."

"Well, the impulse wins," said Doc. "You have forgotten one thing, Old Jingleballicks. Indeed, there have been species which became extinct through their own miscalculations, but they were species with a small range of variability. Now consider the lemming—"

"That is a very specialized case," said Old Jingleballicks.

"How do you know we aren't? What do lemmings do when their population exceeds the food supply? Whole masses of them swim out to sea and drown, until a balance of food and population is reached."

"I deny your right to use lemmings," said Old Jingleballicks. "Hand me the bottle, will you?"

"Deny and be damned!" Doc said. "Is the lemming migration a disease? Is it a memory? Or is it a psychic manifestation forced on part of the group for the survival of the whole?"

Old Jay howled back at him, "I will not be robbed of extinction! This is a swindle." He turned to the Patrón. "Don't listen to that man. He's a charlatan."

"He sure in hell is," said Joseph and Mary admiringly.

Doc leveled a finger between the eyes of Old Jay, holding his whisky glass like the butt of a pistol. "Disease, you say? Infection? Down almost to nonexistence? But tell me, are not neurotic disturbances on the increase? And are they curable or does the cure spread them? Now you wait! Don't you try to talk now. Do you suppose that the tendency toward homosexuality might not also have a mathematical progression? And could this not be the human solution?"

"You can't prove it," Old Jingleballicks cried. "It's all talk—overemphasis. Why, you might as well accuse me of neurotic tendencies and be done with it!" His eyes brimmed with tears. "My friend, my thought-friend, my true friend," he whimpered.

Doc said, "I wouldn't even think of such a thing."

"You wouldn't?"

"Certainly not."

"When are you going to start dinner?" said Old Jingleballicks.

"You've eaten my dinner," said Doc.

"I've got a fine idea," said Old Jay. "While you start dinner, William and Mary can get a fresh bottle of whisky and I'll set up the chessmen."

"It's not William and Mary, it's Joseph and Mary."

"Who is? Oh! My friend, I'm going to teach you the greatest of all games, the ethereal creation of human intelligence. Shall we sugar it up with a little side bet?"

"Why, you dishonest old fraud!" Doc shouted.

"Ten dollars, Mary?"

The Patrón shrugged his shoulders in apology to Doc. "You have to pay to learn things," he said.

"Make it twenty-five," Old Jingleballicks said. "You want to live forever?"

Doc opened a can of salmon and a can of spaghetti and stirred the two together in a frying pan. He grated nutmeg over it. Sadly he put the burned stewpot to soak in the sink.

A little after dark the Patrón went back to the grocery and sent Cacahuete to deliver a third bottle of whisky. Upstairs he joined the wetbacks as in advancing and retreating lines they danced the sad and stately measures of the Tehuanos. "Sandunga," they sang, "Sandunga mama mia . . ."

In the darkening laboratory Doc and Old Jay went softly into the third bottle of Old Tennis Shoes.

"You've had the bed long enough," Doc said. "I want it now."

"All right. As I grow older I expect less and less—and get nothing, even from my so-called friends."

"Look here! You've eaten and spoiled my first dinner, stuffed my second, swilled my beer, taken two drinks for one of the whisky, appropriated my bed, broken two phonograph records, and I saw you put my fountain pen in your pocket. And how you razzle-dazzled the Patrón out of twenty-five dollars I don't know. You shouldn't have told him that under certain circumstances a knight can jump three squares in one direction—that's not honest."

"I know," said Old Jingleballicks. He patted the pillow lovingly. "Now you lie down here and get comfortable. I'll bring you a drink. Feel better now?"

"Oh, I'm all right," said Doc.

"Say, is that place across the street still running?"

A jagged rage whipped Doc upright. "You stay out of there!" he said. "You old fool! Lie down and go to sleep."

"Why shouldn't I go? Am I to deny myself the loveliness of women if the price is right? I can hear the tinkle of their sweet voices and see the heaving of their white roundness—"

"Oh, shut up!" Doc said.

"What's the matter, dear friend? I don't remember that you ever starved for love even when it was less near and less reasonable."

"You go to hell," said Doc. "But you go to hell here."

26

The Developing Storm

At the very moment Doc and Old Jingleballicks were quarreling over a matter neither of them understood, Mack was sitting, body comfortable but spirit disturbed, in Fauna's office bedroom. In his hand he held a Venetian glass bud vase of whisky. He was pouring out to Fauna a problem that had not come up in his life for many years.

"Don't think that there ain't been parties before at the Palace, and fights," he said. "Why, when the news come that Gay had went to his reward we give a memorial shindig that they don't hardly do no better at the Salinas Rodeo. Gay would of been proud of it—if he could of got in."

Fauna said, "There's talk around that three mourners went to join Gay before nightfall next day."

"Well, you got to expect a certain amount of accidents," said Mack modestly. "That was all fine. But this here's something special. Not only are loyal hearts framing their dear friend for a hunk of charity, but we got a double-header. Right in the Palace Flophouse the holy bounds of matrimony got its spikes dug in on the starting line. This here's a halcyon brawl. I and the boys got real delicate feelings about it."

"But no clothes," said Fauna.

"Right! We think somebody got to set a standard. If the loyal friends look like mugs, what'll the mugs look like?"

Fauna nodded. "I see what you mean. How far you want to go—monkeysuits?"

"God no!" Mack said. "Just pants and coats made out of the same stuff and nobody gets in without he's got a necktie on,

and none of them bow ties that light up neither. This is a goddam solemn moment, Fauna."

She scratched her scalp with her pencil.

Mack went on, "I ain't as young as I was. I don't know how
many more parties I can take."

"Don't none of us get no younger," said Fauna. She tapped
her teeth with the pencil. As it happened, she also had a problem, and she intended to ask Mack's advice. Now, suddenly, the
two problems crashed together and a solution for both was
born. Into Fauna's eyes came the light of triumph as she mur-
mured, "I got it!"

"Give it to me gentle," said Mack. "I didn't get much sleep
today."

Fauna got up and found the stick with which she directed as-
trological traffic or whacked a protruding piece of bad posture.
She talked better with the wand in her hand. "This here calls
for a drink," she said, and she poured it.

Mack turned the stem of the bud vase in his fingers and
sighted through his drink. The red glass made the brown whisky
look green.

Fauna said, "There was a queen a long time ago and she was
loaded. Didn't think nothing of paying a couple hundred bucks
for a housedress. Got so many bracelets she couldn't bend her
arms. You know what she done when she had a birthday or a
hanging or something?"

"Overalls," said Mack.

"No, but you're close. Dressed like she's a milkmaid. They'd
wash up a cow and the queen'd sit on a gold stool and take a
whang at milking. And there's another old dame. Just the top
cream of the top cream. Gives them parties can't nobody get in.
She wears a head rag. Done it for years. If you look over the
crowd and don't see a head rag—she ain't there."

Mack's hand shook as he raised the bud vase to his lips. "Is it
what I think?"

"Masquerade!" cried Fauna. "There's only two kinds of people in the world gives a masquerade—people who got too much
and people who ain't got nothing."

Mack smiled inwardly to himself. "Can I have a freshener?" he asked.

"Help yourself," said Fauna. "Masquerade has got other things too. People get kind of bored with who they are. Makes them something else for a while."

Mack spoke with reverence. "They used to say, if you got something you can't figure out, give it to Mack. Fauna, it's your dice. You're a bull-bitch idear dame. God te-tum-tum His wonders to perform."

"Like it?"

"Like it! Fauna, this here's one *Life* magazine would give its ass for an invite."

"We got to have a theme."

"How do you mean?"

"Well, we can't let people just run wild. You don't know what kind of stuff they'd wear. I don't want no tramp and gunnysack party."

"I guess you're right. You got any idears?"

"How about 'At the court of the Fairy Queen'?"

"No," said Mack. "First place, we got no right to hurt Joe Elegant's feelings; second place, the cops—"

"Well, how about then 'Snow White and the Seven Dwarfs'?"

"I seen the picture," said Mack. "I think you got something. Some of them dwarfs looked like mugs. I can't see Hazel as no fairy, but he'd do fine as a great big overgrowed dwarf."

"That's what's nice about it," said Fauna. "Gives you some leeway."

"Do you think this might call for a drink?"

"I sure as hell do! You spread the word, Mack, will you? You come either as a dwarf, a prince, or a princess, or you damn well don't get in. Hold that vase steady."

"But not Doc," said Mack.

"You know," said Fauna, "five'll get you seven Doc wears a tie."

O Frabjous Day!

The communications system on Cannery Row is mysterious to the point of magic and rapid to the speed of light. Fauna and Mack came to the decision that the party should be a masquerade on Friday evening at 9:11½. By 9:12 the magic had started, and by 9:30 everyone who was not asleep, drunk, or away, knew about it. One particularly mean woman who hadn't had a man for a long time commented, "How will you know whether they're in costume or not?"—a statement clearly drawn from her own state of misery. But mainly the news was received with wonder and joy. Mack's tom-wallager had achieved the stature of a bull-bitch tom-wallager.

Consider what was in store for the ticket holders: a party at the Palace Flophouse; a raffle that amounted to a potlatch; an engagement of exciting proportions unknown in the annals of the Row; and, on top of this, a costume party! Any one of these would have been enough. Together they threatened to be a celebration close to a catastrophe.

Fauna breathed a sigh of relief for it solved her greatest problem. She wanted to dress Suzy in a certain way, and Suzy, being the tough monkey she was, would have resisted. Now it was easy. There's little difference between the wardrobe of Snow White and that of a lovely young bride.

There will be those who will consider that Fauna took too much upon herself in engineering a marriage without the knowledge or collusion of either party, and such skeptics will be perfectly right. But it was Fauna's conviction, born out of long experience, that most people, one, did not know what they wanted; two, did not know how to go about getting it; and three, didn't know when they had it.

Fauna was one of those rare people who not only have convictions but are quite willing to take responsibility for them. She knew that Doc and Suzy should be together. And since they were too confused, or thoughtless, or shy to bring about that happy state, Fauna was prepared to do it for them. Her critics will cry, "Suppose she is wrong! Maybe this association has no chance of success." And Fauna's answer to this, if she had heard it, would have been, "They ain't doing so good now. It might work. What they got to lose? And when you look at it, what chance has anybody got? Doc put on a tie, didn't he? And if I'm wrong it's my fault. Sure, they'll fight now and then. Who don't? But maybe they'll get something too. What's the odds for anybody?"

And if it was suggested that people should have the right to choose for themselves after thinking it over, she would have replied, "Who thinks? I can think because I ain't part of it."

And if she had been accused of being a busybody she would have said, "Damn right! Done it all my life!" You couldn't win an argument with Fauna because she would agree with you and then go right on as she had planned. She had taken up astrology because she found that people who won't take advice from a wise and informed friend will blindly follow the orders of the planets—which, by all reports, are fairly remote and aloof. Doc would refuse astrology, so he had to be sandbagged. Fauna expected no thanks. She had given that up long ago. Doc could not interpret the black voice of his guts, but it sounded loud in Fauna's ears. She knew his loneliness. When she was with him, that low voice drowned out all the others.

On Saturday morning she made every girl in the house bring out every article of clothing she possessed and lay it on the bed in her office.

Now Mabel was a natural-born, blowed-in-the-glass hustler. In any time, under any system, after a period of orientation, Mabel would have found herself doing exactly what she was doing in Cannery Row. This was not a matter of Fate, but rather a combination of aptitudes and inclinations. Born in a hovel or a castle, Mabel would have gravitated toward hustling.

The heap of finery on Fauna's bed was impressive. Some of those dresses could have got a girl booked for vagrancy just going out to mail a letter.

Mabel took Fauna aside and spoke to her privately. "My grandma come from the old country," she said when the door of her room was closed. Mabel opened the bottom drawer of her bureau and lifted out a brown paper parcel sealed against air with strips of cellophane tape. "Grandma left it to Mama, and Mama left it to me," she said as she tore the paper. "We ain't none of us needed it." She removed layer after layer of tissue paper and at last spread a dress out on her bed—a wedding dress of sheerest white linen embroidered with sprays of white flowers—stitches so tiny they seemed to grow out of the cloth. The bodice was close-fitting and the skirt very full. Mabel opened a box and laid beside the dress a silver wedding crown. "I guess she wouldn't hurt it none," said Mabel. "Tell her not to spill nothing on it. I'll polish up the crown, it's kind of tarnished— real silver!"

Fauna was speechless for once. Her fingers went to the light and lovely fabric. She was a hard woman to break up, but the dress nearly did it. "Snow White!" she said breathlessly. "I better be careful or I'll get to believing my own pitch. Mabel, I'm going to give you my jet earrings."

"I don't want nothing."

"You want my jet earrings!"

"Aw shoot!" said Mabel.

"Looks like it might nearly fit her," Fauna observed.

"Well, we can kind of tack it where it don't."

"You know, you're a good girl. You want I should go to work on you?"

"Hell no!" said Mabel. "I like it here. There's a veil too in this here bag."

"I don't know if we can get away with a veil, but we'll try," said Fauna.

"Oh hell, she don't know a veil from a hole in the ground," said Mabel.

———

If only people would give the thought, the care, the judgment to international affairs, to politics, even to their jobs, that they lavish on what to wear to a masquerade, the world would run in greased grooves. On the surface Cannery Row was quieter than usual, but below the surface it seethed. In one corner of the Palace Flophouse, Whitey No. 2 gave careful lessons to little Johnny Carriaga in the art of palming cards. Johnny had been borrowed for the occasion—or, more truthfully, rented—since Alberto Carriaga had received sixty-two cents, the price of a gallon of wine, for the use of his firstborn. It was planned that Johnny should be dressed as Cupid, with paper wings, bow and arrow, and quiver. The quiver was added as a hiding place for the winning raffle ticket. For although nearly everyone on the Row knew the raffle was rigged, a certain pride made it necessary to carry the deception off with dignity. Because of a small distrust of Johnny the arrows in the quiver were tipped with rubber suction cups.

Whitey No. 2 had cut a card the exact size of a raffle ticket. "Now try it again, Johnny," he said. "No, I can see the edge of it. Look! Sort of squeeze the edges in your palm, like this. Now try it again. That's right! That's good. Now let's see you get it out of the quiver. You make a pass with the bow—like this—so they look at your other hand, and you say—"

"I know," said Johnny. " 'I'm Cupid, God of Love, and I draw a bead on unsuspecting hearts.' "

"God! That's beautiful," said Eddie. "I wonder where Mack got that?"

"He made it up," said Whitey No. 2. "Now when you shove up the bow with your right hand, you get the ticket out of the quiver with your left. Try it."

" 'I-am-Cupid-God-of-Love,' " said Johnny, and he brandished the bow.

"That's good," said Whitey No. 2. "It will take a little more practice though. Don't look at your left hand, Johnny. Look at the bow. Now here's the bowl. Dig around the cards without dropping the ticket. Go on, practice."

"I want thirty-five cents," said Johnny.

"What!"

"If I don't get thirty-five cents I'll tell."

"Mack," said Whitey No. 2, "this here kid's jumped the price."

"Give it to him," said Mack. "I'll flip him double or nothing later."

"Not with that two-headed nickel, you won't," said Johnny.

"Seems like kids got no respect for their elders nowadays," Eddie observed. "If I ever said that, my old man would of clobbered me."

"Maybe your old man wasn't rigging no raffle," said Johnny.

Whitey No. 1 said, "This kid ain't honest. You know where bad kids go, Johnny?"

"I sure do, and I been there," said Johnny.

"Give him the thirty-five cents," said Mack.

What hidden, hoarded longings there are in all of us! Behind the broken nose and baleful eye may be a gentle courtier; behind the postures and symbols and myths of Joe Elegant there may be the hunger to be a man. If one could be, for only an evening, whatever in the world one wished, what would it be? What secret would come out?

To a certain extent the theme of the Palace Flophouse raffle and engagement party was chosen because of Hazel. He was definitely dwarf material. But when he had reviewed the story, asked questions, and got as clear a picture as he ever got of anything, Hazel elected to be Prince Charming. He saw himself in white silk knee breeches and an Eton jacket, his left hand fondling the hilt of a small sword.

They offered him Grumpy, lovable old Grumpy, the prize part of all. They offered him Sweet Pea the Skunk, but Hazel stuck to his dream. It was Prince Charming or he wouldn't attend. Friendships have foundered on less.

"All right," said Mack, "you go ahead. I was going to help you with your costume, but I know when I'm stumped. Hazel, if you're Prince Charming, you're on your own."

"Who cares?" said Hazel. "Who wants your help? I'll bet you're mad because you wanted to be Prince Charming."

"Not me," said Mack. "I'm going as a tree."

"How do you mean?"

"It's a forest, ain't it?" said Mack. "I want a little anenmity. You can't see the tree for the forest."

Hazel went to sit under the cypress tree. He was gloomy and he was frightened because ideas did not come to him, and when he sought them they ran screaming away. But he was determined. He could not let the office down. A man sentenced to be President could not go as a dwarf. It wasn't dignified. Later in the morning he went to the back door of the Bear Flag and called for help from Joe Elegant.

Joe smiled. "I'll help you," he said maliciously.

All over the Row trunks were being opened, and the smell of mothballs penetrated as far as the middle of the street. And all over the Row the story was being rewritten to fit the wardrobe. By unspoken agreement no one planned to be Snow White.

In Western Biological, Doc awakened wracked with pain from sleeping on the floor. He lay still for a moment, trying to isolate the part of him that hurt worst. Not the least of his agony was his memory of forcing Old Jingleballicks to take his bed. A crazy, alcoholic generosity, probably masochistic in origin, had prompted the sacrifice. He raised up on one shattered elbow and looked at the old bastard sleeping so sweetly—his halo of yellow hair surrounding his polished pink pate, his breath puffing in small comfortable snores.

"Wake up!" Doc shouted in fury.

The pale eyes flickered. "What's for breakfast?" said Old Jay.

"Don't you even have the decency to have a hangover?"

"Certainly I do," said Old Jay with dignity. "How's about some beer?"

"Does your head ache?"

"Yes."

"Do your joints ache?"

"Yes."

"Do you have low-blood-pressure depression?"

"Overwhelming."

"Then I've got you," said Doc. "You get the beer."

The pale eyes rolled despairingly. "I'll pay half if you get it."
"No."

"Tell you what I'll do—I'll loan you the money."
"No."

Old Jingleballicks' eyes were bleak. "Reach me my pants," he
said, and he fished out a quarter and a dime and held them out.
"No," said Doc.

"God in heaven! What *do* you want?"
"I want two dollars."

"Why, that would be six bottles!"

"Exactly. You're trapped, Old Jingleballicks, and you know it."

Old Jay dug deep and found two one-dollar bills. "Maybe I
can write it off to entertainment," he said.

Doc pulled on pants and shirt and went across the street. He
took his time. He drank a bottle of beer quickly and then sipped
a second while he heard the news of the day from Joseph and
Mary.

Back in the laboratory he put the four cold remaining bottles
on the table.

"Where's my change?" asked Old Jay.

"I drank your change," said Doc. He was beginning to feel
good. He saw the stricken look. "You cheap old fraud," he said
happily, "for once you've been had." And he went on, "I wish I
could understand you. You must have millions and yet you
pinch and squirm and cheat. Why?"

"Please give me beer. I'm dying," said Old Jingleballicks.

"Then die a little longer," said Doc. "I love to see you die!"

"It's not my fault," Old Jay said. "It's a state of mind. You
might call it the American state of mind. The tax laws are creating a whole new kind of man—a psyche rather than a psychosis.
Two or three generations and we'll maybe set the species. Can I
have beer now?"

"No."

"If a man has any money he doesn't ask, 'Can I afford this?'
but, 'Can I deduct it?' Two men fight over a luncheon check
when both of them are going to deduct it anyway—a whole nation conditioned to dishonesty by its laws, because honesty is

penalized. But it's worse than that. If you'll just hand me a bottle I'll tell you."

"Tell me first."

"I didn't write the tax laws," Old Jay said, trembling. "The only creative thing we have is the individual, but the law doesn't permit me to give money to an individual. I must give it to a group, an organization—and the only thing a group has ever created is bookkeeping. To participate in my gift the individual must become part of the group and thus lose his individuality and his creativeness. I didn't write the law. I hate a law that stifles generosity and makes charity good business. Corporations are losing their financial efficiency because waste pays. I deplore it, but I do it. I know you need a microscope, but I can't give it to you because with taxes a four-hundred-dollar microscope costs me twelve hundred dollars—if I give it to you—and nothing if I give it to an institution. Why, if you, through creative work, should win a prize, most of the money would go in taxes. I don't mind taxes, God knows! But I do mind the kind of law that makes of charity not the full warmness of sharing but a stinking expediency. And now, if you don't hand me a beer, I shall be forced—"

"Here's your beer," said Doc.

"What's for breakfast?"

"God knows. The party at the Palace Flophouse tonight is a masquerade. 'Snow White and the Seven Dwarfs.'"

"Why?"

"I don't know."

"I shall go as a red dwarf," said Old Jingleballicks.

"A dying star," said Doc. "It kind of fits you with that hair."

When the beer was gone they decided that beer made breakfast redundant. Doc went back for six more bottles, and in a burst of generosity he brought back the Bohemia.

"Now there's beer for you," said Old Jingleballicks. "The Mexicans are a great and noble people. The Pyramid of the Sun and this beer—whole civilizations have produced less. You started to tell me about your paper last night but you got deflected by a girl. I'd like to see that girl."

"I'd like to tell you about my paper. I want to draw some parallels between emotional responses in cephalopods and in humans, and I'd like to observe the pathological changes that go with these responses. Now the body walls of octopi are semitransparent. With proper equipment it might be possible to observe these changes as they happen. Sometimes the simpler organisms can give us a key to the more complex. Dementia praecox, for example, was considered purely a psychotic manifestation until it was observed that there were physical symptoms as well."

"Why don't you write your paper?"

"I seem to be afraid to. A kind of terror comes over me when I start."

"What have you got to lose if you fail?"

"Nothing."

"What have you got to gain if you succeed?"

"I don't know."

Old Jingleballicks regarded Doc benignly. "Have you got enough beer in you so you aren't quarrelsome?"

"I'm never quarrelsome."

"The hell you aren't! Took my head off last night. You hurt my feelings."

"I'm sorry. What did you want to say?"

"Will you let me finish if I start?"

"I'll try."

Old Jay said, "You feel to me like a woman who has never had a baby but knows all the words. There's a lack of fulfillment in you. I think you have violated something or withheld something from yourself—almost as though you were eating plenty but no Vitamin A. You aren't hungry, but you're starving. That's what I think."

"I can't imagine anything I lack. I have freedom, comfort, and the work I like. What have I missed?"

"Well, last night, in every conversation, a girl named Suzy crept in—"

"For God's sake!" said Doc. "Do you know what Suzy is? An illiterate little tramp, a whore! I took her out to dinner because Fauna asked me to. I found her interesting the way I'd find a new species of octopus interesting, that's all. You've always been a goddam fool, Old Jingleballicks, but you've never been a romantic damn fool."

"Who's talking about romance? I was speaking of hunger. Maybe you can't be wholly yourself because you've never given yourself wholly to someone else."

"Of all the esoteric goddam nonsense!" Doc cried. "Why I give floor room to you I don't know."

"Then try to figure out why you get mad," said Old Jay.

"What?"

"Well, aren't you putting a lot of energy into denying something which, if it is not true, deserved no denial?"

"Sometimes I think you're just plain nuts," said Doc.

"Know what I'm going to do?" said Old Jay. "I'm going to buy a bottle of whisky."

"I don't believe it!" said Doc.

28

Where Alfred the Sacred River Ran

Very few people know that Hazel had given the Palace Flophouse its name years ago when the boys had first moved in. Inspired by the glory of having a home, Hazel compounded the name of something he knew about and something he didn't, the known and the unknown, the homely and the exotic; and, ever after, the name had stuck, so that it was known by certain people from one end of the state to the other. And the Palace Flophouse had justified its name over the years. It had been shelter and home base to the boys. Also, some surprising events had occurred there.

The building itself was not impressive—redwood board and bat, tar-paper roof, twenty-eight feet long, fourteen feet wide, two square windows, and two doors, one on each side. Into this simple box Mack and the boys had moved some remarkable articles, the products of their wits, their work, and sometimes their misfortune. The great cast-iron stove was in excellent condition and bid fair to outlast the Colosseum which it resembled. The grandfather clock, once the home of a dog, stood empty now—and Eddie wanted to be buried in it. Each of the beds was canopied as a substitute for mending the roof, and Gay's bed was kept just as it was when he went away—patchwork quilt turned down to reveal a gray tennis-flannel sheet. His copy of *Amazing True Desert Stories,* folded open to page 62, lay on top of the apple box just as Gay had left it; and his prize possession, a collector's item, a ring gear and pinions of a 1914 Willys-Knight, lay on a black velvet cloth in the bottom of the box. On the shelf over his bed the boys kept some kind of nosegay in a swanky swig glass, for Gay had loved flowers. He ate them—particularly red roses, mustard flowers, wild turnip blossoms, and the petals of one variety of dahlia. No one had ever been allowed to sit or sleep in Gay's bed. He might return one day, the boys thought, even though he was reported dead and his Army insurance paid.

Now there had been tom-wallagers in the Palace Flophouse but never such a bull-bitch tom-wallager as was now in the process of exploding. The outside was freshly whitewashed. Beds were pushed together, and the interior was a bower of pine boughs crossed to make a canopy. The great stove was laid out as a bar and the oven was full of cracked ice. In front of the back door a little stage was built, with a painter's dropcloth for a curtain and the door for an entrance—for certain theatrical effects, not counting the raffle itself, were planned for that area.

This forest bower was lighted by Japanese lanterns, and a string of lanterns led down to the chicken walk above the railroad track. The boys were pleased with their effort.

Mack surveyed the scene and put a name to it that was remembered. "A veritable fairyland," he said.

The Patrón had contributed his prize group of musicians, the original Espaldas Mojadas—two guitars, gourds, bones, castanets, and Haitian drum, and last, a guitarón as big as a rowboat. Cacahuete Rivas, the nephew of the Patrón, was scheduled to join his trumpet to the band later, but now he was on the beach, practicing his solo softly.

As evening came to Cannery Row the boys were tired but content. Following Mack's lead, they all agreed to be trees. After all, they were the hosts. Their one sorrow was that Hazel had left them. His yearning to be Prince Charming had overcome his love for his friends. In Joe Elegant's tiny bedroom he was being transformed.

"Caught me with my pants down," Mack apologized for the twentieth time. "Hazel's such a mug you forget he's sensitive. Hell, I could of worked out some kind of charming rig if I'd give it some thought. Don't seem right without him here to mess things up."

It is customary at most masquerades for the arriving guests to be shy, ill at ease, and sober, and to stand around uneasily for

maybe an hour before the party warms up. In this matter of
starting a party Cannery Row is far ahead of some other centers
of culture. The party was to start at 9:00 P.M. sharp. The guests
would be notified by the trumpet of Cacahuete Rivas, playing
"Whistle While You Work."

At least two hours before the signal a series of small earnest
parties, at Wide Ida's, the Bear Flag, and in private homes, were
practicing for the main event. This party was going to begin in
full bloom. Of course Mack and the boys were so weighed down
with responsibility that they didn't get the best out of their liquor;
still, they made progress, and they watched the big hand of the
alarm clock on the back of the stove.

In the Bear Flag the pageantry was spread all over the floor.
Snow White was going to have, as ladies of honor, some of the
best-known and most respected hookers north of San Luis
Obispo. The ladies were dressing in filmy gowns of red, yellow,
and green, and each one was to carry a bottle of whisky gar-
landed with ribbons to match her dress. Fauna was going as a
witch. It was her own idea. The only costume she really needed
was a broom, but she had made a peaked black hat and a black
alpaca wrap-around to carry the part off. But Fauna had a pay-
off. When the big moment came she was prepared to fling off
her black gown, switch broom for wand, and emerge as the
fairy godmother.

Wide Ida's was dwarf country. Eight Happys, four Sneezys, six
Dopeys, and nineteen Grumpys clustered about the bar, earnestly
singing "Harvest Moon" in one-and-a-half-part harmony.

Joseph and Mary had elected to go as Dracula. He hadn't
seen *Snow White*, but to him a moving picture was a moving
picture.

At Western Biological, Doc and Old Jingleballicks were
hopelessly enmeshed in a discussion of tobacco mosaic. When
the dam had burst a flood followed. A garbage can stood in the
middle of the floor, and in it, nestled in crushed ice, the six remaining bottles of a case of champagne bought by Old Jay.

Doc and Old Jay had completely forgotten the party. When Cacahuete's trumpet sounded the call to arms they were shouting so
loud they didn't hear it. When the youth and beauty of Cannery

Row walked gaily up the lantern-lit chicken walk Old Jay and Doc were still screaming at each other.

Suddenly Doc dropped his voice, and it had the effect of a loud noise. "I think I will go away," he said. "I have tried with every sinew and I have failed."

"Nonsense!" said Old Jay. "Young man, you are at the threshold of a great career."

"But what do I care for honors?"

"How do you know? You never got any," said Old Jay.

"Don't try to hold me back, Old Jingle."

"I won't. There's too many of you already. Do you realize you haven't cooked any dinner?"

"I bought a pound of hamburger and you ate it raw before I got it near a pan."

"You shouldn't starve yourself, young friend," said Old Jingleballicks.

Eddie hurled himself up the steps and flung open the door. "Doc!" he cried. "For God's sakes! She's started! They're going to draw!"

Doc picked a bottle from the ice. "Arm yourself, Old Jingleballicks. Forward!"

They had to help Old Jay up the chicken walk.

The drawing was being held for them. Dwarfs, animals, monsters, were drawn up in half-circle, facing the curtain.

"I guess we're all here," said Mack. He looked behind the curtain. "You all right, Johnny?"

"Goddam cold," said Johnny.

And at that moment Hazel entered proudly, his chin up, his eyes flashing with dignity. Joe Elegant had worked all day to get his revenge on mankind, and Hazel was the result. The basis of his costume was long gray underwear, to which were sewed hearts, diamonds, spades, and clubs in red and black. Hazel's army shoes had yellow pompoms on the toes. An Elizabethan ruff of stiff paper was around his neck, and on his head a Knight Templar's hat with a white ostrich plume. From the belt around his middle hung a long scabbard. His right hand proudly held a cavalry saber at salute.

Joe Elegant had concentrated his revenge in one area. The

drop seat of the costume had been removed and in its place, right on the essential surface of Hazel himself, was painted a bull's eye in concentric circles of red and blue.

Hazel was a breathtaking sight. He did not glance around. He knew he was right—he knew it by the silence. Smartly he turned the saber to parade rest and crossed his hands on the hilt. His breath caught in his throat.

"I," he said huskily, "I am Prince Charming." And the company could see now that his cheeks were rouged and his eyelashes beaded. "I proteck dam—damsels," he announced. And only then did he turn his proud head for the applause and approval he knew he merited.

There were tears in Mack's eyes. "You done fine, Hazel baby," he said. "Couldn't nobody do better. Who helped you?"

"Joe Elegant," said Hazel. "What a nice guy!"

Whitey No. 2 moved up at Mack's imperceptible signal. "You want I should go now?"

"Right now," said Mack softly. "Kick the bejeezus out of him."

Hazel moved proudly in on their soft talk. "Mr. Joe Elegant presents his compliments," he said. "He is sorry he cannot attend as he had to leave town on business. Let's see—is that all?—yep, that's all."

"We'll thank him when he comes back," said Mack grimly.

The guests looked at Hazel with stricken eyes, and no one laughed. One glance at Mack's jutting chin and doubled fists stopped that impulse.

"Get on with it," Wide Ida growled.

Mack pulled himself together, advanced to the curtain, and turned to face the guests.

"Fellow citizens," he said, "right here in Cannery Row lives a guy that there can't nobody want a better friend. For years we have took his bounty without sharing nothing back at him. Now this guy needs a certain article that runs into dough. Therefore it is the pleasure of I and the boys to raffle off the Palace Flophouse to buy a microscope for Doc. We got three hundred and eighty bucks. Curtain!"

Doc shouted, "Mack! You're crazy!"

"Shut up!" said Mack. "Curtain."

The cloth was pulled aside to reveal Johnny Carriaga dressed in an aluminum supporter and a pair of blue paper wings. Johnny brandished his bow. "I-am-Cupid-God-of-Love!" he shouted. Then the winning ticket slipped from his palm and fluttered to the floor. Johnny scrambled after it, yelling, "I-draw-a-bead-on-unexpected-hearts." He grabbed the ticket and turned to Mack. "What do I do now?" he asked.

Mack gave up. "Oh, what the hell!" Then he shouted, "Is that the ticket you have drawn, Cupid?"

"I have plucked from the many." Johnny hadn't been near the bowl but he yelled it anyway.

"Give it to me, you little bastard," said Mack quietly. "Friends," he said, "do my eyes deceive me? This *is* a surprise! Well, well! Folks, it gives me great pleasure to announce that the Palace Flophouse has passed into the hands of Doc."

Doc was jarred toward sobriety. He moved close to Mack. "You're crazy!" he said.

"Like a fox," said Mack.

"Who told you you owned it? I didn't tell."

"How do you mean, Doc?"

"I didn't think Chong told anybody but me. He was afraid you'd do something like this."

Mack said, "Let's you and I step outside."

Under the lanterns they faced each other. Doc popped the champagne cork and handed the bottle to Mack, who cupped his mouth over the glistening foam.

"What was you saying, Doc?" he asked quietly.

"Chong wanted you and the boys to have a home. He deeded it to you and put up the money for ten years' taxes."

"Well, whyn't he tell us?"

"He was afraid if you knew you owned it you'd mortgage it or sell it and then you wouldn't have a home."

Mack was shaken. "Doc," he said, "would you do me the favor? Don't tell the boys."

"Why, sure."

"Shake on it?"

"Shake! Have a drink."

Suddenly Mack laughed. "Doc," he said, "I and the boys want to ask will you rent the joint to us?"

"Sure I will, Mack."

"I hope they never find out. They'd skin me," said Mack.

"Wouldn't it be simpler if we just forgot the raffle?"

"No, sir!" said Mack. "Chong was right. I wouldn't trust the boys not to sell her sometime when they need a buck. I wouldn't trust myself."

The visit of Old Jingleballicks had put Doc's system to an outrageous test. Meals had been infrequent, sleep fitful, emotions on stilts, and the intake of alcohol enormous. The raffle had jarred him out of a pleasant swimming state into something resembling sobriety, but not very closely. A fog of unreality like a dream feeling was not in him but all around him. He went inside the Palace and saw the dwarfs and monsters and the preposterous Hazel all lighted by the flickering lanterns. None of it seemed the fabric of sweet reality. The music was deafening. Old Jay danced by, clutching a pale brunette to his stomach as though she were a pain—a disgusting sight, and as unreal as the rest.

Anyone untrained in tom-wallagers might well have been startled at this tom-wallager. Eddie waltzed to the rumba music, his arms embracing an invisible partner. Wide Ida lay on the floor wrestling with Whitey No. 2, at each try displaying acres of pink panties, while a wild conga line of dwarfs and animals milled about. Johnny Carriaga ran wild. Standing on a box, he fired at random but not at unsuspecting hearts. Mrs. Alfred Wong had a rubber-tipped arrow stuck between her shoulderblades. Then Johnny winged a lantern, and it crashed in flames and set fire to three dwarfs, so that they had to be put out with a punch bowl.

Mack and Doc were swept into the conga line. To Doc the room began to revolve slowly and then to rise and fall like the deck of a stately ship in a groundswell. The music roared and tinkled. Hazel beat out rhythm on the stove with his sword until Johnny, aiming carefully, got a bull's-eye on Hazel. Hazel leaped in the air and came down on the oven door, scattering crushed ice all over the floor. One of the guests had got wedged in the grandfather clock. From the outside the Palace Flophouse seemed to swell and subside like rising bread.

Doc cupped his hands close to Mack's ear. "Where's Fauna and the girls?" he shouted.

"Later," Mack cried.

"What?"

"Coming later," and he added, "Better get here pretty soon before the joint burns down."

"What?"

"Skip it," Mack shouted.

At this point Whitey No. 1 fought his way to Mack's side and yelled, "Mack, they're coming!"

Mack rushed to the Espaldas Mojadas and raised both hands at them. Johnny aimed his last arrow at the guitarón and took the fret out clean.

"Hold it!" Mack screamed.

The music stopped, and silence fell on the room. Then the unrealest part of all began to happen.

Very softly the sound of a sweet muted trumpet whispered, and the crazy thing was playing the "Wedding March" from *Lohengrin*, and even as Doc listened the sly brass began playing with it, slid into minors, took a short rhythm ride, and moaned away at blues. The dancers were very still, almost stuffed. Doc found the source of the music—Cacahuete Rivas in the corner of the room, muting his trumpet with a damp sponge.

Then in this dream the paint-splashed curtain was pulled aside, and Fauna, the witch, came through the door, straddling a broom.

Doc thought, God! I'd hate to testify about this. I'd get the booby-hatch!

Fauna barked, "This here's a very happy occasion." She looked around. "Doc, come here."

He moved vaguely toward her.

Four girls from the Bear Flag came through the door, dressed in blinding colors. They ranged themselves two on each side of the door, facing inward, holding their beribboned whisky bottles to make an arch.

Fauna dismounted from her broom and ripped off her black wrapper, displaying a sheath of silver lamé. In her hand miraculously appeared a silver wand tipped with a gold star. She struck a pose, riding on her toes as though prepared for flight. "I am your fairy godmother," she shouted. "I bring you Snow White, the bride!"

Then Suzy appeared in the doorway, a transformed Suzy in a wedding gown. The silver crown was on her head, and from its points a veil was suspended. She looked lovely and young and excited. Her lips were parted.

Fauna yelled, "Doc, come get your girl!"

Doc shook his head to try to wake up. It was a dream, a craziness, the crown, the veil, the virginity. "What in hell is going on?"

It happens that two people standing apart can dip into each other's thoughts. Suzy read his mind or his face. An embarrassed red crept up her neck and darkened her cheeks. She closed her eyes.

And Doc's mind read her pain. His world spun like a top. He heard himself say, "Fairy Godmother, I accept—my—girl."

Suzy opened her eyes and looked in Doc's eyes. Then her jaw muscles tightened and her eyes grew fierce; her sweet mouth hardened to a line. She took off the crown and veil, looked at them a moment, and placed them gently on an apple box.

The crazy trumpet put a samba beat to the "Wedding March" and a guitar took up the throbbing.

"Listen, you mugs," said Suzy over the music, "I could live with a stumblebum in a culvert and be a good wife. I could marry a yellow dog and be nice to him. But good Christ! Not Doc!" Suddenly she turned and darted out the door.

Fauna plunged after her. There was no chicken walk out the back way. Suzy slipped and rolled down the embankment and Fauna rolled after her. On the railroad track they gathered themselves together.

"You goddam grandstanding bitch!" said Fauna bitterly. "What do you mean—'not Doc'?"

"I love him," said Suzy.

Oh, Woe, Woe, Woe!

One of the common reactions to shock is lethargy. If, after an automobile accident, one man is howling and writhing and another sits quietly staring into space, it is usually the quiet man who is badly hurt. A community can go into shock too. Cannery Row did. People drew into themselves, kept their doors closed, and didn't visit. Everyone felt guilty, even those who had not planned the party. Merely to have seen it was enough.

Mack and the boys were doubled up with a sense of unhappy fate. It was their third try at doing something nice for Doc, and it was their third failure. They did not know where to turn to escape their own scorn.

Wide Ida became fiercely taciturn. Her customers drank in silence to escape the guilty rage they knew was just under her muscular surface.

Fauna grieved like a lost setter dog. In a lifetime of preposterous plans she had discovered some failures but never before a catastrophe.

Even the Patrón experienced little flashes of an emotion new to him. Always before he had managed to swap guilt for blame of circumstance or enemy, but now his accusing finger bent like a comedy pistol and aimed at his own heart. It was an interesting pain, but a pain nevertheless. He became kindly and thoughtful of all around him—an attitude that frightened people who knew him. There is nothing reassuring about the smile of a tiger.

As for Doc, he was undergoing reorganization so profound that he didn't know it was happening. He was like a watch taken apart on a jeweler's table—all jewels and springs and balances laid out ready for reassembling. For pain or frustration the human has many anodynes, not the least of which is anger.

Doc quarreled viciously with Old Jingleballicks, ordered him out, and told him never to return. Doc fought with the expressman over the quality of the service he had been getting, although it hadn't varied in ten years. Finally he let the word be passed that he was working and did not want to see anyone from Cannery Row or anyplace else. He sat over his yellow pad, the neat pile of Suzy's sharpened pencils beside him, and in his eyes the bleak look of shock.

Suzy was at once the cause and the victim of the disintegration of the Row. It cannot be said that trouble builds character, for just as often it destroys character. But if certain character traits, mixed with certain dreams, are subjected to the fire, sometimes . . . sometimes . . .

Ella, the waitress-manager of the Golden Poppy, was no less tired at ten in the morning than at midnight. She was always tired. She not only accepted this but thought everybody was that way. She could not conceive of feet that did not hurt, of a back that did not ache, or of a cook with a good disposition. At breakfast the row of gobbling mouths ruined her appetite and she never got it back. In the slack time around ten she cleaned and mopped the moist restaurant and swept the crumbs from under the counter stools.

Joe Blaikey came in for his morning coffee.

"Just making a fresh pot. Want to wait?" Ella said.

"Sure," said Joe. "Say, Ella, you heard what happened down in Cannery Row Saturday night?"

"No. What?"

"I don't know. There was a party. I was going to it. Time I got there it was over. Nobody wants to talk about it."

"I didn't hear," said Ella. "Fight, you think?"

"Hell no. They'd talk about a fight. They love a fight. Everybody seems to feel kind of ashamed of something. Let me know if you hear anything, will you?"

"Okay. Coffee's about ready, Joe."

Suzy came in, dressed in her San Francisco suit—gray herringbone tweed, very neat and smart. She sat down on a stool.

"Hi," said the cop.

"Hi," said Suzy. "Cup of coffee."

"Just going through the grounds now. Say, that's a cute outfit," said Ella.

"Frisco," said Suzy.

"You moving out?"

"No," said Suzy, "I'm staying."

Joe said, "What happened down on the Row the other night?"

Suzy shrugged her shoulders.

"You won't talk neither, huh?"

"Nope."

"Damnedest thing I ever saw!" said Joe. "Mostly they'd break their necks to tell. Suzy, if anybody got killed you better spill it. You ever hear of that material-witness stuff?"

"Nobody got killed," said Suzy. And then, "Your name's Ella, ain't it?"

"Till now."

"Remember you said you wasn't never off shift?"

"Well, I ain't," said Ella.

"Would you give me a try? Watch me a couple weeks. Then maybe you could go to a movie."

"Sister, you come to the wrong place. This joint don't make enough profit to hire no waitress."

"I'll do it for my meals, and I don't eat much."

Joe Blaikey looked away. It was his method of paying attention. Ella said, "What's the gag, sister?"

"No gag. I want a job and I'll sling hash for my keep."

Joe turned his head back slowly. "You'd better tell—" he suggested.

"Sure I'll tell," said Suzy. "I'm going to fix myself up and I ain't going to run away to do it."

"What made up your mind?"

"That ain't none of your business. Is it against the law?"

"Happens so seldom it ought to be," said Joe.

"Come on, Ella," Suzy begged, "give me a break."

Ella asked, "What do you think, Joe?"

Joe's eyes went over Suzy's face. He dwelt for a moment on the dyed hair. He said, "You're letting your hair grow out?"

"Yeah."

"Give her a break, Ella," he said.

Ella smiled a tired smile. "In them clothes?"

"I'll go change. Take me maybe fifteen minutes. I can cook too, Ella. I'm a pretty good fry cook."

"Go change your clothes," said Ella.

Joe Blaikey waited in the street for Suzy to come back. He moved up beside her. "Don't bitch Ella up," he said gently.

"I won't."

"You look excited."

"Joe," said Suzy, "you remember once you said if I wanted to blow this town you'd lend me the dough?"

"I thought you was staying."

"I am. I wonder could you stake me not to blow town."

"How much?"

"Twenty-five bucks."

"Where you going to live?"

"I'll let you know."

Joe said, "I staked kids before. What the hell have I got to lose?"

"You'll get it back."

"I know I will," said Joe.

The boiler that for many years had rested among the mallow weeds in the vacant lot between the Bear Flag and the grocery was the first boiler the Hediondo Cannery ever had, and the Hediondo was the first cannery Monterey ever had. When it was understood that pilchards could be placed raw in cans, doused with tomato sauce or oil, sealed and then cooked in live steam, a new industry came to Monterey. Hediondo started with small capital and skimped and pioneered its way first to success and finally to oblivion. Its first boiler for producing the cooking steam was the triumphant improvisation of William Randolph, engineer, fireman, and president. The boiler itself he got for nothing. It was the whole front end of a locomotive of the Pajaro Valley and Coast Railroad. This engine, encountering a split rail one night, leaped a trestle and dived twenty feet into a mudhole. The railroad company stripped its wheels and valves, whistle and bell, and left the great cylinder standing in the mud.

William Randolph found it, hauled it to Monterey, and set it in concrete at the new Hediondo Cannery. For years it produced low-pressure steam for cooking canned fish, while its tubes blew out at intervals and were replaced.

In 1932, when the cannery was rich and expanding, the old boiler was finally abandoned in the vacant lot to save a moving bill. Old Mr. Randolph was still alive and, although retired, he still hated waste. He stripped out the tubes, leaving only the big cylinder, sixteen feet long and seven feet in diameter. The smokestack was still on it, and its firedoor, two feet wide and eighteen inches high, still swung on rusty pins.

Many people had used the boiler for temporary shelter, but Mr. and Mrs. Sam Malloy were the first permanent residents. Mr. Malloy, who was good with his hands, after stripping out the remaining tubes, added a number of little comforts.

A boiler as a home has disadvantages as well as advantages. Some people would balk at getting down on hands and knees to crawl in through the firedoor. The floor, being rounded, makes for difficulty both in walking and in arranging furniture. The third inconvenience lies in a lack of light.

The advantages of a boiler can be listed as follows: it is absolutely rainproof; it is cozy; and it has wonderful ventilation. By adjusting the damper and firedoor you can have as much draft as you like.

Under the smokestack Mr. Malloy had built a little brick fireplace for cold winter nights. In addition to all of these advantages, the boiler was fireproof, windproof, earthquakeproof, and almost bombproof. These more than balanced the lack of running water, electricity, and interior plumbing.

There are those, particularly in Carmel-by-the-Sea, who say that Suzy's choice of the boiler as a home was a symbolic retreat to the womb, and, while this may be true, it is also true that this womb had economic factors. At the Golden Poppy, Suzy had her meals free, and in the boiler she had free shelter.

Suzy took the money Joe Blaikey loaned her and went to Holman's Department Store in Pacific Grove. She bought a hammer, saw, assorted nails, two sheets of plywood, a box of pale blue kalsomine and a brush, a tube of Duco cement, a pair of pink cottage curtains with blue flowers, three sheets, two pillow cases, two towels and a washcloth, a teakettle, two cups and saucers, and a box of tea bags. At Joe's Surplus she bought a used army cot and mattress pad, bowl and pitcher and chamberpot, two army blankets, a small mirror, and a kerosene lamp. These supplies exhausted her capital, but at the end of her first week of work at the Golden Poppy, Suzy paid Joe back two dollars and a quarter out of tips.

The Row, in its shame, pretended not to see what was going on at the boiler or to hear the sound of hammering late at night. This was good manners rather than a lack of curiosity.

Fauna held out for ten days, and when she did give in to her natural nosiness she went secretly, late on a Tuesday night, when the Bear Flag was closed for lack of customers. From the window of the Ready Room, Fauna could see a little glow of light coming from the firedoor of the boiler. The smokestack put out a lazy curl of smoke that smelled of pine pitch. Fauna went silently out the front door and up through the mallow weeds.

"Suzy," she called softly.

"Who is it?"

"Me, Fauna."

"What do you want?"

"To see if you're all right."

"I'm all right."

Fauna got down on her knees and poked her head through the firedoor. The transformation was complete. The curving walls were pale blue, and the curtains were stuck to the walls with Duco cement. It was a pleasant feminine apartment. Suzy sat on her cot in the light from the little fireplace. She had built a dressing table for her mirror and bowl and pitcher, and beside it stood a fruit jar filled with lupines and poppies.

"You sure fixed it up nice," said Fauna. "Ain't you going to invite me in?"

"Come on in, but don't get stuck in the door."

"Give me a hand, will you?"

Suzy pulled and boosted her through the firedoor. "Here," she said, "sit down on the cot. I'm going to get a chair pretty soon."

"We could make you a hook rug," said Fauna. "That would look nice."

"No," said Suzy. "I want to do it myself. Would you like I should make you a cup of tea?"

"Don't mind if I do," said Fauna absently, and then, "You sure you ain't mad?"

"I ain't mad. You know, I never had no place of my own before."

"Well, you've fixed it up real nice," said Fauna. "I can lend you anything you need. You can use the bathroom over at the Bear Flag."

"They got a shower down at the Golden Poppy," said Suzy.

"Now look," Fauna said. "You got me down and my claws wedged. Don't put the boots to me."

"I ain't."

"This here's a nice cup of tea. I got to tell you one thing, Suzy. I don't care if you want to hear it or not. I been wrong quite a lot, but you're going about this wrong. Don't rub Doc's nose in it. That just makes a man mad."

"What are you talking about?"

"Well, settling here. He can't look out his window without you're in his hair." Fauna braced herself for the explosion, and it did not come.

Suzy looked at her hands. "I got real nice nails," she said. "Down at the Poppy where I got my hands in water all the time I squidge lotion on. Keeps them soft. Fauna, you told me not to run away, and I didn't. I felt like digging a hole in the ground and crawling in and I didn't, because I think what you said was right. I'm going to do it right here in sight."

"That ain't what I said."

"Don't bust in!" said Suzy. "You said about Doc. Now I'm telling you once, and you can tell it all over the Row if you want, then I won't have to tell it to nobody again. You just forget Doc. Doc ain't got nothing to do with me. He come along and I wasn't up to him—wasn't good enough for him. Now maybe it won't never happen again, but if it does—if there's a guy—I'm goddam well going to be good enough for him, inside and outside, public and private; but mostly I'm going to feel good enough. Now you got that?"

"You better watch that cussing," said Fauna.

"I don't cuss no more."

"You just—"

"Don't try to mix me up," said Suzy. "Did you get what I said?"

"Why, sure, Suzy girl! But I don't see why you won't let your friends give you a hand."

" 'Cause then it wouldn't be me done it. Then I wouldn't be no good."

"You borrowed dough from Joe Blaikey."

"Sure, from a cop. The same cop that was going to float me. He ain't a friend, he's a cop. When I get him paid back maybe he can be a friend."

"You sure make it tough on yourself."

"How else? You can't cut off a leg with a banana."

"You wasn't never no hustler, Suzy. At least you wasn't no good at it."

"I know what I was, and I know what I'm going to be."

"Doc?" Fauna asked.

"That's done, I tell you! Get it through your thick head—that's done!"

"Well, I guess I better be going," Fauna said unhappily. She put the teacup on the little dressing table, got down on her hands and knees, and crawled to the firedoor. "Give me a boost through, will you, Suzy?"

Suzy stuffed her through the opening the way you'd stuff a sausage. And then she called, "Fauna!"

Fauna put her head in through the door.

"You been the best friend I ever had. If I'm tough, it ain't at you, it's at me. I was always mad at everybody. Turns out it was me I was mad at. When I get friends with myself, maybe I can get friends with somebody without no chip."

Fauna said, "S'pose Doc come a-begging?"

"I ain't no mantrap," said Suzy. "I wouldn't have him if he come walking on his hands. You can't cure a sock in the puss with a sock in the puss. But if ever I like a guy again, and he lays it on the line, why, I'm going to have something to lay on the other side."

"I miss you, Suzy."

"I'll be back when I'm right. I love you."

"Oh, shut up!" said Fauna. And she clanged the firedoor shut.

30

A President Is Born

Of all our murky inventions, guilt is at once the most devious, the most comic, the most painful. Was it planted by the group pressure of the tribe to keep the potentially dangerous individual off balance? Is it set in the psychotissue, watered and cultivated by ductless glands? Is guilt the unconscious device by which a man cries for attention in an unperceiving world, or can it be that the final human pleasure is pain? Whatever its origin, we scream like cats in copulation, wolf-bay the moon, whip ourselves with the exquisite thorns of contempt, and generally have a hell of a good time at it.

In the pleasure and passions of guilt, Hazel should have been voted the human least likely to succeed. Guilt is a selfish pastime and Hazel had never been aware enough of himself to indulge in it. He watched life as a small boy watches a train go by—mouth open, breathing high and light, pleased, astonished, and a little confused.

Hazel had never amounted to a damn. Mack once described Hazel's education: "He done four years in grammar school and four years in reform school—and he didn't learn nothing either place."

Reform school, you see, where vice and crime are not extracurricular, failed to have any more effect on Hazel than the fourth grade had. He came out as innocent as he had gone in. Hazel didn't pay enough attention to be evil. If Mack and the boys and Doc hadn't been friends, there's no telling what might have happened to him. Hazel thought Mack was the world's greatest human, while Doc he didn't consider human at all. Sometimes he said his prayers to Doc.

But Hazel was changing. Imperceptibly he had begun to pay attention. Perhaps Fauna had planted the germ by reading Hazel's horoscope. After his first protest he never mentioned it again, which should in itself have been suspicious.

Hazel did not want to be President of the United States. If there had been any avenue of escape he would have taken it, but his horoscope closed all doors. When a man is finally boxed and he has no choice, he begins to decorate his box. So Hazel, condemned to the presidency, since he could not escape it, began to ornament it. A man can climb high on the steps of responsibility.

Hazel began to prepare himself for the time when his call should come. He read every word of a copy of *Time* magazine, then went back to the beginning and read it again. He thought about it a great deal and came to the conclusion that it was nuts—which proves that Hazel's problem had been inattention, not unintelligence.

He bought a *World Almanac* and read the lives of the Presidents, and he began to wonder what he would do if the British impressed our sailors or the "Fifty-four-Forty" issue ever came up again.

He had accepted his duty and it made him sick. Sometimes in the morning he would awaken happy in the thought that it was a bad dream. Then he would count his toes and relapse into acceptance of his fate and his duty. What made it worst of all was the loneliness. He couldn't discuss it with anyone. He was set apart and above ordinary experience. When he had offered to fight Mack it was not in anger. He was preparing to defend the weak. When he had flown in the face of his friends, and refused to be a dwarf, and insisted on being Prince Charming, Hazel was not being vain. The dignity of his position was greater than himself. He could not let his future down.

In an ordinary time one of the boys would have noticed Hazel's suffering face, the weariness, the pained nobility, and they would have given him two tablespoons of Epsom salts. But in these times all men's souls were being tried, and women's too, and a tried soul doesn't look around much.

Hazel's attempts to figure out what had happened at the masquerade were fruitless. He remembered how he had been dignified and beautiful and then all hell had broken loose. And the aftermath was horrible. The spirit of the Palace Flophouse, tested under the torques and stresses of so many years, was broken, shattered like granite, which withstands so long as the hammer blows, then suddenly disintegrates.

Mack, who considered life hardly worse than a bad cold, was sickened to death—his eyes were lackluster and his valiant soul was shot. And if Mack was that way, you can imagine what the boys were like—jellyfish washed up on an inhospitable shore.

"What happened?" Hazel asked, and eyes glanced at him and glanced away and no one had the will to explain. For several days Hazel thought it might be the bull-bitch hangover of all time, but it continued into the day of reviving thirst and there was no thirst. Hazel began to be afraid for his friends.

He sat under the cypress tree and he not only kept his mind on the subject, he actually thought about it. It was a time for greatness, and only Hazel had the strength to rise to that bright bait. When he stood up and brushed the cypress dirt from his jeans, he had completed the change. No longer was he Hazel the Innocent, Hazel the Unaware, Hazel the Dope. His shoulders squared to take the weight, and the calm beauty of strength shone from his eyes.

It was dusky in the Palace, moldy and sad. The boys lay on their beds, listless and ruined. Mack stared up at his canopy, and he was the worst of all, for there was no expression in his face. He had not crashed in flames, he was eroding away.

When Hazel sat down quietly on the side of his bed Mack didn't even take a kick at him, although his shoes were on.

Hazel said, "Mack, Mack darling, you should shake the lead out of your pants now."

Mack did not answer, but he closed his eyes and two tears squeezed out and hung there until they dried.

Hazel said gently, "Mack, you want I should kick the hell out of you?"

Mack moved his head quietly back and forth in negation.

Hazel did not hold back. He threw his trump card in, and the hell with it. "I been over to Doc's," he said. "He's setting there with a pencil in his hand. He ain't wrote nothing. He ain't done nothing. He ain't thought nothing. Get off your behind, Mack, he needs us."

Mack spoke sepulchrally. "He needs us like a mud-dauber's nest up his pants leg. Don't blame me, Hazel. I can't fight back no more. I'm down for the count."

"What's happened, Mack?"

Mack's voice was hollow. "When we done it before we wrecked his joint and busted him, but that was mere chaff."

"How do you mean, mere chaff?"

"Oh, it was things busted—glass, records, dishes, books, stuff like that. But this time we've put a knife in his belly. If you keep trying to pat a guy on the head and instead you knock his brains out, you lose confidence." He sighed and turned over and covered his face with his arms.

"You ain't got the right to give up," Hazel said.

"I got the right to do any goddam thing I want."

"Now that sounds better!"

"Or not do nothing," said Mack.

"Look, Doc got to go to La Jolla, you know that. He got to make the spring tides next week. Then, when his new microscope comes, he'll have devilfish and write his paper. We got to help him, Mack."

"Fauna says she used to manage a welterweight name of Kiss of Death Kelly. That's me—Kiss of Death Mack. Everything I touch withers like the sere and yellow leaf."

"Get up!"

"I won't," said Mack.

"Get up, I tell you!"

Mack didn't even respond.

Hazel went outside and looked around. He walked to a broken tar barrel lying in the weeds and pulled out a curved oaken stave. He went back and stood beside Mack's bed.

He judged distance and lift. He hit Mack so hard that his pants split. And only then did Hazel realize how serious it was, for Mack didn't even move. He only groaned.

Hazel fought down panic, and then he remembered his Fate— a sacrifice to Washington where he would have to eat oysters. "All right, Mack," he said softly. "I'll have to do her myself."

He turned and walked out of the door with quiet dignity.

Mack rolled up on one elbow. "Did you hear what that crazy bastard said? Oh, what the hell! Can't do no worse than I done. Mother, make my bed soon, for I'm sick to the death and I fain would lie down."

"You're already down," said Whitey No. 2.

31

The Thorny Path of Greatness

When people change direction it is a rare one who does not spend the first half of his journey looking back over his shoulder. Hazel had chosen, or had been forced to choose, a new path. He had said, "I'll have to do her myself." It had seemed easy. But, sitting under the sheltering branches of the black cypress tree, he had to admit he didn't know who or what in the hell "she" was. He thought with longing of the old time when he was a dope, when he was cared for and thought for and loved. He had paid off, of course, by accepting ridicule, but it had been a lovely time, a warm time.

Doc had said long ago, "I like to have you sit with me, Hazel. You are the well—the original well. A man can give you his deepest secrets. You don't hear or remember. And if you did, it wouldn't make any difference because you don't pay attention. Why, you're better than a well because you listen—but you don't hear. You are a priest without penalties, an analyst without diagnosis."

Those were the good days before Hazel's responsibility. But responsibility required judgment, the choosing between courses, and what was that but thought? Hazel undertook thought, but he did it secretly. No one knew. He was a little ashamed of it. In the sweet old days he would have sat down under the black cypress and then he would have reclined with his head on his arm and in less than a minute he would have been asleep. The new Hazel clasped his knees with his arms and mourned into the future. His mind climbed and slipped like an ant in the treacherous crater of an ant lion's trap. He must plan, he must judge, he must choose. No sleep came. He didn't even itch. He had to do her. But what was she? He never knew how his solution came to him. He dropped off to sleep, forehead on knees, then suddenly his muscles leaped as though under a blow. He had a sense of falling—and there was his course laid out before him. It wasn't an honorable course, but it was the only one he had. It almost amounted to treachery.

You will remember that it was Hazel's pleasant social custom to ask questions but not to listen to the answers. People expected that, depended on it. Suppose, he thought, I was to ask and then listen but not let on I'm listening. It was sneaky, but the intention was clean and the end infinitely to be desired.

He would not only listen, he would remember, and he would put all the answers together. Maybe then he would be able to think her and do her. One question would be enough, he thought. Maybe two.

Hazel was weary from his effort. He reclined, put his head on his arm, and slept the good sleep of work well done.

32

Hazel's Quest

Joe Elegant came cautiously back from his journey ready to take another one at a moment's notice. He expected reprisals for Hazel's costume, and there were no reprisals. In gratitude he made popovers at the Bear Flag three evenings in a row—and the girls didn't even know what they were eating. He wanted to know what had happened but he was afraid to ask. Thus Joe Elegant was glad when Hazel called on him in his little lean-to in the rear of the Bear Flag.

"Sit here," he said. "I'll get you a piece of cake."

While he was gone Hazel regarded the works of Henri the artist on the wall—one from the chicken-feather period and one from the later nutshell time. And he looked at the card table on which Joe Elegant worked at a portable typewriter. There was a neat pile of manuscript on the table, green paper typed with a green ribbon. A sheet of paper was in the machine. It began: "My dear Anthony West, It was sweet of you—"

Joe came back with a wedge of cake and a glass of milk for Hazel, and while Hazel munched and drank, Joe's large damp eyes bracketed him but never hit him.

"How'd it go?" he asked.

"What?"

"Why, your costume?"

"Fine, fine. Everybody was real surprised."

"I'll bet they were. Did Mack say anything?"

"He said I done fine. He almost cried."

Joe Elegant smiled with quiet malice.

Hazel asked vacuously, "Say, what would you think was the matter with Doc?"

Joe crossed his legs professionally and his fingers rippled through the green-typed green pages. "It's the whole and the part and the part is the whole," he said.

"Come again?"

"It's many things and one thing. Doc's libido is driving him one way and his conscience is pulling him another. His myth is the sea, the wind, and the tide, and he relates to it by collecting animals. He carries his treasures to his laboratory. He wants to hide them and perhaps to place the dragon Fafnir on guard."

Hazel nearly said, "He sells them," but that would have given him away as listening. "I knew a dame named Fafnir," he said. "Bertha Fafnir. Third grade. Used to do pitchers of turkeys on the blackboard Thanksgiving. Had starched underskirts, they rustled kind of."

Joe Elegant scowled faintly at the interruption. "Distill the myth and you get the symbol," he went on. "The symbol is the paper he wants to write, but that in itself has impurities, needs distillation. Why? Because it is a substitute, that's why. His symbol is false. That's why he can't write his paper. Frustration! He has taken the wrong path. And so he brings in false solutions. 'I need a microscope,' he says. 'I need to go to La Jolla for the spring tides.' He will not go to La Jolla. He will never write his paper."

"Why not?"

"Wrong symbol. We must go back to the myth, the sea. The sea is his mother. His mother is dead but she is living. He is carrying treasures from his mother's womb and trying to save them. Do you understand?"

"Sure," said Hazel listlessly.

"He needs love. He needs understanding," said Joe Elegant.

"Who don't?" Hazel asked.

"I feel that I could help him if he would let me."

"I kind of thought he'd took a shine to Suzy," said Hazel.

Joe Elegant let a shadow of distaste tighten his mouth. "That would only be a new false path, a new frustration."

Hazel observed, "Some people like one thing, some another."

"Very original!" said Joe Elegant.

It was only a few steps from Joe Elegant's lean-to through the kitchen to the Ready Room. In the Ready Room sat Becky with her feet up, reading her mail. Becky subscribed to "Pen Pals" and had a lively correspondence all over the world. The sheet of rice paper in her hands was from Japan. "Dear Pen Pal," it began, "Your interest missive receipt. How gondola the Goldy State. Japan girl do hair-kink likewise, but not using blitch. My friend, Mitzi Mitzuki very West in minded. Would try if you mailing small little container hydrogen peroxide double pressure."

"Hi!" said Hazel.

Becky laid down her letter. "Ever been to Japan?"

"Nope."

"Me neither. How's Mack?"

"Fine. Say, Becky, what would you say was the matter with Doc?"

"Love," said Becky. "Doc's aching away. Or if he ain't, he ought to be. Nice fella like that."

"He sets like he been pole-axed."

"That'll do it. Poor fella! If it was me, why, I'd go to him and I'd put my cool hand on his brow and I'd say, 'Doc—'"

The door of Fauna's room opened. "I thought I heard voices. Hello, Hazel. Ain't none of the other girls around? Becky's poorly."

"I come to ask you something," said Hazel.

"Well, come on in here. Set down. Want a snort? Is it private? I'll shut the door."

"Yes," said Hazel, and that covered all the questions.

The snort brightened his eye. "What would you say was wrong with Doc?"

"I wouldn't of said it a while ago," said Fauna, "but when he put on that tie—and then, the other night—"

"Hell, he was drunk," said Hazel. "A guy will say anything when he's drunk."

"No, he will not," said Fauna.

"You think it's Suzy?"

"Yes, sir! And if she wasn't nuts, she could go to La Jolla with him and help him work. Why, hell! She'd be in."

"He's trying to write his paper."

"He got himself all bollixed up," said Fauna. "I bet he ain't even thinking about his paper."

"He ain't thinking about nothing."

"That's what I mean. If he could stop not thinking about Suzy, why, he could start thinking about his paper. That's my opinion anyway."

"You think if she went to La Jolla—?"

"I do. But she won't go."

"He wouldn't take her," said Hazel.

"If everybody wasn't such damn fools he wouldn't get asked," said Fauna. "I don't know what we're coming to. Have one more snort?"

"I can't," said Hazel, "I got to see a guy."

It was only a coincidence that Joseph and Mary Rivas was also reading a letter when Hazel entered the grocery. Joseph and Mary was reading and cursing at the same time, cursing in obscure Spanish. The letter was from James Petrillo, and it spoke in no uncertain terms. If the threat in the letter could be carried out, it looked as though what the U.S. government could not do in keeping wetbacks out, the musicians' union could. The Patrón was in a stew. Ordinarily what he could not eliminate he joined. But Petrillo did not give him that choice. Joseph and Mary's mind strayed toward assassination.

Hazel said, "How're you?"

"Lousy!" said the Patrón.

"Ain't nobody feeling too good," Hazel observed. "Doc's setting over there like he's punch-drunk. What you think's the matter with him?"

"Christ knows!" said the Patrón. "I got troubles of my own. Funny thing," he said, "you know, last night I was coming home from Monterey, late, and there was a shadow up in the vacant lot. It moved into that bright spot the street light throws up by the boiler, and I swear to God it was Doc sneaking around up there."

"No!" said Hazel.

"I say yes." The Patrón looked over the vegetables and the piled canned goods and his eyes dwelt on the cardboard Coca-

Cola girl in a swing. "Know something?" he said speculatively. "Before the party I would have said she was just one more tramp. Then she belted loose and moved into the boiler. And then, well—it looks like Doc seen something there. Maybe Suzy's got something I missed. I been thinking I might just take a whack at her."

"You can't," said Hazel. "She's Doc's."

"Hell," said the Patrón, "dames don't belong to nobody. I might just whistle under her window."

"She ain't got no windows," said Hazel.

The Patrón smiled. Petrillo's poison was going out of him. "Yes, sir!" he said. "Maybe I missed something."

"You stay away from her," said Hazel.

Joseph and Mary drooped his eyes, and an Indian looked out for a second. Then he smiled again. "Have it your own way," he said lightly. "I hear she's got a job."

This was the Golden Poppy: long, narrow, high-ceilinged; small octagonal tile on the floor; dark wood counter with small round stools; units at intervals on the counter—jukebox slot, paper-napkin holder, salt, pepper, sugar, mustard, catsup; rear door to the kitchen with window and service shelf; cash register at the front, cigarette machine beside the door; long mirror behind the counter fronted by coffeemaker, griddle, toasters, covered cakes and pies, stacked breakfast foods, doughnuts, rack of canned soup and soup heater, fight cards, movie schedule, bus timetable.

There was nothing to be done about the Golden Poppy. It was a dour and gloomy place dedicated to good coffee and sad, soggy food. It could not compete with the gay and phony little restaurants springing up in Monterey, with their checked tablecloths, showcard murals, low ceilings, and candles in cork floats.

The Golden Poppy did not try. There were many people who preferred it to the newcomers—customers who liked cold, damp doughnuts, stringy stews, and canned soup. These diners distrusted fishnets on the walls and jokes on the menu. To them food was a necessary but solemn sacrament about which there should be no nonsense.

The rush hours were seven to eight-thirty, breakfast; eleven-thirty to one-thirty, lunch; six to eight, dinner. In between these hours there were the coffee customers, the sandwich and dough-nut people. In the evening came two rush times: at nine-thirty when the early movie let out, and at eleven-thirty when the sec-ond show broke. At twelve-thirty the Golden Poppy curled its petals, except on Saturday nights, when it stayed open until two for the early drunks.

The coming of Suzy to the Golden Poppy had a curious but reasonable effect on Ella. She had, over the years, maintained an iron interdict against weariness and pain. If she had allowed herself to realize how miserable she was she would have cut her throat.

Suzy did more than help, she took over: joked with the sales-men, whistled over the sandwich toaster, remembered that Mr. Garrigas like cream of celery soup and remembered his name too.

For a day or so Ella had watched Suzy and refused acidly when Suzy suggested that she go home and lie down for a couple of hours. Then her interdict cracked, and the crack widened. Abysmal fatigue, aching legs, and abdominal pains crept through. Ella was an exhausted woman when she came at last to admit it. Going home to lie down for an hour was first a sin, and then a luxury, and finally a drug.

Now when Suzy said after the nine-thirty rush, "Go on home and get a good night's sleep," it seemed perfectly natural. Not only could Suzy hold the fort, but her terse, professional gaiety was drawing in new customers.

At eleven-fifteen Suzy had the four Silexes filled with fresh coffee, the hamburgers between waxed paper in the icebox, the tomatoes sliced, and the sandwich bread in the drawer below the griddle. At eleven-thirty the customers came in a rush from the second show.

Suzy grew six extra hands: club sandwiches, melted cheese sandwiches, cheeseburgers, and coffee, coffee, coffee! The cash register jangled and the change appeared standing up between the tits of the rubber mat.

"How's about a date Saturday?"

"Sure! Love to."

"Is it a date?"

"Can my husband come?"

"You married?"

"I won't be if I keep that date."

"You're a swell-looking kid."

"You're kind of pretty yourself. Here's your change."

"Keep it."

"Thanks. Cheeseburger coming up. Sorry, eighty-six on the tuna fish sandwiches."

In the seconds between orders, three of her extra hands carried dishes into the soapy water, rinsed and dried them.

"Hey! Mr. Gelthain, you forgot your umbrella!"

"So I did. Thank you." That would be another quarter tip, and the quarter went into a slotted can marked "Joe."

Every morning when Joe Blaikey came in for his coffee a little pile of silver was put before him and checked in the account book. It was amazing how it added up.

At five minutes of twelve Hazel came in and waited against the wall until a stool was vacant.

"Hi, Hazel. What'll it be?"

"Cup of coffee."

"It's on the house, Hazel. How you been?"

"Okay."

Gradually the customers thinned out and then were gone. Suzy's flashing hands put the Golden Poppy to bed: scrubbed the grill, washed down the counter, wiped the necks of the catsup bottles. She looked up to see Hazel sweeping out.

"Say, what the hell are you doing?"

"I figured we're both going the same way. I'll walk with you."

"Why not?" said Suzy. "You can carry my books."

"What?"

"Just a joke."

"Ha, ha!" said Hazel seriously.

They walked down Alvarado Street, all closed up except where the bars splashed neon culture on the sidewalk. At the tip of the Presidio they stopped and leaned their elbows on the iron railing and looked at the fishing boats in the black water of the bay. They crossed the tracks, went past the Army warehouse, and entered the upper end of Cannery Row. And at last Hazel said, "You're a swell dame."

"Come again?"

"Say, what you think's the matter with Doc?"

"How would I know?"

"You sore at him?"

"How'd you like to mind your own business?"

"It's all right," said Hazel quickly. "I ain't bright. Everybody knows that."

"What's that got to do with keeping out of my hair?"

"Nobody pays no attention to me," said Hazel. He offered this as a recommendation. "Doc says I don't listen. He likes that."

They walked on in silence for a while. Then Hazel said timidly, "He done everything in the world for me. Once he went character witness for me and I ain't got no character. Once I'd of lost a foot, but he opened her up and shook powder on her and I still got her."

Suzy didn't answer. Their footsteps were loud on the pavement and echoed back from the iron fronts of dead canneries.

"Doc's in trouble," Hazel said.

Their footsteps filled the street.

"Anybody in trouble, why, they go to Doc. Nobody goes to him now he's in trouble."

Step, step, step.

"I got to help him," said Hazel. "But I ain't bright."

"What the hell do you want me to do?" said Suzy.

"Well, couldn't you go over and set with him?"

"No."

"If you was in trouble he'd help you."

"I ain't in trouble. How do you know he's in trouble?"

"I'm telling you. I thought you liked him."

"I like him all right. If he was in real trouble like if he was sick or bust his leg, I'd probably take him some soup."

"Jeeze! If he bust his leg he couldn't go to the spring tides," said Hazel.

"Well, he ain't busted his leg."

They passed Wide Ida's. Hazel asked, "You want a beer?"

"No, thanks." Then she said, "Ain't you going up to the Palace?"

"No," said Hazel, "I got to see a guy."

Suzy said, "Once, when I was a kid, I made an ashtray for my old man and old lady—"

"They like it?"

"They didn't need no ashtray."

"Didn't they smoke?"

"Yes," said Suzy. "Good night."

Hazel was approaching a state of collapse. In his whole life he had never sustained a thought for more than two minutes. Now his resources reeled under the strain of four hours of concentration. And it was not yet over. He had to make two more visits, and then he had to retire under the black cypress tree to sift his findings. So far he could see no light anywhere. His mental pictures were like those children's kaleidoscopes that change color and design as they are turned. It seemed to Hazel that a slight zizzing sound came from his brain.

It was a catty night. Big toms crept about, their heads and shoulders flattened to the ground, seeking other toms. Lady cats preened themselves in sweet innocence, unaware of what they hoped was likely to happen to them. On the rocks off Hopkins Marine Station the sea lions barked with a houndish quaver. The silver canneries were silent under the street lights. And from somewhere on the beach Cacahuete Rivas's trumpet softly mourned the "Memphis Blues."

Hazel had stopped for a moment in appreciation of the secret night. He looked up at the boiler where Suzy had gone, and into the streak of street light he saw a figure move. From the shape and posture he thought it must be the Patrón. In a way it was none of Hazel's business. He walked up the stairs and knocked on the door of Western Biological.

Doc sat on his bed regarding a heap of collecting paraphernalia: nets, buckets and jars, formaldehyde and Epsom salts and menthol, rubber boots and rubber gloves, glass plates and string. On his table stood a small new traveling aquarium with a tiny pump and motor run by two dry cells. Morosely he watched the mist of white air bubbles sift through the sea water.

"Come in," he said to Hazel. "I'm glad to see you."

"Just come to pass the time of day," said Hazel.

"Good. I'm glad. A man feels silly talking to himself, and at the same time it's private. You're the perfect answer, Hazel."

"Say, Doc, I just remembered. What's ass-astro-physic?"

"You don't really want me to tell you, do you?"

"Not very much. I just wondered. I signed up for it."

Doc shuddered. "I don't think I want to hear about that," he said.

"I brang you a pint."

"That's friendly of you. Will you join me?"

"Sure," said Hazel. "You're really going to La Jolla, huh?"

"Well, I guess I have to. That's one of the things I've been trying to figure out. I've made such a stink about it."

"Lot of people think you won't go."

"Well, that's one of the reasons I have to."

"Don't you want to?"

"I don't know," said Doc softly.

He got up from the bed and disengaged a wire from the dry cell. "No point in wasting juice," he said. "I've been tearing myself down like a Model T Ford in a backyard. Got the pieces all laid out. Still don't know why it won't run. Don't even know whether I can get it together again."

"I could help," said Hazel. "I know about Model T's."

"It might turn out you know about people too," said Doc.

Hazel looked shyly down at his feet. No one had ever accused him of knowing anything before.

Doc chuckled, "That's my good Hazel!"

"Say, Doc, what you think is the matter with you?" Hazel was appalled at his daring, but he had asked. And Doc seemed to find the question reasonable.

"God knows," he said. "Some kind of obscure self-justification, I guess. I wanted to make a contribution to learning. Maybe that was a substitution for fathering children. Right now, my contribution, even if it came off, seems kind of weak. I think maybe I've talked myself into something, and now maybe I have to do it."

Hazel groped among his bits and pieces. "Mack's sorry about what him and Fauna done. He's just sick."

"He shouldn't be," said Doc. "I'm the one who messed it up."

"You mean you would of took Suzy on?"

"I guess so. I've thought about it ever since. For a couple of days there I felt different and better than I ever have in my life. A kind of built-in pain was gone. I felt wide open."

"About Suzy?"

"I guess so. I'm supposed to have this wild free brain without conventional barriers. And what did I do? I balanced a nasty ledger. I weighed education, experience, background, even probable bloodlines. Some of the worst people I ever knew had the best of all those. Well, there it is. Saying it has made it even clearer. I guess I've thrown it away."

"Why don't you give it one more try, Doc?"

"How?"

"Why don't you take a candy bar or a bunch of carnations and knock on her door?"

"Right from the beginning, huh? Sounds kind of silly."

"Well, dames is all dames," said Hazel.

"You may have made a discovery. Have you seen her?"

"Yeah. She got that boiler fixed up real pretty. She got a job down at the Golden Poppy."

"How is she? What did she say?"

Hazel cast about again among his broken pieces. Her vehemence came back to him. "When she was a kid she made an ashtray for her papa and mama—" Hazel let it hang there because it sounded ridiculous.

"Well, what about it?"

"They didn't need no ashtray," said Hazel.

"She told you that?"

"Yep."

"Let's have a drink."

"I can't, Doc. I got one more—I mean, I got to see a guy."

"This late at night?"

"Yeah." And then Hazel confessed. "You been good to me, Doc. I wouldn't do no bad thing to you."

"Of course you wouldn't."

"But I done it."

"What!"

"Remember you always said you liked me 'cause I didn't listen?"

"Sure I remember."

Hazel's eyes were shy and ashamed. "I listened," he said.

"That's all right."

"Doc—"

"Yes?"

"Joseph and Mary's hanging around the boiler."

Hazel couldn't remember ever having been so tired. He had put his mind to unaccustomed tricks, and it was just as he had been afraid it would be. He had got nothing. He had started out hoping to find some kind of light to guide him. What he had got reminded him of Henri's painting in nutshells. He wanted to sleep a long time, perhaps never to awaken to a world in which he now felt himself a stranger. He had made a mess of it. He wondered if he would make as bad a mess in Washington.

He walked wearily through the vacant lot and up the chicken walk to the Palace Flophouse. He wanted to slip into bed in the dark and hide his failure in sleep.

Mack and the boys were waiting up for him.

"Where the hell you been?" said Mack. "We looked all over for you."

"Just walking around," said Hazel listlessly.

Mack moved and groaned. "Jesus! You hit me a crack," he said. "Damn near killed me."

"I shouldn't of did it," said Hazel. "You want I should rub it?"

"Hell no! What you been up to? When you get making plans, the sky is falling on my tail, said Henny Penny."

Whitey No. 2 asked, "Who you been with?"

"Everybody. Just walking around."

"Well, who?"

"Oh, Joe Elegant and Fauna and Suzy and Doc."

"You seen Suzy?" Mack demanded.

"Sure. Went down to the Poppy for a cup of coffee."

"Look who's buying coffee!"

"It was on the house," said Hazel.

"Well, what did she say?"

"She says in the third grade she made an ashtray."

"Oh, Jesus!" said Mack. "Did she say anything about Doc?"

"Yeah, I guess so."

"You guess so!"

"Don't ask me if you're going to be mean to me. That'll just get *me* mean."

Mack shifted painfully to his other buttock.

Hazel felt ringed with hostility. "I guess I'll go outside," he said miserably.

"Wait! What'd she say about Doc?"

"Said she didn't want no part of him, except—I'm going to go on out."

"Except what?"

"Except he got sick or bust a leg."

Mack shook his head. "Sometimes you get me thinking the way you do. God Almighty! I shouldn't of let you out alone."

"I didn't do no harm."

"I bet you didn't do no good either. I bet right now you're trying to figure out germ warfare—how to get Doc sick."

"I'm tired," said Hazel. "I just want to go to bed."

"Who's stopping you?"

Hazel didn't even take off his clothes before he went to bed, but he didn't sleep either; at least not until the dawn crept out from Salinas. His brain was blistered and his responsibility rode him with surcingle and spurs.

33

The Distant Drum

Doc sat for a long time after Hazel left him. His chest rustled with feeling and his throat was dry. His top mind looked at him—a scientist, a thinker trained, conditioned to method, to exactness. No single thing could be permitted in unless it could be measured or tasted or heard or seen. The laws of science were Doc's laws, and he sought to obey them. To break these laws was not only a sin to him but a danger, for violation would let in anarchy. He was frightened and cold.

His middle mind screamed with joy at his discomfiture. "I told you! All through the years I've told you you were fooling yourself. Let's see you get back to analysis, I dare you!"

And the low-humming mind in his entrails was busy too, aching and yet singing that the ache was necessary and good.

Middle mind had its way. Doc thought, Let's look at this. Here is a man with work to do. The girl—what is she? Let's suppose every good thing should come of a relationship with her. It still would be no good. There is no possible way for this girl and me to be successful—no way under the sun. Not only is she illiterate, but she has a violent temper. She has all of the convictions of the uninformed. She is sure of things she has not investigated, not only sure for herself, but sure for everyone. In two months she will become a prude. Then where will freedom go? Your thinking will be like tennis against a bad player. Let's stop this nonsense! Forget it! You can't have it and you don't want it.

Middle mind hooted, "You can't *not* have it too. Whatever happens, you've got her. Take a feel of your pulse, listen to your pounding heart. Why? You just heard the iron door of the boiler clang, that's why. You haven't even thought what that means yet, but you've got a pain in your gut because of that clang and because it's three-thirteen in the morning."

Low mind said, "Nothing's bad. It's all part of one thing—the good and bad. Do you know any man and woman—no matter how close—who don't have good and bad? Let me out! Or, by God, I'll set my claws in you and I'll tear at you for all your life! Let me out, I say! Feel this, this red burning? That's rage. Will you let it out or will it fester here until it makes you sick and crazy? Look at the time. You heard that iron door."

Doc looked at his watch—3:17. "Why that son-of-a-bitch!" he said aloud. He snapped off his light and went to the window and looked out toward the strip of light the street lamp threw on the vacant lot. Then he opened his front door and crept down the stairs. Crossing the street, he followed a broad shadow and hid in it.

The Patrón was sitting on a big rusty pipe trying to work out a puzzle. He had it laid out and the pieces didn't make sense. Here was himself, young, good-looking, snappy dresser, and making dough. And here was a dame, a dime-a-dozen dame, living in a boiler, working for her keep. The Patrón knew methods too, and, if not scientific, they had served him well enough so that he could depend on them. You sweet talk, you promise, you offer, and in reserve you always hold force. Every dame needs a little force. He felt the swelling knuckles of his right hand. This dame was nuts. She didn't listen to his pitch, and when he brought up force she slammed the iron door and damn near took his fingers off. He was going to lose the nails of all four fingers. The dirty bitch! Thus, musing bitterly, he did not hear Doc's approach.

Doc's fingers locked in the collar of the Patrón's striped shirt and yanked him to his feet. By reflex the Patrón lashed out with his foot and kicked Doc's legs from under him. The two fell together and rolled in the mallow weeds. Joseph and Mary tried for the groin with his knee, while Doc's delicate strong fingers laced around the throat. The Patrón felt the thumbs seeking the hollow below his Adam's apple. He tore at the white face with his fingers and Doc's thumbs went home. Flaring lights whirled in the Patrón's eyes and his brain turned red. He knew that in two seconds his thorax would collapse under the thumbs and he would be dead. He had seen it happen. He knew it and, so knowing, he went limp and in sweating terror felt the thumbs relax.

The Patrón lay still, and his sickened mind figured the chances—the groin again or butt of head to chin? But if he missed the terrible thumbs would come again. He was weak and afraid—afraid even to speak for fear the wrong word might draw the seeking thumbs. "Doc," he whispered, "I give up. You got me."

"Go near that girl again and I'll tear your throat out," Doc whispered back.

"I won't. I swear to God I won't."

In the grocery under the seven-watt light, the Patrón tried to get the cork out of a pint with his mashed fingers but had to pass the bottle to Doc.

Doc felt the sickness that follows rage—and he also felt silly. He took a gulp of whisky and passed the bottle over the counter. Joseph and Mary drank and then bent over, coughing and spluttering. Doc had to run around the counter to beat him on the back. When he could speak, Joseph and Mary looked at Doc with wonder.

"I can't understand it," he said. "Where'd you learn that trick? What'd you want to do it for? You might of killed me."

"I guess I wanted to," said Doc. "I must have wanted to." He laughed embarrassedly. "I thought you were making a pass at Suzy."

"I was," said Joseph and Mary. "Jesus, Doc, I didn't know you was that way with her."

"I'm not," said Doc. "Give me a drink."

"You wasn't playing tiddlywinks," said Joseph and Mary. "Now don't get excited. She give me the bum's rush. Hell, she damn near took off my fingers with that door. You ain't got any competition from me, Doc. She's all yours."

"She won't even see me," said Doc.

"Won't? What in hell *is* the matter with her?"

"Who knows?"

They rested their elbows on the counter and faced each other.

"Beats me," said Joseph and Mary. "What you going to do?"

Doc smiled. "Hazel said take her flowers and a candy bar."

"He might have something there. I can't figure her." Gingerly the Patrón let a little whisky dribble down his throat and winced as it passed the bruised place. "I guess she's just nuts," he said. "And if she's nuts, a guy's got to do nuts things. You don't think you could say the hell with her?"

"I have, over and over."

"Don't do no good?"

"Not a bit. I know it's damn foolishness, but there it is."

"I knew guys like that. There ain't nothing to do about it, I guess." His eyes sharpened. "I remember something," he said. "When I was talking to her through that damn firedoor tonight she says, 'When I find a guy that's up to his eyes I'll dive in,' she says. And I says, 'For Doc?' 'Hell no!' she says. 'He's sliced like package bacon.'"

"I guess she's right," said Doc.

"That ain't what I was thinking. Look, Doc, when you had the hooks in me, if I'd went on—well, would you of?"

"I guess so. I can hardly believe it of myself, but I guess I would have. I never did anything like that before. Why?"

"Well, I just thought—a guy that'll do a killing with his hands ain't sliced too thin. Let's finish the pint, Doc, and then I'll help you."

"Help me what?"

"Flowers," said Joseph and Mary. "We got an hour before daylight. Up above Lighthouse Avenue there's front yards just lousy with flowers."

34

The Deep-Dish Set-Down

Joe Elegant was only the cook at the Bear Flag, not the bouncer, with the result that his services were never required late at night. He retired early and set his alarm clock for four. This gave him three or four hours every morning over his portable to tap out green letters on green paper.

The book was going well. His hero had been born in a state of shock and nothing subsequent had reassured him. When a symbol wasn't slapping him in the mouth, a myth was kicking his feet out from under him. It was a book of moods, of dank rooms with cryptic wallpaper, of pale odors, of decaying dreams. There wasn't a character in the whole of *The Pi Root of Oedipus* who wouldn't have made the observation ward. The hero had elderly aunts beside whom the Marquis de Sade was an altar boy. The pile of green manuscript was three inches thick, and Joe Elegant was beginning to plan his photograph for the back of the dust cover: open collar, he thought, and a small, wry smile, and one hand relaxed in front of him with an open poison ring on the third finger. He knew which reviewers he could depend on and why. He typed: "A pool scummed with Azolla. In the open water in the middle of the pond a dead fish floated belly up . . ."

Joe Elegant sighed, leaned back, and scratched his stomach. He yawned, went into the Bear Flag's kitchen, and started a pot of coffee. While it was heating he walked out into a glorious morning. The pelicans were drumming in for a run of tom cod, and little pink Kleenex clouds hung over the bay. Joe saw the flowers in front of the boiler door and moved over to inspect them—a huge bouquet of tulips, early roses, jonquils, and iris.

They might have been anyone's offering, except that their stems were in a museum jar.

Joe Elegant's life had not been in danger since the engagement and raffle party, but he hadn't felt much friendliness in Cannery Row either. He carried his news into the Bear Flag and served it to Fauna on a tray along with her coffee and crullers. By eight o'clock the news was in the Palace Flophouse, and the early men were ingesting it with their whisky sours at the La Ida.

The best seats were in the Ready Room with its windows overlooking the vacant lot. Mack was there behind a drape, munching Fauna's crullers. The girls were there in their best kimonos. Becky had put on her mules with the ostrich feathers. At eight-thirty the audience heard the boiler door screech and shushed one another.

Suzy, on her hands and knees, poked her head out of the firedoor and rammed her nose into the giant floral tribute. For a long moment she stared at the flowers, and then she reached out and dragged them inside. The iron door closed after her.

At nine o'clock Suzy re-emerged and walked rapidly toward Monterey. At nine-thirty she was back. She went into the boiler and in a moment came out, pushing her suitcase ahead of her. The audience was filled with dismay, but only for a moment. Suzy climbed the steps and rang the bell at the Bear Flag. Fauna chased the girls to their rooms and Mack out the back way before she answered the door.

Suzy said, "You told me I could use your bathroom."

"Help yourself," said Fauna.

In an hour, when the splashing had ceased, Fauna knocked on the bathroom door. "Want a little toilet water, honey?"

"Thanks," said Suzy.

In a few minutes she emerged, scrubbed and shining.

"Like a cup of coffee?" Fauna asked.

"Wish I could," said Suzy. "I got to run. Thanks for the bath. There ain't nothing like a good deep-dish set-down bath."

Fauna, from behind a drape, watched her crawl back into the boiler.

In her office Fauna scribbled a note and sent it by Joe Elegant to Western Biological. It read: "She ain't going to work today."

35

Il n'y a pas de mouches sur la grandmère

Doc laid his best clothes out on his cot. There were pale acid spots on the washed khaki trousers, the white shirt was yellow with age, and he noticed for the first time that his old tweed jacket was frayed through at both elbows. The tie he had worn to the dinner at Sonny Boy's was spotted. He found a black army tie in the bottom of his suitcase. For the first time in his life he was dissatisfied with his clothing. It was silly to feel serious about it, but there was no doubt that he was serious. For a time he sat down and regarded his wardrobe and his life, and he found them both ridiculous. And not less ridiculous was the quaking certainty that he was frightened.

He spoke aloud to the rattlesnakes, and they ran out their forked tongues to listen.

"You are looking at a fool," he said. "I am a reasonable man, a comparatively intelligent man—IQ one hundred and eighty-two, University of Chicago, Master's and Ph.D. An informed man in his own field and not ignorant in some other fields. Regard this man!" he said. "He is about to pay a formal call on a girl in a boiler. He has a half-pound box of chocolates for her. This man is scared stiff. Why? I'll tell you why. He is afraid this girl will not approve of him. He is terrified of her. He knows this is funny, but he cannot laugh at it."

The eyes of the snakes looked dustily at him—or seemed to.

Doc went on, "Let me put it this way: there is nothing I can do. They say of an amputee that he remembers his leg. Well, I remember this girl. I am not whole without her. I am not alive without her. When she was with me I was more alive than I have ever been, and not only when she was pleasant either. Even when we were fighting I was whole. At the time I didn't realize how important it was, but I do now. I am not a dope. I know that if I should win her I'll have many horrible times. Over and over, I'll wish I'd never seen her. But I also know that if I fail I'll never be a whole man. I'll live a gray half-life, and I'll mourn for my lost girl every hour of the rest of my life. As thoughtful reptiles you will wonder, 'Why not wait? Look further! There are better fish in the sea!' But you are not involved. Let me tell you that to me not only are there no better fish, there are no other fish in the sea at all. The sea is lonely without this fish. Put that in your pipe and smoke it!"

He took off his clothes and had a shower and scrubbed himself until his skin was soap-burned and red. He brushed his teeth until his gums bled. His hands were frayed with formalin, but he gouged at his discolored nails just the same, and he brushed at his overgrown hair and he shaved so close that his face was on fire. At last he was ready—and still he looked for things to do, to put off his departure.

His stomach was crowding up against his chest, forcing him to breathe shallowly. I should take a big slug of whisky, he thought. But it would be on my breath and she would know why I'd taken it. I wonder if she's frightened too? You never know. Women can conceal these things better than men. Oh God, what a fool I am! I can't go this way. I'm falling to pieces. My voice would tremble. Why, the little—no, don't do that. You can't build your courage by running her down. You're going to her, not she to you. Why do I say "you" when it is "I"? Am I afraid of "I"?

And then he knew what to do. He went to his records and he found the *Art of the Fugue*. If I can't get courage from his greatness, he thought, I might as well give up. He sat unmoving while Bach built a world and peopled it and organized it and finally fought his world and was destroyed by it. And when the music stopped, as the man had stopped when death came to him, stopped in the middle of a phrase, Doc had his courage back. "Bach fought savagely," he said. "He was not defeated. If he had lived he would have gone on fighting the impossible fight."

Doc cried to no one, "Give me a little time! I want to think. What did Bach have that I am hungry for to the point of starvation? Wasn't it gallantry? And isn't gallantry the great art of the soul? Is there any more noble quality in the human than gallantry?" He stopped and then suddenly he seemed to be wracked with inner tears. "Why didn't I know before?" he asked. "I, who admire it so, didn't even recognize it when I saw it. Old Bach had his talent and his family and his friends. Everyone has something. And what has Suzy got? Absolutely nothing in the world but guts. She's taken on an atomic world with a slingshot, and, by God, she's going to win! If she doesn't win there's no point in living anymore.

"What do I mean, win?" Doc asked himself. "I know. If you are not defeated, you win."

Then he stabbed himself in vengeance for having run Suzy down. "I know what I'm doing. In the face of my own defeat I'm warming myself at her gallantry. Let me face this clearly, please! I need her to save myself. I can be whole only with Suzy."

He stood up and he did not feel silly anymore and his mission was not ridiculous. "So long," he said to the rattlesnakes. "Wish me luck!" He took his box of candy and went jauntily down the steps of Western Biological. Crossing the street, he knew he was being observed from every window from which he was visible, and he didn't care. He waved a salute to his unseen audience.

Going through the vacant lot among the mallow weeds, he thought, How do you knock on an iron door? He stooped and picked a rusty tenpenny nail from the ground and he arrived almost gaily at the boiler and tapped a little drumbeat on the iron wall. The firedoor was slightly ajar.

Suzy's voice sounded with a metallic ring. "Who is it?"

"It's I," said Doc. "Or me—somebody like that."

The firedoor opened and Suzy looked out. "Thanks for the flowers," she said.

"I brought you another present."

She looked at the candy box in his hand. Being on her hands and knees, she had to twist her neck to look up at him. Doc couldn't tell whether there was suspicion and doubt on her face or only strained muscles from her position.

"Candy?" she asked.

"Yes."

"I don't—" she began, and then Fauna's words crowded in on her with short punches. "What the hell," she said. "Thanks."

Doc was losing his poise. Suzy had straightened her neck and from her position she couldn't see above his knees. Doc tried for lightness again, and he sounded clumsy to himself. "This is a formal call," he said. "Aren't you going to ask me in?"

"Do you think you can get in?"

"I can try."

"There ain't much room inside."

Doc remained silent.

"Oh, for God's sakes come on in!" said Suzy. She backed her head out of the opening.

Doc got down on his hands and knees. He threw the candy box through the firedoor, then crawled through the opening. He thought with amusement, A man who can do this with dignity need never again fear anything, and at that moment his trouser cuff caught on the door and pulled it closed against his ankle. He was all inside except one foot and he could not free himself. "I seem to be hung up," he said.

"Hold it," said Suzy. She straddled him and worked the cuff loose from the door corner. "I think you tore your pants," she said as she backed off over his shoulders. "Maybe I can mend 'em for you."

Doc's eyes were getting used to the dim interior. A little light came in from the smokestack and met a little more that entered from the firedoor.

"It's hard to see at first," said Suzy. "I got a lamp here. Wait, I'll light it up."

"No need," said Doc. He could see now and something in him collapsed with pity at the pretension of the curtains, the painted walls, and the home-built dressing table with its mirror and bottles. My God, what a brave thing is the human! he thought. And then Suzy brought his rising compassion crashing down.

"There's a welder eats at the Poppy. Know what he's going to do first any day he can? Bring his torch and cut windows in the sides."

Her voice echoed with enthusiasm. "I'll put in little window frames and some flower boxes with red geraniums," she said. " 'Course, I'll have to paint the outside then, white, I think, with green trim. Maybe a trellis like in front. I got a nice hand with roses."

Then she was silent. Constraint and formality sifted in and filled the boiler.

Doc thought in wonder, It's not a boiler at all. Somehow she has managed to make a home of this. He said, "You've done a wonderful job here."

"Thanks."

He spoke his thought. "It's a real home."

"It's comfortable," she said. "I never had no room of my own."

"Well, you have now."

"Sometimes I set in here and think how they'd have to blast to get me out if I didn't want to come."

Doc gathered his courage. "Suzy, I'm sorry for what happened."

"I don't want to talk about it. It wasn't none of your fault."

"Yes, it was."

"I don't think so," she said with finality.

"I would do anything to——"

"Look, Doc," she said, "you won't let it alone, so maybe I got to rub your nose in it a little. It wasn't no fault of yours, but it sure as hell give me a lesson. I had myself a bawl and now it's done. There ain't nothing for you to do. I don't need nothing. Anybody's sorry for me, they're wasting their time. I ain't never had it so good in my life. Got that? Well, don't forget it! There ain't nothing for you nor nobody to do 'cause I'm doing it all myself. If you can get that through your knocker, okay. If you can't, you better take a powder."

He said, "What a conceited fool I've been!"

Then silence hung in the boiler. Suzy broke it when she felt that his nose was sufficiently rubbed in it.

"Know what?" she said brightly. "They got a night class, typing, at the high school. I signed up. Next Saturday I get a rent typewriter. I can learn."

"I'll bet you can too. Maybe you'll type my paper for me."

"You're going to write it after all?"

"I've got to, Suzy. It's all I have. I'm a dead duck without it. I'm going to La Jolla Saturday for the spring tides. I'm glad. Are you?"

"Why not?" she asked. "I don't like to see nobody kicked in the face." She drew up formality like a coverlet. "You want I should make you a nice cup of tea? I got a Sterno stove."

"I'd like it."

She had the situation in hand now, and she talked on easily while she lighted the stove and put her little teakettle on to boil.

"I'm making good tips down at the Poppy," she said. "Paid off Joe Blaikey in two weeks. Ella's thinking about taking a week's vacation. She ain't never had a vacation. Hell, I can run the joint easy. 'Scuse that 'hell.' I don't hardly never cuss no more."

"You're doing fine," said Doc. "Could you tell me, without rubbing my nose in it, what you want in a man? Might help me—another time."

"Tea's ready," said Suzy. She passed him the steaming cup. "Leave it steep a little longer," she said. "Sugar's in the cup on the dressing table."

When he was stirring the sugar in she said, "If I thought it wasn't a pitch you was making I'd tell you."

"I don't think it's a pitch."

"Okay then. Maybe what I want ain't anywhere in the world, but I want it, so I think there is such a thing. I want a guy that's wide open. I want him to be a real guy, maybe even a tough guy, but I want a window in him. He can have his dukes up every other place but not with me. And he got to need the hell out of me. He got to be the kind of guy that if he ain't got me he ain't got nothing. And brother, that guy's going to have something!"

"Except for toughness, you're kind of describing me," said Doc.

"You keep out of this! You told me and I was too dumb to listen. You like what you got. You told me straight. I'd spoil it. Took me a long time to wise up, but I sure wised up."

"Maybe what I said wasn't true."

"When you said it with your face it was true all right."

Doc felt beaten. There was no anger in her tone, nothing but acceptance, together with an undertone of excitement. That was it, excitement, almost amounting to gaiety.

He said, "You know, Suzy, you sound happy."

"I am," said Suzy. "And you know who done it for me?"

"Who?"

"Fauna. That's a hunk of dame! She made me proud, and I ain't never been proud before in my life."

"How did she do it?" Doc asked. "I need some of that myself."

"She told me, and made me say it—'There ain't nothing in the world like Suzy'—and she says Suzy is a good thing. And goddam it, it's true! Now let's knock it off, huh?"

"Okay," said Doc. "I guess I ought to be going."

"Yeah," said Suzy, "I got to go to work. Say, remember that guy you told me about that lived out where we went that night?"

"The seer? Sure, what about him?"

"Joe Blaikey had to pick him up."

"What for?"

"Stealing. From the Safeway store. Joe hated to do it."

"I'll see what I can do. So long, Suzy."

"You ain't mad?"

"No, Suzy, but I'm sorry."

"So'm I. But hell, you can't have everything. So long, Doc. Hope you do good at La Jolla."

When Doc crossed the street this time he hoped no one was watching. He went into the laboratory, walked to his cot, and lay down. He was sick with loss. He couldn't think. Only one thing was sure: he had to go to La Jolla. If he didn't he would die, because there would be nothing left in him to believe in, even to defend. He squinched his eyes closed and looked at the bright points of light swimming on his retinas.

There were footsteps on his porch and the snakes whirred their rattles but not violently.

Hazel opened the door and looked in. He saw Doc's expression and the hope died out of him.

"No soap?" he asked.

"No soap," said Doc.

"There got to be some way."

"There isn't," said Doc.

"Anything I can do?"

"No. Yes, there is too. You know Joe Blaikey?"

"The cop? Sure."

"Well, he picked up a man in the sand dunes. Find Joe and tell him I'm interested in the man. Tell him to be nice to him. I'll be down to see him as soon as I can. Tell Joe the man is harmless." Doc rolled on his side and dug in his pocket. "Here's two dollars. Ask Joe to let you see the man and give him—no, stop at the Safeway and buy a dozen candy bars and take them to the seer and then give him the change."

"Seer?"

"That's the man's name," said Doc wearily.

"I'll do her right now," Hazel said proudly. He went out at a dogtrot.

Doc was arranging himself comfortably in his misery again when there was a knock on the door.

"Come in," he cried.

There was no answer but a second knock and a wild buzzing from the snakes.

"Oh Christ!" said Doc. "I hope not schoolchildren on a culture tour."

It was a telegram, a long one, collect. It said:

EUREKA! GREEK WORD MEANING I HAVE FOUND IT. YOU ARE NOW AN INSTITUTION. HAVE SET UP CEPHALO-POD RESEARCH SECTION AT CALIFORNIA INSTITUTE OF TECHNOLOGY. YOU ARE IN CHARGE. SIX THOUSAND A YEAR AND EXPENSES. GET TO WORK ON YOUR DEV-ILFISH. AM MAKING ARRANGEMENTS FOR YOU TO READ PAPER IN CALIFORNIA ACADEMY SCIENCES AT END OF YEAR. ALL CLEARLY DEDUCTIBLE. CONGRATU-

LATIONS. WISH I COULD HEAR YOUR WORDS WHEN
YOU HAVE TO PAY FOR THIS WIRE.

Doc laid the telegram beside him on the cot. "The son-of-
a-bitch," he said.

36

Lama Sabachthani?

Hazel sat on the end of the steel cot in the Monterey jail and looked with interest at the seer.

"Open up one of them Baby Ruths," he said. "If you're a friend of Doc's, can't nothing bad happen to you."

"I don't know him," said the seer.

"Well, he knows you. That's your good luck."

"I don't know any doctors."

"He ain't that kind. He's a doctor of bugs and stuff like that."

"Oh yes, I do remember. I gave him dinner."

"And he give you candy bars."

"I probably won't eat them."

"Why, for Chrissake, not?"

"Tell my friend Doc that greed poisoned me. I love candy bars. I stole only one at a time and eased my conscience of a little crime. But yesterday an appetite like a whip overcame me. I stole three. The manager of the Safeway says he knew I was stealing one at a time. He let it go. But when I took three he couldn't let it pass. I don't blame him. Who knows what I would have done next? Some other appetite might have driven me. I'll punish myself by smelling these bars and not eating them."

"I think you're nuts!" said Hazel.

"I guess so. I have no basis of comparison so I don't know how other people feel."

"You talk a little like Doc," said Hazel. "I don't get none of it."

"How is he?"

"Not too hot. He got troubles."

"Yes, I could see that. I remember now. He wore loneliness like a shroud. I was afraid for him."

"Jesus, you do talk like him! He got dame trouble."

"That was bound to be. When a man is cold he looks for warmth. When he is lonely there's only one cure. Why doesn't he take the woman?"

"She won't have him unless."

"I see. Sometimes they're that way."

"Who?"

"Women. What do you mean, unless?"

Hazel looked at the seer with level penetrating eyes. This man talked like Doc. Maybe he could help. But with this thought there came also caution.

"I'd like to ask you something," Hazel said.

"What?"

"Well, this ain't none of it true. It's a kind of a—a whatcha-macallit—"

"Hypothetical question?"

"I guess so."

"S'pose there's a guy and he's in trouble."

"Yes?"

"Well, he can't get out of it. But he got a friend maybe he don't know about."

"That's you," said the seer.

"No it ain't! It's some other guy. I forget his name." He hurried on. "Well, s'pose the guy's in trouble and there's one way he can get out but he can't do it. You think his friend ought to do it?"

"Certainly."

"Even if it hurt like hell?"

"Certainly."

"Even if it might maybe not work?"

"Certainly. I don't know what the situation is with your Doc, but I know how it should be with you. If you love him you must do anything to help him—anything. Even kill him to save him incurable pain. This is the highest and most terrible duty of friendship. I gather that what you must do is violent. You must first make sure it can be successful, and you must, second, make sure within yourself that you know you will be punished. It is quite possible that even if you are successful your friend will never speak to you again. That takes a lot of love—maybe the greatest love. Make sure you love him that much."

Hazel caught his breath, "Hell, there ain't no such guy. It's hypa—it's malarky, a kind of a riddle."

"I guess you do love him that much," the seer said.

No one knows how greatness comes to a man. It may lie in his blackness, sleeping, or it may lance into him like those driven fiery particles from outer space. These things, however, are known about greatness: need gives it life and puts it in action; it never comes without pain; it leaves a man changed, chastened, and exalted at the same time—he can never return to simplicity.

Under the black cypress tree Hazel writhed on the ground. From between his clenched teeth came little whimpers. As the night drew on and the moon went down, leaving blackness, so desolation fell on Hazel, so that he cried out against the agony of his greatness as that Other did, feeling forsaken.

Hour after hour the struggle went on, and only about three o'clock in the morning was Hazel saturated. Then he accepted it as he had accepted the poisoned presidency of the United States. He was calm, for there was no escape. If anyone had seen him it would have been a dull man who did not find him beautiful.

Hazel picked his chosen instrument from the ground—an indoor-ball bat. He crept like a night-colored cat out of the black shadow of the cypress tree.

In less than three minutes he returned. He lay on his stomach under the tree and wept.

Little Chapter

Dr. Horace Dormody hated night calls, like everybody else, but Doc was his friend and he responded to the frenzied voice on the telephone. In the lab he looked at Doc's white face and then at his right arm.

"It's broken all right. I don't know how badly. Think you could get to my car? I want to X-ray."

And later he said, "Well, that's that. It's clean and it will take time. Now, tell me your cock-and-bull story again."

"I was asleep," said Doc. "Only thing I can think is that I must have turned over and it was caught between the cot and the wall."

"You mean you weren't in a fight?"

"I tell you I was asleep. What are you grinning about? What's so funny?"

Dr. Horace said, "Have it your own way. It's none of my business—unless the other fellow shows up. The tissue over the break is smashed. It looks as though it's been hit with a club."

"I can't have it!" Doc cried. "I've got to go to La Jolla tomorrow for the spring tides!"

"And turn over rocks?"

"Sure."

"Try and do it," said Dr. Horace. "Is the cast getting hot?"

"Yes," said Doc despondently.

Hooptedoodle (2), or The Pacific Grove Butterfly Festival

When things get really bad there are some who seek out others who have it worse, for consolation. It is hard to see how this works but it seems to. You balance your trouble against another's, and if yours is lighter you feel better.

You would say the situation in Cannery Row was just about hopeless. Consider, then, the plight of the town of Pacific Grove, and you will understand why the lights burned all night in the Masonic Hall and why there was talk of getting rid of the city government. It wasn't a small thing. The whole town was involved. The butterflies had not arrived.

Pacific Grove benefits by one of those happy accidents of nature that gladden the heart, excite the imagination, and instruct the young.

On a certain day in the shouting springtime great clouds of orangy Monarch butterflies, like twinkling aery fields of flowers, sail high in the air on a majestic pilgrimage across Monterey Bay and land in the outskirts of Pacific Grove in the pine woods. The butterflies know exactly where they are going. In their millions they land on several pine trees—always the same trees. There they suck the thick resinous juice which oozes from the twigs, and they get cockeyed. The first comers suck their fill and then fall drunken to the ground, where they lie like a golden carpet, waving their inebriate legs in the air and giving off butterfly shouts of celebration, while their places on the twigs are taken by new, thirsty millions. After about a week of binge the butterflies sober up and fly away, but not in clouds: they face their Monday morning singly or in pairs.

For a long time Pacific Grove didn't know what it had. Then

gradually it was remarked that an increasing number of tourists were drawn to see the butterflies. Where there are tourists there is money, and it is a sin to let it drift away. Pacific Grove had a gravy train right in its lap. And the butterflies came free. It is only natural that the Great Butterfly Festival evolved, and where there is a festival there is bound to be a pageant.

There was ointment trouble at first. Pacific Grove is not only a dry town, but ardently dry. The sale of various tonics of good alcoholic content is the highest in the state, but there is no liquor. The fact that the visiting butterflies came to the dry oasis to get drunk seemed a little unfair, but the town solved this, first, by ignoring it, and then, by hotly denying it. The Butterfly Pageant explains the whole thing: There was once a butterfly princess (sung by Miss Graves), and she wandered away and was lost. Somehow a bunch of Indians (citizens in long brown underwear) got in it. I forget how. Anyway, the loyal subjects searched and searched and at last they found their princess and in their millions came to rescue her. (When they lie flat on their backs their legs are waving greetings to their queen.) It all works out very nicely. The pageant is in the ballpark and tourists can buy butterflies made out of every conceivable material from pinecones to platinum. The town makes a very nice thing of it. Why, the symbol of Pacific Grove on its advertising is the Monarch butterfly.

In all history there has been only one slipup. In 1924, I think it was, the butterflies did not come, and the frantic town was forced to print hundreds of thousands of paper butterflies in two colors and spread them all over. Today a wise city government keeps a huge supply of paper Monarchs on hand in case tragedy should strike again.

Now the time of the arrival is set, give one or two days in either direction. The pageant has been practicing for months, the Indians are trained, the prince has his tights out of mothballs, and the princess flowers toward coloratura luxury.

Perhaps it was an omen. Two days before the insects were due, Miss Graves lost her voice. She was a nice young woman, rather pretty and rather tired. She taught fourth grade, which is enough to tire anyone. Sprays and injections had no effect. Perhaps it was psychosomatic pressure that closed her throat and bottled up all but a dry squawk. Her eyes were feverish with despondency.

And then the days went by and the butterflies did not arrive. At first there was panic in Pacific Grove, and then a blind anger set in and the citizens looked about for someone to blame: The city government was a pushover. It was time for a change. Storekeepers whose bookkeeping was shaky blamed it on the mayor. Moving-picture attendance had fallen off. The city council took the rap for that. The matter became a growl, and the growl a roar: "Turn the rascals out!"

Then there was a hotel fire in King City, sixty miles away, and guess who came boiling out with an overcoat and a blonde? Mayor Cristy of Pacific Grove didn't even trouble to resign. He left town, and just as well. There was talk of tar and feathers. He must have heard. The town hadn't been so upset since the Great Roque War.

The religious block blamed the whole thing on sin without going into details. The cynics wanted to throw the whole council out, together with the chief of police and the water commissioner. More solid citizens placed the blame where it belonged, on Roosevelt-Truman socialism. And the butterflies did not come.

Then the first grade had its scandal. William Taylor 4th brought his crayons home wrapped in the dust cover of the Kinsey report. On being confronted, he panicked and said he got it from the teacher, Miss Bucke. She was questioned, and it developed that her father had signed a petition for the release of Eugene V. Debs in 1918. It had got so nobody could trust anybody.

And Miss Graves went on croaking.

And the butterflies did not come.

So you see, the trouble on Cannery Row wasn't as horrible as you thought.

Sweet Thursday Revisited

Again it was a Sweet Thursday in the spring. The sun took a leap toward summer and loosed the furled petals of the golden poppies. Before noon you could smell the spice of blue lupines from the fields around Fort Ord.

It was a sweet day for all manner of rattlesnakes. On the parade ground a jackrabbit, crazy with spring, strolled in March Hare madness across the rifle range and drew joyous fire from two companies before he skidded to safety behind a sand dune. That jackrabbit's moment of grandeur cost the government eight hundred and ninety dollars and gladdened the hearts of one hell of a lot of soldiers.

Miss Graves awakened breathless with expectancy. She sang a scale in half-tones and found that her voice was back and all was well with the world. And she was right. At eleven o'clock the Monarch butterflies came boiling in from across the bay and landed in their millions on the pine trees, where they sucked the thick sweet juice and got cockeyed. The butterfly committee met in emergency session in the firehouse and got out the crowns of fairies and the long brown underwear of Indians. The mayor pro tem of Pacific Grove wrote a proclamation for the evening paper.

The tide was very low that morning, preparing for the spring tides, and the warm sun dried the seaweed so that billions of flies came on excursion to feed.

People felt good. Judge Albertson discharged the seer on the recommendation of the Safeway manager.

Dr. Horace Dormody whistled through his mask over an appendectomy and told a political joke to the anesthetist, but he didn't mention Doc's broken arm. A patient's problems, no matter how funny, were sacred to Dr. Horace. But he couldn't help chuckling discreetly to himself now and then.

How did the word spread about Doc's arm? Who knows? Fauna heard it with her crullers. Alice, Mabel, and Becky got it with their orange juice. The Patrón heard it from Cacahuete, who thereupon rushed to the beach and played three loud and uninhibited choruses of "Sweet Georgia Brown," using six changes of key.

Wide Ida was siphoning Pine Canyon whisky into Old Crow bottles when she heard it.

Mack and the boys had the news early, and it gave them something pressing to do.

Suzy opened up the Poppy that morning. The counter was crowded with breakfasters who dawdled over coffee. It was well into the morning before Suzy heard that Doc had broken his arm. And then she couldn't do anything about it because Ella was getting a permanent. But after she heard it some mid-morning customers got curious service from a Suzy who looked blankly over their heads when they spoke to her. She called Mr. MacMinimin Mr. Gross, and she called Mr. Gross "you" and served his eggs straight up which sickened him.

Mack was first on the scene. He didn't even put on his shoes. He regarded the new cast, which still hadn't cooled off, and listened to the only explanation Doc could think of—that he had got his arm caught between the cot and the wall.

"What you going to do?" Mack asked.

"I don't know. I have to get south, I have to!"

Mack was about to make an offer when a thought came to him that made him say, "Maybe something'll turn up." He bolted for the Palace Flophouse.

Once there, he went to Hazel's bed and found it pristine and unwrinkled.

"He ain't been in," said Whitey No. 1.

"Well, what do you think of that?" Mack said with admiration. "Why, the sweet son-of-a-bitch!"

Mack went out to the cypress tree and crawled under its low hanging limbs, and he dragged Hazel out the way you'd drag a puppy from under a bed and half carried him up to the Palace Flophouse.

Hazel was far gone in emotional fatigue. "I had to," he said hopelessly.

"Anybody seen Suzy?" Mack asked.

"I seen her go to work early," said Eddie.

"Well, you better go break the news to her. Do it offhand," said Mack. "Now, Hazel, how'd you do it?"

"You mad with me?"

"Hell no," said Mack. "'Course we don't know how she'll work out, but it's a step in the right direction." He turned to the two Whiteys. "I want you should notice Hazel didn't bust Doc's leg. That was good judgment. Doc can walk but he can't work. You, Whitey," he said to Whitey No. 2, "I want you should get over to Doc's and hang around. If anybody offers to drive him down to La Jolla you take care of it. Where's the indoor-ball bat?"

"I throwed it in the bay," said Hazel.

"So that's what it was! Whitey, you get yourself a couple of feet of gas pipe."

Hazel went into collapse. Mack sat on the edge of his bed and placed and replaced cold damp rags on Hazel's feverish brow.

Hazel struggled for speech. "Mack," he said, "I can't do her. I don't care if the stars or even the cops say I got to, I can't do her. I ain't got the poop."

"What you talking about? You already done her."

"I don't mean that. You tell Fauna she got to get somebody else for President of the United States."

Mack stared down at him in amazement. "I'll be damned," he said. "I thought you'd forgot."

"I practiced," said Hazel brokenly. "I don't want to let nobody down, Mack, but I just ain't no good at it. Try and get me off, will you, Mack? Please? Pretty goddam please?"

Mack's eyes brimmed with compassion. "Well, you sweet bastard," he said. "You poor little rabbit. Don't you worry. Ain't nobody going to force you. You done noble stuff. Wasn't nobody with guts but you."

"It ain't oysters," Hazel said. "Hell, I could do that. I'd eat old socks if I had to. It's just—the job's too big for me. I'd mess up the whole country."

Mack said, "You just lay there, Hazel baby, Mack's going to take care of it. There ain't nobody brave as you. Whitey," he said to Whitey No. 1, "you set here on Hazel's bed and kind of pet him. Don't let him get up until I get back." And Mack hurried out.

"You got to do something and do it quick," Mack said to Fauna. "S'pose Hazel gets another noble idea—why, hell, he might kill somebody."

"Yeah," said Fauna, "I can see how it is. Just let me get my stuff together. You think he'd like a nice monkey head?"

"He'd love it," said Mack. "He needs it."

Fauna held her chart in front of Hazel's eyes. "Anybody can make a mistake," she said. "They was a fly speck on the chart. Saturn wasn't in the bicuspid at all."

Hazel said suspiciously, "How do I know you ain't malarky-ing me now just to make me feel good?"

"How many toes you got?"

"I counted them—nine."

"Count them again."

Hazel slipped off his shoes. "Looks like the same as before," he said.

"Look at that little toe kind of bent under. Hell, Hazel, I may of made a mistake with a fly speck, but you miscounted your toes! You got ten. One bent under."

A slow smile began to spread over Hazel's face, a smile of re-lieved delight. Then for a moment the shadow of worry came back. "Who you think they'll get instead of me?"

"Nobody knows," said Fauna.

"Well, he better be good," said Hazel ominously. And then he abandoned himself to pure relief. " 'I got a little shadow that goes in and out with me,' " he sang.

Fauna rolled up her chart and went home.

———

Just before noon the expressman picked his unaccustomed way up to the chicken walk to the Palace Flophouse.

"I got a great big crate for you guys," he said. "I ain't got no call to deliver it up a rope ladder. Come on down and get it."

"It's here!" Mack cried. "God works in his tum-te-dum way his tum-tums to perform."

Hazel and Whitey No. 1 and Mack were wrestling the big wooden case up the chicken walk when Eddie joined them.

"Suzy come!" he cried. "I come with her. Seemed like she was about to take off any minute. She's in there with him now."

"Give us a hand," said Mack. "How's she look?"

"Fireball," said Eddie.

They carried the case into the Palace and Mack attacked it with a hand ax.

"There she is," he said when the lid was off.

"She's with Doc. Say, what you got?"

"Look!" said Mack. And he and the boys gazed down on the instrument, the great black tube of an eight-inch reflector, eye-pieces socketed beside it, and its tripod cradled.

"Biggest one in the whole damn catalogue," said Mack proudly. "Jesus, Doc'll be happy! Eddie, tell us everything that happened, don't leave nothing out."

What a day it was! A day of purple and gold, the proud colors of the Salinas High School. A squadron of baby angels maneuvered at twelve hundred feet, holding a pink cloud on which the word J-O-Y flashed on and off. A seagull with a broken wing took off and flew straight up into the air, squawking, "Joy! Joy!"

Suzy was ahead of her racing feet when Eddie intercepted her. She answered yes and no to Eddie's casual comments on the weather, but not only did she not hear the comments, she didn't know Eddie was beside her.

She went up the steps of Western Biological without seeing Whitey No. 2 standing guard with a sashweight. Her coming relieved him of a duty, but he stuck around to hear.

At the top of the steps Suzy became a breathless, shy girl, and, as anybody knows, there is nothing more indestructible and deadly than a shy young girl. She paused to get her breath and then knocked on the door and went in and forgot to close the door—which was good for Whitey No. 2.

Doc was sitting on his cot gloomily regarding the pile of collecting paraphernalia on the floor.

"I heard you was hurt," Suzy said gently. "I come to see if there was anything I could do."

For a moment Doc's face lightened, then gloom descended. "This shoots the spring tides," he said, staring at the white cast. "I don't know what I'll do."

"Does it hurt much?" Suzy asked.

"Some. It will hurt more later, I guess."

"I'll go down to La Jolla with you."

"And turn over rocks that weigh fifty or a hundred pounds?"

"I ain't put together with spit," said Suzy.

"Can you drive a car?"

"Sure," said Suzy.

"You can't do it," he said. And then, from way down in the deep part of him, there came a bubbling shout, "Sure you can! I need you, Suzy. I need you to go with me. It will be terribly hard work and I'm pretty near helpless."

"You can tell me what to do and what to look for."

"Sure I can. And I'm not entirely helpless. I can use my left hand."

"It's a cinch," said Suzy. "When do we start?"

"I've got to go tonight. If we drive all night we can make the tide at seven-eighteen tomorrow morning. Think you can make it?"

"Cinch," said Suzy. "If you need me."

"I need you all right. I'd be lost without you. But you'll be a tired kid."

"Who cares?" said Suzy.

"I want to ask you something," said Doc. "Old Jingleballicks has set up a foundation for me at Cal Tech."

"Why not?"

"I don't have to work there."

"Fine."

"I don't know whether I oughtn't to throw it in his face."

"Why don't you?"

"On the other hand, there's all the wonderful equipment."

"Fine," said Suzy.

"I don't like to work for anybody."

"Give it back."

"But there's an invitation to read my paper before the Academy of Science."

"Do it then."

"I don't know whether I can even write the paper. What shall I do, Suzy?"

"What do you want to do?"

"I don't know."

"What's wrong with that? Say, Doc, I got to do a couple of things. Take me maybe two hours. That too long?"

"Just as long as we start by evening."

"I'll come back soon's I finish."

Doc said, "Suzy, I love you."

She was headed for the door. She whirled and faced him. Her brows were straight and her mouth taut. Then she took a slow breath and her lips became full and turned up at the corners and her eyes shone with incredible excitement.

"Brother," said Suzy, "you got yourself a girl!"

I'm Sure We Should All
Be as Happy as Kings

In the Palace Flophouse, Suzy sat on a straight chair surrounded by the boys. She wore a look of furious concentration. Her feet were on two bricks and she held a barrel hoop in her hands. Propped in front of her was a board on which were chalked "ignition key," "speedometer," "choke," and "gas gauge." On the floor on her right side stood an apple box with a mop handle sticking upright out of it.

"Try her again," said Mack. "Turn the key and reach up with your right toe for the starter."

Suzy put her foot on a chalk spot on the floor.

"Chug-a-chug-a-chug," said Hazel happily.

"Push out your clutch."

Suzy pushed her left foot down on a brick.

"Now bring the gear to you and back."

She moved the mop handle to low gear.

"Ease up the gas and let in the clutch. Now clutch out, away from you and forward. Give it gas. Now clutch out and straight back. There, you done it good. Now do it again."

At the end of an hour and a half Suzy had driven the straight chair roughly a hundred and fifty miles.

"You'll do all right," said Mack. "Take it slow. If you can get two miles out of town without ramming into something, you can tell him the truth. He ain't going to turn back then. He'll tell you what to do. I'll get her started and kind of lined up with the street."

"You're a bunch of nice guys," said Suzy.

"Hell, if Hazel can go to all the trouble to break—oop,

sorry—the least we can do is see he gets some good out of it. Come on now—whang her through the gears again!"

The evening was as lovely as the day had been. The setting sun pinked up the little white caps on the bay and lighted the serious pelicans pounding home to the sea rocks. The metal cannery walls seemed a soft and precious platinum.

Doc's old car stood in front of Western Biological, its backseat loaded with buckets and pans and nets and crowbars. All Cannery Row was there. The Patrón had set out pints of Old Tennis Shoes along the curb. Fauna's hair blazed in the setting sun. The girls gave Suzy quick little hugs. Becky was in romantic tears.

Joe Elegant looked out his lean-to door. He thought he would go to Rome after his book was published.

Doc held a list in his hand and checked equipment.

Only Mack and the boys were missing. And here they came down the chicken walk, balancing among them the tripod and the long black tube. They crossed the track and the lot and they set the tripod down beside the automobile.

Mack cleared his throat. "Friends," he said, "on behalf of I and the boys it gives me pleasure to present Doc with this here."

Doc looked at the gift—a telescope strong enough to bring the moon to his lap. His mouth fell open. Then he smothered the laughter that rose in him.

"Like it?" said Mack.

"It's beautiful."

"Biggest one in the whole goddam catalogue," said Mack.

Doc's voice was choked. "Thanks," he said. He paused. "After all, I guess it doesn't matter whether you look down or up—as long as you look."

"We'll put her inside for you," said Mack. "Give me one of them pints. To Doc!" he cried, and under his breath he whispered to Suzy, "Turn the key. Now, starter."

The ancient engine roared. Doc was sipping from a pint.

"Clutch out—to you and back," Mack said. "Let in the clutch."

Suzy did.

The old car deliberately climbed the curb, ripped off the stairs of Western Biological, careened into the street, and crawled away, scattering lumber as it went.

Doc turned in the seat and looked back. The disappearing sun shone on his laughing face, his gay and eager face. With his left hand he held the bucking steering wheel.

Cannery Row looked after the ancient car. It made the first turn and was gone from sight behind a warehouse just as the sun was gone.

Fauna said, "I wonder if I'd be safe to put up her gold star tonight. What the hell's the matter with you, Mack?"

Mack said, "Vice is a monster so frightful of mien, I'm sure we should all be as happy as kings." He put his arm around Hazel's shoulders. "I think you'd of made a hell of a president," he said.

Notes

Starred notes below also appear in Robert DeMott and Brian Railsback, editors, *John Steinbeck: "Travels with Charley" and Later Novels 1947–1962* (New York: Library of America, 2007), pp. 979–82.
Special thanks to my research intern, Tracy Kelly, and to Steinbeck
specialist Carol Robles for assistance.

DEDICATION

v Elizabeth R. Otis (1901–81), Steinbeck's literary agent and confi-
dante, and cofounder in 1928 of New York literary agency McIntosh
and Otis. Steinbeck's voluminous correspondence with Otis covered
thirty-seven years, from 1931 to his death in 1968; a sampling is available in *Steinbeck: A Life in Letters* (1975), *Letters to Elizabeth*
(1978), and in the Appendix to *The Acts of King Arthur*. The main
collection is housed at Stanford University Library's Department of
Special Collections and University Archives. Access the individual
Container List of the Steinbeck–Otis correspondence in the John
Steinbeck Collection, 1902–1979, at content.cdlib.org/view?docId=
tf3c6002vx&chunk.id=dsc-1.8.6.

PROLOGUE

xxxv Originally titled "Introduction Mack's Contribution," a
much longer version of the prologue (156 lines long as opposed to 47)
appears in the original autograph manuscript, the typed manuscript,
and the unrevised galley proofs of *Sweet Thursday* (all housed at
the Harry Ransom Humanities Research Center, University of Texas,
Austin). It is not known why Steinbeck excised such a large portion
of the text.

xxxv   that book *Cannery Row*: Steinbeck's earlier roman à clef novel (1945), set in pre–World War II Monterey, featuring the protagonist Doc (based on Edward F. Ricketts) and including in its cast of characters numerous other lightly fictionalized, loosely disguised real-life persons. The novel is dedicated "For Ed Ricketts / who knows why or should." On the dedication page of the copy Steinbeck presented to Ricketts, he wrote, "with all the respect and affection this book implies." In his memoir "About Ed Ricketts" (1951), Steinbeck wrote:

> I used the laboratory and Ed himself in a book called *Cannery Row*. I took it to him in typescript to see whether he would resent it and to offer to make any changes he would suggest. He read it through carefully, smiling, and when he had finished he said, "Let it go that way. It is written in kindness. Such a thing can't be bad." But it was bad in several ways neither of us foresaw. As the book began to be read, tourists began coming to the laboratory, first a few and then in droves. People stopped their cars and stared at Ed with that glassy look that is used on movie stars. Hundreds of people came into the lab to ask questions and peer around. (pp. lvi–lvii)

CHAPTER I

1   Cannery Row: Site of numerous fish canneries, fish reduction plants, and processing and packing houses along Ocean View Avenue, Monterey. The street was renamed Cannery Row in 1958. That section of town was called New Monterey, which, Susan Shillinglaw explains in *A Journey into Steinbeck's California* (2006), was "not Spanish Monterey, not Methodist Pacific Grove, but the shoreline and sloping wooded hills between these places . . ." (p. 107)

*1   "As with the oysters in *Alice* . . .": From "The Walrus and the Carpenter," a poem in chapter four of *Through the Looking-Glass and What Alice Found There* (1871), by British writer and mathematician Charles L. Dodgson (1832–98), whose pseudonym was Lewis Carroll: " 'O Oysters,' said the Carpenter, / 'You've had a pleasant run! / Shall we be trotting home again?' / But answer came there none— / And this was scarcely odd, because / They'd eaten every one."

1   pilchards: California sardine (*Sardinia caerulea*). At eleven to fourteen inches in length, it was the state's most important commercial fish until midcentury. According to a graph in Richard F. G. Heimann and John G. Carlisle's *The California Marine Fish Catch for 1968 and*

Historical Review, 1916–1968, reprinted in Michael Hemp, *Cannery Row* (1986), in 1941–42, the Monterey area sardine catch was a record 250,287 tons. The canning boom driven by World War II saw Monterey become "the Sardine Capital of the World," though in 1947–48, around the time of Doc's discharge from the army, the catch was 17,630 tons (p. 110). Marine scientist Ed Ricketts studied the sardine extensively during his later career, and in his final article on the subject, published in the *Monterey Peninsula Herald* in 1948 (shortly before his death) and reprinted in Ricketts, *Breaking Through* (2006), concluded that if "conservation had been adopted early enough, a smaller but streamlined cannery row . . . would be winding up a fairly successful season, in stead [*sic*] of dipping, as they must be now, deeply into the red ink of failure" (p. 330). As Katherine Rodger asserts in her Introduction to *Breaking Through*, his "pleas for moderation fell on deaf ears . . ." (p. 73). In 1953 to 1954, the year *Sweet Thursday* was published, a greatly reduced Monterey fleet brought in fifty-eight tons.

1 Doc: Marine biologist, pioneering ecologist, and intellectual polymath Edward Flanders Robb Ricketts (1887–1948) was the model for Steinbeck's fictional Doc. Steinbeck's portrayal of Doc is often biographically accurate regarding Ricketts's physical gestures and appearance, his personal habits and tastes, and his cultural interests (especially in music, literature, and philosophy). Steinbeck embroiders, too: Ricketts attended the University of Chicago (1919–22) but never graduated, whereas his fictional counterpart holds a PhD from that institution. The research award Doc receives from Old Jingleballicks in chapter 37 may have been compensation for Ricketts's failure at winning a Guggenheim Fellowship in 1947. On the other side, in order to emphasize Doc's romantic adventures, Steinbeck ignores Ricketts's role as a husband and a father to three children from his marriage to Anna "Nan" Maker in 1922. (The couple later separated but were never legally divorced.) "Half-Christ and half-goat," Steinbeck summed him up in his 1951 elegy "About Ed Ricketts," itself an exercise in paradox, selective memory, and impressionism. Steinbeck's eighteen-year relationship with Ricketts was profoundly beneficial, as Richard Astro established in *John Steinbeck and Edward F. Ricketts* (1973). Besides their collaborative book, *Sea of Cortez* (1941), Steinbeck drew on Ricketts's ideas so deeply and so often that after Ricketts's death in May 1948, Steinbeck told mutual friends in *Steinbeck: A Life in Letters* (1976): "Wouldn't it be interesting if Ed *was* us. And that now there wasn't any such thing or that he created out of his own mind something that went away with him. I've wondered a lot about that. How much

was Ed and how much was me and which was which" (p. 316). Excellent resources with which to survey the world of Ed Ricketts are Katharine A. Rodger's *Renaissance Man of Cannery Row* (2002) and her *Breaking Through* (2006), as well as Eric Enno Tamm's *Beyond the Outer Shores* (2004).

1 Old Jingleballicks: Eccentric Old Jay's prototype has never been positively identified by scholars, though it is possible he was in some way connected with Stanford's Hopkins Marine Station, perhaps its onetime director W. K. Fisher, who was initially critical of the quality and nature of Ricketts's scientific work. In "About Ed Ricketts" (1951), Steinbeck says only that Ricketts "hated one professor whom he referred to as 'old jingleballicks.' It never developed why he hated 'old jingleballicks' " (p. xviii).

1 Western Biological Laboratories: Doc's business was modeled on Edward F. Ricketts's Pacific Biological Laboratories, cofounded in 1923 in Pacific Grove with Albert Galigher (his former University of Chicago roommate). In the late 1920s, Ricketts, by then the lab's sole owner, moved the business to 740 Ocean View Avenue in Monterey. Later, the street was renumbered, then renamed, with Ricketts's lab becoming 800 Cannery Row. The building, now a private social club, still stands. Recently it received a California Governor's Historic Preservation Award.

1 our victory: Victories by Allied forces over Germany and Japan that ended World War II took place in May and August 1945.

2 Palace Flophouse: A shed, once owned by Horace Abbeville and used to store fish meal, that figures prominently in *Cannery Row* (1945). The Palace Flophouse was deeded to Chinese merchant Lee Chong as payment for a grocery debt.

*3 "Rock of Ages . . . St. James Infirmary": "Rock of Ages" (1776) written by Augustus M. Toplady; "Asleep in the Deep" (1897) written by Arthur J. Lamb, with melody by Henry W. Petrie; "St. James Infirmary," a folk song of indeterminate authorship, was recorded by many artists, including Louis Armstrong in 1928.

*3 Bear Flag: The Bear Flag, so named because it featured a grizzly bear (once native to California), was raised at Sonoma, California, on June 14, 1846, by a group of American settlers led by Captain John C.

Frémont in a revolt against Mexican rule. In 1911 California's state legislature adopted it as the state flag.

4   G.I. bill: The popular name for the Serviceman's Readjustment Act (1944), which provided college or vocational education for returning World War II veterans.

5   Fort Ord: Originally called Camp Gigling when it was established in 1917, the Fort Ord Military Reservation (1940–94) was located on the Monterey Bay Peninsula between Marina and Sand City. At more than twenty-seven thousand acres, it was one of the largest U.S. Army bases on the West Coast and housed as many as fifty thousand troops. After World War II it became a facility for basic combat and advanced infantry training. Part of the base is now the site of California State University, Monterey Bay.

7   Point Pinos: Located at the northern end of the Monterey Peninsula, Point Pinos was named by Spanish explorer Sebastián Vizcaíno in 1602. It became the site of the oldest continuously operating lighthouse on the West Coast (established in 1855).

CHAPTER 2

8   egg-heady: Highly academic, intellectual, or studious.

9   pachucos: Members of Mexican-American youth gangs in the southwestern United States from the 1930s to the 1950s. The pachuco style and culture originated in El Paso, Texas, but moved quickly westward and became especially prominent in East Los Angeles. Pachucos sported loose-fitting "zoot suits" (oversized trousers and jacket, with a characteristic broad felt hat), which presented an exaggerated version of gangster clothing of the 1930s. Pachucos spoke a unique dialect called Calo, a hybrid blend of formal Spanish with English and Gypsy words.

9   lagged with loaded pennies: Joseph and Mary may have used illegally weighted pennies for the coin toss that determined who would be first to break ("lag") at pool.

9   badger game . . . Spanish treasure: Illegal or unethical confidence games. The badger game, for instance, is a dishonest trick in which a person is lured into a compromising situation and then blackmailed.

10   François Villon: French poet, thief, and general vagabond (ca. 1431–ca. 1474).

11   muggles: A slang term for marijuana.

11   wetback: Derogatory name applied to undocumented Mexican immigrants in the United States. The term is thought originally to refer to people crossing the border by swimming across the Rio Grande. Generally, Steinbeck's use of racially charged terms such as "Chink" and "spick" reflects the attitudes and habits of his characters, not necessarily of the author. His attitude toward Mexican nationals—if not exactly fully realistic or authentic—is nonetheless generally positive and respectful, especially when it is noted that *Sweet Thursday* appeared during the same year the United States government's Immigration and Naturalization Service launched Operation Wetback (1954), which targeted illegal Mexican nationals in the southwestern United States and eventually succeeded in deporting eighty thousand of them.

*13   Espaldas Mojadas: Joseph and Mary's group is Wetbacks.

*13   "Ven a Mi . . . que Llora": Spanish song titles: "Come to Me, My Sorrowful Girl," "Woman from San Luis," and "The Little White Cloud That Cries."

*13   *charro*: The Spanish word for the colorful, even gaudy, traditional outfit of the Mexican cowboy.

13   I. O. O. F.: Independent Order of Odd Fellows, a fraternal organization devoted to improving and elevating the condition of humanity through friendship, love, and truth. Derived from seventeenth-century British orders, the first American I.O.O.F. lodge was chartered in Baltimore, Maryland, in 1819. In 1851, membership was extended to women.

CHAPTER 3

14   Velella: *Velella velella,* commonly known as By-the-Wind Sailor or Purple Sail, is a jellyfish that resembles a miniature Portuguese man-o'-war. Usually blue in color, these jellyfish travel by means of a small stiff sail that catches the wind. They can become stranded on beaches by the millions.

15 Sistine Choir: Recordings of the Vatican's Sistine Chapel Choir.

*15 William Byrd: William Byrd (1540?–1623) was one of the most celebrated English composers of the Renaissance. His three famous masses (in Latin) were written between 1592 and 1595.

15 *Faust* of Goethe: German author Johann Wolfgang von Goethe's tragedy of a man who sells his soul to Mephistopheles the devil in exchange for unlimited power. Part I was published in 1808 and revised in 1828–29; part II was published in 1832, the year Goethe died.

15 *Art of the Fugue* of J. S. Bach: Johann Sebastian Bach (1685 O.S.–1750 N.S.) was a prolific German composer and organist of sacred and secular works for choir, orchestra, and solo instruments. His final (and unfinished) collection of fugues and canons was composed between 1745 and 1750, and published after his death in 1750. See below pp. 80, 135, and 201.

*15 Diamond Jim Brady: James Buchanan Brady (1856–1917), American businessman, financier, and philanthropist of the Gilded Age, whose appetite for food was legendary.

16 Lao-Tse: Major Chinese philosopher said to have lived in the sixth century BCE; however, many historians place his life in the fourth century BCE. He was credited with writing the seminal Taoist work, the *Tao Te Ching*, and he was recognized as the founder of Taoism.

*17 *Bhagavadgita*: The *Bhagavad Gita* is a passage of 701 verses in the epic *Mahabharata* and is revered as a sacred text of Hindu philosophy. *Bhagavad Gita*, a conversation between divine Krishna and Arjuna, proposes that true enlightenment comes from growing beyond identification with the Ego, the little Self, and that one must identify with the Truth of the immortal Self (the soul, or Atman), the ultimate Divine Consciousness. Through detachment from the personal Ego, the Yogi, or follower of a particular path of Yoga, is able to transcend his mortality and attachment from the material world, and see the Infinite.

17 Prophet Isaiah: Jewish prophet (eighth–seventh centuries BCE) who prophesied during the reigns of four biblical kings and is generally regarded to have authored the Book of Isaiah, which delivers messages of peace, compassion, and justice.

17 Dr. Horace Dormody: In 1930, Dr. Horace Dormody (1897–1984), with his brother Dr. Hugh Dormody, opened Peninsula Community Hospital (renamed Community Hospital of Monterey Peninsula in 1961).

17 Great Tide Pool: An especially rich ecological zone and consequently one of Doc's prime specimen collecting sites. It is located off Monterey's Ocean View Boulevard at the western foot of the Point Pinos lighthouse. In chapter 4 of *Cannery Row*, Steinbeck wrote:

It is a fabulous place: when the tide is in, a wave-churned basin, creamy with foam, whipped by the combers that roll in from the whistling buoy on the reef. But when the tide goes out the little water world becomes quiet and lovely. The sea is very clear and the bottom becomes fantastic with hurrying, fighting, feeding, breeding animals.

19 kraken: Legendary tentacled sea monster of gargantuan size, perhaps inspired by giant squid.

20 Charles Darwin and his *Origin of Species*: Steinbeck is creating a myth here. According to Brian Railsback in *Parallel Expeditions* (1995),

Darwin never claimed his theory "flashed complete" in such a way. However, the inductive process the novelist suggests, in which a theory emerges after a gathering of facts, does indicate his knowledge of Darwin's method. Further, Steinbeck is essentially correct in stating that the naturalist spent the rest of his life "backing it up" (Darwin produced six editions of *The Origin of Species* in his lifetime, the last in 1872, ten years before his death). (p. 26)

CHAPTER 7

39 "Stormy Weather": Blues song written by musician Harold Arlen (1905–86) and lyricist Ted Koehler (1894–1973) in 1933, about a heartbroken woman who has lost her man. Its first stanza sets the tone for the whole song: "Don't know why, there's no sun up in the sky / Stormy weather, since my man and I ain't together / Keeps raining all the time." Ethel Waters first sang it at the Cotton Club in Harlem, but it was also memorably performed by Billie Holiday, Ella Fitzgerald, and Lena Horne, who sang it in the movie of the same name in 1943. In 2004 it was chosen by the Library of Congress to be added to the National Recording Registry.

*40   Jack Dempsey: William Harrison Dempsey (1895–1983). World heavyweight boxing champion (1919–26) known as the "Manassa Mauler." Fifty of his sixty wins were by knockout.

42   spick: Insulting, derogatory term for a Hispanic person.

CHAPTER 8

44   The Great Roque War: An American variant of croquet (the name was derived by removing the first and last letters), roque is played on a rolled sand court with permanently anchored wickets. The mallets, with which the ball is struck, have a short handle (approximately twenty-four inches), and the ends of the mallet are faced with stone. According to Susan Shillinglaw's *A Journey into Steinbeck's California* (2006), "There was no such war, with Greens squaring off against Blues," though in 1932–33 a local tempest erupted in Pacific Grove over attempts to remove the roque courts. Voters resoundingly defeated the move (p. 95).

44   Pacific Grove: Sedate Pacific Grove, Monterey's next-door neighbor on the Peninsula, began in 1875 as a summer Methodist tent camp and religious retreat (on property owned by land baron David Jack), then in 1879 became the site of a Pacific Coast arm of the Chautauqua Literary and Scientific Circle, modeled on the Methodist Sunday school teachers' training camp established in 1874 at Lake Chautauqua, New York. Pacific Grove's roots, as Steinbeck notes, were religiously, philosophically, and politically conservative.

CHAPTER 9

47   Whom the Gods Love . . . : Parody of a line by Greek tragic dramatist Euripides (480 BCE–406 BCE): "Whom the gods would destroy, they first make mad."

*47   *Sorrows of Werther*: *The Sorrows of Young Werther* (1774), loosely autobiographical novel of love and suicide by German writer and scientist Johann Wolfgang von Goethe (1749–1832).

48   A and C: "Ass and collar"—a bouncer's move, used to grab hold of and then eject a patron. Steinbeck mentions the technique in chapter 23 of *Cannery Row* as well.

48 Jackson fork: A mechanical hay fork, used for lifting large amounts of hay.

51 William Henry Harrison: Harrison (1773–1841) was an American military leader, a politician, and the ninth president of the United States (1841), who died thirty days into his term—the briefest presidency in U.S. history and the first U.S. president to die while in office.

52 Quod erat demonstrandum: Latin for "that which was to be demonstrated," indicating that something has been clearly proven. Its acronym, Q.E.D., often appears at the conclusion of mathematical proofs.

CHAPTER 10

*55 Harun al-Rashid: Harun (ca. 763–809), fifth Abbasid caliph, who ruled from 786 to 809, was a munificent patron of letters and arts, and under him Baghdad was at its apogee. He became a great figure to the Arabs, who tell about him in many of the stories of the *Thousand and One Nights*.

55 djinni: In Arabian and Muslim mythology, djinni, or jinni, are intelligent spirits of lower rank than the angels. They are able to appear in human and animal forms and to possess humans.

58 yerba buena tea: Yerba buena (*Clinopodium douglasii*) is a sprawling aromatic herb of the western and northwestern United States, western Canada, and Alaska, and is used to make tea that is both a medicinal and a refreshing drink. Its name, an alternate form of *hierba buena*, which means "good herb," was given by the Spanish priests of California.

CHAPTER 11

60 Holman's Department Store: According to the Pacific Grove Museum of Natural History (www.pgmuseum.org), this landmark Pacific Grove store was started in 1891, when R. Luther Holman bought Towle's dry goods store on Lighthouse Avenue near Seventeenth Street. By 1924, when the store moved over two blocks to its new location at 524 Lighthouse Avenue, son Wilford Holman was in charge of operations. Holman's Department Store, with more than forty different departments, was the largest store on the Pacific coast between Los Angeles and San Francisco, and Highway 68, also known as the Holman Highway, was built in part to bring customers to its doors. The store, having hired a flagpole skater to promote business, appears in chapter nineteen of *Cannery Row*.

*63   "lets concealment . . . his damask cheek": Mack quoting Shakespeare is one of the incongruous comedic effects Steinbeck strove for in *Sweet Thursday*. Spoken by Viola in act II, scene 4, line 111 of William Shakespeare's comedy *Twelfth Night, or What You Will* (ca. 1601–02):

> "A blank, my lord. She never told her love,
> But let concealment, like a worm i' the bud,
> Feed on her damask cheek: she pined in thought,
> And with a green and yellow melancholy
> She sat like patience on a monument,
> Smiling at grief. Was not this love indeed?"

63   Lefty Grove: Robert Moses (Lefty) Grove, one of the greatest pitchers in major-league baseball history. Grove (1900–75) retired in 1941 with a career record of 300-141. His .680 lifetime winning percentage is eighth all-time, but none of the seven men ahead of him won more than 236 games. Grove was elected to the Baseball Hall of Fame in 1947. In 1999, he was elected to the Major League Baseball All-Century Team.

63   absinthe: A distilled, highly alcoholic, anise-flavored spirit derived from herbs including the flowers and leaves of the medicinal plant wormwood (*Artemisia absinthium*).

64   Woolworth's: The F. W. Woolworth Company was a nationwide retail corporation whose five-and-dime stores became a nearly universal presence in America. The first Woolworth's store was founded in 1878 by Frank Winfield Woolworth; the chain closed in 1997.

CHAPTER 12

*66   Flower in a Crannied Wall: "Flower in the Crannied Wall" (1869), by Alfred, Lord Tennyson (1809–92), a popular English

Victorian poet and the poet laureate of England from 1850 to 1892: "Flower in the crannied wall, / I pluck you out of the crannies, / I hold you here, root and all, in my hand, / Little flower—but *if* I could understand / What you are, root and all, and all in all, / I should know what God and man is."

66   Joe Elegant: Various candidates have been proposed as the model for Joe Elegant—notably mythologist Joseph Campbell and novelist Truman Capote—though, given the self-parodying nature of *Sweet Thursday*, Louis Owens, in *John Steinbeck's Re-Vision of America* (1985), plausibly offers the ". . . young John Steinbeck, author of such ponderously mythical novels as *Cup of Gold* and *To a God Unknown* with their naive and heavy-handed wielding of symbols" (p. 194).

CHAPTER 13

68   fusel oil: An oily, colorless liquid with a disagreeable odor and taste. It is a mixture of alcohols and fatty acids, formed during the alcoholic fermentation of organic materials. Fusel oil is used as a solvent in the manufacture of certain lacquers and enamels (it dissolves nitrocellulose). It is poisonous to humans.

69   Oakland Polytech: Oakland Technical High School, in Oakland, California, known locally as Oakland Tech, is a public high school located on 4351 Broadway in North Oakland. It is one of six comprehensive public high school campuses in Oakland. Founded in 1917, it is the alma mater of Clint Eastwood, Rickey Henderson, Huey P. Newton, and the Pointer Sisters.

CHAPTER 14

72   Coca-Cola calendar girls: Illustrators for the Atlanta-based soft drink giant pioneered a type of graphically appealing and colorful calendar art that featured Coca-Cola's Calendar Girls, who, though provocatively posed in bathing suits, were intended to portray wholesomeness as well as beauty. Steinbeck had used the ubiquitous advertising image in chapter one of *The Wayward Bus* (1947).

*72   Romie Jacks: Romie Jack was one of the seven surviving children (out of nine) of wealthy and controversial Scottish-born Monterey

County land baron David Jack and his wife, Maria Christina Soledad Romie. Romie served as manager of the family's David Jack Corporation–owned Abbot Hotel (later Cominos Hotel) in Salinas. The Cominos Hotel is featured in Steinbeck's short story "The Chrysanthemums."

CHAPTER 15

74 The Playing Fields of Harrow: Harrow School (founded in 1572), an exclusive, elite British men's boarding (public) school near London, was famous for its tradition of Harrow football (begun in the nineteenth century), a unique hybrid game exclusive to the school, which combines elements of both soccer and rugby (but which uses a spherical-shaped leather ball). Because Fauna tutors her girls in social/sexual gamesmanship as a route to victory in matrimony, Steinbeck might also be alluding to a statement, allegedly by the Duke of Wellington, that "The Battle of Waterloo was won on the playing fields of Eton."

74 Parcheesi: Brand name of a once-popular board game based on Pachisi, an ancient royal game of India created around 500 BCE, which utilized slave girls and concubines as red, yellow, blue, and green pawns on palace grounds. The trademark name was registered in 1870 by a New York game manufacturer.

75 high Elk: The Benevolent and Protective Order of Elks of the USA (B.P.O.E.), which began modestly in 1868 as a private drinking club to circumvent New York City laws governing the opening hours of public taverns, has evolved into a major American fraternal, charitable, and service order. Headquartered in Chicago, it has local lodges throughout the nation. Both Monterey and Salinas had active Elk Lodges.

76 haute monde: French for "fashionable society."

77 A and P: The Great Atlantic and Pacific Tea Company, better known as A&P, is a North American supermarket chain. The company was founded in 1859 by George Huntington Hartford and George Gilman in Elmira, New York, as The Great American Tea Company. It was renamed "The Great Atlantic and Pacific Tea Company" in 1870, and over the next eighty years went on to become one of the dominant grocery chains in the United States.

77 Arbor Day: American holiday, first observed in 1872, that encourages the planting and care of trees. National Arbor Day is observed on the last Friday of April, but each state has its own date. California's observation occurs March 7–14.

77 Watch and Ward: Steinbeck was both intrigued by and suspicious of civic, social, professional, or special-interest organizations, whether real (Woodmen of the World and I.O.O.F.) or imagined (Rattlesnake Club and Forward and Upward Club). In *America and Americans* (1966), he said, "Elks, Masons, Knight Templars, Woodmen of the World, Redmen, Eagles, Eastern Star, Foresters . . . the *World Almanac* lists hundreds of such societies and associations, military and religious, philosophic, scholarly, charitable, mystic, political, and some just plain nuts. All were and perhaps still are aristocratic and mostly secret and therefore exclusive. They seemed to fulfill a need for grandeur against a background of commonness, for aristocracy in the midst of democracy" (p. 360). His satire on civic hypocrisy is especially sharp here, for he refers to what was probably a local chapter of the New England Watch and Ward Society, founded in Boston in 1878 as the New England Society for the Suppression of Vice, and in 1890 renamed the Watch and Ward Society. It functioned as a watchdog agency against vice and led successful censorship campaigns against books it deemed obscene or pornographic.

78 *Breeder's Journal*: Perhaps *The Guernsey Breeder's Journal*, the oldest dairy breed magazine published by a U.S. breed organization.

*78 Sterling North: Thomas Sterling North (1906–74), author of numerous books for adults and children, including the best seller *So Dear to My Heart* (1947).

CHAPTER 16

80 The Little Flowers of Saint Mack: *The Little Flowers of Saint Francis of Assisi*, the name given to a classic collection of popular legends about the life of St. Francis of Assisi (1182–1256) and his early companions as they appeared to the Italian people at the beginning of the fourteenth century.

CHAPTER 17

86 Suzy Binds the Cheese: An early step in the cheese-making process requires the addition of rennet (plant- or animal-derived substance that contains the enzyme rennin), which binds or coagulates milk.

89 "I love true things . . .": Cf. Steinbeck's appraisal of Ed Ricketts in "About Ed Ricketts" (1951): "He loved true things and believed in them" (p. XVI).

CHAPTER 18

91 "Home Sweet Home" . . . "Harvest Moon": "Home, Sweet Home" was composed in 1852 by Sir Henry Bishop (1786–1855) from an adaptation of *Clari, or the Maid of Milan* (1823) by American dramatist John Howard Payne (1791–1852); "Old Black Joe" was composed in 1860 by Stephen C. Foster (1826–64). The other two songs Steinbeck mentions here have resonance for the romantic plot of *Sweet Thursday*. Tell Taylor (1876–1937) wrote the words and melody of "Down by the Old Mill Stream" in 1910. Its chorus goes: "Down by the old mill stream where I first met you, / With your eyes of blue, dressed in gingham too, / It was there I knew that you loved me true, / You were sixteen, my village queen, by the old mill stream." "Shine On, Harvest Moon," a popular song written by entertainer Nora Bayes (1880–1928) and her husband, songwriter Jack Norworth (1879–1959), debuted in Florenz Ziegfeld's *Follies of 1908*: "Shine on, shine on harvest moon / Up in the sky, / I ain't had no lovin' / Since January, February, June or July / Snow time ain't no time to stay / Outdoors and spoon, / So shine on, shine on harvest moon, / For me and my gal."

93 Woodmen of the World: Widespread national fraternal organization founded in 1890 in Omaha, Nebraska, by Joseph Cullen Root. Lodges, whose members are eligible for a wide array of insurance coverage, conduct volunteer, patriotic, and charitable activities that benefit individuals and communities. The organization is one of the leading donors of U.S. flags to schools and nonprofit groups.

***95** Jiggs and Maggie: *Bringing Up Father*, a comic strip created by George McManus (1884?–1954) that ran from 1913 to 2000, was often called "Jiggs and Maggie," after its two main characters.

CHAPTER 19

101   Sarajevo . . . Pearl Harbor: World War I was precipitated by
the assassinations of Archduke Franz Ferdinand of Austria and his
wife, Sophie, Duchess of Hohenberg, on June 28, 1914, in Sarajevo.
The roots of Europe's entrance into World War II occurred on
September 29, 1938, when Adolf Hitler orchestrated the Munich
Agreement (signed by Germany, Italy, France, and Britain), which
allowed the Third Reich to expand its control over the Sudetenland
area of Czechoslovakia. The Battle of Stalingrad, during which So-
viet troops defeated the German Sixth Army and other Axis troops,
began on August 21, 1942, and lasted over five months. On December 19, 1777, George Washington's ragtag Continental Army entered their winter encampment at Valley Forge, Pennsylvania, where
they remained for seven months while being rigorously retrained
and reorganized. Japan's surprise air attack on the United States'
Pacific naval fleet at Pearl Harbor, Oahu, Hawaii, took place on
December 7, 1941.

*102   *Down Beat*: American magazine devoted to jazz. The publication was established in 1935 in Chicago, Illinois. It is named after the
"downbeat" in music, also called the "one beat."

*103   *"Tío mio"*: Spanish for "my uncle."

CHAPTER 20

107   Hediondo Cannery: Steinbeck's joke: "hediondo" means
"stinky" in Spanish.

CHAPTER 21

112   Imp of the Row: Perhaps a comic and reductive echo of Edgar
Allan Poe's theory of human perverseness ("overwhelming tendency to
do wrong for the wrong's sake") sketched out in "The Imp of the
Perverse" (1845).

115   *tom*-wallager: Slang term that means humdinger, whopper, etc.

CHAPTER 23

123 Orient Express: The Orient Express, which connects Calais, France, on the English Channel, with Istanbul, Turkey, on the Black Sea, is one of the most legendary luxury trains in Europe, and a symbol of exotic adventure.

124 Webster F. Street Lay-Away Plan: An inside joke: The drink was named for Steinbeck's former Stanford classmate and Monterey friend, attorney Webster "Toby" Street (1899–1984).

CHAPTER 24

129 Seconal: Registered name of secobarbital, a barbiturate sedative that reduces anxiety by slowing down brain and nervous system activity. Supposedly available only by prescription.

129 Bohemia beer: Extensive research proves Doc's assessment to be correct. Alcoholic haze that pervades this novel aside, there is something fitting about bohemian Doc preferring this aptly named brand of beer. Brewed exclusively in Mexico since 1900 and named for the beer-brewing region of Czechoslovakia, Bohemia is a smooth, medium-bodied pilsner-style beer with some pronounced hops flavor.

CHAPTER 25

*135 Buxtehude . . . Palestrina: Dietrich Buxtehude (ca. 1637–1707) was a German-Danish organist and a highly regarded composer of the Baroque period. Giovanni Pierluigi da Palestrina (ca. 1525–94) was an influential Italian composer of Renaissance music.

135 Mozart's *Don Giovanni*: Opera in two acts, based on the legend of Don Juan, with music by Wolfgang Amadeus Mozart (1756–91), and libretto in Italian by Lorenzo Da Ponte (1749–1838), first performed in Prague on October 29, 1787. At the opera's end, Don Giovanni, unrepentant seducer, is visited by the ghost of a man he has murdered, and is offered the opportunity to save his soul. When he refuses, he is dragged to hell while he is still alive. The concluding chorus delivers the opera's moral: "Thus do the wicked find their end, dying as they had lived."

*136 Giordano Bruno: Italian philosopher, priest, astronomer/ astrologer, and occultist. Bruno (1548–1600) is perhaps best known for his system of mnemonics and as an early proponent of the idea of extrasolar planets and extraterrestrial life. Burned at the stake as a heretic for his theological ideas, Bruno is seen by some as a martyr to the cause of free thought.

139 Olympus: At 9,570 feet high, Mount Olympus is Greece's tallest mountain. In Greek mythology, it was considered the home of the pantheon of principal Greek deities, led by Zeus, king of the gods.

139 Armageddon: In the New Testament's Book of Revelation (16:12–16), Armageddon is the site where forces of good and forces of evil assembled for an apocalyptic, climactic battle.

*141 Tehuanos: Inhabitants, predominantly Zapotec Indians, of Tehuantepec, in Oaxaca, southeastern Mexico.

*141 "Sandunga": "La Sandunga," unofficial regional anthem of the Isthmus of Tehuantepec, was written by governor and military commander Máximo Ramón Ortiz (d. 1855). It is a sensual, graceful dance song that expresses the grief of a Tehuana (Zapotecan woman) over the death of her mother. The song moves from overwhelming sadness to a sense of acceptance of her loss.

CHAPTER 26

143 Salinas Rodeo: The California Rodeo has taken place each summer at the Salinas Rodeo Grounds since 1911.

145 Life: In 1936, under new owner Henry Luce, Life (which began in 1883 as a humor magazine) became the first all-photography news-magazine in the United States. At its most popular, it sold more than thirteen million copies per week. It published a regular feature, "Life Goes to a Party."

145 the picture: Snow White and the Seven Dwarfs, a 1937 Walt Disney Productions movie, was the first animated film made in Technicolor.

CHAPTER 27

*146 O Frabjous Day!: From Lewis Carroll's nonsense poem "Jabberwocky," which appears in chapter one of *Through the Looking-Glass and What Alice Found There* (1871): " 'And, hast thou slain the Jabberwock? / Come to my arms, my beamish boy! / O frabjous day! Callooh! Callay!' / He chortled in his joy."

154 Dementia praecox: Any of several psychotic disorders, such as schizophrenia, characterized by distortions of reality, disturbances of thought and language, and withdrawal from social contact.

CHAPTER 28

*156 Where Alfred the Sacred River Ran: Parody of ". . . Where Alph, the sacred river, ran / Through caverns measureless to man . . ." from "Kubla Khan or, a Vision in a Dream: A Fragment" (1816), a poem by British Romantic poet Samuel Taylor Coleridge (1772–1834).

156 1914 Willys-Knight: Willys-Knight automobiles were produced between 1914 and 1933 by Willys-Overland Company of Elyria and Toledo, Ohio. In an internal combustion engine, ring gear and pinions connect the car's starter with the motor's flywheel.

157 "A veritable fairyland": According to Susan Shillinglaw in *A Journey into Steinbeck's California* (2006), Steinbeck's portrayal of the culminating costume party at the Palace Flophouse may owe its inspiration to an outrageous benefit party, "Surrealistic Night in an Enchanted Forest," thrown by artist Salvador Dalí at Monterey's Hotel Del Monte on September 2, 1941 (pp. 76–77). See also the short film clip, "Dizzy Dali Dinner," on YouTube at http://www.youtube.com/watch?v=vg6i4EoWoak.

*158 "Whistle While You Work": Song featured in Walt Disney's animated movie *Snow White and the Seven Dwarfs* (1937), with music by Frank Churchill (1901–42) and lyrics by Larry Morey.

159 threshold of a great career: Old Jingleballicks echoes Ralph Waldo Emerson's salutation to Walt Whitman, after the philosopher had read the first edition of the younger man's *Leaves of Grass* (1855): "I

greet you at the beginning of a great career," he wrote Whitman on July 21, 1855.

159   Knight Templar's hat: The Knights Templar is a Christian-oriented organization founded in the eleventh century. Originally, the Knights Templar were laymen who protected and defended Christians traveling to Jerusalem. These men took vows of poverty, chastity, and obedience, and were renowned for their fierceness and courage in battle. All Knights Templar are members of the world's oldest fraternal organization, known as "The Ancient Free and Accepted Masons" or, more commonly, "Masons." The hat Steinbeck refers to is plumed.

*163   "Wedding March" . . . *Lohengrin*: The Bridal Chorus from Richard Wagner's romantic opera *Lohengrin* (1850). Traditionally played at weddings, it is commonly known as "Here Comes the Bride."

CHAPTER 29

165   Oh, Woe, Woe, Woe!: From American Modernist expatriate poet Ezra Pound's parodic "Song in the Manner of Houseman," which appeared in his fifth collection, *Canzoni* (1911). The final stanza reads, "London is a woeful place, / Shropshire is much pleasanter. / Then let us smile a little space / Upon fond nature's morbid grace. / *Oh, Woe, woe, woe, etcetera* . . ."

169   Mr. and Mrs. Sam Malloy: In chapter 8 of *Cannery Row*, the Malloys take up residence in this cast-off cannery boiler.

CHAPTER 30

*175   if the British impressed our sailors: During the administrations of Washington, Adams, Jefferson, and Madison, the Royal Navy impressed thousands of seamen from American ships, claiming that they were British subjects. (The British refused to recognize American naturalization, and often disregarded protection documents issued to native-born American sailors.) American anger over impressment became one of the causes of the War of 1812.

*175   "Fifty-four-Forty": In 1844 James K. Polk was elected president on a platform calling for setting the northern boundary of Oregon at 54°40'N. The Anglo-American dispute over the boundary was settled in 1846 by a treaty setting the border at 49°N.

CHAPTER 32

181 "My dear Anthony West . . .": Steinbeck's satire of Joe Elegant as a novelist continues here in this dig at Anthony West. The British author (1914–87)—novelist, essayist, biographer—published "California Moonshine," an unflattering review of Steinbeck's *East of Eden,* in the September 20, 1952, issue of the *New Yorker*: "Mr. Steinbeck has written the precise equivalent of those nineteenth-century melodramas in which the villains could always be recognized because they waxed their mustaches and in which the conflict between good and evil operated like a well-run series of professional tennis matches" (p. 125). In a letter to Carlton Sheffield on October 15, 1952, in *Steinbeck: A Life in Letters* (1975), Steinbeck registered his dismay: "I am interested in Anthony West's review in the New Yorker [sic]. I wonder what made him so angry—and it was a very angry piece. I should like to meet him to find out why he hated and feared this book so much" (p. 458). Clearly, Steinbeck had the last word.

182 Fafnir: In German composer Richard Wagner's Norse-inspired epic of four linked operas, *Der Ring das Nibelungen* (its first complete production took place in 1876), Fafnir, a giant transformed into a dragon, guards the golden treasure.

184 James Petrillo: James Caesar Petrillo (1892–1984) was a labor leader who became the influential president of the American Federation of Musicians from 1940 to 1958. He rigorously policed the practice of hiring nonunion musicians, such as the members of Joseph and Mary Rivas's band.

189 Hopkins Marine Station: The Hopkins Seaside Laboratory of Stanford University opened in 1892 on Lovers Point, north of its current site at 120 Oceanview Boulevard, Pacific Grove. It has been located on Oceanview since 1917, when it was officially renamed Hopkins Marine Station. It is the oldest marine research facility on the West Coast. Steinbeck attended summer classes at Hopkins in 1923.

189 "Memphis Blues": A song written in 1909 (published in 1912) by songwriter and bandleader William Christopher Handy, self-proclaimed

"Father of the Blues." "Memphis Blues" played a significant role in bringing African American music into the mainstream.

192   Henny Penny: English fairy tale of undetermined origin and variable plot, sometimes called "The Sky Is Falling," "Chicken Little," "Chicken Licken," or "Henny Penny." In one version Henny Penny is hit on the head by a falling acorn and believes that "the sky is falling" and that she must tell the king. The moral of the tale varies from version to version but certainly can be interpreted to mean that danger is imminent.

CHAPTER 35

*200   Il n'y a pas de mouches sur la grandmère: The English translation of the French is: "There are no flies on Grandmother."

204   "no room of my own": Suzy's lament ironically and metaphorically echoes Virginia Woolf's pioneering feminist essay, *A Room of One's Own* (1929), delivered as lectures at Cambridge University in 1928. In the essay, Woolf claims that in order for a woman writer to be successful, she needs space to work in and money enough to support herself.

CHAPTER 36

*209   Lama Sabachthani?: From Matthew 27:46: "And about the ninth hour Jesus cried with a loud voice, saying, 'Eli, Eli, lama sabachthani?' that is to say, My God, my God, why hast thou forsaken me?"

CHAPTER 38

213   Monarch butterflies: Steinbeck has taken some license here by timing the arrival of the butterflies (*Danaus plexippus*) in spring. In reality, they appear annually by the thousands in October to begin their crucial overwintering period in the pine and eucalyptus groves in Pacific Grove, which has established a permanent Monarch Grove Sanctuary.

*215   Kinsey Report: Alfred C. Kinsey (1894–1956), a biologist at Indiana University and the founder of its Institute for Sex Research, published the studies *Sexual Behavior in the Human Male* (1948) and *Sexual Behavior in the Human Female* (1953).

*215 petition for release of Eugene Debs: Eugene V. Debs (1855–1926), four-time Socialist Party presidential candidate, was convicted in 1918 under the Espionage Act for inciting disloyalty in the armed forces by making an antiwar speech in Canton, Ohio. He was sentenced to ten years in prison, but was freed on December 25, 1919, after President Warren G. Harding commuted his sentence.

CHAPTER 39

216 March Hare: The March Hare appears in chapter seven, "A Mad Tea-Party," in *Alice's Adventures in Wonderland* (1865), by British writer and mathematician Charles L. Dodgson (1832–98).

220 Salinas High School: Steinbeck's alma mater; he graduated in 1918.

CHAPTER 40

*223 I'm Sure We Should All Be as Happy as Kings: Poem 25 ("Happy Thought") by popular Scottish author Robert Louis Stevenson (1850–94) in his *A Child's Garden of Verses and Underwoods* (1913): "The world is so full of a number of things, / I'm sure we should all be as happy as kings."

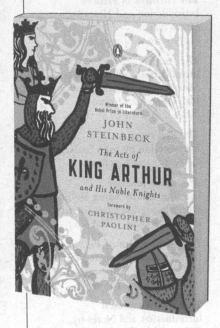

The Grapes of Wrath
Introduction and Notes by
Robert DeMott
ISBN 978-0-14-303943-3

Of Mice and Men
Introduction by Susan Shillinglaw
ISBN 978-0-14-018642-0

East of Eden
Introduction by David Wyatt
ISBN 978-0-14-018639-0

The Winter of Our Discontent
ISBN 978-0-14-018753-3

The Portable Steinbeck
Edited by Pascal Covici, Jr.
ISBN 978-0-14-015002-5

*America and the Americans and
Selected Nonfiction*
Edited by Susan Shillinglaw and
Jackson J. Benson
ISBN 978-0-14-243741-4

*Burning Bright: A Play in Story
Form*
Introduction and Notes by
John Ditsky
ISBN 978-0-14-303944-0

Cup of Gold
ISBN 978-0-14-018743-4

In Dubious Battle
Introduction and Notes by
Warren French
ISBN 978-0-14-303963-1

The Log from the Sea of Cortez
Introduction by Richard Astro
ISBN 978-0-14-018744-1

The Long Valley
Introduction and Notes by
John H. Timmerman
ISBN 978-0-14-018745-8

The Moon Is Down
Introduction and Notes by
Donald V. Coers
ISBN 978-0-14-018746-5

Once There Was a War
ISBN 978-0-14-310479-7

The Pastures of Heaven
Introduction and Notes by
James Nagel
ISBN 978-0-14-018748-9

The Pearl
Introduction by Linda Wagner-
Martin with Drawings by
José Clemente Orozco
ISBN 978-0-14-018738-0

The Red Pony
Introduction by John Seelye
ISBN 978-0-14-018739-7

A Russian Journal
Introduction by Susan Shillinglaw
with Photographs by Robert Capa
ISBN 978-0-14-118019-9

The Short Reign of Pippin IV
Introduction by Robert Morsberger
and Katharine Morsberger
ISBN 978-0-14-303946-4

To a God Unknown
Introduction and Notes by
Robert DeMott
ISBN 978-0-14-018751-9

Tortilla Flat
Introduction and Notes by
Thomas Fensch
ISBN 978-0-14-018740-3

The Wayward Bus
Edited with an Introduction and
Notes by Gary Scharnhorst
ISBN 978-0-14-243787-2